The Magic Pumpkin

THE MAGIC PUMPKIN

by

Benji Alexander Palus

iUniverse LLC
Bloomington

THE MAGIC PUMPKIN

This is a work of fiction. All of the characters, names, incidents, organizations, and dialogue in this novel are either the products of the author's imagination or are used fictitiously.

iUniverse books may be ordered through booksellers or by contacting:

iUniverse LLC
1663 Liberty Drive
Bloomington, IN 47403
www.iuniverse.com
1-800-Authors (1-800-288-4677)

Because of the dynamic nature of the Internet, any web addresses or links contained in this book may have changed since publication and may no longer be valid. The views expressed in this work are solely those of the author and do not necessarily reflect the views of the publisher, and the publisher hereby disclaims any responsibility for them.

Any people depicted in stock imagery provided by Thinkstock are models, and such images are being used for illustrative purposes only.

Certain stock imagery © Thinkstock.

ISBN: 978-1-4759-7048-7 (sc)
ISBN: 978-1-4759-7046-3 (hc)
ISBN: 978-1-4759-7047-0 (ebk)

Library of Congress Control Number: 2013900060

Printed in the United States of America

iUniverse rev. date: 07/13/2013

The author would like to thank

Emily, Virge, Mindy and Marian

for their invaluable input, and generous and loving support

and Keith

for allowing me to share his treasures

For Kaol and Kendall

INTRODUCTION

Owen and Oliver had a magic pumpkin. Now, there are many magical things, people and places. Some are always magical, having begun that way and which obviously will stay that way. Some find their magic and get to keep it forever while others lose it after only a little while. Then there are those things, people and places that have always been magic but that lose it and can't ever find it again. Those are the saddest kind.

Of the many magical things, only one was a pumpkin and it was the one that belonged to Owen and his little brother, Oliver. As far as the boys knew, the pumpkin had always been magical, but whether or not it will be magic forever is something that we shall just have to wait and see…

PART ONE

CHAPTER ONE

The enormous pumpkin flew across the bright pink sky, leaving a trail made of little wisps of its magic glow: autumn colors of red and orange and yellow and green, and even a bit of violet which swirled and faded into nothing a few seconds after the pumpkin had passed. Atop the pumpkin rode two small boys, brothers named Owen and Oliver. Owen was five years old at the moment and Oliver had just turned three, though he didn't know it.

Being the older brother, Owen got to "drive." That is, he sat on top of the pumpkin with his legs around the giant stem and steered with a piece of deep green vine that grew out of either side of the stem into a loop, much like the reins on a horse. In fact, it was this loop of vine that had first given Owen the idea to climb up onto the pumpkin and pretend that it *was* a horse, only to find himself flying away from the ground and from Oliver, who had started to cry, but that is another part of the story. Oliver was not crying now. Quite the opposite; he was laughing, as was Owen.

Riding the magic pumpkin was the boys' favorite thing to do. They looked forward to it every day. After Owen was up and settled at the reins, Oliver would climb up after him. Oliver was much smaller than Owen and often had trouble getting on the pumpkin. Owen would always try to help him but Oliver was determined to do it by himself, every single time, no matter how many tries it took or how many times he fell down.

Sometimes Owen would get impatient and yell at Oliver to hurry up. "Come on already, Oliver! You're never gonna get it! No! Not like that, you're doing it wrong! Put your foot *there*!"

This would only make Oliver more frustrated and half of the time he would sit on the ground, crying and pouting and hitting the pumpkin. "Shut up, Owen! I hate this stupid punkin! I wish we never found it! I don't evuh wanna ride it again!" Of course, Oliver didn't mean any of these things, nor did he mean to yell at his brother, but sometimes his temper got the best of him. He was only three, after all, and was easily discouraged when things did not go his way.

Owen would usually feel bad when Oliver couldn't get on the pumpkin. He never meant any of the angry things that he said, either, and the sight of his baby brother crying would almost always make Owen's anger melt away. That's when he would gently or cheerfully say, "It's okay, Oliver. You can do it!" and then Oliver *would* do it, grabbing at the piece of vine that Owen pretended he hadn't lowered and scrambling up behind him with a giggle or two of excited anticipation as he squeezed both arms around Owen's middle, pressed his head tightly against Owen's back and closed his eyes tight, waiting for the moment when the pumpkin would rise into the air and tickle the bottom of his belly.

The pumpkin flew over the gently rolling hills, carrying the young brothers who laughed at everything, and at nothing. They laughed at the black birds that yelled at them for flying through their flock. They laughed at the singing fish. They laughed at the feeling of the wind in their faces and because the sun and the moon were rising over the horizon together. They laughed because it was so ridiculous and at the same time so wondrous that they were actually riding on the back of a pumpkin that could fly through the air. Mostly they laughed because they loved each other and because they were together.

As close as the brothers were, they did not necessarily look like brothers at first glance. Owen had dark brown eyes, straight and thick dark hair that barely touched his collar in the back, and at age five he was already a bit lanky. It was obvious that he would someday be very tall like his Daddy. Oliver had bright blue eyes and long, reddish-blonde hair that grew out of his head straight, but then landed in curls on his shoulders and just above his eyes. He had lean limbs like his brother but didn't seem as if he would grow up to be quite as tall as him (although at age three it can be hard to tell such things), and Oliver still had some baby fat in his face and a plump round belly that often poked out from beneath his shirt.

Although these differences were striking, if one were to look a little closer they would see that both boys had the same friendly, round nose - nice and short. They would also see that although their eyes were different colors, the shape was almost exactly the same: big and round and bright, and with long lashes. Both of the boys had the same mischievous curl in the center of their upper lip and the same clumsy-looking ear lobes.

Strangely, where the brothers were probably most alike was in their little boys' hands, not just in the shape but in the curious way that they moved them. It was as if each finely shaped finger had a mind of its own and could move how it liked without regard to the rest. That is not to say that their fingers were constantly wiggling in all directions like the tentacles of an addlepated octopus, far from it. Rather, they moved in the way that the fingers of a talented pianist moved over the keys of a piano; all doing what they're supposed to be doing and doing it where they're supposed to be doing it, but no two fingers in the same place, often nor at the same time. Of course, neither boy could play the piano, indeed they had no piano to play even if they could, but this was how their fingers and hands moved no matter what activity occupied them, whether they were buttoning their shirts, picking rainbowberries or waving goodbye to the cow-pies in Springland. Their hands looked nimble even when they weren't doing anything at all. Most fingers rest together, sometimes curled this much and sometimes that much and sometimes laid flat, but Owen's and Oliver's fingers would rest at different angles from each other without the boys even noticing it. It was as if they had been carved by a master sculptor who had studied for weeks to find the perfect position to convey fluid grace, and yet the boys' hands never came to rest in the same position twice. Sometimes Owen would cross his fingers when he was content and sometimes Oliver would lay one finger aside his chin while he thought; it was all very bizarre, this finger business, especially in contrast to how clumsy the rest of their little bodies could often be.

Owen's fingers tightened on the vine as he steered the pumpkin up and over a hillside covered with long yellow grasses and withering weeds. Leaving the fire trees behind, the brothers headed toward the Dead Wood Forest where they liked to chase the leaves that fell from the black hole trees and blew about in the gusty winds. The pumpkin flew lower as it neared a light wood of tall, soft-colored trees whose rich fall foliage seemed to brighten the sunlight that shone through it. The boys were in Autumnland and it was a perfectly crisp autumn day.

The pumpkin landed with a quick bounce and a *fwump!* in a pile of leaves, sending up a rustling shower of red and yellow and orange and brown into which Owen and Oliver jumped and were immediately buried. The boys' laughing heads popped up, bits of leaves in their hair and sticking to their sweaters, and they waded out of the leaf pile. For a while they took turns running and jumping into the piles of leaves, until they had spread them all about, and then the brothers left the leaves and the pumpkin behind and walked off toward the black hole trees, holding each other's hands and knowing that by the next time they visited that place, the wind would have swept the leaves into piles again.

The boys walked hand in hand to a large stand of evergreen trees. It was dark amidst the evergreens, whose dense needles let little sunlight through, but the boys weren't scared. They cheerily strolled in among the trees and soon were walking downhill. The ground grew steeper and steeper until they came to a narrow open glade, enclosed on both sides by the tall evergreens. This was their favorite place to catch leaves. It was one of the few places in Autumnland where the grass was green and soft (for catching leaves entailed much falling down). This patch of grassy hillside sloped down to a place where the ground leveled out for a very short distance before the thick, black trunks of the Dead Wood Forest began. These were the black hole trees, which then continued, following the hillside down again all the long way to the bottom of a deep ravine and back up the other side. The black hole trees that grew out of the side of the hill had only three or four, or at most five dead leaves clinging to their dying branches, and yet few leaves littered the bare dark soil. The grass stopped shortly after the trees started, right at the place where the ground began to steeply slope downward again. These trees that grew out of the slanted ground twisted and turned in all manner of strange shapes and angles, trying to keep their footing in the steep earth. Many of these trees looked as if they would soon fall over, though they never did. Owen and Oliver often crept up to the edge of the grass to look down at this vast forest of black, serpentine trunks and branches that fell to a bottom that they could never quite decide if they could see. They were afraid to climb down among those trees. The evergreens that grew on either side of the glade stopped at the edge as well, as if they, too, were afraid.

A few trees grew almost in a line across the bottom of the grassy glade where the boys chased the leaves. These trees stood on the edge of the grass, just before the hill dropped again. They were also black hole trees, but they grew very differently from the ones growing out of the hillside just below. They were straight and tall, as tall as three-story houses, and they held up their branches proudly to show off the bright autumn colors of their leaves, or perhaps they held them up because they liked the feeling of the wind blowing through them; you never can tell with trees.

Powerful gusts blew through the smooth, black branches, sending their leaves toward the waiting brothers. The wind made a sound that is hard to describe if you've never heard it. It was an exciting sound and a soothing sound, all at the same time. It started with the rustling of thousands of dry leaves, which slowly grew louder and was then joined by the creaking of hundreds of branches. The howling of the wind then grew louder between the trunks, and its whistling reached higher through the tiniest, top branches. Added to this was the deep sound that the wind made as it blew through the wide, deep holes in the tree trunks, almost like a fog horn or someone who never runs out of breath blowing in a jug.

Something in the way that all of these different sounds built up and joined each other made Owen and Oliver feel as if something were building up inside them, like a growing excitement combined with the way that uncontrollable laughter bubbles up. It felt to the boys like life itself filling them and tingling in every single part of them, from the tops of their heads to the pits of their stomachs and even that place behind their kneecaps that made them want to kick their legs in excited anticipation of the giddiness that was about to burst free.

Feeling the strength of the wind build as it blew through their hair and over their skin, and even gently tossed them about, made it seem like a living thing. The wind was like a friend that was happy and excited to see the brothers and to play with them. It blew the leaves from the trees for the boys to jump about and try to snatch from the air. It carried the sound of their laughter as they missed and fell and rolled down the hill, and it shared in their shouts of glee when they actually caught a leaf.

Everything about this simple play of catching leaves filled the boys with a special joy that only children can feel, and being children, they never stopped to wonder at this or to ask why it was so. They didn't think about how long it would last or if they would ever feel it again. They simply enjoyed themselves as if the fun would last forever.

"Owen! I got one! That makes a hunn-jed!" Oliver ran about waving a big, brown leaf.

Owen rolled his eyes in an amused fashion and corrected his little brother, "That's only five, Oliver, and besides, I got eight already!" He had to raise his voice slightly to be heard over the wind.

"Nuh *uh*! A *hunn*-jed! I can count to a hunn-jed, you know!" Oliver confidently waited for an answer to what he felt was an inarguable point.

Owen did not give the answer that Oliver was hoping for. "I know you can count to a hundred, but you're cheating! You can only count the ones that fall from the trees."

Again, Oliver felt that he had the winning point in the discussion. "They *all* fell fum the chwees, Owen!"

Owen was half-frustrated and half-entertained by Oliver's straightforward logic. Rather than explain, he let Oliver think that he was winning. Owen stopped chasing leaves for a moment to watch Oliver. Sometimes, he liked to just watch his baby brother play. He loved him very much, and thought he was very funny. He watched Oliver run all around with his hands in the air, snatching at the leaves that flew by him. Oliver's upraised arms made his sweater lift up so that his belly poked out. Owen felt a warm surge of love and amusement, and grinned widely at Oliver's exposed belly button. Owen couldn't have put his feelings into words, but the term that would describe them best would be *endearing*; at times like that he found his brother's unaffected antics endearing.

But Owen's feelings went deeper than that. Just because he was a child and didn't have the vocabulary to describe his emotions or the experience to help him sort through them, that didn't make them simple. Just because he spoke and thought in unsophisticated terms didn't mean that he felt things that way. Owen might look at a color and call it purple because that was the only word he had for it, but that didn't mean that he couldn't tell the difference between violet, magenta, eggplant and indigo. It was the same with his feelings toward his little brother. He watched Oliver and thought that to do so made him feel *happy*, but only because he didn't know how else to express it, even to himself.

There is a love that grows for the things we take care of, and Owen took care of Oliver. This was something else that Owen would never have thought out for himself: part of the joy he felt when watching Oliver play was the satisfaction of doing a good job. He could be proud of himself because he had worked hard to provide his little brother with all of the things he needed, so that his laughter could come as easily as it did. Sometimes, when Owen felt afraid, he hid it from Oliver because he didn't want him to feel scared, too, and at times like that, Oliver's smiling face would in turn help Owen to find courage.

In this and many other ways, the boys had helped each other through many dark times, sometimes on purpose and sometimes it just worked out that way, but as we have said, feelings are not simple things, even for a five-year-old boy. Every bit as deep a reason for Owen's affections for his brother was something inside Oliver himself, something all his own, for Oliver was a child of incredible light and beauty. His inner glow spread to everything around him and made living things feel lighter inside themselves. Owen was a bit in awe of his little brother, though he didn't realize this, either. It was a fascinating thing; this delight Owen felt in having successfully protected the thing which delighted him.

Oliver jumped at a passing leaf, missed it by quite a lot and fell to the ground. He rolled over several times and sat up with a leaf in his hand that he had grabbed from the ground. "Owen! I got another one! That's *two* hunn-jed!"

"Oliver, that's not right! First of all, two hundred doesn't come after one hundred. Second of all, a hundred and one does. Third of all, that only makes six! And fourth of all quit cheating!"

Owen sounded angry but Oliver knew that he wasn't so he started to sing a song about the two hundred leaves he had caught until Owen interrupted him.

"I'm tired of catching leaves. I'm hungry," Owen said.

At these words Oliver stopped singing immediately and sat up. He asked, "Hungry for whut?"

While the boys had been playing, the bright pink sky had faded to white, and now began to darken to gray. There was a stillness in the air, as if the wind, sensing that play time was over, was resting.

"Well, Owen? What we gonna eat?"

Owen thought for a minute and said, "Let's eat some parrots."

Oliver got that look on his face that he used when he was trying out a suggestion in his head. His squinted eyes seemed to focus on a space up and to his right, then his lips squeezed together tightly and squished over to the same side while his head tilted in the opposite direction and he laid one finger aside his chin. Owen knew what to look for. If Oliver's eyebrows rose up, it meant, *Good idea, but what else have you got?* If only one eyebrow rose up and his nose got a wrinkle, it meant, *Nahhhhh, try again.* If his head tilted back and he looked at the sky, it meant that he was trying not to laugh, and that Owen would shortly see the corners of his mouth twitch into a smile as his excitement for the idea got the best of him. This last was what he did. Parrots it was.

"Race ya to the pumpkin!" said Owen, as he got to his feet and started to run.

Oliver ran after him but couldn't keep up and lost him in the evergreens. Oliver knew exactly where to go, but he had only freshly turned three and sometimes he got scared when he couldn't see his big brother. He yelled for Owen and when he didn't get an answer, Oliver let out a high-pitched sound of fear and started to cry. He ran faster, feeling panic, and he tripped and fell, skinning his knees and his nose on some roots that were poking through the bed of fallen evergreen needles. His whimpers turned to howls of pain and fear. The rain clouds had grown darker and Oliver became terrified that nighttime would come before he could find Owen. He screamed for Owen between high-pitched wails, his face very wet with tears. The eye shadows were coming to get him and he had nowhere to hide.

"MOMMY! *MOMMMMYYYYYYY!*"

Owen was already running back to Oliver as fast as he could. Even though he knew there was nothing to be afraid of, the sound of Oliver's screams cut right through him. His little brother's terror was working its way into him, too. Owen was also afraid of the shadow eyes. He knew that it would be hours before they would come, but still...

Owen found Oliver sitting and rocking back and forth, wailing and holding his knee. He saw the blood on his nose and on his pants and the thought ran through Owen's mind, *It's my fault!* He reached Oliver and crashed to his knees beside him, throwing his arms around him.

"It's all right, Oliver! It's okay! I'm here, I'm here!"

Oliver stopped screaming, but sobbed all the harder now that he felt safe again. He buried his face against Owen and held onto him tightly, as if he were afraid to let go. The two little boys sat wrapped in each other's arms for a few minutes, until Oliver's sobs grew quiet and ebbed to sniffles. Owen looked at his brother's nose, licked his own sleeve and very gently used it to wipe away the blood. He helped Oliver to his feet and held his hand until they were out of the evergreens, then it was Oliver's turn to yell, "We're still racing!" He started to laugh as he got a head start on Owen and was the first to slap his hand on the side of the pumpkin, causing a few swirls of color to thrill through his fingers. "I win!"

Children are remarkable creatures.

CHAPTER TWO

The pumpkin landed beneath the fire trees and Owen and Oliver jumped off to look for parrots. The sky was still pink in that part of Autumnland. The color reflected off of the white trunks of the trees and made them look even more like they were on fire.

The leaves on the fire trees were always yellow. They were not light yellow nor dark yellow, not lemon nor goldenrod. They were *yellow*, in all its primary glory, without blemish or variation. Every time that Oliver saw them he yelled, "Yeh-woh!" It was his favorite color. The leaves were so delicate as to be almost like feathers, and they danced in the slightest breeze like flames that couldn't be blown out. The first time that the boys saw the fire trees, they ran toward them, thinking to enjoy their warmth, but of course they were not actually on fire.

Among these slender white trunks, the parrots grew in the ground. Their deep red leaves were easy to spot growing out of the wheat-colored grass. It was Oliver who had discovered them. He had thought that the red leaves were pretty and had pulled on some with thoughts of saving them for Mommy. He'd been rather surprised and quite pleased with himself when the potato-shaped root pulled easily out of the ground, letting off a smell vaguely of cinnamon and sugar. He broke the root in half and saw that it was orange inside like a carrot. At the time, he had been so hungry that without even thinking (indeed, he had only been very small and would put most anything in his mouth anyway), he had immediately taken a bite and had found that it tasted even better than it smelled.

Owen had been picking fire leaves at the time and placing their stems between his fingers, whose subtle movement made the leaves dance so that Owen could pretend that his hands were on fire. He'd been running around, yelling and laughing, "Ahhhh! Oliver, help! I'm on fire! Ahhhhh!"

When Owen had seen Oliver chewing, he had stopped yelling. When he had stopped yelling, he had heard Oliver making quick, high-pitched yummy noises, as if he thoroughly approved of what he was tasting. When Owen had heard the yummy noises, he had grabbed the root from Oliver and taken a big bite. There had been a tense moment and things could have turned ugly, but luckily there were more parrots among the fire trees than the boys could ever hope to eat. So, after a minor scuffle, some hasty words and a few tears, they'd had a happy little feast and Owen, although he still didn't like Oliver putting just anything in his mouth, had had to congratulate his baby brother on his discovery.

The boys now sat in the grass, each with a lap full of parrots. Aside from the noisy chewing and an occasional "Mmmm!" the boys didn't talk. Owen finished eating first (as he usually did). He tossed what was left of his parrot to a couple of pipchunks that were frolicking nearby. The chubby creatures immediately began to stuff their cheeks with the discarded parrot. Owen and Oliver watched them for a bit and giggled at how silly they looked. When Owen had first seen these funny little gold animals with red stripes on their backs, he had thought out loud that they looked a little like chipmunks. Oliver had said, "Pipchunks!" and both boys had started laughing and repeating the name, over and over. The little animals had been pipchunks ever since.

Owen tossed them another parrot and said, "Ya know what, Oliver? I remember *real* parrots from when I was little."

Oliver looked at Owen as if he'd just said something very foolish. He held up a half-eaten parrot. "It's wheee-all."

"No, Oliver! Real parrots are *birds*. Our neighbor had one that could talk."

"*Whut*? Buhds can't talk!" Oliver gave his big brother an incredulous chuckle and shook his head.

"Can too! Ya know how the fish here can sing? Well when we were at home they had birds called parrots and they could talk!" Owen was trying to be patient but it wasn't easy when his word was being questioned by a three-year-old.

Oliver asked, "Well whut'd they say?"

Owen took a deep breath. He was growing annoyed that Oliver was missing the point. "I don't know! They said 'hello' and 'gimme a cracker'!"

Oliver was intrigued by the word cracker and asked, "What's cwackuh? 'S'at like lightning?"

At this sudden change of subject, Owen's patience was gone. "No!" he yelled, "It's something you eat! Don't you know *anything*?"

Every once in a while, Owen needed to talk about their home from before. He got frustrated when Oliver couldn't remember things. He knew that it wasn't Oliver's fault, but having no one to talk to about things like parrot-birds and cars and video games made Owen feel very lonely sometimes. Every now and then, he wondered if maybe he had dreamed it all, but Oliver still had some memories of their life before, too. At least, Oliver remembered Mommy and Daddy, and he remembered dogs and bubbles. Besides, Owen had proof that it was real.

This unbridgeable gap between the brothers was less hard on Oliver, but it did confuse him when Owen talked about home as if it were something that was gone. The same straightforward logic that exasperated Owen so much brought Oliver to the conclusion that he must not understand the word *home*. He thought that *home* was the cave where he and Owen lived. In fact he knew that Owen said it every day: *Let's go home, Oliver.* Yet sometimes at night, Owen would get sad in the cave. He'd start to cry and say, *I wanna go home.* Oliver didn't quite understand, but when Owen cried like that, it made him cry, too, and it made him miss Mommy and Daddy. Was that *home*?

"Owen, I'm *thuhhsty*," said Oliver.

"Me, too. Are you thirsty for green, gold, blue or white?" Owen asked, hoping that Oliver wouldn't say blue.

Each of the lands had its own river. The rivers were not wide, though they were mostly too wide for the boys to cross, nor were they very deep, though there were places where the boys could not see the bottom. It was as if they were child-sized versions of the rivers that had flowed in the place where the boys had come from.

Autumnland, where the boys were at the moment, had a gold river. It looked like a rippling sheet of gold that reflected light and images on its surface. The illusion had held until a hand had broken the surface of the water and its owner (in this case, Oliver), had found that he could still see his fingers, which had created ripples in the flow of the river.

The boys sometimes went to the Gold River to get a drink and became lost in the grace of their own fingers as they wove patterns in the current of the golden water, just beneath its surface. The boys moved their fingers in a way that they called, "making them shimmer." This was when they held their hands just under the water and all ten of their fingers moved about in what seemed like graceful randomness at first, but looking closer, it appeared that they were actually dancing; each finger paired with its own curling, flitting, undulating reflection of light. If the boys stared long enough, they forgot that they were the ones moving their fingers, or even that they *were* fingers. Their fingers became the gentlemen of the silent waltz, bowing and sweeping and swaying beneath the water, never breaking the plane which separated them from their partners, the ladies of light, who twirled and dazzled and leapt about on its surface. Being children, the boys found many ways such as that to relax their minds and to let their thoughts and imaginations drift along. Just as when they caught the leaves, they never stopped to wonder that they had discovered something of such beauty, nor indeed the marvelous fact that it existed to be discovered at all.

The Gold River's water tasted rich and sweet, like something fermented. When Owen drank it, he was reminded of honey and apple cider and pumpkin pie, though it didn't really taste like any of those things. Oliver thought that it tasted like candy, but when Owen asked him what kind he shrugged his shoulders and said, "I dunno." The gold water made the boys feel happily drowsy and very relaxed.

Summerland had a green river. It was not green like an ordinary river, but a deep, emerald green. The water was very clear and when the sunlight shone through it, Owen and Oliver could stand at the edge and see through the deep pools where the shimmering light penetrated to the bottom. The play of light created the illusion that emeralds were constantly appearing and disappearing. Sometimes the boys called it the treasure river and pretended that it was filled with real gems. They fought off hordes of imaginary enemies who wanted to steal their treasure. Sticks became swords and guns, and the brothers threw stones that blew up when they hit the bad guys.

Sometimes Oliver told Owen to stay back where it was safe, and then he faced the bad guys alone. Once in a while, Oliver pretended to be killed, sacrificing himself for his brother. It's hard to explain how that made Owen feel; sad because his imagination was strong and it was almost like watching it happen for real, but also proud of his little brother's selfless and noble nature. Owen never let the thought quite reach the surface of his mind, but he knew deep down that if it ever came to it, Oliver would actually be willing to die for him. The knowledge made Owen love his brother all the more, and it was a big part of why Owen strove to take such good care of him.

The water in the Green River was very refreshing, and filled with something that was obviously very good for the boys. When Owen first tasted it, he thought of Gatorade, though it didn't taste like Gatorade. The only way to describe the taste of the water would be to say that it tasted *green*; not like lime or sour apple green but the green that was life, the green of living things. The Green River made the boys feel invigorated and full of energy. If they were tired or sore from too much play, they could drink its healing water and feel better.

Springland had a white river. Actually more a shallow stream than a river, it trickled over the contours of its bed of countless pebbles and stones, cascading over tiny waterfalls and rippling around the larger stones in its way. This gave the white water the appearance of a river of tiny blossoms that were weightlessly born along an invisible current. The sound of the White River was a gentle and melodious glubbling that tickled the boys in a place deep inside them; a spot right in their center, below their hearts but above their stomachs. When the boys took off their clothes and played in the stream, adding their plishing and plashing to the babbling and bubbling, it was like a watery symphony.

The White River gently poured over its narrow course, accompanied on either side by the greenest, springiest grass in any of the lands. There were spots where the boys could even jump across from side to side without getting their feet wet. In some places, blossom trees grew by the side of the river. These trees had smooth bark that was a very pale brown with a warm, greenish hue. Some of the trees were filled with white blossoms, some with pink, and just a very few with pale lavender that was almost blue. The petals of the blossom trees shimmered and blew in the breeze as the autumn leaves did from the black hole trees, except as the wind was gentler in Springland, the falling petals gave the impression more of a gentle rain than a gusty storm. It was a funny thing that no matter how many of their leaves or blossoms were stolen by the wind, the trees in the land never seemed to have any less.

The boys took their baths in the White River, in spots where calm pools formed. When the boys sat in these pools, the water came up to Oliver's chest and to the middle of Owen's belly. The blossoms gathered in the pools and added their perfume to the already sweet-scented water. Strange as it was that two small boys actually loved to take baths, and without anyone having to make them, such was the case with Owen and Oliver. They often sat and played contentedly in their springtime bath for a very long time without growing tired of it. Perhaps if all little boys got to bathe outside in magic streams, it would not seem so strange at that.

The water in the White River had a flowery sweetness that reminded Owen of Easter lilies. The water was so light that the boys could barely feel it running down their throats when they drank it, but they could feel its airiness working through them and making them feel buoyant and lighthearted. They often went to the White River to drink when they felt scared, for though they lived in a wondrous place, there were things that scared them, and even things that wanted to hurt them.

Winterland had a blue river. It was a light, cold blue; the blue of glaciers and of deep, deep ice. Much like the White River cut a path through the green of Springland, the Blue River cut a path through the white of Winterland.

The boys couldn't swim in the Blue River. It was much too cold. The uncertain banks of the river were hidden under deep snow, so that the boys always approached it very carefully, never quite knowing when they would come to the edge. They had learned this the hard way, but that is its own adventure, to be told later. The Blue River was not like the others in that it did not invite the boys to come and play in its waters. It was beautiful, but in a different way. It made Owen think of all-white Christmas trees, the kind that Mommy liked to decorate with only blue ornaments. They, too, had seemed not-for-touching.

Of the four rivers, the sound of the Blue River was the most soothing. It was white noise, steady and unvarying, and strangely muted, like snow falling. To sit in the vast whiteness and watch the opaque blue waters flow by was to feel an incredible stillness and peace.

This was not a percipience that Owen and Oliver had found easily. It is not in the nature of small boys to sit and enjoy stillness. The fact that the boys had nearly died in those beautiful waters had given them a new understanding of the different natures of wondrous things. They had learned what it was to love something that could hurt them. They had sacrificed a piece of their innocence to the beauty of the Blue River and received knowledge in return. It is a tragedy that innocence lost can never be regained. Perhaps the greatest tragedy of life itself is that its one unalterable course is that of experience, to each of which a piece of innocence must be offered up as payment. We are born with a finite wealth of it, and spend our lives growing ever poorer, but for all that must be let go, there are also gifts that grow with exploration and even tribulation. The boys certainly felt the safety of the shore more surely after the danger of the waters, and when they went to the Blue River's treacherous edge to drink, they were testing themselves, testing their bravery. They were rewarded with proof of their courage as well as the invigorating, icy water coursing down their throats, with a taste so pure that it cannot be described.

On their way to Springland (for Oliver had chosen the White River, perhaps to help him over the last traces of his scare among the evergreens), the boys felt the rushing wind grow warmer as they flew through the air atop the pumpkin. The sky over Springland was a friendly, pale yellow that day with pillowy white clouds. (Yellow was Oliver's favorite color, but he eyed the sky suspiciously; because of a misunderstanding long ago, Oliver didn't entirely trust yellow skies, though his mistrust never affected his good mood in the least bit.)

The boys were laughing, as they almost always did when they flew on the pumpkin. They were filled with joy by the feat, as they were whenever they were touching the pumpkin, or even near it, for the pumpkin seemed to be *made* of joy. When it sailed across the sky with the boys clinging to its vines and ribs, it was as if it couldn't contain its own happiness, which overflowed and formed its swirling trail of glowing colors. The boys loved the pumpkin very much, and strange as it may be to assign the feeling to a vegetable, the pumpkin seemed to love them back. The pumpkin certainly watched over them, almost as would a parent...

The boys landed under a stand of blossom trees and Oliver watched as Owen blew at a blossom petal that had landed on his nose. After three quick tries Owen took a huge breath and blew with all his might. The petal flew into the air, but just as he was letting out an exasperated groan (as one tends to do after working much too hard to accomplish something simple), the petal gently floated down and perched on his nose once more. This made Oliver fall over from laughing. Owen stamped his feet and shook his fists.

"Gaaahhhhh! You stupid petal!"

Of course, Owen was only pretending to be angry at the petal in order to make Oliver laugh. He secretly felt good about the whole affair because he thought that the petal must like him, and it's always nice to feel liked.

The petal had fallen off when Owen yelled, so the boys crawled over to the stream to have a drink of the white water. The occasional giggle escaped them as they replayed the petal incident in their heads. Their giggling led to a spitting contest. They took turns taking a drink and then spitting it all out with a big laugh. The spitting went on until Oliver laughed for real with a mouthful of water. He choked until tears ran down his reddened face. Owen chuckled at his brother's gracelessness and playfully clapped him on the back until he was done. Oliver's choking didn't ruin the good mood, but it did put an end to the spitting, at least for that day.

The boys took off their sweaters and after using them to dry their faces, hung them on the pumpkin.

Owen said, "Oliver, let's explore the river."

Oliver always liked this idea. It meant that they were going to walk in the stream and that he could splash as much as he wanted. "Which way we go?" he asked.

From where the boys were standing, they could follow the river downstream, where it flowed through a lush, green pasture filled with cow-pies eating yellow flowers, or they could follow it upstream, where the blossom trees grew thick and made the sunlight dance on the water.

Owen said, "Let's go upstream through the trees." He was hoping that more petals might land on his nose.

Oliver scrunched his face to one side and lay a finger on his chin, but only for a moment before he jumped in the stream and started splashing his way toward the blossom trees. He really didn't care which way they went. He would be looking down at his splashing feet.

Chapter Three

The sun was setting before the boys were in sight of the cave they called home. It was much too low in the purple sky for Owen's liking, which made this one of those times when he had to hide his fear from Oliver. Owen willed the pumpkin to fly a little faster toward their cave. Once the sun set there were very few places that were safe from the shadow eyes. However, one of those places was the boys' cave.

The entrance to the cave was located behind a clump of bushes on a steep, grassy hillside in Summerland. As far as the boys knew, they and the pumpkin were the only things ever to go in or out of their cave, except, of course, for what they brought with them. The pumpkin couldn't actually fit into the cave proper, but stayed in an area just inside the opening where it was at least dry.

The pumpkin brought the boys to the entrance of the cave just as the sun's bottom edge touched the horizon. Owen and Oliver nervously hopped down and each gave the pumpkin an affectionate pat.

"Night-night, Punkin!" said Oliver.

"See you tomorrow," said Owen.

The boys crawled through a narrow space about as long as Owen and then yelled, "Woohoooooo!" and slid over the edge, down a short, smooth slope. They landed in a pile of feathery fire leaves just as the echoes died. It was always nice to come home, and the slide made it even nicer.

Theirs was no ordinary cave. The cave was shadowless, which was why it was safe from the shadow eyes. A special kind of rock formed every last square inch of the cave. The brothers called it glow rock, for that's exactly what it did. It glowed with a soft opalescence, so that being in the cave was like being inside of a dim nightlight. Every bit of surface on the inside of the cave was its own omni-colored light source, so that no matter where the boys stood or how they waved their arms or what they put down; *no matter what*, they could not make a shadow. This discovery was so strange and astounding that it had sent the boys into uncontrollable peals of laughter. If one could imagine what it feels like to look at something that is impossible, they would understand the jollity that the boys felt when they found their cave.

After a dip at the bottom of the little slide, the floor continued to slope gently down so that the main part of the cave was shaped roughly like a bowl. If one stood on the edge of the bowl and looked down at the bottom, it would be like looking from the second floor of a house into the living room on the first floor. When the boys ran down to the bottom of the bowl and up the other side, it was as far as running from home plate to the pitcher's mound on a Little League baseball field. Too many times to count, the boys had climbed up to the lip of the bowl and then run back down and up the other side. Dozens of skinned knees and scuffed hands (from each of the times that their clumsy little feet had tripped them up), couldn't keep the boys from doing it again and again and again.

Between the edge of the bowl and the walls of the cave there was a flat ridge that was a very few feet wide and ran all around its edge. There was just enough room between this circumventing ridge and the ceiling of the cave for a tall man to stand up straight. Along the ridge, in the back part of the cave, were three openings in the rock wall. The boys called that part of their cave "upstairs."

One of these openings was a crack in the far left side of the back wall. It made a narrow walkway with high, steep sides and led to a place where a shaft had formed in the rock floor. The boys couldn't see the bottom, even though it had no turns and, like everything else, was lit by the glow rock that formed it. Luckily it was too narrow for the boys to fit through, for it really was a very long way down. This was where the boys went to the bathroom at night. After all, they had to go *somewhere*, since they couldn't leave the safety of the cave. They never wondered where it all went, they just had fun watching it go and laughing at the echos that traveled down the shaft.

In the middle of the back wall, directly across from the little slide, was the boys' bedroom. It was a wide rectangular opening in the rock, roughly the size of the bedroom that the boys had shared before they came to that place. The back of the area was raised like a dais and the boys had gathered lots of soft, feathery fire leaves to sleep on. They also had a blanket which was old and dirty and worn but still soft. They slept next to each other, and on scary nights Owen would hold his baby brother until they fell asleep. Often, Oliver would still be wrapped in Owen's arms when he awoke the next morning. They slept where they did because it gave them a clear view to the opening of the cave. If either brother awoke in the night and felt lonely or especially afraid, they could cast their eyes toward the magic pumpkin and its warm orange glow would comfort them.

To the right of the boys' bedroom was a sloping tunnel that led up to a small room where Owen and Oliver kept their booty piles. These were their treasures. The first thing that the boys always did when they arrived at their cave was to run down the wall of the bowl, up the other side, and go to their booty piles. They would look through them, admiring what they had, and then add whatever interesting bits they had found during the day.

They each had their own pile in different spots in the booty room. Owen's pile was up on a shelf of rock that had formed on the right side of the room. It was so high that he would have had to lift Oliver up for him to see. Owen could climb onto the shelf fairly easily but Oliver couldn't do it without help. Perhaps this was why Owen chose his spot, but he needn't have worried. Oliver was more concerned with his own booty, which was piled in a small cubbyhole in the floor on the left side of the room.

The boys' booty piles were the only areas in which each of the brothers expected and gave the other privacy. They each needed to have something that was all their own; their proof to themselves of their individuality, for they were always together and there was never anyone but them. The boys were so dependent on each other that they had become a part of each other's sense of self. This wasn't necessarily a bad thing under the circumstances. In fact, the brothers shared something incredibly special with each other that was magnificent in its very necessity. Their two little lives were so a part of each other's, so closely shared, that the brothers knew a selflessness that most never would. The boys lived for each other, their own joy and happiness so tied to each other's that personal or selfish desire was almost a thing unknown to them. No decision was made that didn't affect them both. No discovery was made that wasn't shared (except for one, selflessly kept by Owen for a very long time; and his one selfish desire). So they had their booty, none of which was secret, but all of which was sacred as being *theirs*, each their own.

Owen climbed up onto his shelf and emptied his pockets. He had a small haul that day: just a couple of interesting rocks and the pink petal that had kept landing on his nose. Owen sorted through his pile, trying to decide where to put the newest additions. He *could* add the petal to his leaf zoo, except that the reason he'd kept it was because it had seemed to want to be his friend. The zoo was more for leaves that he'd found and brought back just to collect them. He had fire leaves, blossoms of all three colors, black hole leaves, elephant ears, mouse ears, parrot leaves, leopard leaves *and* tiger leaves, he had a whole bough of evergreen needles from Winterland with the berries still attached, he had the big green and silver flutter leaves that only came out on cloudy days, and the pride of his leaf zoo: a giant paint leaf. Owen set the petal aside for now. He would find a special place for it later.

Owen looked over his sticks. The clubs/swords and the ones shaped like guns were set aside in case of surprise attacks by imaginary enemies, but he also had one stick that was shaped vaguely like a man and another that made him think of a fire truck with the ladder extended.

He also had a few mud sculptures that were now dried and crumbling. One was of Oliver and had a big belly. Another was a patty that he'd told Oliver was poop, right before he had thrown it at him. He smiled now at the memory of how mad Oliver had been, and of how he'd laughed and thrown it back at when Owen had told him that it was only mud. By the end of that epic mud battle both boys had been splendidly filthy. Oliver didn't know that Owen had saved that first clump of mud in his pocket.

Owen's favorite thing to collect was rocks. He had more rocks than anything else and he now added the two that he had brought back that day. The new ones were both smooth, round and pearly white. He had found them in the bed of the White River. He also had blue rocks of nearly every shade, red rocks, brown rocks, gray rocks, black rocks, shiny rocks, sharp rocks, smooth rocks, clear rocks (which made everything go funny when he looked through them), speckled rocks and marbled rocks, flat rocks and box rocks. He was running out of room for all of his rocks. He'd have to take some down to the Green River and throw them in.

Owen looked for signs of the bright orange and red lizards that he kept bringing back to the cave. He didn't expect to find any and he wasn't disappointed. The lizards always escaped when Owen's back was turned, though he kept bringing more whenever he could find them.

Owen had a special section for things that Oliver had given to him. In this pile was a tiny speckled egg that Oliver had found in Springland. Oliver had seen a bird's nest in a blossom tree and had climbed up to get it, but in his excitement to show Owen he had fallen out of the tree and all of the pretty, raspberry-colored eggs had broken except for one. Oliver had cried a lot when he'd fallen; he had wanted so badly to share the find with Owen (and also because it was the first time that Oliver had ever had the wind knocked out of him, which had scared him badly), but the nest had broken and the eggs were gone. When Owen had found that one was left, Oliver had gotten excited and given it to him to keep.

Also in this section of Owen's pile was the only bright green rock that either of the boys had ever found. Oliver had found it and knowing that Owen's favorite color was green, he had given it to him. There was also a rock that Oliver had thought looked like a bird. He'd painted it with paintberries and given it to Owen because he had said he liked it.

Finally, tucked behind everything else, there were a few cherished items that Owen prized most of all. These were things that he'd had in his pockets when he and Oliver had arrived in the land. There were two quarters, three dimes and a nickel, two marbled rubber balls, one pink and one blue, and a yellow Matchbox Lamborghini that had belonged to his Daddy when he was a little boy. When everything that Owen remembered seemed very far away, he could look through these things, pick them up and hold them. Sometimes it helped.

Also with these special items was something that Owen had made for Mommy. It was a necklace made of the pinkberry vines that grew in Summerland. It had taken Owen weeks to figure out how to braid the pink vines into a necklace. There had been a lot of trial and error, a lot of frustrated and discouraged tears, and a lot of vines angrily thrown down the bathroom shaft, but Owen had kept trying. He loved his Mommy very much and deep down he had secretly hoped that if he could make the necklace pretty enough, so that Mommy would really like it, then maybe Mommy would come for him and Oliver. She could make everything okay so that they could all go back home again. Eventually, Owen had made something that he was very proud of. He knew that Mommy would love it, and even though she hadn't come, he kept it safe, just in case. He picked it up now and carefully put it on. It helped him to miss her a little less. With one thumb in his mouth and the other absently caressing the pink vine, Owen looked down and watched his little brother.

Oliver had only brought one thing for his booty pile that day: parrot leaves. Since the first time that he had seen them, Oliver had always saved some of the pretty red leaves for Mommy. Every day, he pulled the fresh leaves from his pockets and lovingly put them in this safe place for her. He thought about Mommy's smiling face that he barely remembered, how happy she would be when she saw the pretty leaves that he had found for her, and this made Oliver happy.

In general, Oliver preferred giving to having and so his pile was smaller than Owen's. There were some practical items, though, and some things that were very precious to him. Oliver had a few rocks. He mostly kept them so that he would have something to throw in the Green River with Owen, but he had two special rocks that he would never part with. These were bright silver. Owen had found them and given both of them to him. Owen had also found some gun-shaped sticks for him, and had pulled the twigs from a couple of long ones so that they could be used as swords.

All of Owen's gifts were special to Oliver, who idolized his big brother. He looked up to Owen, who always seemed to know about everything. Oliver had once started a leaf zoo in emulation, but it had annoyed Owen so much that they had fought over it and Oliver had thrown his leaves down the bathroom shaft in a tantrum. Owen had simply wanted something of his own, and he had felt sorry that he had upset Oliver enough to make him throw away his zoo, but of course making Owen feel sorry had been the reason why Oliver had thrown it away in the first place. He hadn't actually wanted the zoo so much as to be more like his big brother, and it had deeply hurt his feelings that Owen hadn't wanted that, too.

Oliver also kept a lot of paintberries in his pile. He loved to paint. The outside of the cave was covered in his and Owen's drawings (almost every time that Oliver started painting, Owen asked if he could have some berries to paint with, too). Oliver also had some flat rocks that he had covered in bright colors. Though Owen kept his berries in careful order according to color when painting, Oliver let his get all mixed up; the brighter the better, he thought. Oliver had tried eating the paintberries once, but they had made him sick. He had thrown up rainbow colors all that morning and had never eaten them again.

Oliver, too, had his prized possessions. They were gifts from Owen; the rest of the items that he'd had in his pockets on the day the boys had arrived. He had once shown them to Oliver when they were talking about home, in the hope that they would help Oliver to remember. When Owen had seen the reverence with which Oliver handled these unique artifacts, he had thoroughly approved, enough to let Oliver keep some. He had given him the three pennies (because Oliver didn't understand that they weren't worth as much), a third marbled rubber ball (this one yellow), and a Matchbox Volkswagen Bus that also had once belonged to the boys' Daddy.

The boys often thought about their Daddy, but they did not miss him in the same way that they missed their Mommy. If they could have analyzed why this was, they would have found that in fact they felt their Daddy's comforting presence all along, but not noticing something that they didn't feel to be missing, the boys never stopped to realize this.

"Owen, let's play caws!" Oliver had finished with Mommy's parrot leaves and picked up the Matchbox bus.

Owen got his car and hopped down from his shelf. The boys went to opposite sides of the lip of the bowl that made the downstairs of their cave. They let go their cars and did their best to have them meet at the bottom in head-on collisions.

Eventually the boys grew sleepy. They climbed up to their bedroom and ate a snack of leftover pinkberries before falling asleep. It had been a very full day for them and they slept soundly, straight through the night.

The pumpkin sat motionless in the entrance of the cave, as it did every night, keeping the boys safe from the darkness outside and allowing nothing that could harm them to enter.

CHAPTER FOUR

Owen and Oliver burst out of their cave under the orange morning sky. They threw themselves down the hill and rolled all the way to the bottom, coming to a stop a few feet from the tendrils of some pinkberry vines. For a few moments they simply lay on their backs with their arms and legs spread out.

"Tha's fun!" Oliver said. "Le's do it again!"

Owen looked back up the hill to see if the pumpkin had followed them. It usually didn't, and it hadn't this time. It was a distance of about half the length of a football field to climb back up to where the bushes hid their cave in the side of the grassy hill. "Let's eat first," Owen said.

After a quick face scrunch, Oliver agreed. He was very hungry, and so his mind switched gears easily (it didn't occur to him that he need climb only a little way up the hill to still enjoy a brisk roll). Without sitting up, Oliver used his legs and feet to push himself head-first through the grass and work himself under the pink vines. Owen watched and started to laugh, then plopped down on his back and did the same thing. Both boys giggled every time they pushed themselves to a new spot, picking and eating the creamy pink berries as they went.

A short time later, the boys lay under the vines with full bellies, looking up at the sky with their fingers interlaced behind their heads. The sky was still orange, but lighter now; the color of peach ice cream. The changing color of the sky was something that neither brother had yet gotten completely used to. Sometimes it was off-putting, giving them a feeling that confused them. If they had been familiar with the term *surreal*, they could have categorized this strange feeling, processed it and understood it better. More often though, the changing color of the sky was just one more thing about the land that amused them. The boys were young enough so that many of the things that come to be seen as most certainly being one way and no other were not yet set in stone for them. They had seen the sky take the hue of every color in the spectrum at one time or another. Once in a while it was even blue.

The sun was not yet at its zenith. Its light shone through the vines, making intricate patterns of shadow that crisscrossed the boys and the ground beneath them. A slight breeze fluttered the green and pink leaves and blew a rolling quiver over the grass, adding a dancing play of sunlight to the fixed shade of the vines. A sweet scent was carried on the wind, of the grass and berries, and something else: summertime.

Oliver rolled over onto his side and planted his elbow in the grass, resting his cheek in the palm of his hand. He watched the play of sunlight and shadow on his brother. They seemed to frolic across Owen's dreamily blissful features. Oliver wanted to ask Owen something, but he was afraid that it would upset him and ruin his good mood.

It was the shadows. Oliver usually didn't want to talk about the eye shadows, but he had been really scared yesterday when he had lost Owen in the evergreen trees, and he needed reassuring. Lying there in the warm grass with a belly full of pinkberries, danger seemed so far away, but still he hesitated. It was finally these nice shadows and how different they were from the eye shadows that made Oliver feel safe enough to speak.

"Owen?" and a pause, "I was scay-ud yestuhrday."

Owen didn't turn. He kept looking up at the sky, his expression unchanging. "It's okay to be scared sometimes, Oliver, but I'm not ever going to leave you all alone."

"Awn't you a scay-ud of the eye shadows, Owen?"

Owen lost his faraway look. He still stared at the sky, but he was back in the moment. He said, "How many times do I have to tell you? They're called *shadow eyes*, not eye shadows. Eye shadow is makeup."

"But they'uh not made up! They wee-uhl!" Oliver argued.

Owen explained, "No! Not *made* up, *makeup*. It's something Mommies wear."

"Whut? Wayuh? Like socks and shuhrts? On Mommy's *eyes*?" Oliver was thoroughly confused. He had wanted Owen to tell him that the eye shadows wouldn't get him, but somehow they were talking about eye clothes. Oliver couldn't picture what eye socks could possibly look like.

"Nooooooo!" Owen yelled. "Makeup is like paint that Mommies wear on their faces."

This made more sense to Oliver, but the picture in his head made him feel afraid. "Why would Mommy paint shadows on huhr eyes? Was she tryin' ta scayuh you?"

Owen smiled and his faraway look returned. "No, Mommy wore makeup to be pretty for Daddy. I don't know why they call it eye shadows. I thought it made her eyes look brighter." Owen had never thought about it before, but it did seem like a strange thing to call it. "She also had something called lipstick that she painted her lips with. It was kinda like a paintberry." Owen's smile grew. He was remembering just how pretty his Mommy was, especially when she smiled at him.

The picture in Oliver's head was much different after this explanation. He was now smiling, too. "Whut cuh-wuh wips?" He was picturing Mommy with bright eyes and bright yellow lips.

Owen answered, "Red, when she wore it. It was always red…or pink, I think."

"Pink I think!" Oliver's mind had switched gears again. He loved to rhyme. He rolled over onto his back again, and so didn't notice that Owen's smile had faded.

As always after enjoying memories of Mommy, Owen felt the sobering realization that she wasn't there and that he might never see her or Daddy again.

"Yeh-woh I theh-woh! Red I said! Guh-ween I mean! Buh-wue I poo poo!"

Luckily Owen had a baby brother to make nonsense rhymes that cheered him up. At "blue I poo poo," he laughed out loud and repeated it with Oliver over and over.

Oliver started to rhyme his brother's name, "Owen is growin' and outside it's snowin'!"

It was harder to rhyme Oliver's name, but Owen did his best, even though he had to cheat a little bit. "Call-iver Oliver to go bring the *ball over*!"

"Owen is slowin' 'cause he stubbed his toe-wen!"

"Oliver is small-iver and wishes he was tall-iver!"

After the boys ran out of rhymes, their laughter died down. Owen started to get up but Oliver held on to his hand, "Wait, Owen."

Both boys were sitting up. Oliver looked a little scared so Owen gave his hand an encouraging squeeze while he waited to hear what was wrong.

Oliver said, "*Awww* you a scayud of the eye shadows, Owen?"

"Yeah," Owen admitted, "but they only come out at night."

Oliver thought for a few seconds while Owen waited patiently. "And they can't get in ow-wuh cave?"

"No, Oliver. They can't get in our cave. They can't even get us in Winterland if we stand in the snow, remember?"

Oliver did *not* remember, but if Owen said so, he knew that it was true. "But whut about punkin? It can't fit in the cave. They can't get punkin?"

"No, Oliver. Pumpkins can't get scared! Besides, the pumpkin *glows*."

There was another pause, this one a little longer. "The eye shad... shadow eyes won't evuh get me again, Owen?" If Owen said they wouldn't, Oliver knew that he could believe him.

Owen was five years old, but to Oliver at moments like that, he may as well have been a grownup. Such was Oliver's trust in him. "I promise, Oliver. They'll never get us again." Speaking the words helped to convince Owen almost as much as it did Oliver, so he continued, "If they try, I'll poke 'em in the eyes!"

This made Oliver laugh and made both boys feel brave. Oliver added, "And I'll *kick* 'em in the eyes!"

"I'll get a stick and stab 'em in the eyes!"

"I'll throw rocks at their eyes!"

"I'll *pee* in their eyes!"

"I'll *poop* in their eyes!"

The boys' laughter dissipated the last of their nervousness after talking about such a scary subject. They climbed back up the hill on hands and knees, taking their time and looking for lizards. Never having any particular place to be or any particular time to be there, the brothers followed their fancies, chasing whatever distractions crossed their paths or entered their heads. They made plans for some days, and sometimes they kept those plans, but just as often they followed wherever the day led them.

There was no one to tell them when to wake up or when to go to bed. There was no one to call the boys home for supper or to make them go to school. Time itself seemed funny there, as if it were passing and not passing. Day followed night, followed by day again, always the same, and yet summer and winter were places to go instead of seasons that passed. It was the boys that came and went while the seasons stood still.

No matter how it may have seemed, time was indeed passing. Every morning, the boys woke up and were one day older. They were growing up. It wouldn't be long before Oliver would be able to hop up on the pumpkin as easily as Owen.

But then what?

Oliver looked forward to getting big like his older brother so that he would be able to do the things that Owen could do, but Owen had an anxiety about it that he didn't know how to express. Indeed, he didn't even know that it was there. It came out through his temper at times when Oliver didn't deserve it.

The first time that Oliver had been able to climb a melon tree and get his own melon, Owen had pushed him down and taken it from him. There had been instant hot tears running down Oliver's cheeks. He hadn't understood why his brother had been angry. He had thought that Owen would be proud of him and had been expecting praise. Like many of his accomplishments, Oliver had gotten his own melon mostly to please and impress his big brother. He'd been excited to hear what a good job he'd done. It had confused him and hurt his feelings deeply when Owen had reacted that way. Oliver had sat and cried while Owen had smashed his melon on the ground.

Owen hadn't done it because he was mean or angry, but because he'd been scared and hadn't understood why. He had been just as confused as Oliver, whose wailing cries had upset Owen even more and so he had yelled at Oliver to "Shut up!" The more upset that Owen had gotten, the harder Oliver had cried, which had only made Owen more upset. Soon Owen had no longer been angry at his brother but at himself for making Oliver cry, though neither brother had understood this.

Afterward Owen, feeling terrible, had climbed up and gotten another melon for his brother, but Oliver hadn't taken it. He'd been afraid to. Even though he had been very hungry, he was so sorry for upsetting Owen that he hadn't felt that he deserved the melon. Oliver trusted his older brother so much that although he hadn't understood, he'd known that he must have done something wrong for Owen to have yelled at him and taken away his food.

Owen had assumed that Oliver had refused the new melon because he was trying to make him feel even worse than he already did, and this had made him start to cry over his guilt and frustration. Owen's tears had made Oliver feel worse and he had started to cry again, too. So they had sat, a few feet apart with their backs to each other, each brother's sobs feeding the other, each of them wanting nothing more than to go home, to their real home with Mommy and Daddy.

There was no one to tell them when to wake up or when to go to bed. There was no one to call the boys home for supper or to make them go to school. And there was no one to pick them up and hold them, no one to dry their tears and tell them that it was okay.

Eventually their tears had dried on their own. The boys had grown calm, the tranquilizing effect of their sobs leaving them feeling lightheaded. When the snuffling and sniffling had died down, Owen had gone over to Oliver and very gently asked him if he wanted to climb up the tree together and have a picnic in the branches.

"Like monkeys?" Oliver had asked timidly, yet hopefully.

Owen had then held out his hand and helped his baby brother up. Both boys had gotten wide grins on their faces, the kind that get bigger the harder you try to stop. They had each been so relieved to be forgiven and to agree on something again that it had made them giddy and they'd had the best monkey picnic in a tree that anyone has ever had.

Owen hadn't understood that what he feared was growing up, and he didn't understand it now. He just knew that he felt uneasy because his shoes were too tight. He stood up, having found not a single lizard.

"Oliver, I think we need new shoes."

Oliver got excited, "Does 'at mean...?"

"Yup!" Owen started to get excited, too.

The boys climbed onto the pumpkin and then they were soaring through the pale orange sky, on their way to Springland.

The make-place was one of the most magical places in that very magical land. It was where the boys went to get new clothes when they ruined or outgrew what they had. There they found clothes for all the seasons: shorts and crocs for Summerland, jeans and sweaters for Autumnland, even gloves and hats and snowsuits for Winterland. Owen and Oliver had no idea where the clothes came from. Every time they went to the make-place new clothes were simply there, under a wide shelf of rock that kept them dry in case it rained. All of the clothing that they found had an unpretentious, even wholesome quality about it, as if it were a gift from a loving but practical grandmother. Somehow it was always what the boys needed most. They grew so used to the fact that they could count on this that they hadn't bothered to wonder about it in a long time.

Owen now needed new shoes and so he knew that that was what would be there, and that they would be the right size. This was one, but hardly all, of the curious phenomena of the make-place.

The path to the make-place was lined on both sides with wedding trees (very thin trees with green leaves, white flowers and little poisonous black berries), whose branches stretched over the path. The sky above Springland was a soft lime green that day, so that when the boys flew along the path beneath the wedding trees, the green sky made it seem even more than usual that they were in a tunnel. This tunnel of trees had the effect of relaxing each of the boys' minds, a very fortuitous approach to such a destination as the make-place.

Owen stared straight ahead, enjoying the way that the trunks of the trees seemed to be gliding past while he, Oliver and the pumpkin seemed to be sitting perfectly still. Oliver looked to the side, his unfocused eyes taking in the blur of green, black and white movement. The boys rounded the third bend in the tunnel of wedding trees and then they were there.

The make-place was at the base of a smooth, light gray stone wall that was as high as a five-story building. This wall formed the foot of a mountain range on the border of Springland. The brothers had been following the White River one day when Owen had seen the wedding tree tunnel in the distance and had thought that it looked like fun. He had guided the pumpkin between the trees to see where they led, while Oliver had hung on and giggled at each turn. Upon reaching the stone wall, the first thing the boys had noticed was the clothestone.

It was also the first thing that they checked now. Sure enough, there were two brand new pairs of sneakers waiting for them, red ones for

Owen and blue ones for Oliver. There was also a pair of jeans to replace the pair that Oliver had torn when he had fallen among the evergreens the day before. The boys put on their new shoes and Oliver his new jeans and they both said "Thank you!" to the clothestone. They left the old clothes that they had just replaced and went and sat in front of the stone wall.

Owen asked, "What should we talk about?" He answered himself, "I know! Do you remember ducks?"

"Ducks? What's ducks?" Oliver answered. His eyes were already bright with anticipation as giggles started to escape him. He knew exactly what ducks were, and that they were very funny.

"Hmmmm, what's my duck look like?" said Owen. "I know! He's all white and fluffy, and he goes 'Quack quack quack quaaaaack!'"

As soon as Owen started to speak, a fluffy white duck appeared, hovering in space a few feet above the ground in front of the wall. The duck began to do everything that Owen described. When the duck started his loud vociferous quacking, Oliver laughed until he couldn't breathe. Owen was trying to describe the duck's waddle, but he was laughing so hard that he could barely speak. He yelled out syllables at a time, "Wad...wad...WADDLE!"

The duck made movements like a terribly poor dancer and made the boys laugh even more.

"What's duck's name, Owen?" Oliver asked.

"Mister Puff Puff! What about your duck?"

Oliver answered, "He's got a gween head, but no body. His name's Daddy and he waddles onnuh cee-wing!"

"*What?* Oliver, that's crazy!" This image of an upside-down, waddling head was too much for Owen. He rolled over onto his back and told Oliver how crazy he was between gasps for air.

Oliver had already gotten his laughter under control. He sat and admired his ceiling-waddling duck with a big satisfied smile on his face. He didn't notice anything else.

This was another moment when Owen felt awe for his brother, and a bit of envy. Owen couldn't help thinking that Daddy was a stupid name for a duck, and that a duck with no body didn't make sense, but Oliver was so delighted by what he'd created that it was as if he didn't even notice how stupid it was. Though this naivety made Owen feel a little jealous at first, he then began to see it differently. He became as delightedly absorbed in watching Oliver as Oliver was in watching his duck named Daddy.

Oliver said, "And den he fawz dowwwwn!"

Daddy the duck head fell from the ceiling and landed upside-down with a loud, indignant, *Quack*! Oliver turned around with bright eyes to see if Owen was laughing, which of course he was. Once again, Owen was feeling a wave of love for his little brother's innocent and unaffected amusement.

But then Owen said, "There's a big red dinosaur chasing Mr. Puff Puff!"

Immediately a Tyrannosaurus Rex appeared and started chasing the fluffy white duck, who quacked his disapproval of Owen's choice quite vehemently. Owen laughed but Oliver was scared by the dinosaur's roar and by his giant, gnashing teeth.

Oliver yelled, "No, Owen! No monstuhs!"

Owen was amused by his little brother's fear. These things weren't real and he knew that Oliver knew it. Owen calmly asked him, "Well, what would you do if a *real* dinosaur came?"

Owen's calmness helped Oliver to settle down a bit.

Oliver said, "I'd chop off his head!" and the T-Rex's head popped neatly off.

Mr. Puff Puff stopped his waddling to turn around and quack at the decapitated dinosaur.

Oliver then said, "An' 'en I'd chop 'im in bits!"

Off popped the dinosaur's arms, legs and tail.

Mr. Puff Puff, with an attitude that all but screamed, "Take *that*!" bit the tip of the dinosaur's tail.

This forced a laugh from Oliver that was made half of surprise and half of relief. He continued, "An' 'en I'd poke him inna eyes with big sticks!"

Immediately the dinosaur was whole again, but no longer scary. Now he looked like a cartoon. He had long staff-like sticks poking out of his eyes and they swung in all directions as the dinosaur looked around. The boys found this disturbing image to be hilarious.

Owen said, "I'd kick him in the berries!" and the dinosaur crumpled to the ground trying to reach between his legs with his little arms. The sticks in his eyes started rolling round in sweeping arcs, each rotating in opposite directions.

Oliver joyously yelled, "I'd kick 'im in the *nawwwds!*" and the dinosaur let out a comical howl, flailing his wee arms in pain and frustration because they were too short to reach what the boys referred to as his "painful place."

After being tortured for a while, the dinosaur became "a hunnjed bunny wabbits" that scampered all around sniffing and twitching their little noses. The bunnies started to do somersaults until they were just fuzzy balls rolling around, bouncing off of each other. Then they started to pop up in the air ("like popcorn!"), making sounds like tiny explosions muted by furry pillows. The popped bunnies floated away like balloons, getting only so high before popping again but this time like bubbles, leaving no trace but a few wispy hairs that dissolved into nothing.

Next there was a great space battle with starships and lasers. Oliver was getting tired so he let Owen make the space ships while he sat and watched. Owen knew a lot more about space ships, anyway. There was a magnificent display of varicolored explosions and intricate maneuvers. Lasers and rockets were flying everywhere. Oliver rejoined the story and the space battle evolved into an alien dance contest. There were the cool aliens (who happened to be two brothers), and the stupid aliens. The cool aliens danced all over to a song without words that Owen and Oliver made up. They leapt way up into the air and spun around and did fantastic flips, and then the stupid aliens either tried one pathetic hop or just fell down on their faces because they were so stupid. Needless to say, the cool alien brothers won every time.

By the end of the seventh dance-off Owen and Oliver started to get hungry so they took a break to gather some rain peas that grew in a field adjacent to the tunnel of wedding trees. Before the boys actually ate any peas, they ran around playing tag with each other, invigorated by the open field and by the sweet smell of the plants and of the flowers that grew from them.

When the brothers had gotten the exercise that their bodies demanded, they each gathered a shirt full of pea pods and took them back to the stone wall. Owen liked to open up the pods and pick out the rain peas, tossing them into his mouth a handful at a time. Oliver liked to put the whole pod in his mouth and then pull it out through his gently clenched teeth, making the peas pop into his mouth one by one. The boys continued to lazily imagine while they munched on their peas, eventually dozing off, causing a group of tennis-playing penguins to grow still and fade to nothing.

After an hour or so Owen woke up to find that the sun was now behind them. It was still shining brightly but was low enough in the sky to cast the boys' shadows on the gray stone wall. The sky was still green above, but made a gradual transition to orange as it reached the tree-lined horizon beneath the sun. Owen sat up, careful not to disturb Oliver, who was still asleep with his head in Owen's lap.

Keeping his eyes on the stone wall, Owen made a graceful, fluid movement with his right hand in the space next to his head. As his hand twisted around, his fingers followed its turns in undulating waves like the hypnotic rhythm of gossamer fins rippling in an undersea current. The movement left a shadow on the stone wall that lingered for few moments after Owen's hand had passed.

Owen's mind emptied and relaxed as it did when he made his fingers shimmer in the Gold River. He moved his hands about in gentle curves and figure eights, crossing them with movements that appeared to weave the shadows of his fingers together for a split second before they freely unraveled again. His movements became automatic, his mind entranced and detached.

Oliver's eyes were open. He was watching the shadows, too. His face was expressionless, absorbed in the play of shadows on the wall. Oliver was in that place between sleeping and waking where his eyes opened before his mind. He had been dreaming, but the dream had faded as quickly as it took Oliver to realize that he was awake, and it left no trace. His thoughts took their time to start forming, letting the little boy contentedly watch his big brother's shadows without the distraction of thinking.

When Owen's hands finally came to rest, Oliver rose the rest of the way into wakefulness.

"Owen, I'm thuhsty."

At hearing his brother's words, Owen made the transition from idle meditation to present awareness smoothly and instantly. "Well get up, then."

Oliver stood up and he and Owen went back to the pumpkin. They had missed it while they were away and were glad to feel its joy. Each of them placed a hand on it, Owen with his free thumb in his mouth, and they walked in silence on either side while the pumpkin floated along between them, looking strangely reminiscent of a grownup holding the boys' hands.

The boys crossed the grassy field and drank from the White River. They were immediately filled with its buoyancy. They dunked their heads and blew bubbles underwater for a few moments before climbing onto the pumpkin.

"Let's go home, Oliver."

As the pumpkin glided away, carrying its pair of giggling boys, several dark creatures emerged from the tunnel of wedding trees. They had been sniffing around the spot where the boys had lain sleeping not long before. The creatures now craned their long necks upward to the sky, to the fading sound of the boys' laughter.

CHAPTER FIVE

The boys stopped to pick some parrots in Autumnland before going home. They arrived at their cave earlier than they expected so they dropped their loads of food and treasure at its opening and ran back outside to enjoy the last little while of daylight. They looked for lizards and chased each other around in the evening sun. They ran and jumped and fell and rolled on their hillside, but stayed fairly close to the entrance of the cave. The pumpkin released a few wisps of color and seemed to glow a little brighter, as if it enjoyed watching the boys play.

Both of the boys were feeling decidedly vigorous. There were times like that, when whatever they felt, they felt more than usual. They were very young boys, and the intensity of their moods actually had the power to enhance their senses. Wherever their eyes rested, images grew sharper and colors brighter (not that their eyes rested anywhere for long). Every little sound registered in their ears. Their noses were filled with the essence of verdure in the life all around them. The warm wind that swept up the hillside nuzzled their skin and ran its fingers through their hair. Owen and Oliver enjoyed the exuberance of youth, specifically the corporeal pleasure that courses through bodies that have spent so few years in existence.

Owen climbed onto a rock that jutted from the side of the hill. The rock was just wide enough for both boys to stand side-by-side on its crown, and was almost as tall as Oliver. Owen jumped off with a yell and hit the sloping ground. He crumpled with the force of his impact into a tumbling roll down the hill.

Owen came to a stop, looked back and yelled, "Okay, Oliver. Your turn!"

Oliver climbed onto the rock but then hesitated, as he always did. It seemed much higher to him than it did to Owen. He put his toes on the edge and squatted down on his haunches, giddy with fear and eager for the sensation of falling. His heart pattering away, Oliver let out an excited squeal and jumped. He felt like he was in the air forever, watching the ground zoom closer and closer until, *BOOM!* He landed and tumbled down the hill as Owen had done. Sometimes Oliver rolled right over Owen with a giggle, but this time he rolled to a stop beside him.

The sight of his brother performing these motions always made Owen laugh. Oliver acted as though he were leaping off a cliff, but he really did little more than hop down from the rock. When he landed and rolled, he pretended that the force of his fall took him all the way to where Owen had landed, but he actually did most of the rolling himself. Owen liked when Oliver rolled over him. He always played along, yelling and groaning as if he were being crushed under Oliver's weight. He was a little disappointed that Oliver had missed him this time.

Oliver looked at Owen, as he always did, with an expression that clearly said, *Whew! We survived!* The boys then ran back up the hill to do it again.

The boys climbed the rock one at a time because of an accident that had happened not long before. They had been standing on the rock together when Oliver had gotten impatient and given Owen an encouraging nudge. Owen had fallen off and cracked his head open on the edge of the rock. At the sight of blood and the sound of Owen's screaming cries for Mommy, Oliver had climbed down and wrapped his arms around his brother. Every time that Owen had pushed him away in anger, Oliver had scrambled back and hugged him again until finally Owen had calmed down and let himself be comforted. Oliver had then taken off his shirt and given it to Owen. The boys had held the shirt to the wound together until the bleeding stopped, which it had long before Owen's tears had dried. They had climbed the rock one at a time ever since.

Finished with their jumping, they lay in the grass, looking up at the massive pink clouds that sat unmoving in a darkening blue sky. The sun would set very soon and yet such was the lingering vibrancy of the boys' moods that they dared to stay outside later than usual.

Oliver stared at a cloud that reminded him of something that he couldn't quite remember. He said, "Wih Mommy and Daddy evuh find us?"

Owen was looking at the same cloud. "I don't know, Oliver. I don't think so. I don't think they know how."

Oliver said, "Maybe *we* can find *them*."

Owen didn't answer this. He said, "We better go inside now."

As they climbed back up the hill, Oliver asked again. "Can't we find 'em, Owen? Can't we tchwy and find Mommy and Daddy?"

"They aren't here, Oliver. They're at home, where we used to live, but we can't go back there."

Oliver asked, "But *why* can't we go back? Aw we 'ost?"

Owen tried to explain what he didn't completely understand himself. "We're not lost, I don't think. We just can't go back. I don't know how we got here. We're *kinda* lost, I guess. I don't know...but I don't think Mommy and Daddy can get here."

Oliver looked at the pumpkin. "Why can't we just whide the punkin back to Mommy and Daddy?"

With a sigh, Owen again tried to explain, "We just can't. Mommy and Daddy can't come here and the pumpkin can't go there."

Oliver asked, "Is 'ere a waull or a tents inna way keepin' us out?"

"It's not *tents*, it's *fence*, and no, not like that. It's just a different place that we can't get there." Owen didn't know how to explain.

Oliver didn't ask any more questions. He was trying to work it out and understand. If he and Owen were in one place, and Mommy and Daddy were in another place, why couldn't they just go from the one place to the other like when they went from Summerland to Winterland on the pumpkin? This wasn't the first time that he and Owen had had this conversation, and it wouldn't be the last.

The boys got up and went back to the cave. They gathered up what they had dropped in the entrance and went inside a few moments before the last rays of the sun sank below the horizon. They gave the pumpkin pats goodnight, slid down the slide and then ran down the bowl of the cave and up the other side to their treasure room. Their conversation hadn't dampened the vitality of their mood so much as changed the flavor of it.

When Oliver arranged the parrot leaves that he'd brought back that day, he did it with even more deliberate purpose than usual. He took his time and thoroughly enjoyed the fact that he was doing something for Mommy. This helped to fill the empty place inside him that came from having a desire that he couldn't attain.

Owen added the sprig he'd brought from the wedding tree to his leaf zoo, lovingly arranging it to show off the contrast between the green leaves, white blossoms and black berries. He was also thinking of Mommy, and of how she would be impressed by his collection. He imagined telling her about each kind of leaf and where he had found it. He imagined her telling him what a beautiful zoo he'd made and what a good boy he was. He let this fantasy drift, imagining both Mommy and Daddy someday finding him and Oliver. They would tell Owen what a brave boy he'd been, and how well he'd taken care of Oliver all by himself. He imagined them both smothering him with hugs and kisses and telling him how much they loved him, and that they were so very proud of him.

In the midst of his daydreaming, Owen realized that he was staring at his elephant ears. They were the first plants that he'd brought back to the cave, the ones with which he had started the leaf zoo. He always made sure to replace them when they started to wilt. He stared at the giant leaves longingly, but didn't pick them up. Instead he put his thumb in his mouth and went back to his fantasy.

Oliver had finished arranging his parrot leaves and had begun to grow bored. He looked up at Owen where he sat motionless on his booty shelf, lost in thought. Oliver wanted to eat the parrots they had brought home but he didn't want to eat alone. He didn't want to disturb Owen, either, so he stared at him and tried to guess what he was thinking. Oliver's head lolled to one side, where it was easier to think.

Owen had said that there was no way to find Mommy and Daddy, but maybe he was trying to think of some way. Owen talked about where they lived before like it was better than this place, but Oliver didn't think that any place could be better than the magical land. On the other hand, Oliver would have given anything to be with Mommy and Daddy again. Was it like choosing between the Green River and the Gold River? Was that what Owen meant? They could be here or they could be with Mommy and Daddy but they couldn't do both? But then, why were they still here? Why hadn't they gone back? Owen said they couldn't go back, but then how did they get here in the first place? And where exactly had they come from anyway? Were they really lost? Oliver thought that being lost was a bad thing, but he and Owen had so much fun every day. All they did was play and fly on the pumpkin. Still, would they be here forever, just the two of them?

"Owen, I'm hungwy." Oliver didn't want to think anymore. He wanted to eat and play with his brother.

Owen wanted to stay in his daydreams a little longer. He had been about to blow out the candles on his birthday cake. Mommy and Daddy had invited all of his friends to his party. The presents they'd brought had been stacked up to the ceiling. When he heard Oliver say that he was hungry, Owen had a wonderful idea.

"Oliver, let's have a birthday party!"

Oliver's head straightened up and his eyebrows rose, which made his eyes get a little bigger. He repeated, "A buthday pawdy?"

"Yeah!" said Owen. "It's a party and you invite all your friends and there's cake and ice cream and everyone gives you presents!"

Oliver liked the sound of this very much indeed. He asked, "When's my buthday?"

Owen said, "We can have your birthday tonight and then my birthday tomorrow!"

"Okay!" Oliver thought this was a marvelous plan, especially since his birthday came first.

Owen and Oliver then decided who to invite to the party. When they finished, the guest list was quite prestigious. It included Mommy and Daddy and Owen, of course. The pumpkin was invited, and Mr. Puff Puff. Oliver wanted to invite Daddy the duck head, but Owen said that they couldn't because their real Daddy was coming and it would just be too confusing. This upset Oliver until they compromised by agreeing to save duck head Daddy some cake. They invited pirates and cowboys and army guys and aliens (the cool brother aliens, *not* the stupid ones). They even thought to invite some puppy dogs. Oliver got a little panicky when he realized that he had forgotten to invite himself, but Owen explained that since it was *his* birthday, he was automatically invited.

Owen helped Oliver to greet all of their imaginary guests, taking each of the imaginary gifts they brought and stacking them in a corner.

Oliver wanted to open them immediately but Owen said that you never open the presents until after cake and ice cream. Owen cut a piece of cake and scooped some ice cream for Oliver. Oliver grabbed a fork that wasn't there and put the imaginary cake in his mouth.

"Mmmm! 'At's good, Owen!" he said. "I yuv cake!"

Next he tried the ice cream. "Mmmmmmm hmmmm! I yuv ice cweam! Mm!"

Owen served all of the guests one by one and then finally served himself. He said, "You're right, Oliver. This *is* good!" Owen then turned to one of the cowboys, "Don't you think this is the best cake you've ever tasted? Yeah, I know! It's so cool!"

This made Oliver laugh. He started to talk to the guests too, nodding vigorously. "Mmm hmm! Yups! It's good!"

The boys had a grand time. Oliver's favorite part was when everyone sang *Happy Birthday* to him. Even Mommy and Daddy sang. Rather, Owen did his best to sound like them. He sang one line as himself, one as Mommy using a high-pitched voice, one as Daddy using as deep a voice as he could, and he quacked the last line as Mr. Puff Puff. That made Oliver squeal with delight and he made Owen do it again and again.

Lastly they opened up all of the imaginary presents. Oliver got a new car, his own private airplane, his own firetruck, his own mansion, all the toys in the whole world, all the money in the whole world ("like, a hunn-jed dolluhs!"), he got to keep the puppies that they'd invited, he got swords from the pirates, along with gold, he got guns from the army guys and ropes and hats and guns from the cowboys, the aliens gave him laser guns and his own space ship, and finally Owen told him to wait a minute while he ran to the treasure room. Owen picked out a quarter and the pink rubber ball. When he presented these gifts to the birthday boy, Oliver yelled, "*Whee-uhl* presents? Woo hoo!" He jumped up and clapped his hands and wrapped his arms around Owen, and then jumped up and down some more. Both boys almost fell over in the excitement.

"Thank you, Owen! I like buthdays!" Oliver was very happy, but Owen was even happier.

Owen got his booty treasures back the next day for *his* birthday, along with a penny for good measure, and a parrot leaf, such was

Oliver's overflowing love and gratitude for his big brother. After that, each brother had birthdays fairly often. In addition to the loads and loads of imaginary presents, their real treasures from the booty piles changed hands several times...well, some of them.

After the boys had said goodbye to their guests, they ate the parrots they had brought back to the cave and threw the skins down the bathroom shaft. They then put on their pajamas and lay down to go to sleep on their bed of fire leaves. Oliver was still very wound up from the party and he asked Owen for a story before they went to sleep.

"Owen, tell me 'bout somethin' from buhfore. Somethin' 'bout Mommy and Daddy."

Owen thought about it for quite a few moments. His mind filled with memories, some happy, and some not so very much. Owen thought for so long that Oliver started to think that he hadn't heard him.

"Owen?"

"I heard you. I'm thinking," Owen said.

Finally, Owen settled on a story to tell.

"One time, when you were a baby, we went to the beach."

"I 'membuh that! I 'membuh beach!"

"Shush, Oliver! You don't remember, you were just a baby! Anyway, Mommy and Daddy took us to the beach and we got to swim in a swimming pool and even in the ocean. They had a cage for you, Oliver, right in the sand. It had a roof to keep you shady. I remember Mommy sat with you and read her book while Daddy took me in the ocean. The water was salty and burned my nose but I liked it when the waves knocked me down."

That got a giggle from Oliver, "The waves knocks you ovuh?"

Owen answered, "Uh huh! The waves in the ocean are huge, huger than me! They're so huge that Mommy had to carry you in the water so you wouldn't drownd."

"What's duh-wound?" Oliver asked.

"It's when you die in the water 'cause you can't breathe. Anyway, me and Daddy found a horseshoe crab and Daddy brought it back and scared Mommy with it." Owen smiled at this memory. He described the horseshoe crab and then went on to tell Oliver about looking for seashells and starfish and sand dollars. He told him about digging in the sand with the bright green bucket with the yellow handle ("Yeh-woh!"), and how if you dug deep enough, the hole would fill with water. He told him about burying his feet in the sand and he remembered how warm it had felt.

Oliver started to get sleepy. Owen was wrong, he did remember some things about their trip to the ocean. Oliver half-listened to Owen and half-drifted off into the dream-like memories sparked by Owen's words. There were images of water that was sparkling blue, and also that was green and endless. He remembered the moon in the sky and the moon in the water that he had wanted to touch. There was the sound of seagulls, and the smell of coconuts, and the warmth of the sand. There was an image that Oliver didn't understand because he couldn't fully remember. He thought it was Daddy's legs but they looked funny, like they were all wiggly and too short...

When Oliver had fallen asleep, Owen got up and very quietly tiptoed to the treasure room. He climbed up onto his shelf and picked up the elephant ears. Behind them was his secret discovery, his one selfish wish. After answering so many of Oliver's questions, it helped Owen to sit and look for a while, thumb in his mouth and a faint smile traced on his lips. At one point he thought he heard the sound of someone crying very softly. Curiously, Owen found comfort in the sound. He stayed there for a while and then he crept back to Oliver and lay down to sleep, feeling better than he had, braver.

In the cave, Owen had just fallen asleep. In Springland, the dark creatures that had come over the mountains were feasting on the cowpies that they had found and slaughtered. The dark creatures were hunters. Their appetites would be sated for a while, but soon they would resume their search for the two strange little animals that had flown away. Having caught such a delicious scent, the creatures would hunt for them until they found them.

CHAPTER SIX

A pair of eyes watched Owen as he searched for Oliver among the melon trees. Owen's footsteps rustled the green brush of elephant ears and mouse ears. The elephant ears were shaped like folded wings with ruffled edges, and were big enough to conceal a three-year-old boy. The mouse ears were shaped like, well, mouse ears, and were just as small. They covered the ground like a raised layer of clover. A single leaf topped each threadlike stem, which reached as high as Owen's shins. Owen liked to pull up his pant legs and feel the mouse ears tickling his bare legs. He was trying to be quiet, peering through the brush for a hint as to where Oliver might have gone. All he saw was a sea of deep green, broken by the lighter green trunks of the melon trees and the occasional yellow of the melons that drooped overhead.

Owen's every move was being closely watched. Something was waiting for the chance to spring. As Owen bent down to look under a fallen tree, a trembling susurration (that sounded suspiciously like someone trying to stifle a giggle), escaped from a nearby tree. Owen did not appear to have heard.

Owen spoke out loud, "I wonder where Oliver could be?" He looked behind a few elephant ears that were growing together. "No Oliver here!" The tremulous sound grew. It was definitely giggling. It seemed to come from directly above Owen and yet his eyes were pointed at the ground as if he still couldn't hear. "Hmmmmm, I can't find him anywhere!"

That's when Oliver swung out of the tree with a, "Raahhhhrrrr!" He hung by his knees from a low hanging branch. He was upside down, holding his hands up like claws.

"Gahhh! Oliver, you scared me!"

Oliver laughed, quite pleased with himself. He dropped his arms and let them dangle above his head. His shirt slid up and exposed his round belly. He enjoyed his swinging at first but soon his face began to turn red and his features strained as he tried with many a grunt to right himself. No matter how he swung his arms, Oliver couldn't get upright; his belly got in the way.

"Owen! Help me I stuck!"

Owen hefted Oliver back up into a sitting position, but only after pausing to laugh at the ridiculous predicament that he had gotten himself into. Owen told him to pick them each a melon while he was up there and then they could go and have a picnic by the pumpkin.

"But Owen, I wanna have a monkey picnic inna tchwees!"

Owen considered the request. He had already let Oliver win at several games of hide-and-seek, *and* he'd just had to save him from falling, but a monkey tree picnic did sound fun, so up he climbed to the sound of Oliver's little clapping hands.

Each of the boys sat in the tree with a melon the size of his own head. The yellow rinds broke apart easily, which let the boys get to the tart purple fruit inside. The color of the sky almost matched the fruit, which was what had given them the idea to have melons for breakfast.

It was one of those days that the boys had planned out ahead of time. They had lain in their cave and discussed it the night before, almost finishing their plans just as they were falling asleep. First, there would be hide-and-seek and breakfast. When the boys had seen the purple sky that morning, the elephant ears and melons of Summerland had replaced the leaf piles and parrots of Autumnland on their agenda, but the rest of their plans remained unchanged. After breakfast, they would ride the pumpkin all morning and afternoon, looking for a place that they had never before seen. Oliver actually just wanted to go for a long ride on the pumpkin. It was Owen that had decided that they should be looking for something. Whether they found something or not, for lunch they would come back to Summerland and eat bluematoes from the vines that grew near the paint bushes, and then they would make pictures on the paint leaves and gather paintberries to bring back to the cave. Oliver had run out of yellow and needed more. The boys had fallen asleep before deciding on dinner plans, but they would worry about that later.

Owen and Oliver sat in the tree, absorbed in the effort of gleaning every last bit of fruit from the yellow rinds. Above them, cumulus clouds had spread across the sky, veiling its purple behind depths of gray and white. At the first tap of a swollen rain drop hitting a leaf, Owen looked up and saw the ceilinged sky. There were many things that made the boys feel the power of the life outside of them penetrate their little bodies and saturate the life inside of them with something more than itself. One of those things was a gentle summer rain. The boys loved weather and the elements - rain, snow, or wind. They were sometimes frightened by thunder and lightning, but if they were safe in their cave, they loved even the bright flash, the loud crash, and the deep rumble that followed.

Oliver's face was buried in his melon. He was oblivious to the rain until an especially heavy drop landed on his head. Startled, he looked up from his feast, purple bits of which were stuck to both of his cheeks. Like Owen, Oliver took a few moments to appreciate the fact that it was beginning to rain. It gave the world a closed-in feel, especially while sitting in a tree surrounded by green. Everything about the boys was hushed, every sound clearer even while gentler. The gray sky muted the daylight, softening shadows and sharpening the shapes of the leaves and branches. The boys looked at each other and smiled, listening to the irregular tapping of scattered raindrops falling one at a time.

The spattering of drops very slowly grew to a steady downpour. As young children will tend to be, the boys were thrilled by this. Unable to find any other way of expressing just how thrilled they were, Owen and Oliver simply began to yell raucously, their shouts accented by moments of screeching laughter.

Once they became soaked through, they calmed down a bit. Occasionally they blew at the drops of rainwater that formed on the ends of their noses, but the drip would always immediately return. For quite a while the boys didn't speak, at least not with words. They communicated all that they needed or desired in that special, wordless language of children that is made of signs and looks, body language, and in this case giggles and laughter.

The boys sat in the tree, holding the rinds of their melons like cups. They collected the rainwater to make melonade with the bits of fruit left uneaten. While they waited for these cups to fill, they discussed where they should go next. Oliver wanted to go to the Dead Wood Forest to catch leaves in the rain, until Owen reminded him that they were supposed to be riding the pumpkin, looking for some new thing.

"Oh, yeah. I fuh-got." Oliver's face scrunched to one side and he put his finger to the side of his chin. "Hmmmmm...."

Owen rolled his eyes and shook his head with a sigh. "I think we should look in Winterland. If it's raining here, maybe it'll be snowing there. It'll make it more fun."

Oliver's eyebrows rose together. He didn't altogether dislike the idea. "Can we go to Autumnland fuhst?" The notion of Autumnland had already set in his mind. Oliver really liked riding the pumpkin over those rolling hills, especially in the rain.

Owen argued, "But what if it stops snowing in Winterland by the time we get there?"

"It won't, Owen! It won't stop snowing, I pom-iss!"

"Oliver, you can't promise it will keep snowing! That doesn't work." Owen scraped a bit of melon from his rind and squeezed its juices into the water that had collected. He was thinking it over.

"Puh-leeeeeze, Owen?"

"Fine! We'll go to Autumnland first."

Owen didn't let on the real reason why he had agreed so easily. It wasn't because of the rain that he wanted to go to Winterland to search that day, and so it didn't matter if it stopped before they got there. An idea had come to him the other night after Oliver had fallen asleep. When Owen had been sitting by his booty pile, watching and listening with his thumb in his mouth, all of a sudden the idea had struck him.

Owen knew that there was special magic in Winterland. He and Oliver had been safe there from the shadow eyes, even at night. Also, it was always winter there, and the trees were almost all evergreen trees: conifers. Even the needleberry bushes stayed green no matter how cold it was. Owen's idea was simple. Maybe Winterland was really the North Pole; not the North Pole on a map where there was nothing but ice, but *Santa's* North Pole where the elves made toys all year long. Owen knew the difference, after all he wasn't stupid. He knew that magic was needed to get to Santa's North pole, and the boys had certainly gotten where they were by magic. Maybe he and Oliver had somehow come to the magic place where Santa Claus lived. Maybe they had actually found it, the home of Santa Claus and the Easter Bunny, the Tooth Fairy, leprechauns, newborn babies, Thanksgiving turkeys! That would explain *everything*. It would explain why they couldn't get back and why Mommy and Daddy couldn't come and find them. And their pumpkin; Owen now suspected that it was the Halloween Pumpkin.

That was why Owen wanted to explore Winterland. If they could find Santa Claus, he would make everything okay and would take them back to Mommy and Daddy when he traveled the world on Christmas Eve. Owen didn't tell any of this to Oliver because Oliver didn't remember Christmas or Easter very well, and Owen couldn't explain holidays to him so that he really understood them.

Owen was so excited at the idea that it never occurred to him to wonder that they had never received presents from Santa since they had come to that place. In his desperate need to believe, it wouldn't have mattered to him, anyway. He had already decided that this would be the best Christmas ever. Santa would give them presents and fill their stockings with candy. He would stay to eat cookies and milk with Owen and Oliver while Mommy and Daddy slept, and then on Christmas morning, Mommy and Daddy would wake up to find Owen and Oliver under the tree with big red and green bows on their heads and gold ribbons tied around them. They would all be happy. Mommy and Daddy would hug them and kiss them and tell them they loved them, just like in Owen's fantasies, and he and Oliver could tell them all about the magical place they had been and about all of the things they had seen and done.

While they waited for Christmas to come, the boys could live with Santa. He and Mrs. Claus would take care of them, and they would play with the elves and eat nothing but candy and cookies and milk. Owen would never have to feel scared or lonely again. He knew that Santa would do all of this because he had been such a good boy and had done his very best to take care of Oliver. He felt sure that Santa would reward him for finding the magical North Pole all by himself. The more Owen thought about it, the more he became sure that he had found a way home for Oliver, and for himself, too.

Unfortunately, wanting something to be true does not always make it so, no matter how good or kind or brave we've been. Owen would not find Santa or the North Pole that day. He was wrong. There was no Christmas, no Easter, nor Thanksgiving in that land. Their magic pumpkin was not the Halloween Pumpkin, and although the boys were very soon to find themselves in a place they had never been, when it happened it would not be their idea, nor would it be a place that they would ever want to be.

Owen drank the water from his melon cup and swung down from the tree. He then waited for Oliver, who had to climb a little slower because he couldn't reach as far as Owen. They walked back to the pumpkin hand in hand. The boys had tied winter coats around its stem for the trip to Winterland. Inside the pockets of the coats were sweatshirts and gloves. The boys retrieved the sweatshirts, which were still mostly dry, and put them on.

The pumpkin was soaked with rain so that even Owen had trouble climbing onto its slippery surface. On his first try he slid right off and landed on his back with an, "Oomph!" It turned out to be lucky that he did. Seeing Owen fall first was the only thing that kept Oliver from having a full meltdown after his sixth fall. Eventually both boys were up and had a good grip, Owen on the reins and Oliver around Owen's waist. The pumpkin lifted into the air and as usual the giddy joy of flying filled the boys, leaving no room for unpleasant thoughts or feelings.

The boys passed a grove of flutter trees on their way to Autumnland. Flutter trees were covered in rough and deeply ridged bark, the color of which was hard to determine. Even from close up, these trees had an almost metallic sheen that seemed to play tricks on the boys' eyes. Were they dark green or brown? Were they silver or black and merely reflecting other colors? The boys never could decide quite what color, or colors, they were seeing.

This was not the strangest thing about flutter trees. Even more curious was the behavior of their foliage, which always hid from the sun. The branches of a flutter tree were bare on sunny days, but at night or when the skies were overcast, buds would push through the thick bark and unfold into slender, smooth-edged leaves that hid all but the trees' trunks. The tops of these leaves were a cool dark green, while the undersides were a light and silvery gray. When the slightest wind blew, the leaves lifted and swiveled about. Sometimes it looked as though the trees were twinkling. At other times it appeared as if waves of silver were blowing across a sea of green.

On that particular day, pouring raindrops battered the individual leaves and made them wink across the rippling surface of silver and green that followed each gust of wind. Owen and Oliver flew around the tops of the trees and under them, streaming their own waves through the leaves and adding the reflections of the warm colors that swirled in the pumpkin's wake as they passed. The boys' laughter intermingled with the sound of the rain and of the wind through the branches, giving a musical voice to the harmony of gleeful sensations with which the boys overflowed.

It is with remissness that childhood is so often defined in terms of mental and bodily development, measured by what children cannot yet do instead of by that which only they can, and without regard to what only a child can see, or the secrets that a child knows and feels that adults have long forgotten.

The boys soon reached the end of the flutter tree grove and were flying over open fields toward the fire trees of Autumnland. The yellow leaves stood out in the distance with dazzling luminance against the contrasting bleakness of the gray sky. The rain slackened to a drizzle as the green fields of summer yellowed and became the wheat-colored hills and valleys of autumn.

This was Oliver's favorite, no matter how Owen steered the pumpkin. Sometimes they followed the lay of the land, making undulating sweeps up and down and up and down. At other times they flew level and steady, and Oliver stared straight down, watching the ground rise up to meet him and then fall away, over and over like giant rolling waves of an earthen yellow sea. He liked to watch until he was dizzy with the movement and then he lifted his head to be refreshed by the rush of cool wind in his face.

It wasn't just the rolling hills; Oliver loved the colors: brown, red, yellow, orange and gold. He loved the smells in the air of dry leaves, hay, and the wet earth. He loved the sweet pungency of trees heavy with ripe fruit. He loved the crispness of the cool autumn air.

Owen swerved the pumpkin toward the top of a hill, where a few lonely-looking trees stood out against a lightening sky. The leaves had all but left the branches of the trees, and in their place were perched hundreds of black birds. The birds resembled crows but were smaller, and their bodies a bit rounder. They were huddled against the wind and rain, silent but for a few scattered caws. Oliver started to make a high-pitched squeal in anticipation. Owen aimed the pumpkin straight at the branches of the trees. Chaos ensued. The sound of the boys' laughter was consumed in a cacophony of cawing and screeching and flapping as the upset black birds took wing all at once. They rose into the air with a roar of beating wings and settled in the stand of trees that crested the next hill, still squawking angrily. The noise was nearly deafening.

Oliver yelled, "Again! Again!" but Owen was already chasing after the birds, shouting and laughing with excitement.

The boys made another pass at the birds and again the flock lifted out of the tree as one. Oliver had one arm around Owen's waist and waved the other about in the air as they flew through the flock. Owen heard Oliver start to scream and he pulled the pumpkin away from the birds.

The pumpkin had almost landed when Oliver yelled, "No, Owen! No land! Chase the buhds!"

Owen turned and saw Oliver rocking his body and kicking at the pumpkin with his heels, trying to get it to go where he wanted. Oliver looked okay to Owen, so back into the air they rose, in pursuit of the black birds.

Oliver had screamed because while swooping his hand about to scare the birds, he had accidentally caught one. When he had felt the bird's struggles in his fingers it had startled him so badly that he had screamed and almost fallen off the pumpkin. He had immediately let go of the bird, and was now swinging a closed fist instead of an open hand so that it wouldn't happen again.

After a few more passes at the birds Owen asked, "Okay, can we go to Winterland now?" The drizzle of rain was now barely a mist.

"Wait, Owen! I wanna pick some leaves for Mommy!"

Owen answered with an exasperated groan, but he circled back toward some fire trees to look for parrots. Minutes later the boys had put on their coats and gloves and were heading to Winterland. Oliver had some leaves tucked in his shirt and each boy had a large parrot in his pocket.

By the time Owen and Oliver arrived in Winterland, the cloudy sky had lightened to almost solid white. Snowflakes floated about in a very slightly blowing wind, seeming to never actually land.

"Owen, my ea-uhs huht."

Owen turned his head and saw that Oliver's ears were a deep shade of scarlet. "Well why didn't you bring a hat? You knew we were coming here!"

"I dunno. I fuh-got! Owen, go slowuh. Too windy!"

Owen reached into his coat pocket and pulled out his own wool cap. It was green, his favorite color. He gave it to Oliver and told him to be careful not to drop it, which of course, drop it he did. It landed in the snow with a puff, and without a word Owen circled around to get it. The pumpkin landed harder than usual and Oliver bounced off and landed on his back in the snow.

"Owen! You did that on puh-pus!" Oliver had fallen in deep enough snow so that he wasn't hurt in the least (in fact, he'd plopped off the pumpkin into snow just like that many times on purpose), but it had startled him and he was already cranky because his coat was still wet and his ears were cold.

Owen had of course done it on purpose because he was annoyed at having to land, but he said, "No I didn't! It's not my fault if you can't hang on right!"

Oliver had stood up, but at Owen's harsh words he sat right back down in the snow and pouted. He didn't care about the stupid hat or the stupid pumpkin or stupid Owen. He would just sit right there forever!

Owen slid to the ground, feeling guilty about bouncing his brother off the pumpkin. He went and picked up the hat and silently handed it to Oliver, wearing a big humble "please forgive me" smile. Owen didn't admit out loud that he'd done it on purpose, but between him and Oliver there was no need. The act of getting down from the pumpkin to retrieve the hat instead of making Oliver get it himself plainly showed that Owen felt sorry. The penitent look on his face and the slump of his shoulders as he offered the hat to Oliver were all the more that was needed. Oliver accepted the hat graciously. This was partially due to embarrassment because he had overreacted a bit, although he would not have been able to explain it that way. He simply knew that his face felt hot, and that he wasn't angry with Owen anymore.

In his chastened attitude toward his baby brother, Owen was able to unfetter himself from the yoke of responsibility for just a few moments and be nothing more than what he was: a little boy. Owen was in charge, all the time, and he did not want to be. By submitting himself to Oliver's forgiveness, he found the closest he could ever come to asking someone's permission, and ironically the associative nuances of this made Owen feel free.

Owen carried a heavy burden, one that no five-year-old should have to carry, and he bore it utterly alone, but such is the nature of childhood that he bore it fairly easily, having no one to tell him that it shouldn't be so. Owen's memories of their life before were very different from their life now, so that he had little basis for comparison. Owen could no longer remember what, if anything, had once been asked of him, although now he couldn't forget for even a second that he was solely responsible for Oliver. He knew that he desperately missed Mommy and Daddy, but he also knew that he had been given the gift of his brother. Though at times Owen felt fear and loneliness in the powerful and consuming way that only a child can, as long as he and Oliver were together, he would not become disheartened.

Some vague and hazy form of these thoughts had gone through Owen's mind as he stood in the whiteness of snow and sky and watched as Oliver took off his gloves to warm his ears with hands, put on Owen's hat and then put his gloves back on. Owen loved his little brother more than anything. Hat on his head, Oliver turned to Owen and the look he saw made him feel warm and safe, for that is what it is to feel loved. Oliver awkwardly ran the few steps through the deep snow to Owen, wrapped his arms around him and buried his head in his chest. He loved to give his big brother hugs. The two little boys stood and held each other in the wintry silence for a moment, and then climbed back on the pumpkin and rose into the sky.

Owen headed away from the Blue River because he couldn't remember having ever heard of a river in stories about Santa and the North Pole. The boys flew all about, but could find nothing new. Oliver, who didn't know that he was supposed to be looking for anything, simply enjoyed the ride and being with the pumpkin. Although not his favorite, he did love the pure white snow and the silence.

The snowflakes stopped falling, but clouds still covered the sky, turning it stark white. The boys had left the river and trees far behind. There were no hills, nothing to cast so much as a shadow. There was no wind, there was no sound. The pumpkin had slowed so that the boys barely felt the air through which they moved.

Oliver had become almost hypnotized. He felt that this was like a dream that he'd had but that he couldn't remember, and soon he began to wonder if he *was* dreaming.

Owen had become lost in the whiteness. He could no longer tell where the sky met the land. He forgot what he was looking for and began to pretend that he, Oliver and the pumpkin were cartoons drawn on a giant piece of blank white paper.

Just when Oliver was positive that he could not be awake, and when Owen started to feel the first pangs of fear lest they should be lost in the whiteness forever, a stand of snow-covered evergreens appeared on the horizon. The boys drew near and Owen landed the pumpkin. The trees had a flaky, henna red bark. Owen took the red and green trees to mean Christmas. He had found the North Pole, or at least he pretended that he had. For a five-year-old boy, sometimes the difference between real and pretend could be set aside if that were required to make him feel happy.

Oliver slid off the back of the pumpkin into the snow and landed on his bottom with a *plunch!* A giggle later and he was fully present. Owen ran from tree to tree discovering imaginary elves and reindeer. Oliver goosestepped through the deep snow, following after as fast as he could. He was oblivious to all but his glee in chasing Owen, and his effort to not fall down. They hadn't gone very far when Owen stopped and stared at a line of bright blue that was cutting a path through the snow not far from them.

"*What*? Oliver! We're back at the river!"

"Whut?" Oliver looked at the blue water, got a very perplexed look on his face and tilted his head to its thinking spot. "Did the ribbuh follow us?"

At this question Owen tilted his own head and said, "I don't know." He honestly didn't. This was a magical place, after all.

The beginning of doubt was nibbling at the edges of Owen's plan, but he pushed it away. Oliver, not sharing Owen's hopes, had none to be dashed so he accepted the reappearance of the river with more amusement than anything. He broke the train of Owen's thoughts in his usual manner.

"Owen, I hungwy."

And they were off to Summerland to eat bluematoes.

CHAPTER SEVEN

The clouds were gone from the periwinkle sky. The boys relished the afternoon warmth of summer after spending half the day in the cold and snow. They soaked up the sun; their coats and gloves, sweaters and hat tossed aside to dry. Dark juice ran down their chins, having burst from each bite they took from the bluematoes.

Each brother was reclining in a natural hammock formed of the bluemato vines. The plants grew in pairs and their sturdy vines interlaced about a foot above the ground. Each pair consisted of one male plant and one female, which were rooted far enough apart that a grown man could stretch out, comfortably suspended on the interwoven vines between them.

Bluematoes were about the size of Oliver's fist. The rich, earthy flesh of the fruit protected its center which was filled with a tangy juice that caused the boys' mouths to pucker. The lustrous, royal blue orbs hung from the indigo-colored vines that formed the odd, suspended cots. Some of the fruit even rested on the ground. The air around the plants was perfumed with the ambrosial blend of salt and sweet from the ripened fruit and from the bright green blossoms from which they matured. The boys had often fallen asleep there, by the banks of the Green River, and after the full morning they'd just had, that day was no exception. Oliver was the first to nod off. He fell asleep mid-bite and continued his slow, slack-jawed chewing after his bluemato had rolled off his chest and onto the ground. Despite Owen's disappointed search for Santa, he fell asleep shortly after Oliver.

That would be the last time the boys would enjoy such blissful afternoon sleep, outside in the open without a care in the world. Soon they would learn that danger existed in daylight as well as darkness. They were about to forever lose another precious piece of their innocence, for danger and fear once discovered cannot be unseen, nor un*felt*, even after they have passed. When a place of safety becomes the scene of peril and deadly horrors, it can never again be what it was. The same channels of memory that filled the boys' hearts and allowed them to relive moments of love and beauty also had the power to take those gifts away. It was almost a betrayal by the land. That which seemed almost specifically designed to nurture and prolong the innocence of childhood would turn on the boys as if trying to destroy the very thing it had protected. Nature could be sustaining, gracious, even generous, but she could also be cruel and brutal in her purity of purpose, even in a magical land.

The boys had done their best. Although the fears they had previously experienced had not left them, they did not control them, either. The boys had faced the terrors of the shadow eyes, and yet still found lightness in their hearts, for they had not been unadept to fear even then. They'd had to learn the cruel nature of existence before they had ever come to that place. It had invaded their safe home, even with Mommy and Daddy there to take care of them. They'd had to learn of things from which Mommy and Daddy couldn't protect them, but still, Mommy and Daddy had been there to hold them and talk to them. In the land it was different. The boys were on their own. In that place there was no one to guide them, no one to warn them. They would soon face a darkness that would not be easily overcome. The existence of remorseless beasts that desired to take away their lives for no more significant reason than a simple meal was a design of nature's savagery as yet beyond the boys' experience. They would have precious few seconds to adapt to this reality or they would not survive, and even if they did, there would still be worse to come.

Oliver awoke first. He didn't wake Owen, but got up and peed in the river before taking a drink (this wasn't something Oliver thought about, but luckily the river had a current). He was refreshed by the emerald green water, and took several gulps. Oliver took off his shoes, socks and jeans and lay down in the warm grass with his bare feet in the water.

He lay on his back, and the curled ends of his reddish-blond locks spread on the ground around his head. He closed his eyes and watched the play of color on the backs of his eyelids. Keeping his eyes shut, he squeezed them tight, both together and then one at a time. There was a wonderland of color and movement behind his closed eyelids. It was like watching strange clouds rapidly form and dissipate across a night sky in which dim stars grew and shrank. Oliver put his hands over his eyes to block out more of the light, and then began to vigorously rub them, causing explosions of color to bloom and showers of stars to appear and fade.

Keeping his eyes closed, Oliver next cupped his hands over his ears to create a low, whistling noise. He moved his hands in and out, faster and faster, and transformed the steady sound of the flowing river into a warbling siren. He then pressed his cupped hands tighter and tighter against his ears, making the pitch of the whistling slowly drop lower and lower until it became a blowing roar and eventually a deep rumbling, like thunder. Oliver did this over and over, and began to imagine himself on a high mountain surrounded by a tempestuous wind. He was climbing higher and higher and higher until finally he reached the top and could see the whole world. There was an ocean and a desert, and woods. He could see a playground filled with laughing children, but he looked away because it made him feel vaguely lonely, and a little frightened. He saw Mommy and Daddy. They were outside feeding the birds and playing with doggy. They looked up and waved at Oliver and he waved back. He saw them and wouldn't lose them and then he was on the pumpkin with Owen and they were flying straight to them.

Oliver's face was expressionless as he lay there by the river. To look at him, one would see nothing more than a very little boy lying on his back with his hands over his ears and his feet in the water, but if one could look inside his mind, the grandeur and detail of the vision would be staggering.

Oliver had his arms wrapped around doggy. Her fur was very soft and she kept nuzzling Oliver with her cold nose and licking his face. Oliver's imagination shifted. He and doggy were super heroes. They wore capes and brightly colored underwear on the outside of their pants (Owen had explained super heroes to Oliver). Doggy wore a blue cape and red underwear over her gray fur. Oliver had a yellow cape and green underwear pulled up over his yellow pants. They flew around without needing the pumpkin and they beat up bad guys. Oliver and doggy saved Mommy and Daddy and Owen from all the bad guys in the world, many times over.

Owen was wakened by the sound of splashing. He looked over and saw Oliver lying by the river and kicking his feet in the water. Owen got up and went to the edge of the bank. Being two and a half years older than Oliver, Owen had the foresight to take a drink and *then* pee in the river. The sound roused Oliver from his daydreams. Now that Owen was awake, it was painting time.

Oliver loved to paint (but then he loved so many things). He sat up and pulled on his socks and shoes, then realized that he had forgotten to put on his jeans and so he had to take his shoes off again. Owen waited patiently and just barely succeeded in holding back his laughter. It was another endearing Oliver moment, as Owen watched him struggle to bend past his belly to reach his feet instead of bringing his feet within his reach. Oliver stood to pull up his pants and rather than make him go through the ordeal again, Owen knelt down and put his shoes on for him, while Oliver leaned a hand on Owen's shoulder for balance.

The brothers raced to the painting patch and Owen won, as he almost always did. These plants, though not edible, were held in an almost reverent awe by Owen and Oliver. The painting patch was saturated with a very pleasant aroma, something like a mix of green onions growing in the wild and freshly cut grass.

Each plant made the shape of a dome that was a little taller than Owen. The outside of the dome was formed by the paint leaves: great oval canvases with a thick waxy surface the color of a freshly peeled white onion. The off-white of each leaf was veined with a very pale green which seemed to seep out from its light green stem. Oliver could stand in front of a leaf that he chose to paint and it would reach from its stem, just above the top of his head, to its tip, just above his knees.

From the top of the plant to the ground, these leaves made a solid covering through which nothing could be seen. When the boys moved the leaves aside, they could step inside the plant and be completely hidden. The trunk of the plant grew in the middle of the dome, and the branches all sprouted from the top, which left an open space inside, much like that of a tent. The boys sometimes just sat on the ground inside these plants and felt safe in the soft, white light that filtered through the leaves.

Where the branches met the trunk, thick bunches of the paintberries grew. The berries were about as big around as a grape, but they were long like beans. The texture of the berries was rather like the flesh of a honeydew melon, but without the seeds or the pulp. They grew in all the colors of the rainbow, and each color had its own scent. Some were sweet, some sour, some bitter and some earthy. Some had a sharp smell while others were bland.

Oliver immediately went inside and started to pick berries while Owen stayed outside and chose one of the giant leaves for himself. The leaves had more than one interesting property. They could not be removed from the plant, at least not by any means that the boys had at their disposal. The one leaf that Owen had been able to bring back to his zoo, he had found lying on the ground, and it was the only one they had ever found detached. The leaf in Owen's zoo was precious to him even though it had lost its other interesting property upon being separated from its plant. When the boys pressed something against the surface of these leaves, a swirl of colors appeared. With his finger, Owen now traced a circle in the middle of the leaf he had picked out. Blazing colors erupted in the path of his finger as if they were all racing to meet it first and got trapped upon reaching the surface of the leaf. Bright red and blue and yellow, green, orange and purple, even black, all swirled together without actually mixing so that each color retained its vibrant intensity.

Owen continued to cover his leaf with colorful lines, shapes and squiggles until he ran out of room. He then moved to a fresh leaf and started to work more earnestly. By the time Oliver emerged with a shirt full of berries, Owen was putting the finishing touches on his first masterpiece of the day. Oliver stood and watched with his head tilted to one side. A few berries rolled out of his shirt.

"Wow, Owen! Yuhr a really good jhraw-uhr!" Oliver was suddenly starting to get the hang of his R's, like when he had suddenly gone from using single words and phrases to complete sentences.

"Thanks. It's not quite finished. I think it needs more boats."

A few more berries landed in the grass. "Yeah! Moah boats!" Of course, when Oliver was excited his R's went away again. Oliver took off his shirt and collected all of the berries he had dropped. He set them aside wrapped in the shirt.

For the rest of the afternoon, the boys went from leaf to leaf, creating. Owen's drawings were very meticulous for a five-year-old boy. He added details that most children far older than him would not have thought to include. He already knew to put people's eyes in the middle of their faces instead of way at the top of their heads like Oliver did, not that Oliver painted many faces. Oliver's works were mostly shapeless designs, or shiny suns and clouds, or birds and trees (although Owen saw one of Oliver's drawings that afternoon that he thought looked like a dog wearing a cape).

When the sun began to sink in the sky, the boys left their artwork. It would all fade back into the leaves overnight. The boys gathered up their things, took a last drink from the river, and hopped onto the pumpkin to go home.

After a short but exhilarating flight, Owen landed the pumpkin at the bottom of their hill. He and Oliver still had the parrots in their pockets for dinner, but he wanted to gather some pinkberries to make a meal of it. Owen filled his pockets and looked at the pumpkin. Oliver was sitting by it with his face pressed against it and holding one of its vines in his hand. Owen saw that his brother looked as tired as he felt, so instead of climbing the hill or getting back on the pumpkin, Owen sat down and grabbed a piece of the pumpkin's vine that hung on its other side. Each boy held on with one hand and the pumpkin dragged them over the grass and up the hill. If they could have seen how comical they looked, perfectly content to be dragged along as if it were a normal mode of transportation, they would have laughed much harder than they did.

After the boys said goodnight to the pumpkin and ate their dinner, they put on underwear over their pants, tied sweaters around their necks like capes and played super heroes. They pretended to fly, running all around on the walls that formed the bowl of their cave, yelling and laughing until they tired themselves out.

When they went to bed, neither brother fell asleep immediately. Their bodies were tired but their minds were wide awake. Neither boy spoke. They lay quietly with their eyes open. After what seemed like a long time, Owen scooched over and wrapped his arms around Oliver, and the boys finally closed their eyes and drifted off to sleep.

It wasn't all the time, but both of the brothers were prone to night terrors; probably as a result of the many hardships they had suffered during their short lives. A couple of hours after they had fallen asleep, Oliver woke with a start. He didn't yell out or do anything else to disturb the silence in the cave. Big, silent tears dripped from his eyes onto the fire leaves that made his pillow. He was comforted by Owen's warmth pressed up against him and by the weight of Owen's arm around him. Oliver lay still and listened to his brother's peaceful breaths. He looked at the pumpkin's soft glow and eventually he cried himself back to sleep.

An hour before the sun rose, Owen was caught in the grips of a nightmare. He dreamt that he and Oliver were visiting a neighbor's house, only the house was in the middle of nowhere. Owen knew little of the plains in the African savannah or the Australian outback, but had they been more familiar to him, that's how he would have described the lonely place in his dream. There was a single dirt road with no turns that cut straight across the plain on a bright and sunny afternoon. A very few trees dotted the hazy landscape. On the road was a single house with shrubbery on either side. The bushes were too high for Owen to see what was behind them.

The man who was their neighbor stood on the front porch and greeted the boys in with smiles. They happily walked around the side of the house. The man was showing them his zoo. It was behind the house, between the tall rows of shrubs. A large chain link fence was closed in on all four sides and above. No grass grew inside the fence, which made a house-sized cage around several species of great cats. Each of the different cat's fur was colored gold and deep red, like the pipchunks. There was a golden tiger with red stripes, and several gold leopards with red spots.

There were others but Owen was too scared to look at them. Oliver was squeezing his hand and whimpering; he was terrified. The cats were fighting and ramming the fence. They were all ferociously growling and roaring and hissing and spitting. Clouds of dust rose around each violent movement of the cats.

Owen turned to run and found a wooden fence behind him, blocking his way back to the road. The door in the fence was locked. Owen turned back around and found that he was inside the cage with the cats, who noticed this at the same time as him. The man was laughing. He told Owen that he better run to the trap door.

Along the right side of the chain link cage was built a double wall of fencing with a space between that was just wide enough for a man. It ran all along the length of the cage, as did a trap door at its base. Oliver was gone, so Owen ran to the trap door and rolled under just as the growling cats lunged at him. The space between the sections of fence was narrower than it had looked. Owen stood up and had to inch sideways toward the way out.

The entire seemingly endless time, the tiger, leopards, and now a mountain lion were trying to get at him. There was nothing but chain links between them. The space seemed to grow narrower with every sideways step, until Owen thought that he would get stuck. He felt the great cats' claws and hot breath. It was loud, impossibly loud. The high ringing of the metal fence, the sound of the cats; Owen thought he would die because it was so close and loud in his ears.

He was trapped, unable to move, and they were going to get him. Owen was screaming, being mauled, stuck in the narrow space and unable even to drop into the fetal position; and then he was through the fence and running away, far away. When the house was in the distance, he saw the leopards get through the fence and start running toward him. Owen was screaming and crying as he ran. The leopards had almost reached him. They were so big. They were so fast. It wasn't fair...

Owen woke up screaming, covered in sweat. Tears coursed down his cheeks. Oliver had been shaking him, trying to wake him up. Oliver was crying, too. Owen's clear, high-pitched screams echoed off the walls of the cave as Oliver held on to him as tightly as he could.

Owen screamed, "*The tigers! There's tigers!*" over and over.

Oliver tried to calm him. "Theyuhs no tiguhs, Owen! Theyuhs no tiguhs! I pom-iss!" But Owen would not be comforted for a long time.

Oliver was still awake after Owen had exhausted himself and fallen back to sleep. He stayed up for a while, keeping his big brother wrapped in his arms and watching over him, feeling scared and very small.

The boys rose later than usual the next morning. Their fear from the night before still lingered in the bright daylight, refusing to be washed away by the sun. The boys sat in their room and nibbled on some pinkberries for breakfast.

Oliver froze with his second berry halfway to his mouth, and gently let his hand fall away. His head dropped and he stared in his lap. He had suddenly remembered his own dream from the night before.

Owen noticed this. "Oliver? What's the matter?"

Without looking up, Oliver answered, "I had a dream...about Mommy."

Owen paused, not sure he wanted to hear the dream about Mommy that made Oliver act like that. He very timidly asked Oliver what happened.

Oliver saw the fountain in his mind and tried to describe it to Owen. "They-uh was a fountain, like the hoss-piddle, but it was big."

Owen started at the mention of the hospital. He thought that Oliver had forgotten all of that. As Oliver described the fountain with the statue of the little girl, there could be no doubt in Owen's mind that he was describing what had been his favorite hospital fountain. Owen said nothing. He continued to listen and hoped that Oliver would not remember any more.

Oliver went on with his dream, "But it was big, too big. It scay-uhd me. Peoples stahted jumpin' in, but they wuhr all sinking. I couldn' see the bottom." Oliver could see in his mind the way that the greenish-yellow light had reflected on the dark water and danced across the giant statue of the little girl. He saw the splashing water but could not hear it. "Den the man jumped in to save 'em. But he sank, too."

Here Oliver paused. He had not raised his head nor looked up once. Owen saw a large tear drop from one of Oliver's downcast eyes.

Oliver continued, and his fragile voice shook. "So then Mommy jumped in." Oliver's chest hitched once as a single rapid breath was drawn into his lungs and released. He did not go on.

Owen knew what happened next, but he couldn't help hoping that it wouldn't, so he asked the question anyway, "Did Mommy save 'em?"

Oliver shook his head and simply said, "She died."

Oliver didn't sob or wail. He didn't roll on the ground yelling. He simply sat and cried, overcome with sadness. Owen got up and sat next to Oliver and held him, as Oliver had held him a few hours before. When the boys got up and went outside with the pumpkin, Owen suggested that they go and take a bath in the White River. Oliver eagerly agreed. Just the thought of that pearly white water made him feel better. He looked up and saw that the sky was a rare and familiar shade of blue.

CHAPTER EIGHT

For once, Oliver let Owen help him up onto the pumpkin. Oliver thoroughly enjoyed the ride to Springland. His sadness had passed by the time the pumpkin rose into the air, and he was just as overwhelmed with the happy feeling that replaced it. He reveled in the warmth of a new day, in the wreath of joy in which the pumpkin wrapped him, and in the immutable bond of love that he shared with his brother.

Oliver was enjoying the elation that children often feel after being so upset. There really is no feeling to compare to it - the heightened emotionality, experienced through the paradox of calming exhilaration. He was pressed up against Owen's back with his eyes closed, using Owen's shirt to dry his tears (and to wipe his still-sniffling nose). The gentle aromatic breeze was like the physical embodiment of all that was good and it became the entire world to Oliver on that ride. He forgot to care when, if ever, they would arrive at the White River.

Soon enough the boys did arrive, and immediately took off their clothes and jumped in a deep pool. They drank the pearly water and felt themselves lightened in body, heart and mind. Their thoughts took on a weightlessness that made the nightmares and fear of the past several hours seem almost silly. Those memories floated away for the time being and left the boys' full attention free to focus elsewhere.

The boys became enrapt by a study of how many different sounds could be made with splashes. They quickly exhausted the catalog of standard splashes and moved into new territory with whizzing splashes that were done by making quick, shallow cuts through the surface of the water with their straightened fingers. Owen discovered the *puh-lump* caused by forcefully submerging his cupped palm. Oliver discovered the tinkling sound made by drumming his fingers on the surface of the water, as well as the bubbly sound of quickly submerging his spread fingers and pushing them through the water just under the surface. The latter came with the bonus sensation of how it forcibly caused his fingers to wiggle. Owen found the sharp crack of slapping the surface of the water, though it made his palm sting. Oliver saw him wincing so he tried the easier approach of tapping the water with just one finger pad ("Look, Owen, just one finger doesn't huht"). Owen eventually took the study to new levels when he submerged his whole head to hear the different splashes from under water.

The boys were enjoyably lost in their play as the morning wore on into the early afternoon. They didn't notice when the blue sky turned gray. Their fingers and toes were extremely wrinkled by the time their rumbling bellies finally drove them out of the water to find something to eat.

Owen had seen a patch of purple parryguss on the edge of a field over which they had flown on their way to the river. After having sat so long in the water, the boys decided to run across the field to the parryguss rather than ride the pumpkin.

Owen said, "Stay here, pumpkin. We'll be right back!"

Oliver gave the pumpkin a hug and giggled at the swirls of color that it released around him. The boys then turned and raced across the field.

Owen reached the parryguss first. He stood panting and bent over with his hands on his knees. He watched Oliver's clumsy gait as he ran straight toward him as fast as he could. The smile on Oliver's face made Owen smile, too. Oliver never even slowed down. He started laughing and ran right into Owen with his arms outstretched to give him a hug. Owen caught him but they both fell over. After knocking Owen down, Oliver gave him a kiss and rolled off of him and onto the ground. The boys lay on their backs, laughing and panting until they caught their breath.

Owen yelled at the sky, "Oliver, you're crazy!" To which Oliver replied with a wild look and a mischievous smile.

Purple parryguss stalks grew all around where the boys lay. The strange plants looked a bit like little, purple palm trees. They grew no taller than halfway to Owen's knees. The plants had not looked like food to Owen when he'd first come across them, even though they'd had a tempting smell, like chestnuts roasting. It was the young Mister Oliver, with his talent for putting anything in his mouth, who had discovered the purple stalks' edibility, having swallowed several bites while Owen wasn't looking, just as he had with the parrot roots.

The little clusters of leaves that grew out of the top of the stalks were good for the boys, but rarely did they bother to eat the bitter stuff. Usually they popped that part off like the head of a dandelion and just ate the stalk, which tasted even better than it smelled. It had a buttery taste, like sauteed pistachios, not that the boys had ever tasted pistachios (if they had, they might have called these vegetables mustachios instead of parryguss, and held them to their upper lips to act like grown-ups).

Soon the grass around the boys was littered with discarded leaf clusters. Owen and Oliver thoroughly enjoyed popping these "heads" off, usually accompanying the flick of their thumb with a smack of their lips, which made an audible *POP*! They popped a few more "heads" and saved the stalks in their pockets for later. They had decided to go for a walk.

The boys went no further than a few steps when they began to be pelted with fat raindrops. It was the second day of rain in a row. Owen and Oliver could hardly believe their luck, for rain never stopped the boys from doing anything; rather, it added a sense of occasion. A rain storm turned a walk into play. Taking a bath in the rain was such a bizarrely sublime experience that both boys were tempted to go back to the White River, though neither said so out loud. They stopped walking for a few moments and tilted their heads back so that their faces pointed straight up toward the sky.

The boys loved to feel the rain on their faces. There was an intimacy to it - facing a rainswept sky. Being outside in the rain was fun and refreshing. It was an activity in itself: *being in the rain*. Rain on their faces, however, was more of a feeling. It was still playing in the rain but different, in the way that whispering secrets in each other's ears was still talking to each other, but different.

Owen and Oliver walked across an open field. They held each other's hands and swung them as they walked. From a distance their laughter sounded like faint music. Still holding hands, the boys took turns hopping and swinging each other forward. This lasted until Owen swung Oliver too hard and down he went. He landed awkwardly and painfully because Owen was still holding one of the hands he would have needed to catch himself. It took a few seconds for Oliver to register what had just happened and then he started to cry. Owen picked him up and put him back on his feet.

"C'mon, Oliver. You're all right!" Owen took his hand again. "Let's not hop anymore today, okay?"

Oliver stopped crying. He gave Owen a sniffle and a nod and it was like it had never happened. The boys walked on through the open field and enjoyed the spring shower. Tiny white flowers dotted their way and Oliver stopped to pick some with thoughts of Mommy. Owen could see that the flowers were far too delicate to make it back to the cave, but he said nothing to ruin his little brother's cheerful diversion.

After a short while, Owen paused to look up into the clouds and to feel more of the cooling drops on his face.

Oliver stopped and did as Owen did.

Owen lifted his arms and held them straight out to either side with his palms up.

Oliver did the same.

Owen lifted his right leg.

Oliver lifted his left, checked again, and switched to his right.

Owen jumped up and down on one leg while flapping his arms like a bird.

Oliver did his best to copy this, too.

The sight of each other made both of the boys start laughing. Oliver fell over after a very few hops, still laughing. Falling down looked as fun as it did funny so Owen fell over, too. Still without a word spoken by either brother, Oliver stood back up with his head leaned back and his arms out again. It was his turn to lead.

Owen got up and did the same.

Oliver started to spin around and around.

Owen mimicked him.

Oliver chanted, "Uh-whoa-uh-whoa-uh-whoa-uh-whoa," until he spun out of control and landed with a laugh in a patch of the little white flowers.

Owen had started the same chant with Oliver and was still spinning, growing louder and faster until he, too, hit the ground. He was so dizzy that he could have sworn that he had still been upright and that the ground had risen to meet him.

For a few moments the boys were too dizzy to stand up. They fell over every time they tried to plant even one foot. Owen eventually got up and started to spin again, but Oliver, once his head cleared, stopped and tilted it to one side.

"Owen, what's 'at smell?" Oliver's nose wrinkled in distaste.

Owen stopped spinning and when he did, lost his balance and fell down. He was still laughing as he answered, "I don't smell anything! Just the flowers!"

Oliver was looking at something past the next flower patch, not too far from the boys. There were odd-looking lumps in the grass. Oliver couldn't tell their shape or color through the thick sheets of rain.

Owen's head was beginning to clear, now that he had stopped spinning. He smelled it, too. It was a sickly sweet smell, vaguely familiar. "I smell it now." He followed Oliver's gaze to the great lumps in the grass.

Both boys felt uneasy. They sat and stared for a few moments, trying to puzzle it out.

"Owen? What's 'at?"

Oliver crawled on his hands and knees to where Owen was sitting. He stopped and sat next to him, putting his big brother between himself and the shapes in the grass. For several heartbeats the brothers sat in the rain and looked at the odd lumps.

"Stay here, Oliver."

Owen stood up and walked toward the strange heaps. In his imagination they were sleeping dragons and he was going to slay them all before they could get his little brother. He drew his pretend sword and bravely marched toward them, but the closer he got, the stronger that reeking smell grew. Owen slowed down. His uneasiness had ebbed at first but now it was back.

Oliver had gotten to his feet and was following Owen a few steps behind, trying to be quiet. He began to feel scared. When Owen came to a stop, so did Oliver.

Owen said, "I think they're cow-pies."

This statement caused Oliver to scrunch his face in confusion. "*Cow-pies*? What'uh they doin', Owen? Sleepin'?" The boys had never seen cow-pies lying down before. "They look funny."

Owen answered, "They're not sleeping, Oliver. They're dead. I don't know...they sure smell bad!" The sound of his and Oliver's voices was reassuring to Owen and he stepped closer to get a better look. The smell was awful. It made it hard to think.

Oliver stepped up behind Owen and peeked at the cow-pies from behind him. Neither boy could quite make sense of what they were looking at. The great lumps were definitely cow-pies, but there was something wrong with them. They weren't whole. The carcasses had swollen and begun to break apart after the rains of that morning and the day before. Their insides were on the outside, and there were what Oliver thought to be big white sticks actually coming from inside of them. Owen knew that these were bones. Much of the animals was actually missing, but with the swelling they were so misshapen that it was hard to tell.

Oliver had no memories of eating meat, and so he had no previous experience of any kind to which he could link the sight before him. He and Owen had seen a dead bird once, but it had still looked like a bird was supposed to look. Oliver stared at the ragged and lacerated husks in confusion. He could not understand why he was growing more and more afraid as he stood in that spot, but at three years of age, the reason behind the fear was much less important than the fear itself. Small children, like Oliver, have strong instincts, and they are generally correct. Oliver took his brother's hand and held it. He had an almost irresistible urge to get away from that place, but he waited to see what Owen would say or do.

Owen was working it out for himself. A part of him, deep down inside, instantly understood that the cow-pies had been eaten, and that it meant that there was something, maybe nearby, that had eaten them. He knew that *that* meant whatever it was might want to eat him and Oliver as well.

This was far too much for him to face all at once. His child's mind was slowly letting the information seep from his unconscious knowledge up through the surface of his thoughts where he could gradually grasp what this might mean. Owen started to breath a little faster. What he was afraid to know was threatening to overwhelm his thoughts just as the rancid smell of the dead animals was overwhelming his senses.

Owen felt Oliver take his hand. Oliver was standing so close to him that he was pressed up against his back. He heard Oliver start to whimper very softly and felt him tug at his hand. Oliver wanted to get away. Owen used it as an excuse to halt the dawning realization before it could fully form. It was too much for him. He was only a little boy, after all.

Oliver hadn't been able to wait any longer. He needed to get away from the cow-pies and from the stench of their rotting bodies. He had been near to panic when he finally broke down and began pulling at Owen's hand. Owen let himself be pulled away, back toward the safety of the pumpkin's glow. Relief washed over both of the boys with each step that increased the distance between themselves and the cow-pies. They half-walked and half-ran across the rain-drenched field.

The boys did not speak until they reached the White River and each took a drink next to the pumpkin's comforting orange glow. Unlike before, they now gave in to the desire to take a bath in the rain. However, they left all of their clothes on. The boys thought that they did this because it would be funny and because they were already soaked through, anyway. Both of these reasons were true, but there was something else. Finding the cow-pies had left Owen and Oliver with vague feelings of being exposed, and taking their clothes off to bathe would have increased those feelings, whether the boys were soaking in the waters of the White River or not. This was the payment due on their innocence for what they had just seen. Fortunately, that didn't change the fact that it was indeed fun, and funny, to take a bath in the rain with all of their clothes on.

The boys sat in a bathing pool, hunched over so that they were submerged up to their necks. Only their faces were exposed to the rain and to the tickling splashes made by the drops that hit the surface of the water. The submerged parts of them felt insulated and protected, much more so for the layer of clothing they wore. When they held their breath and listened to the rain from underwater, they experienced a sensation of warmth and safety reminiscent of being in the womb. It didn't matter that it was only an illusion; the boys felt like nothing could hurt them.

After a short while, Oliver felt relaxed enough to ask his brother about what they had seen.

"Owen? Whut happened to 'em?"

Owen paused before he answered, "I don't know."

Oliver tilted his head to the side and scrutinized his brother from beneath a crinkled brow. "But why'd they die? Wuhr they sick?"

"Maybe."

"But how'd they *get* like that?"

Oliver's questions were starting to make Owen feel scared. He looked at his baby brother and saw him looking back with confusion in his face. Owen could not bring himself to tell Oliver the truth that he had barely even let himself glimpse. He decided to protect Oliver with a lie. The decision made, Owen felt a comforting warmth spread through him and a lightness, as if it had become easier to breathe. It countered the weight of this one more added burden on his shoulders. He smiled at Oliver and said, "They were just old and mean. They weren't nice like most cow-pies, so the rest kicked them out."

Oliver wasn't satisfied. "But whut *happened* to 'em? Why'd they *look* like that? And *smell* like that?"

"I told you, because they were mean and wanted to hurt the good cow-pies, so they kicked 'em out and then they only could hurt each other. They were fighting and that's why they got like that. That's why they're dead, 'cause they were so mean." Owen began to believe his own explanation.

Oliver smiled, "And stupid?"

"That's right! They were stupid, too!" That made Owen laugh.

Oliver started to giggle. He asked, "Is 'at why they smelled so bad?"

"Yeah, and because everything smells bad on the inside."

"Whut?"

Owen was amusing himself but once he had said it, it seemed to make perfect sense. "Yeah, you know how farts smell bad? Well, it's the same thing."

"*Whut*? We smell like fahts on the inside?" Oliver found this fact to be delightful.

"Uh-huh! And when the cow-pies were fighting they ran at each other and exploded and their guts fell out and that's what they smell like on the inside."

"*Whut*?" Oliver's eyes were glistening with mirth now. He was very amused at the stupid, smelly cow-pies. "Like this?" He rammed his closed fists together and threw his fingers open on impact, making a big splash as he simulated an explosion. "Bam!"

"Yeah! Like *this*!" Owen did it, too.

Both boys laughed and made explosions with their hands until they no longer felt the least bit scared. Oliver's lightheartedness was Owen's reward for shouldering the truth, but it was also a fact that in sparing Oliver, Owen was sparing himself as well. He was able to hide for a time under the same veil of fabricated safety that he'd thrown over his baby brother. Safe in their pool, the boys made splashes and laughed, as they often did, because they loved each other and because they were together.

It did not take very long for the boys' anxiety to melt away, at least as far as they could tell. Still, when Oliver spoke about his idea to go to the Paint Patch next, his need to continue feeling that he was in a safe place was apparent.

"Owen, let's go to the paint place and sit unduhr the leaves."

"But I wanted to go and catch leaves in Autumnland!" Owen was also still feeling some influence of the strange experience, but he craved the release of physical activity.

The boys faced a tough decision. On the one hand, to sit in the softly colored light under the dome of a paint tree on a rainy day was a magical experience. It was like being inside of a giant, living umbrella. The boys would be protected from the rain, but able to watch the tiny river of each drop as it made its watery course down the outside of the dome of translucent leaves. There was a single, faint pulse of color where each drop landed in a splash, and a barely perceptible tint beneath where the drops beaded. The hint of color followed along as the beads swelled and lightly flowed down the leaves with a gentle caress. The delicate dance of colors complemented the sound of the raindrops pelting the outside of the enclosed space. It was a very emotional sound. It could take on nuances of whatever mood the boys were in. The sound could be sublimely melancholy, or it could convey joviality. It could also instill the boys with serenity, as if the gentle sounds of the raindrops were massaging their spirits. The whole experience created a feeling of being protected.

On the other hand, to catch leaves in a blustery rain was to vie with the elements in a vigorous contest of skill (however much it may look to the unknowing eye like two small boys jumping around and falling down in the rain). The howling wind in the boys' ears and the stinging rain on their faces added an almost primal nature to the joy excited by the physical exertion of their game. The experience gave the opposite feeling of sitting under the dome of a paint plant. It made the boys feel wild and untamed and reckless, exposed in the midst of life's uncontrolled exhilaration. It's amazing, what is not conveyed by a child's simple sentiment: "That's fun."

The boys' discussion did not last very long. Both brothers were willful by nature, but Owen had the edge, already having twice successfully assuaged his brother's fears that day. Oliver was easily won over by Owen's confidence, on the condition that they stop at the cave for dry clothes and raincoats.

The boys got out of the pool of pearly-white water and made the few steps to the pumpkin. They played with their wet clothes and laughed at how heavy they were. In fact, their clothes were so heavy with water that even Owen had trouble getting on the pumpkin. The boys did not get frustrated. Having soaked so long in the White River, it would have taken much more than that to upset them. Both boys actually had an attack of the giggles. Owen was laughing at his own clumsiness and Oliver was laughing both at Owen and at himself, as he squatted down to hear the squishy sound of air escaping through his wet jeans. Even the pumpkin released a few wisps of color as if it, too, was amused. Once the boys were up, the pumpkin soared away and carried its gigglers back to their cave to suit up for their leaf-catching adventure.

When the boys set out for Autumnland, they were clothed in dry shoes, jeans and sweaters, which were protected underneath raincoats and galoshes. Owen's coat and boots were green and Oliver's, of course, were bright yellow. Both boys wore their hoods with the drawstrings pulled tight around their faces. The gray sky had gotten darker and the air had a slightly greenish cast to it. The gusts of wind gathered more force as they neared Autumnland, and the drops of rain grew heavier and colder. The boys grew more and more excited as the weather became more severe.

The boys did not stop to scare the black birds or to jump in the piles of leaves. Owen landed the pumpkin and he and Oliver waded through the leaf piles as fast as they could, anxious to get to their leaf-catching glade on the edge of the Deadwood Forest. The peals of their laughter were like wisps of sound that the wind carried away no sooner than they had left the boys' lungs. The brothers held hands through the stand of evergreens. They were pelted by pine needles that bounced off of their slickers. Needles, leaves and pieces of grass stuck to their wet boots.

As they had the day before, the boys made a riotous clamor of happy and excited sounds: laughs, shouts, squeals - all but inaudible over the howling wind that instantly swept the sounds away through the trees. There was a loud crack as the branch of a dead tree was snapped from its trunk by the storm winds. Both boys jumped and screamed in surprise, then laughed even harder at their folly. Oliver began to sing a song.

I love the rain!
I love the wind!
It blows on my head,
It blows like my nose!
The leaves in my hand!
I love to stand!
Rain! Rain! Rain! Rain! Rain! Rain! RAIN!

Just as the last *RAIN!* was fading from Oliver's lips, the glade opened before him. The scene that met the two brothers was unlike anything they had expected. Instead of the trickle of leaves blowing on the wind, the air was filled with rain and leaves, twigs and branches, and even struggling black birds, all blowing straight at the boys.

As soon as they stepped out from the trees, it was as if they were under attack. Oliver turned his back and hunched over to protect himself, squealing with laughter. Owen threw his arms out and was yelling, "Ahhhhhh!" at the top of his lungs as he tried to catch everything at once. The boys had never been there during such a violent storm and they were loving every minute of it.

Owen pulled at Oliver's arm. "C'mon, Oliver! They're everywhere!" He had to shout to be heard over the storm and the constant moaning of the wind blowing through the holes in the trees.

"Aaaaaahhhhhhh!" said Oliver. It was all that his overstimulated mind could come up with.

In the chaotic contest that followed, neither boy was clearly winning or losing, and neither boy stopped laughing except to take a breath or to call out their exuberance in a language of grunts, yowls, squeaks and squawks.

Owen had already had more leaves blow right into his hands than he'd ever been able to catch before.

Oliver tried to keep hold of everything he caught, even while he tried to catch more. In the crook of his arm, Oliver dragged a long, thick branch that nearly tripped him at every step.

The confusion was such that the boys nearly ran right into each other several times. They were hit by much more debris than they actually caught.

Owen ducked to avoid a twig that was flying right at his head and he moved directly into the path of a great wet leaf that smacked into his face and stuck.

Oliver turned to his left to avoid a flying stick only to feel a bird get blown into his back. He turned to shoo the bird and got hit with a twig. He was laughing so hard that he could barely breathe, as was Owen.

The boys both spotted a single, bright yellow leaf flying straight toward them and they both jumped for it at the same time. Neither brother caught it.

Oliver felt himself knocked to the ground and heard his branch snap underneath him. He instantly went into tantrum mode. He opened his mouth to yell at Owen but no sound came out. He couldn't yell. He couldn't speak, couldn't breathe, couldn't move.

Owen rolled a ways down the grassy hill. He got up and took two running steps before he stopped to wonder why he was running. Pain flared in his back and he looked around for Oliver so that he could yell at him. At first, Owen just stared, uncomprehending.

A great, dark creature that he had never seen before held Oliver in its jaws. Owen could not even see his brother's right shoulder beneath the creature's immense teeth. The rest of Oliver's body was pinned to the ground by one giant, claw-covered paw that spread across his belly and sank into his left thigh. Oliver's eyes were staring straight in front of him. There was a lot of blood, and Owen saw something long and light-colored sticking out of the creature's mouth. His panicking mind formed the thought, *That's Oliver's spine!* Owen looked in the creature's eyes and saw them staring right back at him.

Owen couldn't move. He started screaming in terror, crying hot, helpless tears.

Oliver heard Owen start to scream and finally began to realize that something was very wrong. His stare shifted to Owen's face and he saw him looking back, crying and screaming, his features contorted in a way that Oliver had never seen. Oliver began to feel panic. He tried to get up but couldn't. The slightest movement caused sharp, piercing pain to shoot through his body. Oliver finally looked down at himself. He saw the giant paw. He saw the sharp claws disappearing into him. He realized that he could not turn his head because an animal was in the way. He felt the hot breath and the pressure in his shoulder but still did not come to the conclusion that something had him in its mouth. Oliver was so deeply in shock that he could make sense of very little. He started to cry. Something hard was pressing into his back that hurt worse than everything else. He felt himself lifted off the ground and then there was pain everywhere.

Owen had almost completely lost his senses. He was absolutely terrified. He stood still, crying. His mouth was stretched wide open, belting out a constant, high-pitched wail. He stared at his brother. He did not have thoughts of saving him. He had no thoughts at all. The creature lifted Oliver off the ground and took a single step forward and Owen turned to run away. He didn't even take a single step. Behind him were several more of the dark creatures. Owen's wailing became raw and broken. He hated the creatures. It wasn't fair. They were everywhere.

Oliver's body hung limp and lifeless. Any movement at all just caused him more pain. It hurt him just to breathe. He closed his eyes, hoping that would make it all go away.

Owen thought that his brother was dead like the cow-pies. He thought that he was all alone and that the creatures were going to get him and eat him. The creatures advanced on Owen from all sides, including the creature that held Oliver in its jaws. Owen slowly crawled backward toward the black hole trees, keeping his face toward the bulk of the creatures. He came to a stop when he felt his foot go over the edge of the steep slope. There was nowhere left to go. The rain still beat down heavily in the glade. The gusts of wind carried the sound of hungry growling, mingled with Owen's cries.

Owen screamed at the creatures. "Go away!" but they did not even pause. His tears blinded him so he lowered his head. "Go a-WAY!" He closed his eyes tightly, screaming it over and over with one hand held straight out, as if he could ward off these monsters that had appeared from nowhere. "Go away! Go a-WAY! *GO AWAY-EEEEE!*"

Oliver, hearing this last scream, put up one last struggle to get free. At that same moment, lightning flashed across the sky overhead, casting the creatures in brilliant light. Oliver finally saw what had him and he started screaming, too. At the moment of Oliver's struggle and the long flash of lightning, the creature that held him in its jaws tossed him up in the air to get a killing grip, the way that a dog will toss up a bone. When the creature had pounced, the branch that Oliver had been dragging around had gotten wedged between his back and the creature's lower jaw. When the creature had instinctively tried to break Oliver's back with its initial lunge, the branch had kept its jaws from snapping shut. The branch, which Oliver had looked so silly dragging around, had saved his life.

When Owen heard his brother's scream, he looked up. The creature's head was thrashing from side to side, shaking Oliver about like a rag doll. There was a sound of tearing fabric, and then Oliver was tossed through the air, over the edge of the glade and out of sight. Owen did not hear him land. He wanted to find him but he couldn't look away from the creatures. Owen's own cries hadn't stopped. He was all alone. He had never felt so sorry for himself. His hand was timidly half-withdrawn now, as if he were afraid to hold it out straight. His face was red and hot tears flowed steadily from both of his eyes, mixing with the rain on his face. His voice faded, but he continued to whimper the words, "Go away...go away...*please* go away..."

"Owen!"

The sound of his own name, screamed at the top of Oliver's terrified voice, finally broke Owen's paralysis. Without a moment's further hesitation, over the hill he went, to his brother's side. However, the scene below him was even more terrible than the one he had left above.

Oliver was far below, lying against one of the twisted black hole trees. His yellow raincoat was torn and splashed with bright red. He was screaming. Owen slid through the steep mud as fast as he could.

His need to reach Oliver was as strong as his need to get away from the creatures above. Owen suddenly realized why Oliver was screaming and when he did, he lost his footing and began to tumble down the hill, slamming painfully into the trunks of the trees and crashing through their branches.

When Oliver had been shaken in the creature's mouth, he had become so disoriented by the pain and the thrashing movement that he had not realized when he had torn free. He had suddenly seen the ground rushing toward him at an impossible speed and had experienced the most intense moment of fear in his very young life. He had been unable to draw breath to scream. The burst of adrenaline had dimmed his vision and then he had been violently jarred by impact, losing his breath yet again. He had rolled and slid through the mud and come to rest against one of the black hole trees.

The boys had been right to fear those trees. No sooner had Oliver found himself able to breathe again than the trees had seemed to come alive. He had finally realized that he was all alone and had screamed Owen's name as loud as he could.

Owen came to a stop about ten feet above his brother. He was on his back. The top of his head was pointed toward the bottom of the ravine. He stared straight up, frozen by what he saw. A flash of lightning lit the hillside and revealed movement everywhere. At first, Owen thought that the black hole trees themselves were alive and thrashing about, but after a few seconds he realized that something lived *inside* the trees. Long, black tentacles reached out through the holes in the trunks, lashing with violent movement in all directions. Whatever they were, they had been roused when Oliver had landed amidst the trees and when both Oliver and himself had slammed against so many of them.

Owen was still crying. This was too much; to escape the dark creatures and end up in that terrifying place. Owen felt like bursting. He was scared, hurt and frustrated; disoriented, lonely, sad and outraged at the unfairness of it all.

Owen screamed at the top of his lungs for it all to just "STOP! STOP IT! GO AWAY!"

He heard Oliver crying, too, but couldn't see him. Owen looked down at his feet, which were actually pointed up, and saw the silhouetted shapes of the dark creatures against the leaden gray sky. They were following the boys over the edge of the glade and coming down the hill very fast. Owen panicked and his movements caused him to slide through the mud, right past his brother.

Oliver's senses were fading. He had lost a lot of blood. He was still bleeding. The blood blossomed in the streams of water running over his raincoat, making it look like there was even more than there actually was. The sight of his own blood badly scared him. He sat still, trying to be quiet but not able to stop crying. The tentacles were all around him, looking for him. He hurt all over. Finally he saw Owen falling down the hill toward him.

Lightning flashed and lit the hillside. More of the black tentacles came out of the trees as Owen crashed into them. Oliver saw Owen slide to a stop a short distance above him and lay there unmoving. He couldn't see Owen's face. Oliver thought his brother was dead. In a flash, he understood everything about the cow-pies and what had happened to them. He started to cry louder, but then he heard Owen screaming at him to stop it, to go away, and this made Oliver want to die. He was so sad. Owen slid past him. Oliver made one final effort and rolled away from the trunk that had caught him. He had to be next to Owen, even if Owen did not want him to be.

Oliver slid right into Owen, who grabbed him tightly and made him wince and cry out in pain. It was worth the pain to feel Owen holding him that way. Owen looked over his shoulder and started to make a noise like a stuttering whimper. He saw a tentacle lash out and catch one of the dark creatures around its throat. The creature roared and squealed.

Owen's panic got him moving fast. Keeping one arm around Oliver, he scooted down the hill as quickly as he could, pulling Oliver along with him as tentacles whipped all about just above the boys' heads.

Oliver let out a painful yell with each scoot but he did not struggle, nor did he say anything. Now that the brothers were together again and Owen was taking care of him, Oliver's mind all but shut down. Owen never stopped moving. He never stopped crying. He never stopped his rapid whimper. When there was a noise worse than in his dream, a noise that seemed like it would go on forever, Owen sped up his panicked pace to get himself and Oliver away.

Thunder boomed. Branches and trees snapped and crashed. The roars of the dark creatures were deafening, as were their squeals. A battle raged upon the hillside but the brothers did not look back. There was an anarchy of sound so overwhelming to the boys' ears, they knew that surely the world must split apart and end. There could be no existence but the deafening noise all around them.

Oliver's eyes were squeezed shut. He was sobbing, "Too loud! Too loud!"

Owen's whimpers grew louder as he felt himself swallowed by the din. Neither of the boys could hear their own voice. They felt the very earth shake.

And then, it was over. The boys stopped shouting but did not stop moving. They still did not look back. The only sounds now were that of the rain and distant thunder, the scrape of the boys sliding over the ground, Oliver's soft cries and Owen's heavy, exhausted breaths that came between each whimper.

The boys reached the bottom of the ravine just as the rain lightened to a drizzle. When they finally looked back up the steep hillside, they saw nothing but the twisted shapes of the black hole trees and the pale gray sky behind them. They did not know it then, but the boys would never see any sign of the dark creatures again, nor would they ever know what had happened to them.

Oliver looked down at himself, at the blood and filth, and began to sob inconsolably, a scared, three-year-old boy.

Owen, only five years old himself, did not know what to do. He saw that Oliver was still bleeding from his leg, stomach, shoulder and neck. Owen looked around. He noticed the pale glint of a narrow stream that ran next to them, along the bottom of the gully. He went to get some water but stopped when he got close.

This was a new river that he had not seen before. Its brackish waters were jet-black, and they seemed to let off an almost tangible sadness. The ground around the boys was covered with a deep layer of dead and rotting leaves. All color seemed to have drained from the narrow floor of the ravine, where very little light could reach. It was a place of darkness and shadows.

Owen did not want to be there.

Oliver's sobs were growing louder.

There was no way out of the ravine without climbing through the black hole trees and the tentacled monsters that lived inside them. The boys had lost the pumpkin and it would not be able to find them all the way down there.

Oliver's sobs rose in pitch until Owen felt as if they would pierce his brain. Owen turned and hit Oliver on his arm as hard as he could and screamed at him. "Shut up, Oliver!"

Owen immediately started to cry. He said, "I'm sorry, Oliver. I'm sorry," over and over but Oliver was shrieking now. They were just two frightened little boys, alone in a dark and scary place. They were both hurt; Oliver was hurt badly. Owen was afraid that he might die, and there was no one to help them. Owen collapsed next to Oliver and the two boys cried until they exhausted themselves.

"Ooowww..." Oliver was moaning. His tears had almost dried but his nose was still running, his chest still hitched with shaky breaths, and the occasional tremor still shook his bottom lip.

Owen slowly and painfully got up. "What's that?" he said to himself.

There was something buried in the leaves that had gathered at the bank of the stream. It was pale and looked soft. Owen pulled it out of the leaves and brushed it off. It was an old and very dirty stuffed dog. Through the gray stains of filth and neglect, Owen could see that it had once been cream-colored with brown ears, brown spots, and a brown patch around one of its eyes. Owen held it up and looked at it in disbelief. Finally, with a sad smile on his face and a tear in his eye he pressed it to his chest and hugged it. He then stepped back over to where Oliver lay.

Oliver's moans didn't seem to match the way that he was staring expressionlessly into space. Owen took Oliver's hand and put the dog in it. Oliver's eyes pointed at the dog. At first there was no reaction, but then...

"*Odie...*" Oliver came alive and held the dog to himself with his uninjured arm. He closed his eyes and rocked the stuffed dog. He murmured softly. "*Odie...Odie...Odie...*"

Owen curled up next to Oliver where he lay, wrapped him in his arms, and rocked with him. Soon both boys fell asleep. In their weariness they had taken no notice that it was growing dark and that they had no shelter. The shadow eyes would come soon and Owen and Oliver could not hide. The boys did not know it, but the very river next to which they slept was the shadow eyes' home. It was that which made the water black and filled it with sadness.

END PART ONE

PART TWO

CHAPTER NINE

It was Owen's fourth birthday. He had just woken up and was lying in his bed, staring up at the ceiling. He wondered if anyone would remember. He looked over at Oliver's empty bed and felt a hot flush of guilt for thinking about himself. He wondered if today would be *the* day, and a wave of fear washed over him. Owen didn't get up immediately. He had a lot on his mind for such a young boy.

There were normal morning sounds coming from the kitchen. *Granny must still be here*, he thought. *She'll remember my birthday*! But as with every happy thought that he had these days, it was immediately followed by a pang of bitterness as he thought about his brother. Owen wondered if Oliver would want some cake, and then wondered if his little brother would even be allowed to eat cake or ice cream.

Owen had a sudden, selfish moment that overrode his guilt. It wasn't fair! Oliver got everything and he got nothing. Everyone loved Oliver more and wanted to be with him all of the time (it was very sad that Owen actually believed this). Owen knew that his family loved him, but he thought that they loved Oliver so much more. Of course it wasn't true, but nothing that anybody said or did could convince him otherwise. He sometimes felt that he was just a bother that was passed off on others so that Mommy and Daddy could spend time with Oliver and not with him.

Mommy and Daddy had not even slept at home last night like they'd promised they would. All week long they had promised to wake up with Owen so that just the three of them could go to Owen's favorite restaurant and have strawberry pancakes with whipped cream for his birthday breakfast, but then late last night Granny had come over so that Mommy and Daddy could leave to go to the hospital. They hadn't even come into Owen's room to tell him they were leaving. He had lain in bed, listening in the dark to their hushed voices and soft crying and he had started to cry, too, but nobody had heard him.

Sometimes Owen thought that everyone would be happier if he were sick instead of Oliver. A few tears escaped his eyes and he silently wished this with all his heart, as he did every day: that he could be the sick one so that Oliver could get better. One of the reasons he believed that everyone loved Oliver more was that he felt that way himself. Owen loved his baby brother much more than he loved himself, and so it seemed natural to him that everyone else would too, even if it did hurt very much. All of these thoughts and emotions lived in Owen and made him a very confused and emotional little boy.

Although nobody had told him, Owen was afraid that Oliver was going to die. He was afraid that was the reason why Mommy and Daddy had left the night before and why he had heard them crying again. A few more tears escaped his eyes as he whispered a very special birthday wish, "Please don't die, Oliver. Please don't die. My birthday wish is for Oliver to get better and play with me again."

After making his wish, Owen felt a little better. He smiled and got out of bed to see what Granny was going to do for his birthday. He went into the kitchen and saw Granny standing at the sink, staring out of the window above it. Her shoulders shook ever so slightly.

"Granny? Whatcha doin'?" He heard her sniffle and there was a pause.

When she turned around her eyes were red but she was smiling and she said, "Happy Birthday, angel!"

Owen smiled back and looked at the kitchen table for a card, or presents, or a cake. There was nothing. "Granny? Where's my cake?"

"We're gonna get your cake, sweetheart, and ice cream, too, but first we're going to see your brother. He's very sick and he had a very bad night."

Granny's eyes were wet with tears. Her face pinched with pain, but only for a moment before the smile was back. Owen felt bad even before he asked his next question. He knew that it would only upset

Granny but he had to ask anyway. "Can we go have pancakes for my birthday first?"

She said, "Oh, Owen honey, we can't, not today. But we'll make it up to you. I promise!"

Owen had seen the answer in her face before she had started to speak. His own face grew red as his tears started to fall. "But it's my birthday!"

"I know, angel, but..."

"All I wanted was stupid strawberry pancakes and Mommy and Daddy promised but they lied! They *always* lie! They're not even here! I'm never gonna get cake and ice cream! I bet I don't even get any presents!" Owen choked out these words between sobs and gasps for air. He had been told *we'll make it up to you* for months, and he no longer believed it. Now it just made him more upset to hear it. He had hoped that his birthday would be different, *special*, but it wasn't.

"Owen!" He had been right. Granny was upset. "Your brother is very sick! Mommy and Daddy wanted more than anything to be here for your birthday, but they had to leave last night to go and take care of him, just like they'd take care of you if you were sick!" Her anger subsided quickly and she said gently, "Now, come on, sugar. Go and get dressed. You can wear whatever you like because it's your birthday."

Owen turned and stormed back to his and Oliver's room. His birthday was ruined and it was all Oliver's fault. Owen kicked one of Oliver's fire trucks and the ladder broke off of it. He was glad it did and he felt bad for it, all at once. He didn't get dressed, but threw himself down on his bed and cried hot tears into his pillow. He was so scared.

Owen heard the phone ring and heard Granny answer it. He heard her use her most flowery voice to say, "Hold on one second while I get him."

Granny came into his room and knelt down next to the bed where Owen still lay face down. "Somebody wants to say something to you, sugar." She had a big, gentle smile.

Owen took the phone. He sniffled a couple of times to clear his nose and put the phone to his ear. "Hello?"

"Happy Buss-tay, Owen!" Oliver's voice sounded very weak, very shaky, and very happy. He was very young and couldn't quite pronounce Owen's name. It came out sounding something like *Whoa-wen.*

Owen replied in a voice that was just as happy as his brother's. "Oliver! Me and Granny are comin' to see you!" Owen couldn't understand Oliver's reply, but he could tell that Oliver was excited to see him. "Are you all right, Oliver?"

Oliver said, "Yups!" Owen heard whispering and then he heard Oliver say, "Buh-byes!"

"Bye, Oliver. I love you, Oliver!"

Daddy's voice came through the phone next. "Happy Birthday, buddy!" He sounded strange, but Owen was very happy to hear his voice.

"Daddy!"

"How're you doin', Owen? Are you being good for Granny?"

"Dad, Granny says we can't have pancakes. Can't we stop first 'cause it's my birthday before we come to the hospital?"

"Buddy, I really need you to be a big boy today, and come straight to the hospital as quick as you can. Mommy and me will talk to you when you get here. Okay?"

"But..."

"No 'buts' today, Owen. Here, talk to Mommy for a second."

Mommy came on the phone. "Happy Birthday, baby! Mommy's so sorry we weren't there this morning, but Oliver really needs us right now."

"Mommy? Is Oliver gonna be okay?"

There was a slight pause before she answered. Owen heard his mother take a breath. "We'll talk about it when you get here, baby. Can I talk to Granny real quick?"

"Okay, I love you, Mommy."

"I love you, too, sweetheart. Happy Birthday."

Before Owen could hand the phone to Granny, he heard Oliver start to yell. It sounded like he was yelling, "Up! Up!" He heard Daddy say something to Mommy and then the phone hung up.

Owen handed the phone back to Granny and started to get dressed. He picked out his favorite jeans and Oliver's favorite shirt, the one with all the frogs on it. He made a quick scan of the room to see what he could bring to the hospital. Granny always let him bring some toys. He filled his pockets with a couple of his favorite matchbox cars, some swirly bouncy-balls, and some change to throw in the fountain.

On the way to the hospital, Granny was very quiet. She was acting even more strange than usual and it scared Owen. He sat in the back in his car seat and stared out of the window. He wondered if Oliver was going to die on his birthday, and this thought made him very sad, and even more scared.

Owen really didn't understand why Oliver was sick, or what was wrong with him. He had overheard so many different things that he couldn't make sense of them. Leukemia and cancer were two of the worst things that Owen knew about. He knew they were bad because nobody ever said them in front of Oliver. Owen didn't understand what these things were, but he knew that they scared him, and it sounded like Oliver had both of them. He knew that something was wrong with Oliver's blood. That was why they were always giving him new blood. Two days ago he heard a doctor say that Oliver had infections on the inside, and ammonia. Owen didn't know what ammonia was, but it had made Mommy cry.

Everyone always had to wear a mask over their mouth to go in Oliver's room so that he wouldn't get germs. They all said that they couldn't let Oliver get sick because of his moon system (Owen wondered if this might have something to do with nighttime), but then all they ever talked about was how very sick he was. It didn't make sense. They even gave him something called chemo that made him sicker.

It confused Owen enough to sometimes make him cry out of pure frustration, and the fact that he couldn't understand made him even more afraid. Even worse, whoever was talking always said these kinds of things in a tone that clearly let Owen know that he was not to ask questions.

When they got to the hospital, Granny gave Owen one of Oliver's clean, soft blankets to carry. It was still warm from the dryer. They walked past the little girl fountain and Owen asked Granny to stop so he could make a birthday wish for Oliver to get better. Owen dug in his jeans for the coins he had brought but Granny stopped him.

"Here, sugar. I have some change. You keep yours because it's your birthday."

She took the blanket from Owen and he tossed the coins in the fountain one at a time. He wished for presents and pancakes for himself, and then he wished the same for Oliver, even though it wasn't even his birthday. He saved the quarters for last. Owen closed his eyes and concentrated. He thought of all the times that he and Oliver had thrown coins in that fountain together. He thought the words, *Please don't let Oliver die. Make him all better so he can play with me and never let him get sick again*, and he pictured the two of them having a pillow fight. In Owen's imagination they could hit each other as hard as they wanted because Oliver wasn't fragile anymore.

Owen opened his eyes, took a deep breath, and tossed his three quarters in the fountain. He looked at the statue of the little girl. He just happened to be standing directly in front of her, so that when he looked in her eyes she appeared to be looking right back at him. Owen turned, took the blanket back from Granny and hugged it as if it were Oliver himself.

Upstairs in his room, Oliver was waiting for his big brother. Oliver had had a very rough night, and the morning wasn't turning out any better. He couldn't stop throwing up, and his head hurt. He felt like he couldn't catch his breath and whenever he coughed, the tube in his nose moved and tickled his throat in a place he couldn't scratch. His cough was wet but he couldn't clear his throat. His lips felt dried and cracked and he didn't even have the strength to lift his hand to rub them. Nothing felt good in his current position, but he lacked the strength to try and roll over. His whole body felt wrong anyway, like no matter how he lay he would be uncomfortable. He just ached all over. They gave him medicine through his tubes that helped a little with the pain, but it made everything fuzzy. It was hard for Oliver to think. He had made them turn the TV off because the noise hurt his ears and they kept the room dim because the light hurt his eyes. He really could not remember what it was like to feel good.

Oliver was eighteen months old. A third of his life had been spent in the hospital. He had been in that particular room for thirty-seven days.

Mommy and Daddy had come to be with him all night. They were taking turns with him. One lay in his bed and cuddled him while the other sat and held his hand. Daddy was in the bed with him now and he was holding the blue blowing-tube to his face. They said it was to help him breathe. The nurse had tried to put the mask on his face but Mommy and Daddy had stopped her when he had cried. They were being extra nice to him today because it was Owen's birthday. They had even let him take the sticky wrap off of his toe, and he didn't have to take any of his meds. Nobody had to wear a mask today, either, so Mommy and Daddy could give him as many kisses as they wanted.

There was a gentle knock on the door. Oliver made a strenuous effort to turn his head so he could see if Owen had arrived. He saw Granny, so Owen must be there, too. But where was he?

When Granny came in, Grampa followed. Oliver heard Owen outside in the hall. Why wasn't he coming in?

Daddy said, "I've got to get up for just a minute, baby. Me and Mommy want to talk to Owen and give him big birthday hugs, and then he can come in and you can tell him 'Happy Birthday' and the two of you can snuggle for a while. Okay?"

Oliver moaned out a "Nooooo..."

Mommy kissed his nose and said, "Only for a minute, baby. I promise."

Mommy had a big smile on her face. She was looking at him and rubbing his head as Daddy eased himself out of the bed. Daddy had to be careful of all of Oliver's tubes. They ran from lots of places on Oliver's body to his pole. Granny and Grampa sat down on either side of him. Granny held his hand while Grampa held the blowing-tube and they both whispered nice things to him.

Grampa said, "They'll be right back, sweetheart. How're you feeling today?"

Granny said, "Good morning, angel!"

Oliver closed his eyes and murmured, "Hmmm..." He was saving his strength for Owen.

When the door had closed behind them, Daddy picked up Owen and both Mommy and Daddy told him "Happy Birthday!" and covered him with kisses. Daddy asked him about his morning as he carried him down the hall to a private room for the patients' families. Owen told his Daddy about the wish he had made for Oliver and that Granny had given him the coins so that he wouldn't have to throw his own. Mommy followed behind. She smiled at Owen, but he thought that she looked very sad.

They went into the private room and Daddy sat down with Owen on his lap. Mommy pulled a chair over and sat so that her knees touched

Owen's legs. Owen felt more scared than he ever had before, but he was with Mommy and Daddy, and that helped him to be brave.

Before anyone else could speak, Owen said, "Is Oliver gonna die?"

Owen felt his Daddy's head bow and come to rest on the top of his own head. He heard his Daddy start to cry. Mommy got up and pushed the chair away. She knelt down in front of Owen, so that her face was level with his. She put a hand on each of his shoulders, then Mommy looked directly into Owen's eyes and she and Owen both started to cry. She didn't say a word, and neither of them looked away, not even when hot tears blurred Owen's vision and then spilled down his cheeks.

Owen's throat hurt. His lips hurt. Most of all his heart hurt. After many moments, Mommy and Daddy hugged him together, and hugged each other around him. Mommy was saying how sorry she was that this had to happen on his birthday but Owen didn't care about that anymore. All he cared about was being with Oliver.

"Can we go see him now?" Owen had spoken in a very timid voice that shook as Oliver's had shaken that morning.

Mommy and Daddy let him go. Mommy passed tissues around and they all blew their noses. She said, "Dry your eyes, baby. We don't want Oliver to know that we're sad. We have to stay happy for him, okay? And don't tell him anything. He doesn't need to know."

When they returned to Oliver's room, Owen stopped at the sink outside his door to wash his hands and to put on a mask.

Daddy said, "It's okay, Owen. You don't have to worry about that today."

Owen barely understood why, but that almost made him start to cry all over again. He took a few deep breaths and pushed on the handle of Oliver's door. Mommy and Daddy each had a supportive hand on his shoulder as they all walked in together. The two brothers each experienced something very different and something very the same when Owen entered the room.

Oliver was so happy to see Owen that he even managed to wave his fingers at him. Grampa got up from his chair and told Owen to sit down. When he did, Oliver held out his hand and when Owen took it Oliver told him, "Happy Birthday."

Owen thanked him and told him about his wish for him to get better. Oliver smiled. He was happy because Owen had used his special birthday wish to make him better. He couldn't wait to play with him. The room started to swim. Oliver needed to throw up again.

Owen was very happy to be near to Oliver, but the sight of his brother upset him so much that he had trouble speaking. Oliver's long, blond locks had fallen out long ago. His bald head was nothing new, but that morning it was covered in a splotchy red rash. He had more tubes coming out of him than he'd had when Owen had been there just two days ago. There was even a tube in his nose again. The places around Oliver's eyes had a hollow look, and the skin had a bluish tint. Oliver's breaths were very rapid, like he had just finished running as fast as he could, but he didn't seem to be getting any air. Grampa was holding a blue tube by Oliver's face. The tube made a blowing sound. Owen walked to the bed and stopped at its foot. Oliver was smiling and waving his fingers at him. Owen waved back. His lips felt numb but he managed to say, "Hi, Oliver."

Grampa had gotten up and was directing Owen into the chair by Oliver's bed. When Owen sat down, Oliver held out his hand and Owen took it in both of his. With his other hand, Oliver was hugging his beloved Odie to his chest. The stuffed dog had been Oliver's best friend since he first came to the hospital. The two of them had been through a lot together. When Oliver spoke, it was one syllable at a time, quickly spoken between each of the forced breaths that he took.

"'Appy...buss-tay...Owen."

"Thanks, Oliver! My birthday wish was for you to get better! Granny gave me some coins so I could wish in the little girl fountain. Remember all the wishes we made there, Oliver?"

Oliver nodded his head and smiled.

Now that Owen was close up, he could see that Oliver's lips were stained red and black, and he saw how dry they were. Oliver closed his eyes and his smile disappeared. He groaned at first and then started yelling, "Up...up...up!"

Everyone jumped to their feet. Grampa pulled on Owen's chair and slid it, and Owen, out of the way so that Mommy and Daddy could lift Oliver into a sitting position. Daddy held the pink tub under his face while Mommy rubbed his back. Both of them were speaking in soft, soothing voices, "It's okay, baby. It's okay."

Owen watched as Oliver threw up. He'd seen it many times before but this time was different. Oliver didn't even heave. It just came up and out of his mouth, and was red with blood. Owen was scared but he couldn't look away.

When Oliver was done, Mommy and Daddy laid him back down, wiped his mouth and nose and dried his tears.

Daddy said to Grampa, "Okay, time for Owen to go now."

"No!" Owen felt something very close to panic at the thought of being taken away from Oliver. He started to cry. "I'm okay, I promise! I wanna stay!"

The grownups all looked at each other. Mommy was shaking her head no.

Daddy said, "Buddy, it'll be okay. Oliver needs to sleep now. Come on, let Grampa take you for your birthday breakfast."

Everyone started to get up. Grampa put a gentle hand on Owen's arm, but Owen pulled away.

In the quiet moment, just before Owen's whimpers could turn to sobs, Oliver said, "Owen...stay!" His voice was weak, shaky, and had a wet croak to it from having just been sick.

Mommy seemed close to tears. She said, "Baby, Owen will come and see you again in a little bit. Okay?"

Daddy agreed, "After your nap, sweetheart."

But Oliver wouldn't be calmed. "No...Owen...stay! Owen...snuggle... me!...pom-ist!"

Owen saw that Mommy wasn't going to say no to Oliver. He was already feeling relief when she said, "Shhhh, baby. Shhhhhh. Owen can stay a little while longer. Owen? You wanna climb in and snuggle with Oliver?"

"Okay."

Owen felt relieved and sad and happy and scared all at once. He felt his love for his brother like he never had before. He climbed in bed next to Oliver, careful not to pull on any of his tubes. Daddy covered them with the fresh blanket that he and Granny had brought and then he placed the blowing tube on the pillow next to Oliver's face.

All of the grownups were standing. Daddy said, "We're going to be in the hall for just a minute, right outside the door. If Oliver needs to be sick, Owen, just yell and we'll come running. Okay?"

"Okay, Daddy."

The boys' Daddy bent over, gave them each a kiss and left the room, followed by Granny and Grampa. Mommy was the last to leave. She looked down on Owen and Oliver and said, "My boys, my big boys. Mommy's so proud of both of you! I love you both so much!" Then she bent over and tickled their necks with Mommy-kisses before she stood up and followed the others out of the room, closing the door gently and quietly behind her.

The boys didn't speak. They simply lay next to each other and snuggled with Odie in the dim hospital room. The only sounds were Oliver's quick, shallow breaths, the blowing-tube and the beeping machines. Within seconds, the boys fell asleep together. When they awoke, they would think, at first, that they were sharing a dream.

CHAPTER TEN

Owen woke first. Before he even opened his eyes, he sensed that something was different. He kept his eyes shut and tried to figure out what it was. Then it came to him: he was outside. He opened his eyes and the first thing that he saw was a bright, cloudless yellow sky. He and Oliver were still under the blanket, but the hospital and everything else were gone.

Oliver stirred and rolled over. He propped himself up on one elbow easily. His eyes were wide as he, too, stared at the sky and the rolling hills of grass all around them.

"Owen!" Owen was in his dream!

"Oliver!" Owen thought that Oliver was in *his* dream.

Both boys giggled and hugged each other tightly. They sat up and Oliver pulled the blanket off of them. He was wearing his fuzzy pajamas but his tubes were all gone. Oliver was happy to see that Odie was in the dream, too.

Oliver took a deep breath, his first in a long time. It felt so good to breathe! Oliver took another breath. He felt as if his lungs would never fill, and when they did, he let out a jubilant, "Wooooooooo!" He struggled to his feet. The warm grass felt good under his bare toes but he fell over before he could manage to take even a single step. His legs were very weak.

"Owen! Up!" Oliver sat with his arms held out to his brother, waiting to be helped up.

Owen felt just an instant of panic at the word "up" but then he remembered that it was a dream and so he excitedly grabbed Oliver's hands and pulled him to a standing position. However, he pulled too hard and toppled over backwards with Oliver landing on top of him. This made both boys laugh.

Oliver did not roll off of Owen at first. He lifted his head and put his hands on Owen's face. He squished Owen's cheeks and made himself laugh, then he laid his head on Owen's chest and closed his eyes. Oliver felt good, really *good*; even better than when he got his special medicine.

Owen lay on his back. He could feel his brother's deep breaths and his heartbeat.

When Oliver sighed, "*Hmmmmmm*," Owen felt the vibration on his own chest and wrapped his arms around his baby brother.

Owen tried it, "*Hmmmmmmmm*."

It tickled Oliver's chest and ear, and he let out a giggle. The boys hummed a bit more, all else forgotten in their child's enjoyment of this simple happiness.

An idea occurred to Owen. "Get up a minute, Oliver," he said.

Oliver rolled off of his chest and gathered Odie in his arms. Owen sat up. He clenched his teeth and pinched himself on the arm as hard as he could.

"Ow!" He did it again. "Ow-wow!" He looked at his baby brother, who sat in the grass, looking back at him and smiling. "Oliver! I didn't wake up!"

Oliver's eyes grew big, and afraid. He squeezed Odie tighter. "No wakes up! No, Owen!"

As soon as Owen had said the word "wake" Oliver had thought about the hospital and all of the terrible things that he would have to go back to when this dream was over.

"No, Oliver! I mean I think we're already awake!"

Oliver looked at his smiling brother for a few seconds, then he involuntarily contracted his neck and shoulders, as if he were a turtle that could hide in its shell. Owen's words did not make him feel afraid, exactly, but overwhelmed and unsure. Oliver's hands were pressed together in loose fists against his chest, his elbows drawn in against his body. His bald head still tucked in and unmoving, Oliver's wide eyes looked all around from under raised eyebrows, as if seeing this strange and wonderful place for the first time. He was unsure quite what to make of it.

Owen jumped up and began to dance around and clap his hands. He was so excited that he could hardly stand it. He danced in a circle around his brother three times and then stopped in front of him. He picked Oliver up under his arms and lifted him off the ground. Oliver let out a squeal of delight. He had always loved to be picked up and bounced before he had gotten too sick. He dropped his stuffed dog, wrapped his arms around Owen's neck and held on. Owen held him tight and jumped up and down until he exhausted himself and the brothers fell over. They rolled around in the soft grass, still clutching each other and laughing. Owen had never felt so happy, though he still hadn't quite realized just why he felt that way.

Oliver said, "Again!"

So Owen picked him up and did it again. This time when they fell down Owen landed next to a bright orange lizard. His hand shot out but the lizard slipped through his fingers. Oliver tried to catch it, but being only a very small boy he crushed its tail under his fist (he had forgotten to open his hand), and the lizard got away, crawling through a tiny hole in the grass.

Owen said, "Aw, man!" as he watched the crooked orange tail disappear. He started scanning the ground around them for more lizards.

Oliver sat with his bald head tilted to one side. He said, "Whiss?"

Owen stopped looking for lizards and instead looked at his brother. The boys stared at each other, and their two pairs of eyes grew very big. *That* was why Owen felt so happy: his special birthday wish had come true.

Owen asked, "How do you feel, Oliver?"

"Yups!" was Oliver's only reply.

This may not have answered the question had it been asked by an adult, but Owen needed no further explanation. Oliver did not feel sick anymore. Owen stopped and took the time to notice how much better his brother looked. Oliver's eyes were bright, without the bluish shadows. His bald head no longer had a rash, and the greatest improvement: Oliver was smiling a smile that Owen had not seen in a long time.

"Oliver! You're all better! You're not sick anymore!"

Owen again jumped up and started to dance. His heart was flooded with happiness. He cheered and clapped and jumped and danced as

Oliver watched with happy amusement. Oliver tried to dance with Owen but he fell over. His legs felt like jelly, so he crawled over to Owen like a baby would, his hips swishing excitedly. When Oliver reached his big brother, Owen knelt down and wrapped his arms around him, still laughing. He held his baby brother tight. He was the best birthday present that Owen would ever get.

The boys did not yet question what had happened, or how. They were young enough to still believe that wishes came true. Owen had wished for his brother to not be sick so that he wouldn't die, and so that he could play with him again, and that was what had happened. It was simple. It was enough.

But things were *not* simple, as the boys slowly began to realize.

Oliver said, "Mommy? Daddy?"

At those words, Owen felt the first pangs of fear. He loosened his hold on Oliver and looked around again, this time with a very different point of view. Where were they? He had never seen a yellow sky before. What were they going to do?

Oliver was looking at him. "Mommy?"

Owen looked around again. There was nothing but grass and trees as far as he could see. The boys were lost. How did they get there? Which way was home?

Oliver was getting more frightened by the moment. When he spoke again, there was real fear in his voice. "Mommy!"

Both of the brothers were suddenly very scared. Oliver started to cry for Mommy over and over. Owen started to cry, too. He had no idea what to do. Each boy's fear fed the other, until they were both panicking. Owen tried to tighten his embrace on Oliver but Oliver pushed him away and continued to yell for Mommy until Owen couldn't take it anymore.

"Stop it, Oliver! She's not here! She can't hear you!" But when Oliver stopped crying for Mommy and began to sob, it was even worse. Owen started to call for his parents now. "Mommmmmyyyy! Daddyyyyyy! Shush, Oliver! I can't hear! What if they're tryin' ta call us?"

Oliver did his best to be quiet and listen, but the only sounds that the boys could hear were the blowing wind and Oliver's sniffles.

Owen called again, "MOMMMMMYYYY! DADDYYYYYY!" But there was no answer.

Oliver couldn't hold back his tears any longer. He started to wail. The sound filled Owen with hopelessness. It was the sound of a child's consuming fear and sadness. All things that make children feel loved and safe are epitomized to them in the vision of their parents' faces, the feel of their parents' warmth, and the knowledge that their parents are there to take care of them.

When a small child is lost in a mall or a supermarket, the fear they feel at losing their safety and security floods them. Still, whether they consciously know it or not, a part of them is sure that they will soon be found. When they stray too far from home and realize that they are on a strange road and don't know how to get back, the fear is even greater. It could be a long time before they are found because no one knows where to look for them. Owen and Oliver did not have even that small hope to cling to. They could intuitively feel that they were far, far from home, though this knowledge wasn't expressed even in their own minds. In their panic, the knowledge was translated into pure fear, as from a language they couldn't understand into a language that they could. Knowledge that a child's mind cannot process takes the simpler, purer form of emotion. For Owen and Oliver, *Mommy and Daddy may never find us* translated into overpowering and paralyzing fright.

Both boys began to scream for Mommy and Daddy as loud as they could, over and over. They called for them until their voices were raw. Owen knew that they wouldn't hear, but he yelled for them anyway because he didn't know what else to do. Eventually he stopped when he saw that Oliver was much more frightened than him. Owen's protective instincts toward his brother rose to the surface and helped to give him something else to focus on.

Oliver was indeed far more frightened. It was much worse for him, for he had been the focus of his Mommy and Daddy's intense care and affection for so long. He had spent only one night without at least one of them in his bed since he had gotten sick. Even for that one night, Granny had been there to snuggle him. Oliver had never been alone like this in his life, without the security of a grownup whom he knew and loved, not even for an hour. After having gotten so used to his Mommy and Daddy's presence, it was far more traumatic for him than it was for Owen to have all of his feelings of warmth and safety ripped away from him. He was, after all, hardly more than a baby.

Although still terrified, Owen felt the impact just a little less. He had been the neglected one, often left to himself or told to go and play in the other room when Oliver had had to take meds or get poked by needles or be held down for some procedure.

Owen had stood outside the door of Oliver's hospital room and listened to his brother scream, and though Oliver had been in pain, he had also been wrapped in loving arms while Owen had stood alone outside his door, sad and afraid. No one ever knew that Owen heard those things, and Owen never told them.

He had learned to go about Oliver's floor of the hospital by himself. He had found the play room and had learned to use its computer to play video games. For the past month he had slept at home in their bedroom alone, with Oliver's empty bed to remind him that his brother was sick and might never get better. At age three, Owen had already had a taste of self reliance, and also of what it felt like to need his Mommy and Daddy but not have them. Now it was his fourth birthday, his brother needed him, and he began to feel like a big boy.

Oliver's continued cries for Mommy and Daddy, which a few moments before had fed Owen's fears, began to have the opposite effect of calming Owen down. He saw that no one else was there to help Oliver and that he would have to do it himself.

Owen unconsciously mimicked his Mommy's behavior. He retrieved Odie from where Oliver had dropped him. He then went to Oliver, gave him the stuffed dog to hold and put a hand on his shoulder.

"Shhhhh, Oliver. Shhhhhh. It's all right, Oliver. It'll be all right."

Oliver stopped screaming for Mommy. He clutched Odie to his chest and closed his eyes. He was exhausted.

Owen knew that it was okay to hold him now, so he gathered Oliver up and did just that. Oliver buried his face in his big brother's chest and cried. It was the first time that he did this. It would be the first of many, but in that moment something changed for the brothers. Owen could never replace Mommy and Daddy, but from then on Oliver would look to him for safety and comfort, and Owen would do his best to give them. From that moment, Owen would take care of Oliver. The boys sat in the warm grass under a yellow sky and slowly began to feel better.

After a while Oliver stirred. He raised his head from Owen's chest and said, "Chicken nuggets." He was hungry.

"We don't have any chicken nuggets, Oliver."

"Chicken nuggets!" Oliver was getting angry.

This was too much for Owen's patience, of which a newly-turned-four-year-old has little to begin with. "We don't have chicken nuggets, Oliver! Where do you think I could get chicken nuggets around here?"

"CHICKEN NUGGETS!" Oliver started to cry again, but at least it was not all because of fear or sadness. He was cranky.

Food. This was something that had not yet occurred to Owen. What would they eat? Owen now felt hungry, too. Even worse, he was very thirsty. He looked around, but saw nothing that would help. The boys were still sitting in the same spot where they had woken up.

"CHICKEN NUGGETS! CHICKEN NUGGETS! CHICKEN NUGGETS! CHICKEN NUGGETS!"

"Stop it, Oliver! We don't have any!" All Owen wanted to do was sit there and pout. It wasn't easy to care for his brother when he was being so irritating. "Shut up! We don't have chicken nuggets!"

Oliver stopped shouting for chicken nuggets. Instead he started to wail like a siren. Owen was being mean to him.

Owen pushed Oliver away and stood up. He started to walk away.

This made Oliver even more upset. He tried to get up and follow but his legs were too weak and he fell. Oliver had gotten sick at such a young age that he had never really learned to walk very well, and after spending the last month in a hospital bed, he would have to learn all over again.

"Sop! Sop! Owen!"

Owen stopped and turned to his brother. "Fine! I'm waiting! Come on, Oliver! I don't have all day!"

Oliver stopped crying and crawled toward Owen, dragging Odie through the grass. When he had almost reached him, Owen turned and started to walk away again.

"Sop, Owen! Wait fuh me!"

Owen let out an annoyed groan, but he stopped and waited for Oliver. This was nearly impossible for him. Now that he was moving, he wanted to *move*. He didn't know where he was going but he felt the need to get there fast.

When Oliver finally caught up to him, Owen wrinkled his nose. He tried very hard not to cry, but this was too much: Oliver needed to be changed. Owen had no idea how to change a diaper. It didn't even occur to him that he had no new diaper to change Oliver into.

Owen saw that they had left the blanket lying in the grass. He really felt that he needed to cry. Without a word, he ran back to get it and then returned to Oliver's side. His quick excursion had been accompanied by Oliver yelling at him to "sop."

"Come on, Oliver." Owen ignored the smell and walked on at a slower pace so that his brother could keep up with him.

Oliver crawled beside him. He felt better, too, now that he was moving. He waddled along, not caring that his diaper was leaking all over his pajama bottoms.

The boys soon noticed a sweet smell that was being carried to them on the warm breeze. It made their tummies rumble and their mouths water. Owen began to walk a little faster and Oliver did his best to keep up. The boys soon reached a patch of pink vines that grew at the foot of a grassy hill. Pink and green leaves grew from the vines, and little pink berries that were about the size of grapes but were perfectly round.

Owen reached the berry patch first but he hesitated. He looked at the berries while his stomach growled angrily at him. He had never seen anything quite like them before. He was unsure if they would be safe to eat. Oliver had no such qualms. He crawled right past his brother and pulled a berry from the vine, but Owen stopped him just before he could put it in his mouth.

There were instant tears and frustration from Oliver. He didn't understand why Owen had taken his berry away.

"Wait, Oliver! They might be poison!" Owen held the berry and inspected it. He gently squeezed it. No juice came out. It felt as if it were made of a very thick dough, and it kept the shape into which he had squeezed it.

Oliver was watching. His eyes never left the delicious-looking fruit. He started to whimper with impatience. Owen bit into the berry and immediately a grin spread on his face. It tasted like candy, but it was creamy. It was like eating fudge, but fruit-flavored, and yet a fruit that was more delicious than any that Owen had ever tasted.

"It's okay, Oliver!"

Owen needn't have spoken. As soon as he'd smiled, Oliver had begun pulling berries off the vine. He put six in his mouth at once so that he almost choked. He happily chewed and chewed, fighting between swallowing and breathing, oblivious to his watering eyes.

Owen ran in among the vines and tripped. He fell face-first into a bunch of berries and greedily gobbled them up, then he sat up and ate some more. A contented silence followed while the boys glutted themselves on their delectable feast.

When they were full, they lay down in the grass at the foot of the hill.

"We have to remember this place," said Owen.

"Mmm hmmm..." Oliver was getting drowsy. His diaper had filled up even more, but neither boy cared at the moment.

Now that Owen had eaten his fill, he was more thirsty than ever. He said, "We have to find something to drink."

This made Oliver realize that he was thirsty, too. Once he acknowledged this discomfort, he rolled over and grew upset at his full diaper.

"Owen! Change me!"

"I can't, Oliver. I don't know how!"

Oliver started to whine. "Change meeeee! Change me, Owen!"

"I told you I can't! Come on, Oliver."

Owen got up and started to walk away again, but this time Oliver sat where he was and pouted.

"CHANGE MEEEEEEE!"

"Just come on!" Owen walked over to Oliver and tried to pull him up by his arms. "Just *walk*, Oliver!"

"NO! Want Mommy!"

"You're such a baby! Get up, Oliver! Get up!"

Owen pulled harder on Oliver's arms, but Oliver refused to even try to stand up, so Owen dragged him across the grass and made him cry.

"Odie! Odie!" Oliver had dropped his dog and was shrieking for him.

Owen let him go after a few feet and Oliver dropped in the grass. He started screaming at Owen. He was angry, uncomfortable, thirsty, and he wanted Mommy.

Owen strode away, which made Oliver scream even louder. He didn't want to be left behind. Owen was at a loss. He had no idea what to do next. He just knew that he was thirsty and that he couldn't make Oliver move. Owen plopped down in the grass and lay on his face, doing his best to out-cry his brother.

Seeing this made Oliver feel sad. After a few minutes Oliver stopped crying. He retrieved his dog and crawled over to where Owen lay.

"Owen?"

"Hmm!"

Owen was mad at him, and this made Oliver feel very small. He put a hand on Owen's back but Owen shrugged it off.

Poor Owen, he was trying his best but he was only a little boy. It was all too much to ask of him. He thought that if his wish came true that everything would be okay, but now they were lost and Oliver was depending on him and he was scared and angry and didn't know what to do.

Oliver put his hand on Owen's back again and gently said his name. "Owen?"

This time Owen didn't shrug him off. Oliver set Odie on the ground by Owen's face. Owen sniffled a bit and then sat up. He picked up the stuffed dog and hugged him, then he raised his head and looked at his baby brother. Oliver was afraid to look at him, and this made Owen feel hot all over.

"I'm sorry, Oliver. I'm sorry I dragged you."

Oliver then looked at Owen and smiled. Owen smiled back at him. He felt very relieved.

Owen asked, "Can we find something to drink and then we'll fix your diaper?"

Oliver nodded. He had already forgotten about his dirty diaper. Owen got up and again ran to retrieve the blanket. He trotted back and then gently took his brother's hands and lifted him to his feet. Owen handed Odie back to Oliver and the two of them walked on together. They moved very slowly. Owen supported Oliver and helped him to walk.

Together the two boys hobbled clumsily away from the grassy hill that would someday become their new home. The entrance to the glow cave could not be seen from the bottom of the hill, hidden as it was behind a clump of bushes, and its glow could not be seen in daylight. If the boys had only climbed the hill that day, they might have been spared many of the horrors that followed, but they would not return to that place for many days.

CHAPTER ELEVEN

The boys were frightened. They were tired. They were dirty. They were very thirsty. Owen still held his brother up, but Oliver's legs were really hurting him. They had gone from feeling like jelly to feeling like lead, and a sharp pain cut through the back of his right thigh with each step. Although it seemed to the boys that they had been walking for a very long time, they had actually traveled only a short distance. Their progress was slow. They would have moved faster if Oliver had simply crawled along next to his brother, but neither boy wanted that. They needed to feel each other; it gave them courage.

The contents of Oliver's diaper had leaked through his pajama bottoms and was trickling onto his bare feet, making the grass beneath them feel sticky. Owen could feel the wetness soaking through his jeans, but he made sure to keep the blanket clean by letting it drag on the ground behind him. Oliver had Odie clasped tightly to his chest with the hand that wasn't wrapped around his brother. Neither boy focused on how messy they were getting. It was enough for them to put one foot in front of the other, careful not to trip each other.

Owen's arms burned from supporting so much of Oliver's weight but he was determined to hold him up until they got where they were going: to water. They must find something to drink. The boys didn't speak. They just walked.

The afternoon was wearing on before Owen finally heard the sound of flowing water.

"Oliver! Do you hear that?" Owen didn't just hear it, he could smell it. "Water!" Owen felt new energy and he picked up his pace.

Oliver had been in a daze, watching his own dirty feet moving through the grass. He lifted his head and listened. "Thuhsty!" was all he said. He leaned into Owen and did his best to keep up, but it was hard for him.

The boys reached the banks of a strange river of emerald green water. There was a sparse wood in the distance, but no trees grew by the river. Owen gently set his brother down within reach of the water and then he got down on all fours, right at the edge of the grassy riverbank. Though Owen was very young, he knew enough to hesitate before drinking green water; but it was so beautiful, and the scent of the river overpowered his uncertainty. Oliver watched him closely as he scooped up the emerald liquid in his cupped hand and sipped it. At the first taste, Owen immediately knelt so that he could use both hands to drink.

Oliver still watched him. "Iss good, Owen?"

"Yeah, it's good! Drink some!"

Oliver scrambled on his belly to the edge of the river and dipped his free hand in the water. He pulled it out and sucked the water from his fingers. When the first drop touched his tongue he immediately felt new vigor begin to spread through his tired body. He lay on his belly with his head over the water and brought handful after handful to his mouth.

Once the boys had drunk their fill, they both paused to stare in wonder at the shimmering river before them. The sunlight sparkled through the water, through which they could see all the way to the sandy bottom.

Oliver got excited and started to yell. "Fiss! Deh's fiss!" The fish made him giggle.

Owen followed his brother's eyes and saw the fish, too. "They're big!" Owen started to giggle as well.

The brothers watched the fish for a while. They had never before seen real fish in a real river. Owen watched one fish swim away from the others. It swam to a spot just a few yards upriver where the water looked shallow enough to touch the bottom. Owen caught a waft of Oliver's dirty diaper in his nose and finally knew what to do.

He said, "Okay, Oliver, time to change you."

Oliver looked up from the fish and obediently rolled over onto his back.

Owen pulled his pajama bottoms off.

"Ewwwww! Oliver, that stinks!" Owen didn't say this to be mean. To a young boy, stinky things are quite funny.

Oliver laughed and kicked his legs, making the mess worse, although he was very careful to protect Odie. Owen told him to stop it, but he was laughing, too. He looked for a way to get Oliver's diaper off of him.

"Li' *diss*, Owen." Oliver pulled the adhesive straps.

Owen held his breath and pulled the dirty diaper from under Oliver, careful not to touch his sticky legs. He threw the diaper in the river, which made the fish scatter and dart away, but he had been careless.

"Ewwww! I got poop on my hands! Ahhhhhh!"

Oliver laughed as Owen ran to the water and washed his hands. Owen then carefully picked up Oliver's soiled pajama bottoms with the tips of his thumb and finger and walked to the shallow part of the river.

"Come on, Oliver."

The Green River had given Oliver a boost of energy. He stood up on wobbly legs and gracelessly made the few steps to his brother. Owen caught him and righted him just as he was about to fall over.

Owen pointed at the water. "In you go!"

Oliver narrowed his bright blue eyes and tilted his bald head to one side. He was skeptical.

"Inna wahttuh?"

"Yeah, Oliver, in the water. You're all dirty!"

Truth be told, Oliver wanted more than anything to jump in the water and make a big splash, but he could not shake the feeling that this was not allowed. He couldn't remember a time when he had not been sick, and so he couldn't remember ever being allowed to do anything like this. Oliver looked all around and over both shoulders, as if Mommy or Daddy were about to yell at him and tell him "No!"

"Come on, Oliver! Look!" Owen took off his shoes and socks and jumped in the river. He had left his jeans and shirt on because they had poop on them and needed to be washed anyway.

When Oliver saw Owen jump in the water, his misgivings evaporated. He set Odie on the grass and in he jumped. His feeble legs crumpled under him and he fell forward into the shallow water. His face smacked the surface and traveled downward until he was completely submerged.

Oliver felt Owen's hands lift him from the water. He coughed and spluttered in surprise, splashing Owen. Owen splashed him back and the boys played in the water, laughing and enjoying themselves.

Owen soon remembered why they had jumped in the river. He waded to the bank and retrieved Oliver's pajamas. He rinsed them as best he could in the Green River's gentle current.

A sandbar had formed this shallow spot where the water was little more than a couple of feet deep. Oliver was thrilled to find that he could easily stand in the buoyant water, which rose only to his chest. He could jump! He jumped up several times and came back down, looking rather like a bobbing cork.

Owen threw the pajamas on the grass to dry and started taking off his own clothes. He lost his balance and fell over, making a big splash. He righted himself and watched Oliver play while he worked to get the poop out of his clothes. Owen was watching his brother do something that he never could before. The joy in Oliver's face touched Owen in a place deep down, the place where love grows.

Oliver was a very little boy, and what very little boys like to do more than anything is to play and to feel the energy of youth. Oliver hadn't been able to do that for a very long time. Now that he could, it was as though he were making up for the six months spent in a hospital bed. He felt that he could never tire of jumping up and down. He threw out his arms to make bigger splashes. There was water everywhere and each drop that hit him infused new life into him, for this was magical water, healing water.

Owen threw the rest of his clothes onto the grass and joined his brother. He pulled Oliver's pajama top off over his head, shabbily rinsed it and tossed it with the other clothes to dry. He wanted to play. Down to his bare skin, Oliver felt the exuberance of the splashing water even more. The boys played and splashed as the sun sank lower in the sky, which slowly turned from yellow to orange.

The boys of course missed their Mommy and Daddy; as night fell, they would find out just how much they missed them, but while they played in the sparkling emerald river they enjoyed a piece of childhood so pure and so perfect that the presence of any adult could only have marred its innocence. Indeed, had a grownup been there, they probably would have stopped the boys from jumping in the river at all.

If the boys had asked themselves whether they would rather stay in this magical place or be with Mommy and Daddy, they would not have hesitated to go back to their parents. But they did not ask themselves this question. They accepted what was: Mommy and Daddy were not there.

What the boys learned that first day was that they could do whatever they wanted. There was no one to tell them, "No." Without realizing that they were learning anything at all, they gained a wisdom that some live their whole lives without finding. The boys were granted an intuitive understanding of the duality of any existence; that the things they wanted both helped and hurt them, just as the things they didn't have they sometimes needed and yet were sometimes better off without. They would face terrible, dark times when they would give anything for just a small reminder that Mommy and Daddy still existed and were somewhere loving them and missing them, but they would also enjoy times made of pure light that could not have happened under the guidance of their parents. The boys were free, free to enjoy the ecstasy of childhood with every fiber of their being and nothing to hold it in check, yet they had no protection from sadness or pain, nothing to blunt the edge of the fear that would sometimes consume them. It was this unconscious understanding that helped them to travel from one peak to another, from darkness into light, though it was not always an easy journey, and the light was ever the more fragile.

The boys eventually had their fill of play and climbed out of the water to dry on the warm, grassy bank. They lay on their backs, resting and relaxing. However, the afterglow of their play did not last long. Once all of their immediate needs had been met, the boys became troubled. Neither said anything at first. It took a while for their vague restlessness to form the actual thought: *What now?* The boys had each had their daily routine. Without it, they began to feel anxious but could not determine the cause.

Owen thought about asking his brother what he wanted to do next, but he didn't voice his question. It seemed silly. They knew next to nothing about this place. He turned his head to look at Oliver and saw that Oliver was looking back at him with an expression that Owen didn't understand.

Oliver was thinking about his bed at home, wishing that he was curled up with his stuffed animals and about to take a nap. He looked at Owen, wanting to ask if they could go there but not knowing how to say it.

Finally Oliver asked, "Home now?"

"We can't, Oliver."

"Home!"

Owen began to have that frustrated feeling again, like he wanted to cry. Was Oliver going to do this for everything? Didn't he understand anything?

"Home! Home! Home!"

"Oliver, we *can't* go home! I don't know how!"

Oliver started to cry. He did *not* understand.

Owen had to do something, but he had no idea what it could be. He, too, was scared. It was so hard to think when Oliver was crying like that. Finally, Owen stopped thinking, and that was how he found the answer.

"Okay, Oliver, but first we have to get dressed."

Oliver's tears subsided immediately. He asked in a soft, hopeful voice, "Home?"

"Yup, I see it right on the hill over there." Owen pointed to a stand of trees, not far from where they sat. "See it, Oliver?"

Oliver looked where Owen was pointing. "See it! Home!"

Oliver scrambled to put his pajamas on. They weren't quite dry yet, but he hardly noticed. Owen got dressed, too, and then helped his brother. The cool dampness of their clothes actually felt good to the boys after lying in the warm sun.

"Can you walk, Oliver?"

Oliver carefully stood up. He took a few shaky steps before calling, "Help!"

Owen had picked up Odie and the blanket. He handed the stuffed dog to Oliver and then put a supporting arm around his middle. He slung the blanket over his shoulder and the boys walked toward the home that existed in their imaginations.

A child's imagination is a most powerful tool. Anything is possible within a child's mind. It can provide them with friends when they are lonely, toys and games when they get bored. It allows them to escape from reality when reality is too painful or frightening; or, as with Owen and Oliver, it can provide a home when they are lost.

Owen pointed at nothing and said, "I see Ripley tied in the yard!"

Ripley was the boys' dog, an old weimaraner. Oliver looked and saw her, too. He giggled. He loved that old dog. He liked to hold her tail while she pulled him around in an effort to get away.

The boys happily walked toward their imaginary home, their worries all but forgotten for a while. A small flock of bright red birds flew by overhead. Oliver excitedly pointed to the sky. He was still at an age when any living creature captured his attention and enthralled him. It didn't matter how many birds he had seen before. Every time was still like the first time. The boys stopped to watch them.

Owen let out a giggle. He was excited by the birds as well. There was something reassuring in the sight of them. True, he had never seen birds quite like them, but they were still a familiar sight. They provided Owen with the company of other living creatures and helped him to feel less lonely.

After the birds had passed, the boys walked on and soon reached the stand of trees. They stopped at the first tree to pat their imaginary dog before they walked through the door of their imaginary home.

Owen looked up into the branches above. "What the heck? There's trees growing in our house!"

Oliver looked at him and started to laugh. He emulated his brother, matching his tone and even his posture. "Whut zuh heck!"

Owen laughed, too. The boys felt safe.

Owen said, "Let's go in our room and watch TV."

Oliver thought this a delightful idea. "'Kay!" He strolled down the hall and sat on the ground, approximately where the boys' bedroom would have been.

Owen followed, but instead of sitting next to his brother he remained standing in front of him.

"Look, Oliver! I'm on TV!"

Oliver's eyes grew big and he clapped his little hands. Owen handed him a pretend bowl of popcorn to eat while he watched his big brother on television. He sat holding the bowl and gobbling the pretend popcorn. He made chewing motions and the occasional *Mmmm!* sound. He also shared his popcorn with Odie, who was seated next to him.

Owen began his performance. He started with a song. He sang the ABC song, one of the few that he knew. He sang it like an opera singer, holding his arms out and waving them in dramatic fashion, his whole head trembling at times with the deep passion that he put into his rendition. He held the letters G, P, T, U, V and Z as long as his breath lasted, with his head thrown back and shaking from side to side. It was a powerful performance.

Oliver tried to sing along with the last bars, but he only knew every third or fourth lyric.

"Now you know your ABC's..."

("*C's!*")

"Next time..."

("*Ime!*")

"Won't you sing..."

("*Inng!*")

"With Meeeeeeeeee!"

("*Eeeeeeeee!*")

When Owen was finished, he made a grand, sweeping bow to Oliver's delighted applause and then he fell over, exhausted by his effort. This released the laughter that was waiting just behind Oliver's open-mouthed smile.

Owen went straight into a slapstick routine. He got back up only to trip over his feet and fall over again. "What the heck?" He was fed by Oliver's peals of laughter. He got up and fell again.

This time Oliver supplied the dialogue. "Whut zuh heck!"

Over and over Owen fell down and each time Oliver laughed and repeated the phrase, "Whut zuh heck!"

Owen got up for the sixth time and walked into a tree. He bounced off and he and Oliver said it together, "What the heck!"

Owen looked up at the tree's melon-laden branches and said in an outraged tone, "There's trees in our *bedroom*, too! What the heck?"

Oliver could not stop laughing. He thought this to be the funniest thing he'd ever seen, but then Owen surprised him by leaping up and grabbing the lowest branch. Oliver sat and watched in amazement as Owen swung himself up and into the tree.

Owen climbed just a little ways up and batted at one of the low-hanging melons. It fell to the ground and broke open.

This forced an incredulous, "Whut zuh heck!" from Oliver, who started laughing again, this time at his own cleverness.

Owen had taken extreme delight in watching the large melon fall and burst. He knocked down another one, and another, and another as Oliver yelled at each one, "Whut zuh *heck*? Whut zuh *heck*? Whut zuh *heck*?"

The ground in the boys' "bedroom" was soon littered with smashed melons. Owen climbed out of the tree and joined his giggling brother. Oliver picked up a piece of melon and was about to bury his face in it when Owen yelled, "Oliver, stop!"

Owen picked up a broken melon by its yellow rind and sniffed the purple fruit inside. It smelled delicious. He took a small bite. "Okay, Oliver! It's good!"

Both boys had gotten hungry again. They feasted on Owen's accidental discovery, laughing at each other's slurping noises. The fruit was so juicy that it quenched their thirsts as well.

The sun dipped behind a row of low, rolling hills, leaving the boys to eat in the purple glow of the magic hour of that strange place. The sky overhead still had a lavender quality but was deepening to violet with every passing minute. The boys continued to eat without noticing how quickly the light was fading. As the light followed the sun, leaving the boys in darkness, so they would fall from the peak of lightness they had ascended in their hearts to a very dark place indeed. The shadow eyes were coming.

CHAPTER TWELVE

Oliver held a piece of melon in his hands. He suddenly didn't want it anymore. He threw it on the ground angrily and then looked at it. He stared at the broken fruit; it looked so pathetic. He had mangled it into a shapeless lump. The fruit had been ripped apart and hung from its rind, stretched across the ground. Oliver had killed it. It was the saddest thing he had ever seen. He felt more sorry than he ever had. He couldn't take it back. He couldn't fix it. He couldn't make it better. He had killed it forever.

When Owen saw Oliver throw his food on the ground, he was surprised. Why would Oliver want to treat the fruit that way? It made Owen sad. He looked at the melon that he held in his own hands. What had he done to it? He had hurt it. Owen dropped his melon. He felt an emptiness in his chest, where his heart should be. How could he do such a thing?

The last bits of daylight faded from the sky, but the boys did not look up to see.

Oliver started to cry.

The sound made Owen wish he were dead. He could not bear it. He would rather die than to know that his baby brother could ever feel so sad.

Night had descended on the brothers. The shadow eyes had come.

Oliver's tears continued, and were joined by Owen's. The boys were not sobbing nor wailing; not yet, for the shadow eyes worked slowly. The boys cried a gentle flow of tears. Their throats hurt in that place just beyond the roofs of their mouths, as if their heartache were building up in that spot too fast for their tears to release it.

The boys finally saw that the darkness had closed in around them. Fear was now added to sadness. They were two very little boys, all alone in the night of a strange place without their Mommy and Daddy. They didn't know what lived in the dark that enveloped them. They began to think of monsters.

All children have lain in their beds at night, hidden under the covers, afraid of the monsters that live in their closets and beneath their beds, or that scratch at their windows trying to get in, but what if there were no windows to keep them out? What if there were no bed, no covers to hide under? What if there were no light shining from the hall to remind them that their parents slept in the next room? Owen and Oliver had no light. There was no hall, no bedroom, no home. They had nowhere to hide, and Mommy and Daddy were far, far away.

Oliver's eyes were closed tight. He was too terrified to open them. He imagined that he could feel the monster's breath on the back of his neck. If he opened his eyes he would see the claws that were reaching out to grab him. He began to let out a sound. It was a high-pitched note that came from the same place in his throat where fear had now joined his heartache. He knew that the monsters would hear him but he couldn't stop.

Owen looked around wildly. Everywhere he looked, he thought he saw movement, as if the monsters were trying to sneak up on him. They became still only when he looked at them. He tried to look everywhere at once so that the monsters couldn't move, but of course he couldn't. Every time Owen glanced around, the phantom movement seemed to get closer. No matter where he looked, he could feel something creeping up behind him. The monsters were closing in on him.

Owen heard Oliver start to make that high-pitched sound that was something between a cry and a whimper. He saw that Oliver's eyes were closed. Owen needed his baby brother to open his eyes. With his eyes closed, Oliver had left him. It made Owen feel all alone. Owen started wailing and he lunged at his brother and started to shake him. When he did that, Oliver began to scream.

Oliver had heard Owen's cries and become even more terrified. The monsters had gotten Owen. Oliver felt something grab him and start to shake him. Oliver had never experienced such violence of movement. He lost himself in his screams.

Owen shouted Oliver's name as loud as he could. He shouted it over and over as he continued to shake his brother with all his strength, but Oliver put his hands to his ears and continued to scream. Owen tried to pull Oliver's hands away but in his terror Oliver fought like an animal and soon the brothers were rolling on the ground.

Owen was desperate to make himself heard over Oliver's screams, while Oliver screamed all the louder, trying to block out the sounds of what he imagined were the monster's roars. Oliver's terror grew while Owen's turned to rage. Each of these emotions were fed by the terrible din that the boys made in each other's ears, and in their own.

There was no other sound; not even the wind. The shadow eyes watched in silence. They had not had such nourishment before. They were all around the boys, but they did not yet reveal themselves.

Owen was on top of his brother. He held Oliver by the arms and began to slam him against the ground. Oliver's screams were cut short as the air was forced from him. Owen let out one last howl of rage, and of the agony in his child's soul, and then he was spent. He collapsed next to Oliver and began to weep for his Daddy.

Everything was wrong. What had he done? Oliver's screams resumed as Owen was overwhelmed by remorse, and fear, and helplessness all at once. He was broken. This was worse than any nightmare he'd ever had. He drew his knees up, closed his eyes and covered his own ears, trying and failing to block out his brother's screams.

Oliver had curled up, trying to make himself small. He still hadn't opened his eyes. His hands still covered his ears. He wet the ground with his hot tears. His screams had become jagged in his throat. After a very long time, they stopped. Oliver lay weeping. He did not understand anything that was happening.

Oliver's conscious mind shut down. He found himself in a place in his mind that he had never been before. It was endless...infinite, and it terrified him. He felt lost, adrift in the vastness of the unknown even as he felt panicked with claustrophobic horror as if he were buried in the ground. There was a roaring noise so loud that he could not even hear it. He saw the blackness so bright that it blinded him. He felt encased in stone so rough and unyielding that it hurt to touch, even as he passed through it like foam. He experienced every sensation of which his child's mind was capable and beyond, to every extreme, and he experienced them all at once so that his fragile mind seemed to explode inside his head, even as it collapsed upon itself. He finally opened his eyes and the night itself seemed to him to shake with the violence of his own sobs.

That change in the tone of Oliver's cries broke Owen from the paralysis of his remorse. He looked up at Oliver from where he lay in the grass and saw that his brother was reaching for him. Owen crawled to him and felt Oliver's hands wrap around the back of his neck so tightly that it hurt him. Owen was glad to feel it. He locked his arms around Oliver and the two brothers held each other and let loose yet another torrent of tears. These were not gentle tears, but they were natural and comforting.

Oliver was inconsolably shaken up by what he had just experienced. The memory would actually haunt him for the rest of his life, and he would continue to relive it in his nightmares for a very long time. Being so very young, Oliver's mind was far more open than Owen's, and far more vulnerable.

The boys felt an inexplicable sadness begin to overwhelm them once more. Less than half an hour had passed since the light had left the sky. What the boys had just been put through was only the first probe from the shadow eyes' efforts to unlock the pain that dwelt inside them. Many hours had yet to pass before the dawn would come to the boys' rescue.

For the next hour, the boys were tortured by the shadow eyes. Their minds and memories were picked apart by something that they could not see. Neither one of them could understand. Their deepest fears danced around them, tormenting them. Their delicate hearts were broken over and over again as the shadow eyes searched the brothers for the one thing that would hurt each of them the most.

Owen saw his Daddy yelling at him and taking his game away. Owen was so sorry that he'd been bad but Mommy and Daddy didn't care that he was sorry...

Oliver saw Ripley, the boys' dog. He saw her whimpering because she missed him and wanted to play with him. She was sniffing his empty bed...

Owen heard Mommy screaming. She was screaming because Oliver was being born. It was Oliver's fault. He was hurting Mommy. Did she scream like that when Owen had been born? Had he hurt his Mommy, too? Owen wished he had never been born so that he never had to hurt his Mommy...

Oliver saw Mommy and Daddy throwing all of his toys away. They were angry at him because he had come here without their permission...

Owen became convinced that a scary man had followed them to that place. He had once seen this man at the park by his house and had known that the man had wanted to hurt him. His Daddy had pulled Owen behind him and protected him from this man, but his Daddy was not there now. The man was the one who had brought them there so that no one could stop him from doing whatever he wanted to do to Owen and Oliver. He had been watching them all this time. Owen was so frightened, but he couldn't move. He knew that the man was there, hiding in the night, but Owen couldn't run away. What if the man took Oliver and left Owen here all alone? The man would hurt his little brother and Owen would never see him again. What was the man going to do to Oliver? *Oliver...*

Oliver thought that he was back in his hospital bed. He was listening to the doctors talk to Mommy and Daddy about what was wrong with him. He heard things that he had not known he had remembered. He heard the words, *less than ten percent chance.* He did not know what those words meant but he knew that they were about him. He saw his Mommy and Daddy start to cry. Oliver couldn't see the doctor but he could hear her talking to Mommy and Daddy as if he weren't there. She was saying that she was sorry. Oliver heard the doctor say the word, *die,* and though he didn't understand what was happening, he became very afraid. He looked at Mommy and she was sadder than he had ever seen her in real life, but Oliver could no longer tell that this was not real life. *Mommy...*

Oliver...

Mommy...

And the shadow eyes withdrew.

Owen opened his eyes. He looked at Oliver, and only at Oliver. He wasn't brave enough to look anywhere else, so scared of what he might see. In that moment, Oliver was everything that Owen needed him to be. He was familiar. He was comfort and love. He was crying as if his heart were broken and he needed Owen. Owen held him and for a moment, found that he was brave enough.

When Owen held Oliver to him, Oliver felt safe. Whatever had been happening, it was over. Still Oliver cried and cried. His throat was raw. His head hurt. He was so thirsty, but he was safe with Owen. He could cry and be sad and wish to go home while Owen kept him safe.

A gentle breeze began to blow through the trees. The boys felt it lift their spirits and they looked at the grass before them, watching the blades bend in the wind. Oliver stopped crying. There was no moon, but where the starlight filtered through the trees the boys saw the dancing grass and the broken melons that littered the ground. It seemed so long ago that they had laughed as Owen had knocked them from the trees. The boys had never felt so tired.

And then it all started once more. Oliver began to cry again. It was the most hopeless sound that Owen had ever heard, and he joined in. Owen gave up. It was even worse than before.

Oliver's entire self was rebelling against what was happening. As he felt the sadness and fear permeate him, he actually fought it. *No...NO... NO...NO!...NOOOOOOO!* He was angry that something was making him feel so sad. He felt betrayed. He had trusted...trusted what, exactly? His outrage did not last long, however.

Both of the brothers were staring at the same spot on the ground. There was a patch of shadow that they could not look away from. They were afraid of that shadow...and then they saw it. Oliver squealed in fear and revulsion. Owen whimpered, as if he were marching toward a punishment that terrified him but from which he knew that it was no use running away. A solid black eye had opened in the grass where the boys had been looking, and it was looking right back at them.

The shadow eyes had found the greatest source of pain in each of the boys, and then they had withdrawn, only to let the boys recover long enough to think that it was over. Now, the feast would begin in earnest.

Oliver...

Mommy...

What hurt each of the boys most was the thing that each of them loved most. It was what each of them was most afraid of losing.

Owen squeezed his brother all the tighter. It didn't matter that they had come here. Oliver was going to die, anyway. It didn't matter that he had gotten better. It was only for a day. Oliver was going to die in his arms that very night and then Owen would be all alone...

Oliver was never going to see his Mommy again. She didn't love him anymore, didn't want him anymore. Even if he went home, she wouldn't let him in...

Eyes began to open all around the boys. Every shadow became filled with them. The eyes were silent and unblinking. They simply looked at the boys, filling them with heartache, fear and hopelessness. The boys couldn't look away, couldn't shut their own eyes. Everywhere they looked, there was a shadow, and in each shadow they saw the dull black sheen of eyes looking back.

Eyes opened in the grass, along the shadows cast by the trees and branches. They opened in the bark of the trees themselves, and in the pieces of melon that lay smashed on the ground. The brothers could not fight anymore. They surrendered to despair.

And still, the shadow eyes wanted more.

Oliver felt a sensation like something had landed on his arm. He looked to see that an eye had opened in the flesh on the inside of his elbow. His rapid screams increased in pitch. He was too frightened even to swat at it. He held his arm out and away from him. When the starlight hit the eye, it went away. It did not disappear with a poof. It did not show emotion or pain at having been forced into the light. The eye simply closed, as if it were still there under his skin.

Owen had watched in horror, and then he felt an eye open on the inside of his own thigh. It opened on his jeans but he felt it in his skin. He kicked his leg out, exposing the eye to the stars, and it closed.

Each time an eye closed another opened somewhere on the boys' bodies. Finally the brothers stopped moving. They had no will left, no energy but what was needed to voice their shrieks and shed their tears. They could feel the eyes looking out from their own skin as well as from the shadows all around them, but they could do nothing about it. They sat still, holding each other, and endured the unimaginable.

The boys' cries and screams would carry on throughout the night, but there was no one to hear them, and no one to help them.

What the boys did not yet know, was that they were not alone. Help was there; they just hadn't found it yet. They thought that they had come to the magical land by themselves, but this was not so. Something had followed them, something that would fill them with the joy from which it was made. It was growing, waiting for them to find it so that it could play with them and watch over them.

As the boys had lain sleeping, before they had awoken under that magical sky for the first time, a single vine had poked through the ground, far from where they lay. From this vine had sprouted a single bud that looked vaguely like an ear of corn. As the boys had been waking up, this bud had opened to reveal that it was a large, beautiful yellow blossom. The blossom had opened in the shape of a child's star, its five points spreading to release the sweet perfume inside. As Owen had been realizing that Oliver was no longer sick, the beginnings of a round fruit had begun to grow at the base of the blossom. As the blossom had withered, the fruit had grown to an enormous size, so that by the time the boys had found the Green River, they both could have sat comfortably on top of the fruit's dark green rind. As the boys had played in the river, the green had faded from the fruit, revealing a soft and comforting orange glow.

The boys had brought the pumpkin with them, or rather, it had come to be with them. They would never know that they, themselves, were the source of the joy from which the pumpkin grew.

CHAPTER THIRTEEN

When the morning light sent its first tendrils of pink into the dark sky, the shadow eyes closed and were gone. The boys had not slept, neither had they moved. Released from the shadow eyes' hold, the boys did not release their hold on each other. They held on and wept, washing away the long night with their tears. They were both dirty. Even Owen had soiled himself, having been unable to move from where he had sat.

The boys felt the shadow eyes go. Relief coursed through them, a physical sensation spreading through their little bodies like ripples in a pond. Their relief fed their tears, helping to wash away the darkness that much faster.

The first to open his eyes was Oliver. Strange as it may seem, he was recovering faster than his older brother. Just as Owen had already had a taste of independence from Mommy and Daddy, so Oliver's resiliency to suffering was the more developed of the two. Although he was only a year and a half old, Oliver had already spent many long days and nights in sickness and pain. In his illness and its treatments, he had learned to bounce back.

He had been held down and stuck with needles and had spent many hours with his face in the pink bucket getting sick. He had been tied up in restraints and unable to move or even to sit up for days at a time when he had been put on the ventilator, a tube which they had inserted into his mouth and pushed down into his lungs. He had suffered through all of that and much more, and when each trial had been over, he had learned to laugh and play again.

The tears had not yet stopped flowing from his eyes, but Oliver opened them and was granted the gift of the dawn. He was touched by its beauty, which was reflected in his glistening tears. Brilliant waves of gold seemed to have been frozen just as they were crashing upon the shores of the warm, pink sky. Behind Oliver, the last stars faded low on the horizon, but he did not look that way. He faced the rising sun. It had barely crept into the sky when it was joined by the moon, a pale yellow sliver that almost seemed to be winking at the little boy who watched it rise.

Owen did not see this display. His eyes were still closed. He held his brother and continued to sob until he heard the singing of birds overhead and looked up to watch them pass. It was a comforting sight. It seemed to confirm that the shadow eyes were indeed gone. The sky would remain a bright pink that day. The color lifted Owen's spirits.

Oliver felt his brother look up and he leaned back to see the comforting vision of his face. Owen still looked sad and his cheeks were still wet with tears, but the sight of him made Oliver smile. Owen looked back at him. When the brothers' eyes met, they started to cry again: yet another release. They were overcome with emotions too complex for either of them to voice, and they had no other way to express them.

The boys finally released each other. Owen stood up, and gently lifted Oliver to his feet. The movement of the their clothes on their skin made both boys think that they felt eyes opening on their bodies. They both squealed and Owen dropped his brother. With panicked, jerky movements Owen lifted his shirt, but there was nothing there. Oliver was wriggling around on the ground, still squealing. Owen dropped to his knees beside him.

"There's nothing there, Oliver! They're not there!"

Owen pulled off Oliver's pajama top and made him look at his own belly. Oliver stopped his spasms and again started to sob.

Owen stood up and pulled his brother unwillingly back onto his feet. He slung Oliver's shirt around his shoulders, then he wrapped Oliver in a hug and lifted him off the ground. Oliver wrapped his arms and legs around his brother and hid his face against Owen's chest. Owen turned and stumbled back toward the Green River, struggling to bear his brother's weight.

The boys sat in the warm water in silence. They had drunk their fill and Owen had again rinsed their clothes as best he could. The water had rejuvenated their bodies, but their minds were still troubled.

Finally, Oliver spoke. "Mommy mad?"

The question confused Owen. "Why would Mommy be mad?"

"Mad a' me!"

"Mommy's not mad at you, Oliver!"

"She not?"

Owen didn't understand why Oliver thought Mommy was mad at him, but then he thought about the long night that they had just spent. "No, Oliver. Mommy loves you."

"Shoo-uh?"

Owen thought about Mommy and Daddy leaving him alone so that they could be with Oliver. "I'm sure, Oliver."

Oliver finally smiled. He was very relieved. "'Kay!"

The boys climbed out of the river and got dressed. Owen smiled as he watched Oliver struggle to pull his pajamas over his head. After a few moments Owen helped his brother dress.

"Stay here, Oliver" he said.

"Noooo!"

"Oliver, I'm just gonna get Odie and the blanket!"

Owen walked back to the stand of melon trees and picked up the stuffed dog. He stood over the blanket and stared down at it. He was afraid of what might be under it. Owen took a deep breath, grabbed one corner of the blanket and jerked it up into the air as he took a few panicked steps away. There was nothing under the blanket but grass. Owen picked the blanket up and shook it out, just to make sure, then he walked back to Oliver, who had been watching him closely.

"Let's get away from here," Owen said.

Oliver nodded vigorously. He fully agreed with this notion. In his anxiousness to get away from the scene of the night before, Oliver did not wait to be helped up. He crawled away on his hands and knees as quickly as he could. Owen had to trot to catch up to him.

Had the boys gone back the way they had come the day before, they would have found themselves in Autumnland before the day's end. They may have even found the pumpkin before the sun set. However, they did not go that way.

It was not long before exhaustion began to take its toll on the boys, especially Oliver. Crawling used up much more energy than walking. The vitality of the Green River ebbed from the boys and they felt the need for sleep. They had not yet reached the edge of Summerland when they stopped. They were hungry and frightened, but they could not go on.

Owen looked back. He could no longer see the stand of trees where they had experienced the nightmare of the shadow eyes. He looked down at Oliver. His little brother had already fallen asleep where he had stopped, his arms and legs still bent as if he had collapsed mid-crawl. Owen lay down next to him, put his thumb in his mouth and closed his eyes.

The boys slept fitfully. The shadow eyes had been banished by the sun, but they remained in the boys' dreams.

Only three hours passed before Owen woke to find that his face was wet with tears. He fought and lost a battle with the panic left over from his dream. He called out for his Mommy and Daddy until he remembered that he and Oliver were alone. It was a long time before he calmed down.

Oliver whimpered in his sleep. He had soiled himself again. Owen looked back the way they had come. He was so unsettled by his dreams that he felt he could not stay where he was. He needed to put more distance between himself and the place where the shadow eyes had caught him. He put a gentle hand on Oliver's shoulder.

"Wake up, Oliver."

Oliver bolted up with a cry and began to beat himself all over. He had been dreaming that the shadow eyes had covered his body.

Owen was frightened by this display. "Oliver, stop! You were having a nightmare! It was just a nightmare!"

Oliver looked at his brother and started to scream for Mommy. It was some time before Owen could calm him. Oliver still sniffled as Owen pulled down his pajama bottoms and cleaned his brother the best he could, which was not very well at all. He made Oliver scoot on the grass, having nothing to wipe him with. Then the boys moved on, feeling very hungry.

They soon entered an orchard of melon trees. The ground around the trees was lush with plant life. A sea of tiny leaves on long, thin stems made an almost solid layer of green a few inches above the ground, in the way that algae covers a still pond. About the bases of the trees grew clusters of very large plants that Owen found familiar.

"Elephant ears!" Owen smiled at the giant leaves. They reminded him of home.

A giggle escaped from Oliver in spite of himself. "Eh-wuh-fent ee-uhs?" He was amused that Owen called them that.

Owen ran in amongst the trees and pulled on one of the "ears" until he uprooted it. He carried it back to Oliver and fanned him with it, to Oliver's delight. The sound of Oliver's laughter had a healing power for Owen, who started to laugh with him. Owen ran and pulled up another of the ears. He brought it back to Oliver and put the two leaves to his head.

"See, Oliver? Elephant ears!"

Oliver's eyes grew wide with mirth. This was just too funny. Owen began to flap his "ears" and lurch around, doing his best impression of an elephant. Peals of laughter sounded from both boys.

Oliver crawled in among the trees to try and pull up ears of his own. However, he was distracted by the hovering layer of tiny leaves. They tickled Oliver's chin when he crawled through them. He stopped and picked a couple and then held them to his head.

"Mousey ee-uhs!"

The sight of Oliver holding the mouse ears to the sides of his bald head, blue eyes bright and smiling, sent waves of whimsy through Owen. He was very pleased by his brother's cleverness, almost as pleased as Oliver himself.

Oliver dropped his leaves and crawled around with his head lowered so that it parted the mouse ears. They whispered over the bare skin on his head, across his nose and around his ears. Owen watched with merriment as Oliver crawled around in circles, tickling and amusing himself.

Owen would remember the sight. This was what he was protecting; for his baby brother, yes, but also for himself. This was the source of the strength that allowed Owen to shoulder the burden of his brother's care. Owen didn't consciously think this out. In the boys' innocence, neither could see what they gave to the other.

Owen sat down against the smooth, light green trunk of a melon tree with his thumb in his mouth. He ran the fingers of his other hand through the mouse ears around him and watched his brother play. It never occurred to him that he had initiated playtime by presenting the elephant ears in the first place. He simply felt a vague gratitude toward his brother for making him feel so light of heart, even after the terrors of the night before. He saw Oliver through the eyes of love, and the sight made him happy.

It would never have entered Owen's imagination to see himself through Oliver's eyes. If he could, he would see that Oliver could only offer him this gift because he felt safe. Oliver had his big brother to lead the way, to take care of him and watch over him. Each brother saw the other through the gifts that they received, never fully realizing the gifts that they were giving back. They felt each other's love, but neither of them could comprehend that they were as important to the other as the other was to them. Such is the generous nature of innocence. The bond that this love created between Owen and Oliver would be severely tested in the nights and days ahead, but it would not break, for its strength was born of giving, not taking, whether the brothers knew it or not.

Owen climbed the tree he had been leaning against and hopped back down with a melon for himself and one for Oliver.

"Are you hungry, Oliver?"

"Yip! Yip yip yip!"

Oliver was in "puppy mode." He crawled to his brother, wagging his bottom excitedly; that is, until Owen held out the melon.

"No want dat!"

Oliver's good spirits evaporated in a heartbeat, as will tend to happen with one-year-old's who are overly tired, hungry and that have just been through a more terrifying experience than most adults will ever know.

"This is all we have, Oliver!" Owen tried to be patient, but his mood was just as fragile as his brother's.

"NO!"

Oliver rolled over onto his back and proceeded to throw a fit. He shook his arms and legs and shrieked his anger at the top of his lungs. The pain that the shadow eyes had put him through was still there. It had been waiting just under the surface for one little thing to call it forth.

Owen dropped the melons and started to cry, too. It was hopeless. They would never get home. He would just give up. He was so hungry. Each of Oliver's angry wails cut through Owen. He looked at the fruit on the ground and the sight made him depressed. He wanted to eat it but he couldn't, not with Oliver acting like that.

Oliver started screaming for chicken nuggets. This turned Owen's sorrow into anger. Oliver knew that he didn't have chicken nuggets. He was being impossible and he was doing it on purpose!

"Shut up! Oliver! Shut UUUUUUPPPPPPP!"

Oliver was startled into silence, but only for a moment before he redoubled his efforts and screamed even louder.

Owen instantly regretted yelling at his brother. In a heartbeat, his anger was spent and he was again depressed. He felt more lost than ever. Owen pleaded with his brother.

"Please stop crying, Oliver. Please!"

He offered Oliver his stuffed dog, but it was ignored. Owen knelt by his brother and put his hand on Oliver's belly but Oliver knocked it away.

"NO! No want you! Want Mommy!" The anger in Oliver's voice melted into a forlorn moan. "I want my Mommy! I want my Mommy! I...WANT...MY...MOMMMMMMYYYYYY!"

Owen bowed his head, feeling utterly defeated. He wanted Mommy, too. He wished they could go home. Owen crawled back to the tree on his hands and knees, picked up his melon and started to peel it. He did it with absolutely no joy.

Left alone, Oliver soon tired himself out. He sat up and watched Owen, who had his back to him. Oliver was very hungry. He tried to see what Owen was doing. Oliver leaned to one side and then the other, but he could not see. His chest was still hitching, although the flow of his tears had stopped. Oliver very timidly crawled a little closer. He saw Owen put something in his mouth and felt his belly rumble. Oliver went back into "puppy mode," but now he was sad puppy. He slowly crawled to Owen, whimpered softly and nuzzled Owen's elbow with his nose.

Owen turned and looked at Oliver's sad puppy eyes. It awakened a tender feeling in him. "Awww, are you hungry, puppy?"

Oliver whimpered, "Mmm hmmm."

Owen pulled free a wedge of fruit and fed it to Oliver by hand. Oliver wolfed it down, and Owen fed him another. The boys sat among the trees, in the elephant ears and mouse ears, and they ate. Owen took turns between eating a piece of melon and feeding one to his brother. When they finished eating, Oliver laid his head on Owen's lap. Owen stroked and petted him, as he would have with a real puppy.

The next thing Owen knew was that he was waking up. The sun was low in the sky, which was turning from pink to violet. Oliver was still asleep with his head on Owen's lap. Owen felt an urgency to move on. Trying his best to spare Oliver from the anxiety he felt, Owen gently shook him.

He said in a sing-song voice, "Time to wake up, puppy."

Oliver stirred and lifted his head from Owen's lap. "Woof! Woof!"

"Do you want to go for a walk, puppy?"

"Arf!"

Puppy did.

Owen picked up the blanket and stood up. He handed Odie to Oliver, who took the stuffed dog in his mouth as a puppy would. Owen walked out of the trees and across the open grass with Oliver crawling along beside him.

Owen did not know where he was going. He had no plan. He simply led his brother on, occasionally casting a nervous glance back the way they had come. He was worried that the eyes would return. He was thirsty, and worried because they had left the Green River behind and he didn't know if they would find more water. He was worried because he felt that the farther they walked, the more lost they became, as if their chances of getting home were getting smaller with every step they took. He had no idea what they would do when it got dark, but he knew that he was afraid of the coming night.

Oliver felt none of this. He pretended to be a puppy. He frolicked around next to Owen holding Odie in his teeth, taking in this strange and beautiful landscape. He could be a happy puppy or a sad puppy, or even a scared puppy. It wouldn't matter because it would not be him feeling these things but the puppy.

The boys crested a gentle hill and saw a stand of strange trees growing below them. They were strange because in all of the land that the boys had traveled through, these were the only flora that appeared to be lifeless. They had no leaves. Their bare branches made them look out of place, and that wasn't their only bizarre quality. The trees' deeply ridged bark had an iridescence that from a distance fooled the boys into thinking that they saw lights shining from them.

The brothers excitedly rushed toward the trees. They reached them just as the sun sank below the horizon. Up close, the colors that were reflected in the bark by the sky and the setting sun seemed to move as the boys' vantage point moved. The boys were confused. They couldn't figure out where the lights had gone.

"What the heck?"

Owen had meant to be funny, but as the words left his mouth, Oliver started to whimper. Then Owen felt it, too. The shadow eyes had returned. The boys had thought they would be safe so far from where the shadow eyes had caught them the night before. They were very wrong.

There were no clouds in the sky, nothing to hold and reflect the light of the sun now that it had set. The mystical light of magic hour faded too quickly.

Oliver was still on his hands and knees. He curled up, his hands over his head and his backside exposed to the fading light in the sky. He still whimpered his puppy cries.

Owen looked all around in a panic. He knew the shadow eyes were there but he couldn't see them. He looked at his brother. Oliver was in the open, holding his stuffed dog over his head as if he could hide beneath it. He looked so small and so vulnerable.

"Come on, puppy! Come on, now!"

Oliver did not look up. His whimpers came more rapidly, and more desperately. Owen pulled Oliver's hands away from his head and tugged.

"Come on, puppy, that's it. Good puppy! Come on, now..."

Oliver let himself be led toward the trees, still crawling like a puppy. He held Odie tightly in his hand. Owen felt the need to be among the trees. He somehow felt that they would be less exposed. Owen was just a little boy, and he was already too scared to think. The urge to find a place to hide was instinctive. He didn't stop to realize that the trees would only create more shadows.

Once among the wood, Owen collapsed and gathered his brother to him. He could not protect him. The shadow eyes would take him, and Owen would be all alone. Owen gave voice to his breaking heart, as the shadow eyes began to open all around him.

Oliver clung to Owen. He was so scared that the sounds he was making were little more than rapid peeps. His eyes were shut tight. He was a puppy...he was a puppy...*he was a puppy*! Oliver felt as if his eyes were opened against his will. He saw the tree next to him, and saw the dull sheen of a black eye open in its bark. He was not a puppy. The shadow eyes would not let him hide in that way. He was a little boy. He had cancer and he would never get better and his Mommy didn't want him anymore. Oliver's whimpers turned to cries and soon he was screaming for his Mommy.

Above the brothers, the flutter leaves poked through the ridged bark of their branches. As night fell, the leaves spread and seemed to catch the twinkle of the emerging stars. A gentle breeze blew through the wood and lifted the swiveling leaves one at a time to sparkle for the blink of an eye. The trees and the night sky seemed joined in a communion of beautiful light, as if the trees felt love for the twinkling of the stars and answered in adulation.

This luminance would continue until the last star faded and the leaves retreated from the light of the rising sun, but the boys would not see it. They were below in the shadows. They would see only the lightless eyes that surrounded them, invading their minds and defiling their flesh throughout the long, terrible night.

The sun rose and cast its first rays upon the weeping brothers. Again, the boys had not slept. They had endured a second night of torture that had seemed to go on forever. Once the shadow eyes took them, the nightmare had no beginning and no end. It became all they had ever known, or would ever know.

The boys felt the shadow eyes go, but it took much longer that morning for their sobs to die down and become sniffles. They were drenched with sweat and with cool morning dew that made them shiver.

Oliver did not witness the dawn. The sun was shining brightly in a turquoise sky when he finally opened his eyes. Pale yellow clouds stretched overhead like cotton that had been pulled apart by clumsy fingers.

Owen wept from closed eyes. He didn't think that he could ever feel safe or happy again; the shadow eyes would come every night.

Owen's heart broke for his own plight. He was trapped here because of Oliver, and because of his own wish. For just a moment, he wished that he could take it back. In that moment Oliver started to whimper like a puppy and Owen was terrified that *this* wish would also come true. Owen tightened his hold on his baby brother and opened his eyes to make sure that Oliver was still there.

The boys locked eyes and again, their tears were renewed. After several minutes they released each other. The boys were again dirty, and now they had no water to clean themselves.

Owen did the best he could and then he stood up. He picked up Odie and the blanket. He did not give the stuffed dog to Oliver, but held on to it. He needed it.

"Ready, Oliver?"

Oliver sat where he was. He shook his head and continued to whimper.

"Come on, Oliver. Let's leave, okay?"

Oliver whimpered vehemently until Owen finally understood.

"Okay, puppy. Wanna go for a walk?"

At this, Oliver nodded his head. His whimpers took on a strangely relieved tone and the boys set out toward they knew not where.

CHAPTER FOURTEEN

Owen walked slowly and Oliver crawled beside him. They emerged from the flutter tree wood to a sight that made them pause.

A comfortably cool breeze blew up a gentle slope toward the boys, carrying with it the perfume of endless blossoms. It swept the hair from Owen's face and caressed Oliver's bald head. Spread below them, as far as they could see, were trees covered in these sweet blossoms. The trees grew in a meadow of new, light green grass. The blossoms were pink, or white, and some were almost blue. These colors seemed to be reflected in the grass under each tree where its petals had softly floated to the ground. Petals also tossed about on the breeze, filling the air with playful movement. Dotting the ground were clusters of plants that were laden with large magenta-colored berries. In the distance, there was a shining white stream that wandered through the trees. The boys had reached the border of Springland.

"Wow! Look, Oliver!" Owen pointed at nothing, and everything. He was quite overstimulated. A pair of bickering blue birds chased each other from tree to tree. Owen watched them in open-mouthed wonder.

Minutes before, the boys had been sobbing in each other's arms. Now, Oliver actually started to laugh. He didn't wait for Owen. He excitedly scrambled down the slope on his hands and knees, filled with giddiness.

Oliver was giggling, but crawling downhill was not so very easy. He quickly gave it up and simply rolled over the soft grass to the bottom. Owen had started laughing, too, and he joined his brother. There is nothing like a brisk morning roll to lift the spirits of two very young boys.

The brothers thought that they had found a safe place. The relief they felt gave them a momentary reprieve from the lingering fear of the night before. Oliver lay on his back with Odie on his chest until he caught his breath, and then he actually stood up and ran through the grass. Owen caught up to him and ran beside him, holding the blanket up over his head with both hands to catch the wind. The boys were running away from the land of the shadow eyes. They were running into a land that seemed filled with hope and joy. They became infused with the life all around them until they overflowed and scintillated their beautiful youth. They were running because there was joy in their hearts that the shadow eyes could enshroud for a time but could not take away, for the boys loved each other and they were together.

Oliver didn't make it very far before his legs started to hurt. He plopped down in front of the first berry plant that he came to and waited for Owen to tell him that they were okay to eat.

The plants grew in small clusters low to the ground, so that they were partially hidden by the young grass. Each short stem bent under the weight of a berry that was roughly the size of an egg. The shining magenta skin of the berry was speckled with tiny, light blue seeds. Each berry had its own corona of dark green leaves that spiraled like ribbons and were covered in tiny fibers that made them feel like velvet.

Owen picked a berry, thinking that it reminded him of a strawberry, and nibbled at it. He was surprised and delighted to find that the inside of the berry had many layers of colors, fading one into another like a gobstopper. Under the magenta skin, bright red melted into orange, which blended into green, which wrapped around a bright yellow center. Of course, Owen was even more delighted by how delicious the berry tasted.

As with the pinkberries, Oliver couldn't wait for his brother's approval. As soon as he saw the look on Owen's face when he bit into the berry, Oliver picked one and popped the whole thing in his mouth. It filled his cheeks. The berry was so big that he couldn't even close his mouth while he chewed. Colorful juice ran down his chin in a rainbow. Oliver bit into a second berry and marveled at the layers of color inside. He offered a bite to Odie, adding the rainbow-colored juice to the stains that already covered the stuffed dog.

When the boys had eaten their fill, exhaustion took over. They laid down their heads and fell asleep in the warm grass. They felt safe. It wasn't just that the boys had found a new place that they instinctively knew was different, they were learning a sort of routine, and that gave them a sense of structure. In the mornings they found food and slept. They knew that when they woke up they would keep moving. It removed some small bit of the scary unknown before the boys and gave them an obscure sense of something that they could count on. It would be far too much to say that they had come to trust the land; the veil of the shadow eyes' darkness would not allow that, but they felt just a little less lost.

Unfortunately, the boys' sleep was just as fitful and filled with nightmares as it had been the day before.

Oliver woke first. He had been crying in his sleep, and immediately upon waking he began to sob. He had been dreaming that the shadow eyes were Mommy. Oliver had wanted her to hold him but she wouldn't. He had kept trying to hug her but there was a dream-barrier that wouldn't let him get close. Then Mommy had looked at him and her eyes had been the dull, solid black of the shadow eyes. Oliver had tried to look away but couldn't. His Mommy had stared at him through those black eyes and he had been forced to stare back while she made him feel all of the things that the shadow eyes had. She didn't love him. She didn't hate him. She didn't know him. He had screamed her name over and over but her face had stayed expressionless and unmoving. She hadn't even blinked. After forever, Oliver had tried again to look away. He had tried to run from Mommy but he hadn't been able to move. He had been pulled into her black eyes where he had again experienced the sensation of everything at once. That was when he had finally woken up.

Owen was having a similar dream except for him the shadow eyes were Oliver, only Oliver was dead. The shadow eyes covered Oliver's body and stared at Owen through Oliver's lifeless, half-closed eyes. Eyes started to open on Owen's own body and he knew that he was dead, too. He knew that soon he would see only blackness when they finally took over his own eyes.

Owen woke to Oliver screaming his name. He was completely disoriented. Oliver was dead and yet he was still screaming. The adrenaline that pumped through Owen made him lightheaded. When Oliver tried to bury his face in Owen's chest, Owen pushed him away. He thought it was the shadow eye-Oliver. Owen tore at his shirt but found that no eyes were on him. He jerked his head in every direction in a panic, and finally realized that it had been a dream. He grabbed Oliver and held him while both of the brothers sobbed together. This, also, had become a part of their routine.

Owen was fiercely relieved to hold his brother and to feel his warmth. Even the movement of the sobs that shook him were a comfort. Oliver was alive and well.

Oliver had no such reprieve from his nightmare. Mommy was not there to reassure him with her presence. He cried her name.

"Mommy mad...Mommy mad...Mommy mad..."

His child's mind could not comprehend the unfeeling blackness in his mother's eyes. The closest he could come to understanding it was as the emotion of anger, so that was how he perceived it.

Owen rocked him back and forth. "Shhhh, Oliver. Mommy's not mad. She's not mad. Shhhh, Shhhh. Mommy's not mad."

There was no consoling Oliver. He needed to cry it all out. It was quite awhile before he started to calm down. When his cries turned to wordless moans, Owen tried to cheer him up.

"Ya want some more rainbowberries, Oliver? Remember the white river we saw? Wanna go and find it? We can take a drink...we can swim some more..."

Oliver was dirty again and Owen was wet.

Oliver grabbed at Odie and clutched him tightly. He lifted his head and looked at his brother. He began to make puppy noises. Through a series of puppy yips, facial expressions and body language, Oliver told Owen quite clearly that yes, he would very much like to go to the White River for a drink and a swim.

Off the boys went, across the field and under the trees through a gentle rain of blossoms that glowed brightly with the sunlight that shone through them. Oliver's legs had gotten all the exercise that they could handle for the day and so he crawled along next to Owen. The knees of his pajamas had worn through, showing the grass stains and bruises on the skin underneath. He was happy enough at the moment, though vague memories of his nightmare and of the long night before lingered in his head.

Owen couldn't help but feel uplifted, but his fears lingered, also. He occasionally cast a glance at his brother, unconsciously looking for signs that his sickness had returned. Indeed, a hollowness had returned to Oliver's face.

If Owen had looked in a mirror, he would have seen the same hollow look in his own face and he might have worried for himself as well, though needlessly. Oliver's sickness had not returned. The boys were simply exhausted. The emotional and mental onslaught of the shadow eyes also wore on the brothers physically. They weren't getting enough sleep, and what sleep they did get was not restful.

When the boys reached the stream, Oliver did not even slow down. He crawled straight into the shallow water and started to splash around, though the stones on the bed of the stream hurt his bruised knees and after a few seconds he crumpled and fell over, getting a face full of water.

While Oliver lifted his face from the stream and sputtered a bit of the pearly water from his lungs, Owen yelled at him.

"Oliver! You got Odie all wet!"

Oliver looked down at his submerged hand and found that Odie was still in it. The stuffed dog was weaving in the current of the stream. He lifted Odie from the water and reprimanded him.

"Odie! No! Bad dawwwwg!" Then he laughed and tossed Odie onto the grass.

Owen stepped into the water with his shoes on. He questioned aloud, "What the heck?" He had been expecting a river, not a shallow stream. He sat down and began to lift handfuls of water to his mouth. As soon as Owen tasted the water, all dark thoughts left him and he decided that a soaking wet Odie was indeed funny.

After drinking his fill, Owen stood up. He was so full that he could feel the weightless water sloshing around in his belly as he stomped around in the stream making splashes. He was having too much fun to watch where he was going and he took one step too many. When his foot stomped down and kept going instead of hitting the bed of the stream, he fell forward with the force of his movement and *SPLAT*! He did a face-smacker on the surface of a pool that had formed where the bottom of the stream had suddenly dropped.

Oliver had been watching him and he let loose peals of laughter. He was so amused that he forgot to be a puppy. He cried, "What zuh *heck*?" and then laughed even more, delighted by his own cleverness in mocking his brother.

When Owen had hit the surface of the water, he had discovered a strange sensation. The pearly white water was so light that it was like falling face first into a pile of feathers that gave way beneath him even as it supported him. The pool was not deep, and yet Owen softly came to rest without so much as scuffing his nose on the pebbles that formed its bed. He put his hands on the bottom and pushed his head above the surface of the water.

"Gaaaahh! What the HECK!"

This was met by more laughter from Oliver, and Owen laughed with him. As it would countless times, the boys' laughter blended with the trill of the trickling stream in a playful, canorous harmony.

Owen stood up and waded back to the shallow part of the stream, where he proceeded to turn an about face and march into the pool with another *splat*!

Oliver lay back in the stream and kicked his arms and legs in his hilarity. He enjoyed the feeling of the shallow stream rippling past his bald head and trickling around his ears.

Owen's head broke the surface of the pool, "What the HECK!"

"Owen! Up! Up!"

Oliver was holding out his hands to be helped up. He wanted to play, too.

For a while, all else was driven from the boys' minds. There were no thoughts of home, or Mommy and Daddy, or shadow eyes. Even Oliver's soiled clothes were forgotten as the boys played, falling face first into the water over and over, each time followed by a sputtering, "What the HECK!"

The sun passed its zenith in the sky, which had deepened from turquoise to a deep teal. The scattered clouds that slowly lumbered by overhead had very faint tints of blue and green where the sun did not shine directly on them.

By then the boys had taken off their clothes and were enjoying their very first bath in the shallow pool of the White River. The water came up to Owen's chest but Oliver had to sit up straight to keep his chin above its surface. The boys had tired themselves out but did not want to get out of the water. Their bodies were exhausted, but their minds were fresh and giddy. The boys were talking.

"Home now, Owen?"

The river had lifted Oliver's spirits so that he didn't see any reason why they couldn't simply decide to just go home. The *how* didn't seem to matter.

"No, Oliver. We can't. I don't know how."

"Whiss?"

Owen hadn't thought of this. "Okay, let's wish."

Both boys closed their eyes and wished they were home. Of course, nothing happened.

"Maybe it has to be a birthday wish," Owen mused aloud.

"Iss *you-uh* buss-tay, Owen!"

"Oliver," Owen said with a trace of impatience, "birthdays only last one day. It's not my birthday anymore."

Oliver tilted his head to one side, dipping his chin in the water. He was thinking.

Owen was thinking, too. He was thinking that Oliver had been going to die, but that now he wasn't. Owen watched Oliver scrunch his face in thought and reflected on how much he loved him, and again that his brother was the best birthday present that he had ever gotten.

"Besides, Oliver, there's no fountain here."

"Whisst inna foun'in?"

"Yeah, the fountain at the hospital, remember? You know, your favorite! With the little girl!"

Oliver thought about the fountain and smiled. He had loved to throw coins to the girl in that fountain.

"Mommy come?" Oliver asked.

"Maybe."

"Daddy come f'us?"

"Maybe. If he can find us."

Oliver tilted his head to the other side.

"Why no'?" Oliver thought that his Daddy could do anything.

Owen had no answer to this at first. He, too, thought that their Daddy could do anything. Finally he said, "I guess he will."

Oliver lifted his hands out of the water so that he could clap. The movement threw him off-balance and his head dipped under water just as he was taking a breath to yell, "Woo-hoo!" Owen lifted him and Oliver came up choking and spitting. Owen tried not to laugh, but he couldn't help it. He was relieved when Oliver laughed, too. It was a nervous laugh, accompanied by a "Whoa!" The water of the White River made the boys feel happy, even when it went down the wrong pipe.

"Daddy come?"

"I dunno. Maybe him and Mommy are here now, looking for us."

Oliver yelled, "Woo-hoooo!" but this time he didn't clap.

Both boys thought for a few moments about their Mommy and Daddy finding them, and of how happy they would be.

Oliver broke the silence. He lowered his head and took a drink of water, then spit it out. With his bottom lip below the surface and his top lip above it, he proceeded to make fart noises, pausing now and then to laugh at himself.

Owen played along, pretending they were real farts.

"Ewww! Oliver! Say, 'Excuse me!'"

Fart noise, "Sooz me!" *Fart noise*, "Sooz me!" *Fart noise*, "Soooooozzzzz ME!"

This went on longer than was acceptably tasteful in polite company, but they *were* little boys, after all.

Eventually the boys got out of the water and Owen helped Oliver to put his pajamas back on. The boys wandered in the grass and stopped at some rainbowberry plants. Once they had eaten their fill, Owen had to go to the bathroom. He wasn't yet comfortable going "number two," as he called it, without a toilet. He went by a tree if one were near, but sometimes he had needed to go in the open.

"C'mon, Oliver. I wanna show you something."

Oliver obediently followed his brother to a space where a group of three blossom trees were growing close together.

"Okay, stand in front of this tree."

When Oliver was in place, Owen pulled his pajama bottoms down to his ankles.

"Owen! Sop it!"

"It's okay, Oliver. I'm showing you how to go bathroom." Owen was tired of rinsing Oliver's clothes.

"NO!" Oliver crumpled into a ball on the ground, trying to pull his pants back up.

"C'mon, Oliver! You can't keep going in your pants! Now stand up."

"NOOOOOO!"

Owen couldn't hold it anymore. "Okay, then just watch me!"

Owen dropped his pants and leaned against a tree across from Oliver. When he was done, he scooted across the grass.

Oliver had been getting angry, but this display made him giggle in spite of himself.

"See, Oliver? It's easy!"

"NO!"

Owen was getting frustrated with Oliver, who had almost succeeded in pulling his bottoms back up. Owen grabbed them and pulled them down again.

"Owen Sop! Sop it! Sop it!"

Oliver started to cry until Owen stopped. He let out an angry but victorious, "*MMM!*" and curled up again, pouting.

Owen looked at Oliver and tried to think. How could he get his brother to pull his pants down and poop? Owen was close to tears himself. The littlest thing made him feel how frightened and alone he was, and this minor failure was more than enough to do just that. Any four-year-old can easily get discouraged at the best of times, and under the circumstances Owen's confidence and patience were incredibly fragile. He had always been a very sensitive boy. Through a tremendous effort of will, Owen rallied and tried again.

"Okay, Oliver. You don't have to go number two. Let's just pee on that tree." He pointed to the third tree.

Oliver propped himself up on an elbow, tilted his head to one side and eyed his brother suspiciously. He suspected trickery.

Owen walked over to the tree and dropped his own pants again.

"C'mon, Oliver. It's fun!"

"No, Owen! No haff to!"

"Just try, Oliver! I promise it's fun!"

Oliver just looked at his brother. His silence told Owen that he was intrigued.

"You wanna watch me do it first?"

"Mm hmm."

Owen peed all over the tree. He swooped and dipped and pushed to make it go higher, all accompanied by his raucous yells, "Whoo-uh-whoo-uh-WHOAH!"

At "WHOAH," he pushed too hard and passed a squeaky bit of gas. A chuckle escaped Oliver, followed by his high-pitched laughter.

"'Sooz me,' Owen!"

Owen turned red, feeling slightly embarrassed, but he was laughing, too. It *was* funny.

"Okay, Oliver. Your turn! I bet you can't get your pee higher than mine."

Oliver scrambled to his feet and walked up to the tree on shaky legs. When he was in place, Owen pulled his pajama bottoms down for him. With one hand, Oliver pulled his shirt up to his chest. He had to lean forward to see past his belly. When Oliver peed all over the tree and in the grass on both sides of it, he found that Owen was right. It *was* fun. Oliver was sometimes a mischievous little boy and with his last push he turned and peed on his brother.

"Oliver! Gaahhhh! You peed on me!"

Owen wasn't really angry. He was too amused not to laugh at the joke, even if the joke was on him.

Oliver giggled happily, very pleased with himself. It was the first time that he had stood up to pee like a big boy, *and* he'd managed to pee on Owen. Oliver wished he had more but he didn't so he shook the last drops at Owen, who quickly jumped away, laughing.

Now that Oliver was having fun, Owen pushed his advantage.

"Okay, ready to poop?"

"No!"

Owen good-naturedly encouraged his brother, "Aww, come on, Oliver! It's so easy!"

"NO! No haff-too!"

Owen could see by the way that Oliver was standing that he *did* have to, and badly.

In his pockets, Owen still had all of the treasures that he had brought to the hospital on that magical morning. He had carefully made sure of each item every morning, and each time he had rinsed his jeans or put them back on. He hadn't told Oliver that he had them. He was afraid that Oliver would lose something, and truth be told, Owen didn't want to have to share them.

Oliver stood, slightly hunched over in his need to go to the bathroom. With his pants around his ankles, he watched as Owen rummaged in his pocket. Oliver really had to go, and was having trouble holding it.

Owen pulled the Volkswagon bus out of his pocket and held it up.

"I'll let you play with this if you go poop against a tree."

Oliver's eyes grew very big when he saw the toy. Oh, he wanted to play with it so badly.

"Keep s'it?" Oliver asked.

"You don't have any pockets, Oliver. But I'll let you play with it whenever you don't poop your pants."

Oliver didn't have to consider this offer very long at all.

"He'p, Owen!"

Oliver couldn't walk by himself with his bottoms around his ankles, so Owen helped his brother shuffle back to the first tree and then helped him to lean against it. Owen lifted Oliver's shirt and held him up under his arms while Oliver went to the bathroom. Then Owen helped him to scoot across the grass, the whole time telling Oliver what a good, big boy he was. This wasn't a very efficient way to wipe, but it was better than nothing, and little boys don't concern themselves overly much about such things, anyway.

Owen tried to fix Oliver's pajama bottoms but Oliver didn't make it easy. He snatched at the toy car until Owen handed it over so that he could finish pulling up Oliver's pants. Owen took out the yellow Lamborghini ("Yeh-woh!"), and the boys played cars together, running them over the grass and making revving and screeching sounds.

Owen experienced the delightful gratification of sharing. Absorbed as he was in his own amusement, he still couldn't help but notice how much Oliver was enjoying the magic bus. Owen had done this, given Oliver this gift of play. He felt empowered and humbled by it at the same time.

Everyone has the power to upset someone, to take away a bit of their joy, but the power to give someone happiness when they're upset, to help someone accomplish something as he had helped Oliver to go to the bathroom like a big boy, that *is* power, true power. Such is the twofold gift of sharing of one's self. Oliver would still have accidents, and for some time he would wake up dirty most every morning, but Owen would remember his success that day and it would help him to be patient with his little brother.

The boys played happily for awhile, but as the sun sank lower in the sky, Owen began to grow uneasy. They had been in one spot for too long and he felt an urge to move on before nightfall. He didn't question this need to keep going, he just felt it and obeyed.

He had no destination in mind. After all, how could he? Part of the urge to move on was his need to get away from the shadow eyes, as if he could outrun them, but there was more to it that he didn't understand, and that had nothing to do with fear. He was a little boy, and he had a boyhood sense of adventure that was kindled by exploring the wonders of that strange land (Oliver had it too, perhaps even more than Owen, which was partly why he so readily followed his big brother).

And yet there was something else, something too complex for Owen to see clearly. He had another need that was driven partially by fear, and somewhat of love. There were so many emotions intertwined throughout this need that was not unique to the boys, but universal. Owen was looking for *home*. He did not understand this need because in his mind, home was the house where he and Oliver had lived with their Mommy and Daddy. He had not yet come to think of the land as his and Oliver's. Being there was like being a guest in a stranger's house. He could play and enjoy his time there but it wasn't *his*. Owen was searching for some place that he and Oliver could call their own, a place that didn't feel so strange. Nowhere in his conscious thoughts could he conceive of such a place without his Mommy and Daddy, and so he couldn't accept the possibility of its existence in that new place without them. It is impossible to look for something whose existence we cannot comprehend, and yet Owen's instincts drove him on in search of just such a thing. Owen didn't understand what he was searching for because he didn't know that he was searching for it. He just felt its absence.

"C'mon, Oliver. Let's go for a walk."

"Wheh-uh walk?"

Owen stood up. He handed Odie to Oliver and took the little bus back. He put it in his pocket with his other car.

Oliver gave Odie a big hug and then looked at Owen and waited for him to answer.

Owen pointed and said, "This way."

That was good enough for Oliver. He stood up and took a few awkward steps before continuing on all fours, following along beside his big brother.

Owen saw that the rainbowberries were growing sparse. He stopped to pick some for later, and carried them in the blanket, using it like a bindle.

The sun was dipping into the horizon when Oliver stopped crawling. He missed his Mommy. He couldn't go on without her.

Owen stopped when he realized that Oliver was no longer beside him. He turned and saw his baby brother staring into his own lap. The sky had deepened into the color of the deep ocean, a dark blue-green. Oliver wasn't going to come with him. He would have to go on alone.

Both boys started to cry. The shadow eyes had found them again.

CHAPTER FIFTEEN

Oliver had stopped in the middle of an open field. His shadow stretched far across the grass to where Owen stood waiting for him, and then it was gone. The sun had gone over the horizon, leaving the boys in twilight.

Owen turned and began to walk away. His silent teardrops fell to the ground as he walked. Oliver was just going to sit there until he died. He didn't care about Owen at all.

Owen couldn't take it. How was he supposed to go on alone? He had saved Oliver's life with his wish. He had brought him here so they could always play together and now Oliver didn't want to be with him anymore. Owen had never felt so sorry for himself. He was lost here alone and he would be alone for the rest of his life, and all because he loved his baby brother and tried to take care of him...

Oliver missed his Mommy. He sat and cried for her. She loved him more than anything in the world and Oliver loved her too. He needed her so much and she needed him. She had told him so, countless times, and it had always made him feel special. Now she didn't know where he was and he would never find her again. She would die without him and it would be all his fault...

The shadow eyes worked very slowly. They had probed and tortured the boys for two long nights and had learned how to draw even more pain and fear from them. Oliver's memories revealed his confidence in Owen and his trust in him. On both previous mornings Owen had been there to tell Oliver that Mommy was not mad at him, that she loved him, and Oliver believed him. This diminished, by the most miniscule shade, the feast that was Oliver's pain, but the shadow eyes felt this hindrance and worked to remove it. They searched deeper and found what they were looking for. Owen could reassure Oliver that Mommy was not mad at him because she loved him, but he could not make her appear to assuage Oliver's unbearable longing for her.

Oliver began to see images in his mind of Mommy distressed and crying. She was terrified, not because she was mad at him, but because she loved him. Mommy didn't understand why Oliver didn't love her anymore. Mommy's heart was broken because her little Snuffer had left her. This change in the shadow eyes' tactics disguised their presence from Oliver. He did not yet know that they were there, even as he felt his little heart breaking in his chest, and yet even this was not enough for the shadow eyes. They had discovered something far worse for the boys, and were twisting their hearts and minds to achieve it.

Owen walked across the dark, rolling fields until Oliver was out of sight. Confused thoughts flashed through his mind: that he would be better off without Oliver, that he would be able to do whatever he wanted and that he would never have to wait for Oliver or clean him or feed him. If Oliver didn't want him, then he wouldn't want Oliver, either. Owen thought, *I bet he cries for me once I'm gone*, and the thought made him glad.

Once Owen had walked far enough, the shadow eyes released him. He suddenly thought about the way that Oliver got so excited to eat and he was immediately overcome with remorse. He stopped walking and realized that he could no longer hear Oliver's cries. Owen looked around wildly but saw only the silhouette of the sloping horizon against the night sky. He could not remember which way he had come. Oliver was gone.

The shadow eyes also released Oliver. He cried for Mommy. His head was down and his eyes were shut. He sat in the grass and very slowly calmed down, until his sobs were no more than an irregular hitching in his chest. Oliver finally opened his eyes. Night had fully come. Owen was nowhere to be seen.

"WHOOOOAAAA-WENNNNNN!!!"

He was answered only with a terrifying silence. Owen was gone.

The boys were separated. The feast could begin.

Owen began to run. He ran in the direction from which he thought he had come, calling out Oliver's name as loud as he could. He was running the wrong way. With each step he put more distance between himself and Oliver. It was so dark that he could barely see.

Owen began to picture his brother, lost and scared. He imagined all sorts of terrible things happening to him. He pictured Oliver being attacked by monsters, and by the scary man. Oliver was just a baby! Owen had to find him. He called out for him some more, and kept running.

A child cannot run in fear without the fear growing. Little by little, Owen's fears for Oliver shifted to himself. He soon forgot that he was running toward something. In his panic he began to feel that he was running *from* something. The *something* was right behind him. It almost had him. He was too scared to turn around and look. If he stopped, it would get him. Driven by terror now, Owen ran even faster. His side hurt. He couldn't breath. He let out a whimpering cry as he ran.

When he tripped in the darkness, he could not bring himself to get back up. He tried to curl up but such was his fear that he couldn't move. He lifted his face out of the grass and stared at the ground, waiting for whatever it was to grab him, or claw him, or bite him. None of these things happened.

Inches away from his face, a single black eye opened in the grass and stared at him. *No! It wasn't fair! He had escaped! The eyes couldn't be here!* But of course they were. The eyes were everywhere that shadows lay. Owen began to scream.

Oliver hadn't moved. He was too scared to think. He could feel his rapid heartbeat. He screamed his brother's name. His voice was choked with fear and outrage.

"WHOA-WENNNNN! *Owen!*"

Oliver felt betrayed. He couldn't accept that his brother had actually left him all alone. Oliver felt a rush of emotions so powerful that it left him lightheaded. He may as well have just been slapped in the face by his mother for telling her that he loved her. It could not have shocked him any more than finding himself abandoned by Owen. It could not have made him cry any harder than he did, nor could it have thickened his throat-wrenching screams.

Oliver suddenly felt the presence of something behind him, something that was not Owen. He grew silent, but the thing already knew that he was there. He stared at the grass between his legs. He tried to stay quiet, but a high-pitched sound escaped him. An eye opened in the grass where he stared, and was joined by another, and another; yet another betrayal. He had thought that he was safe from them. The shadow eyes devoured Oliver's fear, but they could not be sated.

What followed was to be the boys' worst night. They were taken by the shadow eyes in a waking nightmare too terrible to be conceived. Such fear and sadness can only be felt by children, unable as they are to form even a single clear thought to defend themselves when these emotions consume them.

Clouds covered the stars, leaving the boys in almost total darkness. There was no light to close the eyes that opened all over their bodies. By the time the clouds cleared, the boys were lost in their minds and no longer struggled.

All through that long night, every terrible sensation was made worse, not only by the incredible loneliness that each boy felt, but also by the knowledge that the other was also alone, and both boys' thoughts were twisted to convince them that their brother's suffering was their own fault. The night slowly crept toward a dawn that seemed to never come, and the lifeless black eyes watched, and fed.

These two boys, each so alone and so small in a vast darkness that they didn't understand, had been abandoned by everything that is kind, and good, and light. No one would ever know the suffering they endured that night. No one would ever understand what light they had inside them that saw them through it. After that endless night, to see the boys laugh and play again like any other children, no one could ever guess how special was even the most fleeting smile, nor could they truly grasp how precious was each dearly bought piece of their laughter.

Owen felt the shadow eyes close all over his body. He jerked and twitched in revulsion at the sensation. He lay curled up on the ground and sobbed. The eyes were gone and yet he felt little relief. Oliver was lost. Owen was all alone.

When he opened his eyes, it was to a sight that he would never see again. He was in a vast field of what he thought were flowers. A beautiful, joyful green light was growing in the sky where it met the land. This smudge of bright and happy chartreuse seemed to seep into the indigo night sky, swallowing up the stars as it grew.

Owen watched through his tears and received the gift of the dawn as Oliver had received it after that first long night. The quality of the spreading light was such that the world around him appeared to glow. Every blade of grass seemed to swell with its own translucent green light, as did the leaves and blossoms on the distant trees. The tears in Owen's dark eyes caught a sparkle of green as they welled up and rolled down his cheeks. When the sun rose, there was a soft flash of white light that spread in both directions along the horizon, causing Owen to gasp in wonder. It lasted only for an instant, but it was so beautiful that Owen's innocent heart broke and he wept.

Oliver did not witness this. He was racked with spasms as the shadow eyes left him, but his wails remained. They were his only company. He clutched at the grass, wishing that it was Odie in his hand, but he couldn't open his eyes to look for the stuffed dog. He was cold and dirty and alone. For the first time in his young life, he was all alone.

When his wails died down he began to softly whimper his brother's name.

"Owen...Owen...Owen..."

His thoughts turned to images of Mommy and he cried harder, but still it was Owen's name that he chanted. He would not move, nor open his eyes, until Owen eventually found him, and he would still be repeating his name, over and over.

Owen was also dirty. He cleaned himself up as best he could. He rushed, his only thoughts being for Oliver. There would be time for him to dwell on his own plight: that there was no escaping the shadow eyes and that they would come every night...that he might never find a way home.

He was hungry and thirsty and exhausted, but for now finding Oliver was all there was, allowing him to push aside the rest. Owen automatically started walking back the way he had come. Free of the shadow eyes' hold, his instincts guided him. He called out his brother's name, but his voice was so hoarse that it was little more than a whisper.

Owen had so little left in him that he did not sob. His tears simply fell, as if of their own accord. Clouds began to cover the sky as he topped one hill and then another. Owen grew worried. He did not remember coming so far, nor did he remember these rolling hills. He called for

Oliver as best he could and then stopped to listen. When he heard nothing, he had to fight against panic. It was a losing battle. He had been through too much.

Owen looked all around and saw only an unfamiliar landscape. His breathing was growing faster, as was the rapid heartbeat that he could feel pounding in his chest. Adrenaline uselessly coursed through him. He was completely lost. He sat down, wrapped his arms around his knees and cried.

Clouds overtook the sky and the first falling drops of rain made Owen lift his head. It was a light rain, little more than a softly falling mist. Owen needed his brother. He couldn't stand to be alone anymore. Without thinking about which way he should go, he got up and started to jog clumsily over the grass. He was very soon out of breath, but still he called Oliver's name as he went.

Owen stumbled and fell several times. He had never been so tired. Each time he fell, he picked himself up and jogged on. He kept calling for Oliver, but all he heard when he listened for an answer was his own labored breaths. He finally topped a rise and spotted his little brother curled up in the grass.

Oliver heard his name being called in a strange voice. Still he didn't move. He was so drained that he thought it was part of a dream. The voice was getting closer now and he could hear footsteps. Was it Owen? It didn't register as reality. Oliver was sure that he would never see his brother again.

Owen reached Oliver and fell on top of him, wrapping him in his arms. Even though it hurt, Oliver still didn't move. He was so deeply in shock that he didn't react at all. He kept chanting Owen's name.

"Oliver! Oliver! I'm sorry, Oliver! I'm sorry!" Owen choked the words out. He had found him. He had found Oliver.

Oliver still didn't snap out of his shock. He began to speak as if Owen wasn't there.

"Owen mad a' me! Owen mad a' me! Owen mad a' meeeeee..."

"No! I'm not! I'm not mad, Oliver! *Oliver*!"

But Oliver would not be comforted. His voice grew louder as he grew more and more upset. He kept repeating those same words, "Owen mad a' me!" over and over, until he was screaming them. Tears flowed out between his closed eyelids.

Owen lifted his brother into a sitting position and held him. He cried with him. Oliver was purging his horrors of the night.

When Owen felt Oliver's little hands squeeze him back, he tried to soothe him like he thought Mommy would. "Shhhhh, shhhhh. I'm here, Oliver. Shhhhhh, it's okay."

Oliver squeezed him tighter and kept repeating the words, "Owen mad a' me...Owen mad a' me," but more softly now.

And then, he was done.

Owen tried to get up, but Oliver wouldn't let him go. The soft rain was still falling. The boys were cold and frightened, but they were together. Owen didn't try to get up again. He rocked Oliver in his arms and let him cry. Then, in a shaky but clear and gentle voice, Owen started to sing:

Itsy bitsy spider climbed up the water spout...
Down came the rain and washed the spider out...
Out came the sun and dried up all the rain...
And the itsy bitsy spider climbed up the spout again...

Oliver stopped crying. Owen sang it again. He kept one arm around Oliver and with the other he walked his fingers in the air like the spider as Oliver watched.

Itsy bitsy spider climbed up the water spout...
Down came the rain and washed the spider out...
Out came the sun and dried up all the rain...
And the itsy bitsy spider climbed up the spout again...

As the spider climbed up the spout again, Oliver reached out and walked his fingers next to Owen's. Owen kept his hand held out and Oliver pressed his thumb to Owen's pinky finger. Owen sang it one more time. Swiveling their wrists and meeting thumb to pinky, Owen's and Oliver's fingers climbed and fell together in perfect unison, Owen's right and Oliver's left, as if they were one person.

Itsy bitsy spider climbed up the water spout...
Down came the rain and washed the spider out...

Out came the sun and dried up all the rain...
And the itsy bitsy spider climbed up the spout again...

Never again would the brothers let themselves be separated. No matter what the shadow eyes might unearth in their minds, no matter how abandoned or angry the boys might feel, the memory of the pain and fear of that single night without each other would always be greater.

When Owen finished singing, the boys did not let go of each other. The hands that had danced through the air now held each other in warm comfort. Oliver tilted his head back and finally looked up at Owen. His tears had not yet dried, but he smiled. Owen smiled back. They were sad smiles, but after such an ordeal as the boys had been through, those sad smiles were like the sun.

Oliver reached up and poked one of the frogs on Owen's shirt.

"Wibbit," he said.

Owen looked at him with a gentle smile that was a little less sad.

Oliver poked another frog, and another.

"Wibbit, wibbit."

Oliver's finger traced the different breeds of frogs on his brother's shirt, the sadness slowly leaving his own smile as well. He was finding his way back to the light, and bringing Owen with him. This momentary reprieve from the dark didn't last long, but it didn't need to.

Owen thought about the morning of his birthday when he had picked out this shirt to wear because it was Oliver's favorite. It seemed so long ago.

The boys were soon asleep. Such was their weariness that they fell asleep as they were, sitting up in each other's arms. Their dreams were worse than ever and it wasn't long before they woke each other with their fitfulness.

"*Home...*" Oliver cried.

Owen had no answer to this. His dream had been awful. It brought to the surface all of the things he had pushed aside in his search for Oliver. They would never get home. The shadow eyes would take them every single night for the rest of their lives. The reality of it completely filled his mind so that he couldn't see past it.

"HOME!" Oliver was growing more upset. He cried harder.

Owen remained silent. He wanted to go home, too. He didn't know what to say. He couldn't make his little brother stop crying. Oliver's yells grew louder in his ears. There was no way out of this. No one would ever find them. Owen finally broke.

"Shut up, Oliver! We can't GO home!"

Owen became hysterical. He pushed his wailing brother away and crawled a few feet on his hands and knees. He bowed his head to the ground and began to beat his fists in the grass. His anguish came out in terrible sounds that no four-year-old should ever be driven to make. He was rebelling against what he knew to be true. In his mind, a single word repeated. *No no no no NO NO NOOOOO!*

This display frightened Oliver. He watched in timorous desperation as his brother's violence spent itself. He had never been afraid of Owen before. Oliver grew very quiet. He was afraid that the rage he was witnessing would be turned on himself. Oliver closed his eyes and covered his ears. He tried very hard to stifle his own whimpers.

Owen collapsed onto his side and sobbed. To learn what it is to feel despair is something that no child should go through, but that doesn't change the fact that they do, and rarely do they learn it as well as Owen did just then.

Oliver opened his eyes. Owen no longer looked angry, just very upset. Oliver cautiously said his name, very quietly.

"Owen?"

Owen didn't react, at least not visibly. Hearing his name spoken in Oliver's small and timid voice was like a soothing balm on his emotions, but it did not lessen his sobs.

Oliver looked around. He felt very unsure. When he spotted Odie lying in the grass, he crawled over and retrieved him. He then crawled to Owen.

"Owen?" Oliver held out the stuffed dog. "Odie!"

Owen grabbed the dog from him and clutched it tightly to his chest. His sobs began to ebb into sniffles. The storm had passed.

Oliver mimicked his brother's mimicking of their Mommy.

"S'kay, Owen. S'kay. Shhhhh... Shhhhh."

Owen looked at his brother and smiled through his tears. Oliver's innocent gesture had touched him in a place deep down. When Owen's breathing came a little easier he said, "Want me to change you, Oliver?" This was how he asked for forgiveness.

Oliver looked down at himself and saw that he was very dirty. He obediently lay on his back. He thought about the toy bus. Owen had said that he could only play with it when he didn't mess himself.

Owen would have gladly given it to Oliver right then, but he never thought of it, and Oliver was afraid to ask.

Owen found the rainbowberries in the blanket but they had been smashed to jelly. The boys licked what they could from the soiled blanket and then it was time to go.

The boys marched along into the afternoon. The sun had come out to warm them and bring the land to life, but the boys barely noticed. They had no eyes for the beauty around them. Oliver got more cranky and more whiny as they went. The boys had had nothing to eat or drink. They were tired and miserable. The progress of the sun overhead was a subliminal reminder that the shadow eyes would come again once it had set. Owen wanted to give up with each step that he took.

The boys grew annoyed with each other and bickered back and forth, but they stayed close together. After the previous night, the boys held each other's hands as they walked and did not let go, even as they argued.

Oliver kept having to stop to rest, but though this made Owen angry he had no thoughts of storming off. When Oliver needed to rest his legs, Owen sat with him and kept hold of his hand, all the while calling him a baby and telling him to hurry up. This, of course, made Oliver more stubborn at each stop. Owen grew more and more impatient with his brother's weariness, and his own exhaustion made his temper flare easily.

And so that long day passed. Evening came and panic began to force its way through the boys' bleary and tired minds. They knew what was coming. They knew they were helpless.

As the dark of night began to swallow up the green sky, Oliver tried to retreat into the puppy. He got down on all fours and started to whimper. Owen couldn't take this. It was like being left alone. He yanked at Oliver's arm until he cried out in pain, but Oliver would not get up, so Owen sat on Oliver's back until he collapsed under the weight and yelled at Owen to get off. The boys were very angry with each other, but at least Oliver had spoken, though he did not get up.

Oliver felt Owen's grip tighten painfully on his hand. Owen was angry. Owen was going to hurt him. Oliver remembered the way that Owen had beat on the ground and he knew that Owen was going to beat on him in the same way. He felt an urge to get as far away from Owen as he could...

Owen looked down at his brother almost with revulsion. Oliver was such a stupid baby. Owen would never get to a safe place, never get anywhere as long as Oliver kept going so slow. Owen longed for the satisfaction of hearing Oliver's screams as he left him behind...

The shadow eyes had come.

Oliver started to cry and scream. He tried to pull his hand away from Owen but Owen would not let go. Owen was hurting his brother and it fed his anger and made him glad. Owen took the blanket and covered Oliver with it, holding it over his face. A lifeless black eye opened on the inside of the blanket and Oliver began to have hysterics. He screamed and fought and struggled but he was not strong enough to fight Owen off.

A part of Owen's mind watched all of this happen as if someone else were controlling him. He watched in horror as his own hands held his brother down. The part of his mind that was enjoying it made him hate himself. He didn't deserve Oliver. He would go away where Oliver could never find him and then Oliver would be happier...

Owen released his little brother, who threw off the blanket and started to crawl away. Owen watched him go and was filled with loneliness and self-pity, but then Oliver stopped just a few feet away and looked back. He saw Owen weeping and he hated him for holding him under the blanket. Owen looked up and the brothers' eyes met. For a fleeting instant a realization broke through the shadow eyes' hold, a realization that filled both boys with incredible fear. They immediately crawled to each other and locked themselves in an embrace as the eyes opened in the grass all around them.

Through that long night, the boys screamed and wept as the shadow eyes tortured them, but they did not let each other go. They screamed for Mommy and Daddy. They screamed at each other. They became lost amid images of Mommy and Daddy suffering, angry, weeping. Monsters surrounded the boys. Bad men came to hurt them. Still they held on.

When the sun finally rose, both of the boys beheld it. Their faces were pressed cheek to cheek.

They were still together.

They had won.

When pale orange clouds stretched into the bright yellow morning sky, the dawn's beauty was reflected in pools of the brothers' shared wretchedness. Their tears had collected like dew where their features touched. This dew of tears overflowed, and the reflected beauty ran down their faces in trails of light, marking the paths worn by night's heartache.

The brothers held each other and sobbed for a long while. Finally Oliver spoke in a very small and sad voice.

"I sowwy, Owen."

This made Owen lean back and look at his brother. Oliver was looking up at him with big, penitent eyes, hoping to be forgiven. Forgiven for what, Owen didn't know, but he remembered with shame some of the images that had flashed through his own mind during the night.

"It's okay, Oliver. I'm sorry, too."

Owen smiled at Oliver but Oliver did not smile back. He cast his eyes downward and held Owen tighter. After another few minutes Owen was able to coax his baby brother into letting go. He got up and cleaned himself, and Oliver, as best he could.

Oliver was silent. Owen thought he seemed very sad. In happier times to come, Owen would sometimes wonder what Oliver had experienced to make him so sorry and sad that morning but he never asked, and Oliver never told him.

The morning was very chilly. Dew caught the morning light and sparkled in the grass all around the boys, though they were far too miserable to marvel at its beauty. The boys licked the grass. They were very thirsty, and this little bit of moisture made them feel their thirst all the more.

The boys' spirits were broken. The day ahead of them didn't seem to matter. They had no thoughts for what wonders they might find or what beauty they might explore. All was shrouded by thoughts that night would come and bring the shadow eyes.

Owen stood up and retrieved Odie and the blanket. He took Oliver's hand.

"Let's go, Oliver."

Oliver let himself be helped up without a word. He still hadn't spoken since telling Owen that he was sorry.

The boys started their day's journey through blossom trees and fields covered in bright flowers which they hardly noticed. Their empty stomachs ached and rumbled. They made slow progress. Oliver's poor bare feet were so cold that he could barely feel them. The boys were exhausted but they didn't even think to lie down and sleep.

After an hour Oliver began to whine.

"Hungwyyyyyy."

It took a massive effort on Owen's part to not explode on him.

"Hungwy!"

"I know, Oliver! I heard you!"

Oliver started to resist until Owen was pulling him along, but Oliver's legs were still weak and he soon stumbled and fell. Oliver's wail started very small and slowly built up strength like a siren. He hadn't hurt himself. He was just upset.

The sound grated on Owen, but it was no worse than Oliver's silence.

"Hate dis puh-wace!" Oliver shouted.

Owen had no energy. He didn't yell at Oliver, nor comfort him. He simply watched him and felt very low.

Oliver was actually wishing that he could get sick again so that he could go back to the hospital. He didn't care if he never got better. He wanted his hospital crib and he wanted his Mommy in it with him. He wanted his meals brought to him and toys to play with. He wanted to watch the kids play baseball in the park outside his window. He wanted his Daddy to hold him in the rocking chair and read to him, and his Mommy to change his diapers and keep him clean and loved.

Owen sat down and let Oliver cry until he was done. When Oliver's sobs began to die down, Owen offered him his stuffed dog. At first Oliver pushed Odie away, but the second time he was offered the dog Oliver took him and held him.

Owen said, "C'mon, Oliver. There's something to eat right over there." He was pointing on. He had no idea if there was food. He just wanted to start walking again.

Owen helped Oliver up and wrapped the blanket around him. The boys marched on.

As luck would have it, there *was* food right over there. The day was warming up. A breeze blew in the boys' faces and it carried a sweet scent. The boys topped the next rise in the land and came upon a vast field of plants that resembled pea pods, but that were covered in tiny white flowers. A light drizzle fell from a few scattered clouds and the moisture made the plants glisten in the golden light of the yellow sky.

The boys' hunger became unbearable at the sight and smell of food. All else was forgotten as they waded into the plants. Owen picked a pod and pried it open. He gobbled the peas down and picked another. Oliver didn't even open his pod. He shoved the whole thing in his mouth and ate it, peas and pod together. He spit out the tough stem and picked several more.

The vegetables comforted Owen especially. He thought of a funny memory that he had of eating something very like them that Mommy had called snow peas. He remembered laughing at the name because the peas had been green and not white, and because Mommy didn't know why they were called that. What did they have to do with snow? He started to giggle to himself as he ate.

Oliver heard the giggle and looked at Owen as if he were making a sound that he had never heard before. He tilted his head to one side, looking at Owen and trying to figure out if he were "cuh-wazy." Then Oliver started to giggle with him.

Owen looked up into that strange rain that fell while the sun was shining. He looked out over the field and said, "Rain peas!" Then he laughed out loud at the cleverness of his own joke.

Oliver jerked his head up at the rain falling from the yellow sky. He said aloud in a perfect mime of adult indignation, "Waining *pee?*" He didn't like that at all.

"No, Oliver! *Rain peas!* That's what we're eating! They're like snow peas, but it's not snowing. It's raining!"

Oliver gave Owen a querulous look and decided that perhaps he was "cuh-wazy" after all. Oliver suspiciously eyed the yellow sky and sniffed his hand. It didn't *smell* like pee. He went back to eating, but he never fully trusted yellow skies after that.

It was a very light shower that ended before the boys were even very wet. When Oliver was full he crawled over to Owen, put his head in his brother's lap and fell asleep. Owen pulled the blanket over both of them as best he could and soon both boys were deep in their dreams.

Owen woke with a start. A shadow eye had opened on his face. He sat up and beat at his face, jarring Oliver awake to instant tears. The first thing to register in Owen's mind was that the sun was still shining brightly overhead. The second was that Oliver was covered in shadow eyes. Before Owen even had time to react he realized that they were not eyes, but colorful wings. Oliver sat up and a dozen insects that had alit on his sleeping body took delicate and beautiful flight.

"Oliver! Look!"

Oliver stopped crying and the boys looked around.

Oliver yelled, "Futtuh-byes!"

All over the field, thousands of insects resembling butterflies were landing on the white flowers and fluttering through the air. The boys watched in silent awe. They were surrounded by a sea of color. Magnificent blues and majestic purples, shining oranges and deep reds, metallic greens and delicate yellows all caught and reflected the sunlight.

Owen got up and ran deeper into the field. The insects took flight all around him and made Oliver laugh. Owen jumped at them, trying to catch them. Oliver crawled after him, releasing a rising trail of colorful wings in his wake. The insects' wings tickled his body and made him squeal with delight.

Within minutes the entire swarm rose and slowly flew away. The boys watched them go and then looked around. The afterglow of the boys' wonder faded quickly and the oppressive fear of the shadow eyes returned to darken their moods. They never saw the swarm of insects again, though it was a memory that they would always keep safe.

As the boys moved on through the bright fields, the air took on a chill. They slowly grew colder and colder until they were walking huddled together under the blanket. The rain peas and the beautiful wings of the insects had boosted their spirits for only a few precious moments. The clusters of blossom trees that dotted the landscape went unnoticed. As the day shortened, so did the boys' tempers. They fought over the blanket, each yelling at the other for every bit of their bodies that was exposed to the cold air. Oliver's bare feet ached with cold and he whined with every step. The yellow sky turned gold, and then deepened to a sienna that strangely contrasted the cold that the boys felt.

At the first hint of purple on the horizon, the boys became very afraid. It was hopeless. They couldn't face another night with the shadow eyes. The boys stopped fighting and huddled even closer together. They both started to cry. Their cries were expressive of their fear, their sorrow, and most of all their absolute helplessness to stop what they knew was coming.

The gentle roll of the land had leveled out and the boys had left behind the last of the blossom trees. The boys walked on, following their own shadows which stretched very far in front of them now. Their fear grew to panic when the sun set and their shadows were overtaken and dissolved into the sunless land. Oliver tried to stop but Owen was pulling him along, trying to go faster. He knew that he couldn't escape, but he felt the need to try, anyway.

There was a line of tall, dark evergreen trees growing just a short distance ahead of the boys. Owen was trying to reach it. As before, he didn't stop to think about how much darker it would be among the thick branches. He just felt the instinctive need to hide.

Oliver's feet were freezing. He couldn't go on. He fell over and Owen picked him up, his terror pumping adrenaline through him. Oliver's arms and legs were wrapped around Owen, who held him under his bottom and struggled to go on as fast as he could. The first stars appeared in the sky and went unseen by the brothers.

Owen realized that Oliver was going to freeze to death. Owen was freezing as well. He stumbled and fell, landing painfully on top of Oliver. An eye opened in the frozen grass where the boys had landed and caught them in its stare. Owen closed his eyes tight. He and Oliver both started to scream. Owen struggled to get up; he was so close to the trees. Oliver curled up and clutched Odie as tightly as he could.

The assault of the shadow eyes was intense and all at once. The boys were fed no sad thoughts, nor anger. They immediately became terrified. Owen's fear flooded his body. With an incredible effort he picked up Oliver with one arm around his shoulders and another across his legs. His movements were panicked and jerky. Holding Oliver tightly to him he ran toward the trees. The eyes fed his fear even more. His only thought was for escape. He *had* to get away.

Oliver was screaming at the top of his lungs. He didn't know that Owen had picked him up. He thought he had been taken by a monster that was going to eat him.

Owen was sobbing so hard that it was difficult for him to breath. He crashed into the line of trees as the shadow eyes hit him with fear like they never had before. A branch whipped across Owen's eyes and blinded him. Still he ran on. He felt Oliver sliding out of his grip and still he did not stop. With his eyes shut and stinging, Owen collided and bounced off of heavy branches. He crashed right through the smaller ones. He heard them snap and thought that it was his and Oliver's bones breaking. The stiff evergreen needles scratched and jabbed the boys like endless teeth. Oliver's screams continued to blare in Owen's ears until he felt like he would explode.

Owen felt cold wind on his face. In his panic he didn't notice that something was different. His eyes were still closed. He stumbled and almost fell. If he fell they would get him...

There was a strange crunching sound with every step he took. Just as he realized that he was no longer running into trees or branches, Oliver's weight became too much for him to bear and he fell.

The boys rolled when they landed and felt sudden cold all over. Owen opened his eyes. He and Oliver were lying in snow. Owen could no longer feel the shadow eyes.

Oliver was still screaming. He was covered in welts from the whipping branches and Owen had hurt him when he had landed on him for the second time. Oliver heard Owen shouting his name. He opened his eyes to see that he was surrounded by white.

The line of trees behind the boys creaked scarily, but before them the pure white landscape was dotted by only a few scattered evergreens in the distance. The boys looked upon a vast expanse of snow that glittered in the bright starlight. The boys had reached Winterland. There were no shadows here. The boys were safe.

CHAPTER SIXTEEN

Oliver's feet were painfully cold. He had opened his eyes and seen that it was Owen that had landed on him and not a monster. He now clutched at his brother, still sobbing. He tried to tuck in his bare feet to get them out of the snow but he had nowhere to put them. He was still terrified. He did not yet understand that the shadow eyes were gone.

Owen did not yet realize this, either. He thought that the eyes were trying to trick him. Oliver was grabbing and fussing at him as if he were trying to crawl inside him. Owen pulled the blanket over their heads, held his brother as best he could and waited with dread for the eyes to open around them. He was very cold and he ached all over. He tried to cry as quietly as he could.

The boys sat in the snow and waited. They huddled together, forehead to forehead, hidden under the blanket. There was nothing else in the world but each other and Odie, whom the boys were holding together. They were comforted by the warmth and closeness of each other's breath.

Oliver tried to pull himself in even closer to his big brother. Nothing would get him *here*, under the blanket, with Owen to protect him.

Owen held Oliver tighter. He was the most precious thing in the world, what Owen treasured most. As long as Owen had Oliver in his arms, everything would be okay.

Little by little, the flow of the boys' tears eased and their cries quieted. They began to speak in whispers.

"Oliver, I want to look."

"No!" Oliver barely breathed the word, but the night was so quiet that he startled himself and tried to whisper even more quietly. "Finds us!"

Owen was afraid of this, too, but he wanted to know for sure. He whispered, "I think they're gone."

Oliver shook his head vehemently. His fear convinced Owen that perhaps it was best to stay hidden for a while longer.

If the boys could have seen themselves, their feeling of safety would have dissolved. They would have seen a lump under a blanket with four little feet sticking out in the middle of a field of white. They could not have been more conspicuous, but in their minds they had finally found a place to hide and they were more than reluctant to expose themselves lest they be found. It was the oldest defense that innocence has against the dark: if they couldn't see the monsters then the monsters couldn't find them.

In this case, it certainly seemed to the boys to be working. It was working, of course, because they were not in danger. Nothing was trying to find them. The shadow eyes could not cross the open expanse of starlit snow to get to them.

However, the boys were hiding from more than just the eyes. They were hiding from being lost. They were hiding from their need for Mommy and Daddy. They were hiding from the dark and from their fear of losing each other, from the cold and from the fact that they were just two little boys, alone in a strange and faraway place; but they could not hide forever.

The boys continued to calm down and began to feel even safer under the blanket. Owen started to grow restless. He got that feeling like when he played hide-and-seek and realized that whoever was "it" was no longer seeking him.

He again whispered, "I think they're gone."

Oliver whispered his frightened reply, "No, Owen!"

"Oliver, you can stay under here. I'll just peek."

Owen was starting to feel almost giddy with bravery. Under the blanket, he and Oliver were in their own world. After spending enough time in that world of their making, Owen had unconsciously made up rules for it. That was how he'd decided that it was okay for him to safely peek out.

Oliver whimpered in answer to this. He didn't want Owen to look. He wanted him to stay under the blanket with him.

"It's okay, Oliver, just a real quick peek."

Oliver was very frightened for Owen, but he was also in complete awe of his courage. Owen was his hero. It was like he was a grownup. Oliver knew that grownups weren't afraid of *anything*.

Owen parted the blanket just enough so that he could see out with one eye.

Oliver tensed his whole body in anticipation of he knew not what. The suspense was such that he felt he couldn't breathe.

Owen saw only snow. He had exposed himself enough to see out and nothing had happened. He sensed no danger so he pulled the blanket back and poked his whole head out, careful not to expose his brother. Aside from a burst of adrenaline, again nothing happened. Owen saw only the peaceful winter night. The eyes were gone.

He excitedly said, "It's okay, Oliver!"

Oliver hesitated for a moment, then he parted the blanket and looked out with just one eye, as Owen had done. He did what Owen referred to as his "turtle thing," hunching down and trying to tuck his head between his shoulders as he sometimes did when he felt unsure. He, too, saw only snow. He heard Owen gasp in wonder. Oliver's curiosity, fed by his trust in his brother, forced him from hiding. Oliver pulled the blanket down to his tensed shoulders and followed Owen's gaze up to the night sky.

For the first time since they had arrived in that land, the boys looked up at the stars. The vision was overwhelming. It was a perfectly clear night, without so much as a wisp of cloud to disrupt the endless sea of stars, the likes of which the boys had never before seen.

Owen and Oliver had lived in a city whose lights and haze of pollution had brightened the night sky and hidden most of the stars. In the magical land there were no lights. The boys saw more stars than they could ever perceive, each one twinkling brightly through the clear, cold night air.

The boys sat in stunned silence with their necks craned upward. Their breath froze in the cold and wafted up, lit by starlight. Each breath lingered in their vision for just a moment before fading into nothing. They were a little frightened by the vastness of what they saw. It was all so big, and it was all for them.

Oliver whispered, "*Whisses...*"

From the first time that Oliver had sat on his Mommy's lap and made a wish on a star, he had called them wishes.

Owen said, "I bet you couldn't make that many wishes in your *whole life.*"

This made Oliver giggle. He picked out a star and made a wish. He wished that someday Mommy could see these stars with him. He knew that she would like that.

Owen wished that someday he and Oliver could find a way home. Then he lowered his gaze to the endless snow.

"Oliver! Look at the snow! It's magic!" Owen no longer whispered, but still his voice was hushed in reverence of the peaceful stillness around him.

Oliver made one more secret wish and then looked down at the snow where the boys sat. He picked some up and put it in his mouth. It didn't *taste* magic.

"No, Oliver! Look out there!" Owen pointed out over the frozen plain.

Oliver looked and saw yet another sight to fill him with wonder. The clean, unbroken snow was sparkling with starlight. As he moved his head, Oliver watched endless points of light appear and vanish, as if the snow were made of glitter.

"Oliver, your feet!"

Owen had looked down at his brother's poor, frozen bare feet and became alarmed. They were scarlet with cold. Immediately Owen grabbed them and tried to warm them in his hands. He was frightened by how cold they felt.

Oliver whimpered as he let Owen warm his feet. It was painful and the alarm in his brother's voice had scared him.

The enchantment that winter's beauty had cast over the boys was partially broken. They felt the cold once more. Owen pulled Oliver up onto his lap and wrapped the blanket more tightly around them. He made sure that Oliver's feet were inside the blanket.

"Owen, I col'," Oliver whined.

Owen put Oliver's unprotected bald head against his chest and covered it with the blanket. In order to protect Oliver's feet, Owen had not left enough blanket to cover his own head. His ears were red and starting to ache. He felt his backside going numb in the snow. It didn't matter. His brother, his treasure, was safe and warm. Under the blanket, Oliver snuggled against Owen's warmth and soon fell asleep. Owen did not sleep for a long time. The brothers' shared body heat would keep them from freezing but they would still have to endure a long, cold night.

Since Owen did not feel sleepy, he sat and looked out over the frozen land. He was moved by its beauty. His eyes drifted up to the sky. All of those stars made him feel small, and very lonely. It wasn't quite a sad lonely, and it didn't necessarily make him wish for company - not even his Mommy and Daddy's.

Owen was feeling something new, something very grown up. He liked that he could feel Oliver's chest rise and fall with his breathing. Owen's flight into Winterland had saved them from the shadow eyes. He thought about this, and it made him feel another new thing. It gave him hope, and made him believe in himself. He was four years old. He was a big boy now. He could take care of his baby brother.

Owen watched the stars move across the sky. He saw several falling stars and they made him feel special. He knew that no one else saw them but him. After a while Owen parted the blanket just enough so that he could kiss his sleeping brother's bald head. When he did, he felt the first bits of fuzz that would become Oliver's long, strawberry locks. This also filled Owen with hope. Oliver really was all better.

Owen whispered, "I love you, Oliver," and then he finally went to sleep.

The boys were awakened by a snorting sound. They were disoriented, having forgotten where they were or how they had gotten there. They both shivered with cold.

Oliver let out a low, moaning vibrato through his chattering teeth, "Unnuhnuhnuhnuhh..."

Owen was so cold that he didn't want to move. His legs and backside were numb, and the rest of his body was wracked by violent shivers.

As his senses woke up, Owen looked around. Several large animals were wading through the snow all around the boys, their breath seeming to fill the air with steam. Owen was slightly alarmed, though the animals did not look mean.

Oliver pulled the blanket from his head with shaking fingers and saw that the sky was a pale shade of lavender. He then saw the animals and let out a shaking exhale that was as close as his chilled body could come to producing laughter. He shared none of Owen's concern. In fact, Oliver was delighted by the animals. He had as much trouble speaking as he'd had laughing, but he stuttered the word, "Mmmuh-mmuh-muh...muh-muh-*moo-moos*!" He thought they were cows.

Oliver's amusement made Owen feel silly for having been afraid of the animals. He laughed with the same shaky breaths as Oliver.

The animals did look a bit like cows. They had shaggy, piebald fur and large, liquid eyes, but their bodies were lower to the ground than any cows that Owen had seen, and they had a strange wedge shape. The animals' haunches were wide, at least five feet across, with tails that dragged in the snow, but then their bodies narrowed so that their shoulders were only half as wide as their backsides. They had funny ears that made Owen think of his neighbor's pet lop-eared rabbit.

Every time one of the animals snorted, its breath shot out in a frozen plume that made Oliver laugh. Owen laughed, too, but more at Oliver's delight than at the animals themselves, though they were indeed funny.

Oliver threw back the blanket and stood up in the snow. He wanted to pet the funny animals. He took two steps before his bare feet felt frozen.

"Owen! Up!"

Oliver stood there, hopping from one foot to the other and holding out his arms for Owen to pick him up. He ignored his own shivering and his chattering teeth. He *really* wanted to pet the moo-moos.

Owen's lips were blue and he was still shaking uncontrollably. He tried to stand up but his legs were so numb that he fell over. When the snow touched the bare skin on his hands and arms, Owen shook worse than ever. He suddenly felt like crying. He had never been this cold in his life.

Oliver daintily limped through the snow and grabbed Owen's hands. He pulled, trying to get Owen to stand up. Owen saw that Oliver was also shivering uncontrollably, but that he wasn't letting it stop him, so, Owen stood up. As soon as he did, Oliver tried to jump into his arms to get his freezing feet out of the snow.

Owen cried, "Wait, Oliver!" but it was too late. Both boys tumbled over into the snow.

"I said '*wait*,' Oliver!"

Owen angrily picked himself up. He felt slightly warmer, now that he was moving. He picked up the blanket and shook the snow from it.

Oliver was on his back, holding his hands and feet out of the snow. He was yelling at Owen to be picked up, but Owen ignored him and stomped around in a circle, warming himself.

"*Pet a moo-moooooos!*" Oliver was whining now.

Owen looked at his brother, lying in the snow and crying. His anger melted away. He wrapped Oliver in the blanket and picked him up. It wasn't easy, even as thin as Oliver's cancer had made him.

Still shivering, Owen cautiously approached the nearest of the animals. When he got close enough, Oliver reached out and stroked the creature's fur with one timid finger. The animal gave a loud snort and both boys jumped. Owen almost dropped Oliver. The boys laughed nervously at themselves. They were in a very excitable state, thrilled by the unexpected interaction with such a beast. The animal turned its large head and looked at the boys, who looked back and giggled uncontrollably. The moo-moo's dull stare seemed awfully friendly, so with giddy anticipation Oliver reached out again, this time burying his whole hand in the creature's fur.

Oliver's eyes grew big with delight. "I'ss wah-um!" He leaned over and pressed his face against the side of the animal and let out a satisfied sigh. "Mmmmmmmm..."

The animal seemed to like this. It turned its head to the boys again and with its soft, wet tongue it licked Owen's face.

"Ewwww! Stupid cow! Gahhhh!"

Oliver squealed with delight. His eyes grew bright and he chuckled, his smile so big that he couldn't close his mouth.

Owen pretended to be angry but he, too, was delighted. The animal liked him.

Some of the other animals nearby had paused in their march to come over and inspect Owen and Oliver. Their backs only reached about as high as Owen's chest. They sniffed and snorted all over the boys, who cackled with laughter. It would not quite be accurate to say that the boys were scared, for they were having too much fun; a better word would be exhilarated, like when the merry-go-round started moving before they were ready. The animals apparently decided that the boys were not a threat, or perhaps that they weren't very interesting, because they shortly began to move on, all except the one that Oliver had been petting.

Owen's arms were burning after holding Oliver for so long. He had a sudden impulse and he followed it without thinking it through. He heaved Oliver up and onto the lingering cow-creature's back.

"*Aaaiiieeeeeeeeeeeee!*" Oliver did not agree that this impulse should have been obeyed. "No, Owen! Down! Down! Down! Down! Down!"

The animal started to move and Oliver started to cry.

Owen laughed at his brother, and it must be admitted that not all of his laughter came from a good-natured place. Big brothers *will* pick on their younger siblings, after all.

Owen trotted a few steps and caught up to the beast. He tried to hand the blanket to Oliver but he refused to take it. Oliver clutched Odie tightly, afraid that he was going to fall off of the moo-moo or worse, be carried off without Owen. Owen threw the blanket across the animal's back and heaved himself up. It was tricky with the animal moving, but he managed not to fall.

"See, Oliver? It's okay, like riding a horsey! You always wanted to ride a horsey!"

Oliver was already digging his cold feet in the warm fur, but he stubbornly refused to admit that he liked being on the animal's back. "*No* hossy, *Owen!*" Oliver spit these words angrily.

"I know it's not a horsey!"

"Down, Owen! No like diss!"

The cow-like animal trod along, oblivious to the bickering boys on its back. It had rejoined the herd. Some of the other animals glanced at the unusual sight, but they didn't seem very interested.

"Oliver! You don't have any shoes! You can't walk in the snow!"

Oliver pouted, "Cay-wee me!"

"I can't carry you all stupid *day*! You're too heavy!"

Oliver let out an angry, "Hmmmm!" but Owen could swear he saw a smile trying to force its way onto Oliver's face. Oliver's eyes were squeezed menacingly and his lips were pressed tightly together, but the corners of his mouth were twitching, and his dimples didn't show like that when he was truly angry.

Owen inched over so that he was next to Oliver. He was very careful that he didn't fall off. He wrapped the blanket around them both and said, "Hyah! Hyah!" to the animal.

The beast took no notice of this but Oliver finally started to laugh. He mimicked his brother, "Hi-*ya*! Hi-*ya*!" as if he were karate chopping.

The boys began to enjoy their ride in warmth and safety. Once Oliver had gotten used to it, he was in heaven. Every time the animal slipped, Oliver squeezed its fur and yelled, "Whoa!" Every time it snorted (which was often), Oliver had another attack of the giggles.

Owen couldn't decide if he was having more fun riding the moo-moo or watching Oliver. After awhile, he jumped down to gather some snow for them to eat, after which they lay down together on the creature's warm, wide haunches and fell asleep.

The boys' dreams were affected by the swaying movement of the animal on which they slept. For the first time since arriving in the land, both of the boys had good dreams.

Owen dreamt of Mommy. They were lying in a hammock together. It was summertime and there was green grass all around, and flowers and a warm breeze. Mommy was holding him and telling him that she loved him over and over as they swung from side to side. It was just the two of them, and it made Owen feel very special.

Oliver dreamed that Daddy was carrying him. Daddy was there in the magical land with him. He had come and found Oliver. He was taking Oliver to something, a special surprise. Daddy walked across fields and over hills with Oliver in his arms. Oliver started to get excited when he knew they were getting close to his surprise. Daddy was climbing a hill and when they reached the top he would see it. There was the top; they were almost there. They crested the grassy hill and Oliver saw that his surprise was Daddy. He was standing at the bottom of the hill, waiting for Oliver. Daddy seemed to be glowing. There was an orange light all around him and he was smiling like Oliver had never before seen him smile. Oliver ran to him and Daddy picked him up and hugged him. Daddy never said a word. He just held Oliver and Oliver held him back, and was happy.

Owen awoke slowly. He felt rested, but he also felt very hungry. The herd of animals had stopped and were eating tiny red berries from bushes with pointy green leaves. The lavender sky had turned gray, and snowflakes softly drifted down.

Owen had to go to the bathroom but he didn't want to leave Oliver alone. He was afraid that the animal would run away without him. Owen smelled that Oliver was dirty and that was when he noticed that they were both wet, although he couldn't tell if he had wet himself or if it were Oliver's.

Owen gently shook his brother's shoulder.

"Oliver? Are you awake?"

Oliver opened his eyes and smiled. *Daddy's here!*

"Oliver, I have to get down. You wanna stay up here?"

Oliver nodded, then he saw that the herd was eating and said, "Owen, hungwy!"

"Me, too. Just wait a minute."

Owen hopped down and almost fell over. Away from the animal and the blanket, Owen immediately felt the cold hit him and he shivered. The animal paid no attention. The herd was gathered around all of the bushes so Owen walked a short distance and went to the bathroom in the open snow. Oliver watched and giggled at the rising steam.

When Owen was done he grabbed a handful of snow and wiped himself. It was very cold on an extremely sensitive part of his body and he yelled out. His whole body tensed and he involuntarily raised up on his tippy-toes. It wasn't altogether an unpleasant sensation, so when he finished laughing at himself, he did it again.

Oliver was laughing so hard that his face was turning red, until Owen started to walk back toward him and said, "Your turn, Oliver!"

"*Whut?* No, Owen!"

"*Yes*, Oliver!" Owen though to himself, *this is going to be funny.*

"No way! No way! No WAAAYYYYYY!" Oliver was shaking his head so hard that he made himself dizzy.

"Yes way! C'mon, Oliver! You're all stinky! If we don't wipe you off, the moo-moo's gonna knock you off its back!"

Oliver looked mistrustfully down at the moo-moo. Then he looked back at his brother.

"No sooz, Owen!"

"You can wear mine. It's only for a minute!"

Owen approached the animal that Oliver was sitting on while Oliver's mind raced to think of more excuses why he couldn't get down. He couldn't think of any, but Oliver always kept an ace up his sleeve: "NO! No no no no no no no no no no no no *NO!*"

Owen let out an exasperated groan and rolled his eyes up to the sky. "Fine! You can stay up there."

Owen bent down and started packing together clumps of snow. He stopped after each one to warm his hands in his shirt. When he had three good-sized snowballs he piled them on the animal's broad back, next to his brother. Oliver realized what Owen was doing and he knocked the clumps of snow to the ground.

"Oliver! Stop it!"

"No no no! Hungwy!"

Owen was getting very cold. He was wearing only his t-shirt and now it was wet from warming his hands. His teeth started to chatter. His next words came out shaking.

"I'll check the berries *after* we wipe you, and I'll let you play with the car."

"*Beh-weees!*"

"C'mon, Oliver. I'm *cold!*"

Oliver looked at his brother and saw that he was shaking. He didn't want Owen to be cold. In a sad and resigned voice, he said, "'Kay, Owen."

Owen made three more clumps of snow, put them on the animal's back and climbed up. This got a snort and a tail-swish from the moo-moo, and then it went back to grazing. Before cleaning his brother, Owen wrapped himself in the blanket with him to warm up. He didn't wait very long, though. He was afraid that the animals would finish eating and leave the berry bushes behind.

When Owen was ready, Oliver lay on his back and obediently put his feet in the air. He held on to the animal's thick fur. When Owen pulled his pajama bottoms off and the winter air hit Oliver's bare bottom, his eyes opened very wide and he sucked in a breath of air in surprise.

"'At's *col'!*"

Both boys laughed and Owen said, "It's gonna get a lot colder!"

"No, Owen!"

The boys made a comical sight. Oliver lay on his back with his feet resting on Owen's shoulders to keep his dirty bottom off of the animal's fur. Owen tried his best to shake the poop out of Oliver's pajama bottoms while trying to balance Oliver's legs, all the while laughing so hard that he could barely breath. Owen then turned the pajamas inside out and rubbed them with a clump of snow while Oliver repeated in a throaty whisper, "Iss col'...iss col'...iss col'..."

Owen laid the pajamas across the animal's shoulders and picked up a clump of snow.

"Ready, Oliver?"

Oliver was giddy with anticipation. His legs started to shake, making him bounce up and down. His brows rose high over eyes that were dancing with gleeful trepidation. There was a laugh ready and waiting behind his nervous smile. When the cold snow touched his bottom, Oliver cried out in surprised amusement. As Owen did his work, Oliver made noises that were somewhere between laughing and screaming. It was *really* cold and it tickled. Oliver's legs straightened reflexively, trying to get his bottom away from the cold snow. His heels dug painfully into Owen's shoulders, but Owen kept working.

When Owen finished, he helped Oliver put on his cold and wet pajama bottoms and the boys huddled under the blanket. The animal's heat soon had them warmed up and no longer shivering. That was the high point of the day. It would be hard to say which of the brothers had a better time. Unfortunately, the good mood didn't last.

The berries ended up tasting awful and Owen spat them out. To ease Oliver's whining at this, Owen actually let him try one. Oliver, too, spat it out and started to cry.

"*Hunnnnngwyyyyyyy!*"

"I know, Oliver! Me too!"

Nothing could cheer Oliver up after he found that the berries weren't good to eat. Sitting atop the moo-moo was but a temporary distraction. Eventually Oliver wanted to get down but without shoes he couldn't. To pass the time, he did his best to annoy his big brother so that he would be miserable, too.

Owen tried not to get angry. He talked about nice things and made faces to make Oliver laugh, but nothing worked. When Oliver threw the matchbox car in the snow, Owen stopped trying to be cheerful and just let him pout for a while. Owen had to get down from the warm animal and dig in the snow to find the car. By the time he did he was so cold and angry that he told himself he would never let Oliver play with it again. Of course, Oliver screamed at him to give it back until Owen was fighting the urge to push his brother off the moo-moo's back.

The boys grew so aggravated with each other that they started slapping at each other's legs and arms. They made each other cry and scream until the beast beneath them finally grew annoyed and gave its rump a shake. The boys almost fell off and it scared them into stillness as efficiently as would a sharp word from Mommy or Daddy.

After a few seconds of silence, Oliver started to quietly sob. Without the distraction of fighting with his brother, he was no longer angry, just hopelessly sad. The cold and hunger, Owen not letting him have the toy; these were merely portals through which much deeper traumas flooded into him.

Everything bad that had happened, not just since they had come to this strange land, but since he could remember, seemed to fill him up. This little boy, who was hardly more than a baby, had been through so much.

Oliver was weary in his heart, weary far beyond his tender age. His illness had taken so much from him. He had sat by the window in his hospital room and watched other children laugh and play outside in the sun, knowing that he couldn't join them but without understanding why. He couldn't even run around his room because he was attached to an IV pole, and often he was too nauseous or in too much pain to want to move, anyway. He had been ripped from the safety of his crib at home and made to sleep in a metal crib in a strange place. Instead of hearing his brother's voice and soft breathing when he lay down to sleep at night, he had heard machines beeping and unknown children crying and screaming in the rooms next to his.

The doctors had cut him open and put something under his skin in his shoulder, and every few days the nurses had poked needles through it. He had been constantly poked and pricked by needles; in his arms, his hands and fingers, even in his feet. When he couldn't breathe they had held him down and forced a mask over his face. The mask had forced air down his throat and it had hurt his insides. He had fought as hard as he could and screamed and screamed but they wouldn't stop, even when he had begged them, even when he had screamed *please!* It had been the same when they had pushed the tube in his nose and down his throat, all the way to his stomach. He had gagged and choked and screamed but they had held him down and made him swallow it all.

He had loved apples and strawberries but the doctor had said that he wasn't allowed to eat them anymore, not even bananas. They hadn't even let him eat chocolate. There had been a time when he hadn't been allowed to eat a single bite of food for weeks, and another time when they hadn't let him have even a drop of water for days. His lips had dried and cracked and his tongue had swelled; he had been so thirsty.

Several times they had strapped him down and put him in a big, scary machine. The machine had been so loud that it had given him nightmares.

There had been more, so much more, and all of it came crashing in on him. His heart hurt so much. Now he was here with Owen in this scary place without Mommy and Daddy. Owen was being mean to him and the black eyes hated him and wanted to get him. They *would* get him. It would be worse than ever. He ached for his Mommy. He wanted to go home.

Oliver did not specifically think about any of this but it was all there, in vague but powerful and upsetting images. He was far too young for such pain to have faded, even when most of the actual details of his memories hid from him as they did now, so that he didn't understand why his heart was breaking. The pain behind these memories rose to the surface, joined and overlapped into something that he didn't recognize and it overwhelmed him.

Oliver was generally a very happy child. His good memories far outnumbered the bad, even during his illness, but sometimes they weren't enough, and so he wept.

Owen was frightened by the quiet intensity of Oliver's tears. He wanted them to stop, but he didn't know what to do. Whenever Oliver had been like this before, Mommy or Daddy had always been there to comfort him. Owen made a clumsy attempt to cheer him up with a pat on the shoulder. When it did nothing, Owen felt discouraged. He had been through his own bad times, after all, and he didn't quite have Oliver's resiliency.

Owen had more of a tendency to dwell on things, keeping them inside. He had developed this natural trait even more throughout Oliver's illness. The adults around him had become so sensitive that often Owen had suffered in silence rather than ask a question that would upset them, or express a fear that he would only see mirrored in their expressions. This had made Owen's emotional state more delicate, but constantly having so much just under the surface also steadied him in a way.

When a storm of emotions hit Owen, he did not become quite so lost in it as did Oliver, to whom it was so rare. Owen just had to dip below the surface to succumb to his emotions, and so he did not have as far to travel back up into the light. When Oliver was overwhelmed, he sank much deeper, and was often lost in the darkness much longer. Even Mommy and Daddy had always had to work very hard to cheer him up, and they were *grownups*. Still, Owen couldn't just sit and watch his baby brother's heart break, so he did the best he could to find a happy Oliver and bring him back into the light.

The herd had finished grazing and was moving on across the frozen fields. The light snowfall had stopped and the lavender sky had returned slightly darker, for the sun had traveled a good part of the way toward setting.

Owen offered the matchbox bus to Oliver (against his better judgment), but Oliver ignored it. He next offered to climb down and get some snow for them to eat, but it was as if Oliver hadn't heard. He laid Odie across Oliver's lap, but this, too, was ignored. Owen sat back and played with the cars, hoping to draw Oliver's interest. This sort of thing had worked before, but now Oliver didn't seem to notice. He simply continued to cry to himself.

Finally Owen tried talking to him.

"I don't think the eyes will ever come back, Oliver. Doesn't that make you happy?"

Oliver didn't answer.

Owen thought for awhile. He asked, "Do you miss Mommy?"

Oliver's chest hitched and he softly mumbled, "Mmm hmmm."

"I miss her, too. I wish she was here."

"Mmm hmm."

"Do you love Mommy?"

"Mmm hmmm."

"Does Mommy love *you*, Oliver?"

"Mmm hmm."

"Ya think she's thinkin' about you right now?"

Oliver looked up with sad eyes and nodded his head.

Owen said, "I bet when Mommy and Daddy find us they'll give us kisses and hug us for the rest of our lives."

Oliver exhaled a few soft, sobbing breaths, and then he smiled. "Mmm *hmmm.*"

"Odie's here. Does *he* love you?"

Oliver picked Odie up and hugged him. "Mmm hmm."

Owen smiled now. He said, "Where do ya think the moo-moos are goin?"

Oliver looked around. He shrugged his shoulders. "Mm-*mmm*-mm."

"I bet they take us to the North Pole!"

Oliver's eyes grew big. The *North Pole?* He giggled. He didn't know why.

Owen went on. He knew all about the North Pole. "We'd be on the tippy-top of the whole world!"

Oliver raised his eyebrows in appreciation of this grand notion. He smiled a little more. He liked when Owen talked silly like this.

Owen said, "And then they'll jump from iceberg to iceberg until it's warm again, and then they'll swim across the ocean and take us to the jungle. Lions and tigers will try to eat us, but the moo-moos will sit on their heads and squish 'em with their big butts!"

This made Oliver laugh. He finally spoke, "Squish!"

Owen had led his brother back to the light. He talked on about all manner of silly things as the herd of animals trod along. He showed Oliver how to make the animal's fur spasm by lightly touching it. He held Oliver steady while he tickled the animal's ears, and both boys laughed at the way they twitched in annoyance. When they had to go to the bathroom, Owen showed Oliver how to get on his knees and pee off of the side of the animal. The boys laughed at the trail of yellow snow that they made.

The boys were restless, cold, hungry and stiff, but they made the best of things. Oliver's resiliency proved capable of overcoming even these circumstances, and once it did he took over the lead, keeping Owen's spirits up with his light laughter.

With every step, the animal brought the boys closer to the magic pumpkin that would change everything for them. It would change the way they saw the land. It would take away their fear and show them safe places. It would help them to keep and explore the innocence that remained in their hearts and in their fresh, young minds. The pumpkin couldn't keep them from missing their home, nor their Mommy, but it would restore much of their joy. The pumpkin would help to give the boys what they were missing more than anything else: it would make them feel watched over and loved.

As night fell, the herd of animals did a strange thing. They gathered together for warmth with their heads all together and their haunches pointing outward. Their wedge-shaped bodies fit together neatly, allowing them to form tight circles, each consisting of six animals.

Owen looked around and exclaimed, "They look like cow pies!"

CHAPTER SEVENTEEN

The boys spent a very warm and comfortable night curled up in the blanket and in the cow-pie's fur. If they had any nightmares, they did not remember them when they awoke the next morning to the movement of the herd pressing on.

Waking up to find that one is on top of a moving animal can be very disorienting. Both boys woke to the sensation of falling. Their sudden shifts to catch themselves almost caused them to tumble from the cow-pie for real. They sat up and waited for their heart rates to slow and then Oliver said, "Whoa."

The understatement in this single word made Owen laugh. *Whoa* was right. They were riding a strange creature across a frozen tundra under a brilliant purple sky in a magical land. Owen looked around. "Whoa," he said.

It was then Oliver's turn to laugh. After a couple of chuckles he laid his face against the cow-pie's fur and stroked it, murmuring, "*Good moo-moo...*"

Owen checked Oliver's pants and found that he hadn't messed himself. He was relieved at first, but then it occurred to him that it was probably because they'd had nothing to eat in a day and a half. Owen lay back down and stretched himself out on the cow-pie's back. Just this little bit of movement started his hunger pangs, and they were painful.

Oliver continued to coo into the cow-pie's fur but Owen started to get nervous. Where would they find food? He thought about the shadow eyes. He didn't want to go back to where they could get him. He looked across the vast field of snow they had traveled. Could he make the cow-pie turn around? Owen's worries overtook his young mind. He couldn't think when he got like that. Too many questions flooded him at once. He did not know what to do. He looked at Oliver and felt envious of him.

Oliver was hungry, too, and very thirsty, but he was busy introducing Odie to the cow-pie so that they could be friends. The introductions were expressed in a series of wordless sounds, mimicking the tones that Oliver had heard in grownups' voices. Oliver finished and rubbed his stuffed dog on the cow-pie's back and cooed. Now that they were all friends, Oliver proceeded to have a three-way conversation with himself, again voicing no words. He copied the tones of polite conversation in an animated series of hums. Questions were asked, agreements excitedly made, stories were told. Owen became absorbed in his brother's quiet play and forgot about his worries for a while. The cow-pies made their slow progress through the snow, carrying the boys with them.

It wasn't long before Oliver stopped his play and looked up at Owen. "Owen, I doody."

"Oli*verrrrr...*" Owen sighed and checked his brother's pants. It was just a little bit. "You're okay, Oliver. Do you have to pee?"

"Hmm-mm." Oliver said this, followed by a mischievous grin and a devilish twinkle in his eye. He was peeing himself at that very moment and thought it was very funny.

"Oliver! Uhhhh!" Owen rose to his knees and peed as well, sprinkling the passing snow with yellow, as well as getting a few drops on the cow-pie, who didn't seem to care. Owen giggled.

Oliver's amusement quickly faded when he felt a hunger pang cut through his tightened stomach.

"Owen, hungwy!"

"Me too."

"Owennnnn! *Huuunnng*wy!"

"I know, Oliver! I am, too!"

Oliver started to emit a cranky, whining cry.

Owen jumped off the cow-pie and rolled in the snow.

Oliver started to cry harder. He thought that Owen was leaving him (actually, he didn't think that at all, but he told himself that he did so he would have an excuse to grow more upset).

Owen shivered as he packed together two clumps of snow and then he ran and caught up to the cow-pie. He climbed back up with difficulty and offered Oliver some snow. Oliver batted it away.

"No *want* dat!" he whined. He was careful not to bat it so hard that Owen dropped it. Oliver wanted the snow, but he was making a point of being difficult.

Owen did not take the bait. He was growing depressed and had no energy for fighting. He put Oliver's clump of snow on Oliver's lap and then began to eat his own in silence. Owen's hands were cold from holding the snow, and eating it spread a chill through him, but it was better than nothing.

Oliver was fighting an internal battle with himself. He didn't like being ignored. He wanted to knock his snow on the ground to show Owen that he was angry, but he also wanted to eat it. He knew that if he threw the snow on the ground, Owen would not get down to get him more. Oliver was frustrated and couldn't decide what to do, so he did neither. He sat and cried while he watched his snow slowly melt.

As the morning wore on, the boys' moods did not lift. The cow-pie had become like a prison. Oliver couldn't get down without shoes and Owen couldn't leave him. They were stuck there. The boys were bored and irritable. Their hunger pangs grew worse and their young muscles ached for some sort of exercise. They missed their warm beds and their swing set and Mommy and Daddy.

Owen's emotions bounced all around. He was scared and angry and sad, and he was confused by all of the thoughts in his head, none of which offered any comfort. Oliver's constant angry cries did not help. Owen was falling into despair. It wasn't fair. It wasn't fair that they had nothing to eat. It wasn't fair that he had to take care of his little brother when all he did was get mad and cry. It wasn't fair that there was no one to help him. It wasn't fair that they had escaped the shadow eyes, only to be marched across the cold snow forever until they died.

Oliver did not share these thoughts. He was too young to sort through his reasons for being upset, so he was taking everything out on Owen. He didn't even go so far as to think to himself that it was all Owen's fault. He was cranky and there was simply no one else at whom he could direct his crankiness.

Oliver said, "*Hate s'pace!* Hate s'moo-moo! Hate *SNOW!*" and he finally knocked what was left of his snowball onto the ground. Once it was gone, he wanted it more than ever and he had a full meltdown. Oliver had been sitting up, but now he threw himself back against the marching cow-pie and beat on it with his arms and legs. His kicking legs were hitting Owen.

"Stop it, Oliver! Stop it!"

When Owen yelled at him, Oliver started belting out a loud, angry cry. Owen tried to grab Oliver's feet but this only made him kick harder. Owen's temper got the better of him and he punched his brother on his thigh. With a scream of rage Oliver kicked out and his foot caught Owen right in the face. That was too much. Owen's face contorted as tears began spilling down his cheeks and he started wailing loudly. Oliver stopped kicking when he saw that he had hurt his brother but it was too late. Owen was shocked and deeply hurt. With an angry and aggressive grunt, he roughly pushed Oliver off the cow-pie.

Oliver hit the snow and started screaming even louder. Owen did not look back. He sat with his back hunched and his head bowed and he cried. Oliver's spastic shrieks rang in Owen's ears. Owen put his hands over his ears and started to shout, trying to drown out his brother. The cow-pie didn't react. It simply lumbered on.

Oliver rolled around in the snow flailing his arms and legs in a tantrum as other cow-pies stepped around him. He let out one final scream of rage and then lay on his back, sobbing loudly. His feelings were hurt more than anything. He lifted his head and saw Owen moving away atop the cow-pie. Owen was leaving him there. Oliver's anger combined with fear. He screamed his brother's name, both emotions fighting for dominance in his voice.

At the sound of terror in his brother's shouts, Owen looked back. Oliver was already about thirty feet behind him. Owen was still angry. Instead of getting down to go and help, he yelled at Oliver, "Stay down there!" Owen's words could barely form through his sobbing. "I used muh-my suh-special wish to mm-mm-make you better...buh-but all you wanna do is kuh-kick me in the *FACE* an-nnnuuhhh-nnd not play wuh-with me!"

Oliver realized that his brother was not going to help him and he became hysterical.

"Sop, Owen! SOOOOOOOPPPPPP!"

Oliver was crying so hard that Owen did not understand what he had said. Oliver panicked. He got up and started running after the cow-pie, crying as he ran. His bare feet felt frozen. He covered about half the distance before he stumbled and fell. Oliver wanted to stop and curl up where he had landed, but he was too scared of being left behind. His panic forced him to his feet and he continued to chase the cow-pie, still wailing loudly.

Owen watched as Oliver fell twice more. Owen was painfully conflicted but he refused to help. His anger was forcing him to make Oliver do it himself.

Crying harder than ever, Oliver picked himself up for the fourth time and clumsily ran the last bit to the cow-pie. He held out his arms to Owen, who finally relented and heaved his sobbing baby brother up onto the cow-pie's back. Owen brushed the snow from Oliver, put Odie in his hands and wrapped him in the blanket.

The boys looked at each other. Owen looked at Oliver shivering and crying and thought, *Good!* Oliver looked at the swollen red blotch on Owen's face where his kick had landed and suddenly felt very sorry. The cow-pie finally turned its head and looked at the boys with its dull stare. It gave them a loud snort and then went back to the business of moving along.

The boys rode on in silence. Owen buried his hands in the animal's fur, but he did not join Oliver under the blanket. He didn't feel so cold anymore.

As the herd traveled, the air continued to grow warmer. A heavy snow began to fall. The snowflakes stuck together, looking almost like tufts of cotton gently falling from the sky. The cow-pie that the boys rode began to slip more frequently. The animal's slips caused the boys to look up and pay attention.

They had entered a forest. The boys looked confusedly at each other. Where had all those trees come from? They were not evergreens. The bare branches of these tall trees stood out against the cloudy sky and the snowy landscape. The bark of the trees was very smooth, and a warm, dark gray. The snow continued to fall, muffling the sound of the cow-pies' hooves. It clumped on the boys' eyelashes and covered their heads. Within minutes, the trees were covered in soft snow. The boys were spellbound by the enchanted presence that the snow gave to the winter forest. Every last branch, down to the tiniest twig, was swathed in a heavy, yet delicate, layer of snow. The boys did not speak. They simply gasped at the wonderland around them that had seemingly come out of nowhere.

As quickly as it had come, the snowfall ended, casting a colossal stillness upon the land. The clouds began to clear, letting just enough sunlight through to make the snow on the ground and in the trees sparkle endlessly. The boys' necks craned in every direction, taking in every last detail that they could.

A mist slowly began to form, giving the winter landscape an eerie look and feel. Soon the trees became vague shapes that seemed to pass the boys like ghostly forms. The mist thickened until the boys could no longer see the ground over which they passed. The only sound was that of the herd's hooves crunching in the snow, but even that was muffled by the mist. There was a heavy dampness in the air that saturated the boys' clothes.

The boys were not scared. They were roused from their trance, excited by this new phenomenon that they were discovering. They had forgotten that they were supposed to be upset. There was a change happening. The boys sensed it and it awakened an alacritous feeling inside them. They looked all around into the haze that surrounded them.

Oliver pulled the damp blanket off of himself. It was still cold enough for the boys to see their breath, but after the two frozen days they had just endured, the air felt comfortably warm.

"Dis cuh-wazy," Oliver said. His voice sounded harsh in his own ears after the long silence.

Owen said nothing, but the beginnings of a smile formed on his face. He peered into the fog ahead. He could see tall shapes looming toward them.

Oliver tilted his head, listening. There was a new sound. It was a faint and sporadic dripping sound. Unable to see, Oliver used his ears. He tuned into his hearing without the distraction of sight, intrigued by this new and interesting way of perceiving his surroundings. He tilted his head the other way. There was another new sound! He analyzed it. It was the sound that the cow-pies' hooves made, but now the crunch was different. He heard the snap of a twig.

Oliver leaned over the side of the cow-pie and peered at the ground. Owen leaned over the other side. The boys could just make out the dark brown earth through the fading mist. They could see the ground!

"Snow?" Oliver asked.

The question made Owen laugh. "I dunno," he answered.

The boys were transfixed, staring down at the ground as it gradually became more visible. They watched shapes become clearer.

"Owen! Weaves!"

"I *see* 'em!"

"Owen! Wocks!"

"Uh huh!"

"Owen! Duht!"

"Yup!"

"Owen! Yeh-woh!"

"That's not yellow." Owen peered harder. "It's like tan."

The boys had entered the rolling hills of Autumnland. They sat perched on the cow-pie, staring at the ground and watching the wheat-colored grass go by, occasionally seeing dead leaves and sticks that had fallen to the ground. For quite a while they didn't think to look up. It's quite an amazing ability that children have, that they can tune out so much and be fully present to their fascinations. Perhaps even more amazing is their ability to find the most commonplace of things so fascinating, such as the ground passing beneath them.

The boys did not look around them until the cow-pie came to a stop and began to graze on some strange plants. Even then, Oliver continued to study the cottony floss that had burst from the heads of several fibrous weeds growing in a patch below him. Oliver felt Owen tap him on the back and he finally pulled his attention upward.

As with their first view of the starlit sky, the boys sat in open-mouthed wonder at their first sight of Autumnland. They were at the bottom of a wooded hill that sloped up toward a rose-colored sky. There were trees of all shapes and sizes. Some towered into the sky, taller than any trees the boys had seen. Some had broad branches that stretched outward and mingled with the branches of other trees. Some twisted and grew around each other, their gnarled trunks looking ancient and strong. All were filled with fall colors. Some had bright yellow leaves, ("Yeh-woh!"), and some had deep red. Others had brown leaves or orange. Some of the trees had leaves that were red at the base of the stem but which faded into gold with bright yellow tips. Seeing the sun through the leaves was like looking through living stained glass windows. The wheat-colored grass gave way at the foot of the hill to bare earth that was mostly hidden under a layer of fallen leaves that blanketed the ground with warm colors.

Owen hopped down from the cow-pie and then helped Oliver to the ground. The boys were stiff, hungry and thirsty, but they could not resist the urge to explore these colorful woods. The stiff grass was cold and a little painful on Oliver's bare feet, so he dropped to his hands and knees and crawled toward the wood. Owen walked alongside him carrying Odie and the blanket.

Oliver only crawled a few feet before he stopped to look back at the cow-pies. He crawled back to the one that had carried them through the snow. With a big smile, Oliver stood up and wrapped his arms around its neck. The cow-pie ceased grazing and leaned its head against him.

"Good moo-moo," Oliver whispered. He closed his eyes and gave the cow-pie one last squeeze, and then he stepped away and dropped down on all fours to crawl back to where Owen stood waiting.

Owen waved and said, "Bye cow-pies! Thank you!"

"Sank'oo!" Oliver added, and then the boys turned and entered the wood.

The hill was not too steep but the boys made slow progress. They stopped often to inspect pretty leaves that had fallen or to look under them for interesting bugs. The ground was cold but the layer of leaves made it soft so that Oliver could stand up to climb when he had to. His legs were growing stronger with use and with the healing power that was contained in the land's fruits and rivers. Still, the boys made many stops to rest. They grew tired easily, having gone so long without food.

The tallest trees were laden with strange-looking fruit, but those trees had no low branches and their trunks were too thick to climb. The fruit was roughly twice the size of an apple but was ribbed like a pumpkin. The boys looked longingly up at the gold and purple orbs poking through the wine-colored leaves, but could see no way to reach them.

"Owen, hungwy."

Owen craned his neck upward at the fruit high above them. "Me, too."

"Thuhsty!"

"Me, too."

Owen sighed and continued to climb. Oliver followed. The initial awe of Autumnland quickly faded behind the boys' growing need for sustenance. Both of the brothers thought about the cow-pies and felt an urge to go back to them. They had left them behind so easily in their eagerness to explore a new place. Now that the herd was out of sight, the boys again felt very alone. They missed the cow-pies, and they missed their Mommy and Daddy.

Oliver started to whine in a torrent of wordless moans. Owen took his hand to help him up the thickly wooded hill but after a few more steps Oliver sat down and started to cry.

Owen did not grow angry with him. He understood just how he felt. He wrapped the blanket around Oliver's shoulders and sat down next to him. He offered Odie and Oliver took him and held him. Owen put his thumb in his mouth and simply felt the comforting closeness of his brother.

The boys rested, letting the beauty around them slowly recharge their spirits. After a while, Owen looked up at the red sky. It was the first time he had seen the sky take that hue. What had at first accentuated the autumn colors of the trees now began to unnerve him. The sun had already disappeared behind the crest of the hill and the bright red of the sky made it hard to gauge how much of the day had passed. A familiar fear began to creep into Owen's mind.

"Oliver, let's go back."

Oliver's mind had been drifting into sleep. He was roused by his brother's voice. He looked around and saw long shadows everywhere, cast by the tall trees. Night was coming. The realization made him very afraid. He looked at Owen with scared eyes and nodded several times. The boys held each other's hands and slowly made their way back down the hill.

The pumpkin was very close now. Just on the other side of the hill it had begun to glow a little brighter, as if it sensed that the boys were near. It waited to share its joy with them, but first Owen and Oliver would have to endure one more encounter with the shadow eyes, and one more night alone.

The boys' progress down the hill was slow at first, but soon the sky had grown unmistakably darker. From red, it had deepened into maroon and the beginnings of panic sped the boys on faster.

Oliver whimpered nervously. He looked up at the unnatural sky. It did not change hues into purple or deep blue. It simply darkened, as if its red tone were being absorbed by the blackness behind it. The last bit of daylight faded from the sky and Oliver became fully caught in the grip of panic. He squealed with fear and squeezed his brother's hand painfully.

Owen fought between a hopelessness that made him want to give up and stop, and the stark terror that kept him scrambling down the hill. He felt Oliver squeeze his hand and he caught his panic.

The sound of the rustling leaves under the boys' feet seemed to bounce between the trees and come from behind them. They heard an unearthly moaning that seemed to come from everywhere. Monsters were coming down the hill to get the brothers and eat them...

The boys had once again been caught by the shadow eyes.

The boys' haste made them clumsy. The hill seemed much steeper hurrying down than it had climbing up. Owen lost his footing and fell, pulling Oliver down with him. Together they slid through the dead leaves, uncovering dozens of the lifeless black eyes. The boys' skin crawled in revulsion. Oliver's whimpers turned to shrieks and Owen wailed loudly. A dead branch caught at Owen's shirt. It was the monster's claw. It almost had him...

When the brothers' slide came to a stop they did not take the time to even stand up. They scooted down the hill as fast as they could, gripping each other's hands. They pumped their legs and used their free hands to push themselves along. More of the remorseless eyes were unearthed with each swath that the boys' movement cut through the layer of dead leaves.

It was fully dark now. The boys' minds were assaulted with terrible images. They each became terrified that something was under the leaves; something they did not want to see. Again the shadow eyes attacked each of the brothers with what they loved most.

Owen could not shake the certainty that he was holding the hand of some creature that only *looked* like his brother and that the real Oliver was somewhere buried under the leaves.

Oliver saw his Mommy buried beneath the leaves. Where bits of moonlight shone through dark branches, Oliver thought he saw glimpses of Mommy's skin. The hand that Oliver was using to push himself landed on one of the shadow eyes. He felt the cold, wet orb and started to scream hysterically, thinking that he had put his hand on his Mommy's lifeless face.

The boys reached the bottom of the hill and Owen tried to run, but Oliver was too scared to move. Owen pulled desperately at Oliver's hand until his screams of fear became screams of pain as well.

Owen remembered that this was not his brother. Still, he had to save it, whatever it was. If he abandoned it, he would be left all alone. In the grips of his fear, Owen was not thinking clearly. If Oliver was buried in the leaves, then he could not leave him, but he couldn't climb back up the hill.

Overwhelmed by his anguish, Owen drew in a deep breath but his scream was cut short by a rustling in the leaves above him. In his mind's eye he saw Oliver rising from the leaves and coming for him. In the same way that a nightmare can feed a sleeping mind with comforting and familiar images that terrify against all reason, so the phantom-Oliver's approach made Owen feel more afraid than anything that the shadow eyes had yet tortured him with. Owen grabbed the hands of the screaming thing that looked like his brother and started to drag him away from the hill.

Oliver was screaming for Odie. He had dropped him in his haste to descend the hill. He tried to turn back but something had hold of his hands and was dragging him away. He felt the first eyes open on his body and he tried to roll and kick them off, but the monster that held his hands was too strong. He felt himself being dragged through the grass and then he, too, thought that he heard something (*Mommy*), climbing out of the leaves on the hill. Oliver stopped fighting and let himself be dragged away from that sound that scared him so.

Owen felt the Oliver-thing stop struggling. He lifted him to his feet but Oliver fell forward on his face. His legs had become tangled in the blanket. Owen picked up the creature that had replaced his brother and ran back toward the mist, barely able to see through the darkness and through the tears that blinded him.

The moaning that the boys had heard grew louder. The sound was inhuman and filled with fear. It was all around them. Owen felt an undeniable urge to drop the Oliver-thing that he was carrying but his fear of being all alone outweighed his revulsion. He ran on blindly, the awful moaning seeming to thicken the very air through which it became more and more difficult to move.

The shadow eyes were everywhere, assaulting the brothers' minds with fear and heartache in rapidly changing and confusing images. The mist thickened about the boys. Clouds passed over head, blocking the light of the moon and the stars. Now in shadow, the lifeless eyes opened upon the mist itself, like smoky apparitions.

The shock of this grotesque vision almost stopped Owen dead in his tracks. The shadow eyes were always a terrifying sight, but these ghostly, substanceless forms were worse. As a sunbeam will illuminate bits of dust in the air, so the shadows cast from the clouds in the night sky revealed the shadow eyes' presence, as if they were always there, even when unseen.

Oliver's eyes were shut tight. He was paralyzed with terror. The monster that carried him had already eaten Owen and was going to eat him, too. It was going to eat his hands first...

Owen began to think that the mist was made of the unearthly moaning. It was Oliver's ghost that was moaning. Owen would become trapped in the sound, forever wrapped in his dead brother's misery and loneliness...

With one last effort of will, Owen ran on through the eyes, passing through them as if they were projected images. Oh, but he was so tired. The Oliver-thing was too heavy for his weary arms. Owen stumbled and fell.

The boys were forced apart when they hit the ground and Owen was left clinging to the empty blanket. He instantly lost sight of the Oliver-thing in the thick mist. His mind was assailed in terrible ways, but a memory fought through the storm of the shadow eyes' nightmare: he had escaped them before.

The moaning grew louder than ever, accompanied by deafening thuds as if heavy objects were being slammed together. The boys could hear each other screaming.

Oliver hugged himself and rocked back and forth, unable to do anything else. The monster had dropped him and was looking for him. His panicked cries were swallowed up by the terrible moans all around him. It was his Mommy that was moaning because she could not find him. Oliver was terrified that Mommy would take him and hold him and moan in his ears forever.

Owen swatted at the shadow eyes that hovered on the mist all about him. His hands went right through them, dissipating their forms only to have them immediately reappear elsewhere. He had to run. He crawled toward the sound of Oliver's cries. The mist was so thick that he put his hand on Oliver's leg before he saw it. Oliver screeched and pulled away, as did Owen in surprise.

Owen's yell pierced Oliver's haze of terror and he threw himself in his brother's direction. Having found each other, Owen pulled Oliver up. Holding each other's hands, they ran.

Oliver suddenly felt snow under his feet. Owen heard it crunching under his. The mist was clearing as the temperature dropped. The boys could see each other. They left the mist behind, and with it the shadow eyes. The boys would not see them again for a long, long time.

Oliver dropped in the snow. His feet were too cold to keep going. He instantly huddled into a ball, weeping.

Owen looked around wildly at the whiteness of the snow-covered trees. He saw that they were in a small, shadowless clearing, beyond the reach of the shadow eyes.

He looked at the Oliver-creature. Was it his brother? It was not a nice feeling for Owen to look at his brother, whom he knew and loved so intimately, and feel that he did not know him at all. He stared at Oliver as if he had never seen him before. Being made to doubt such a fundamental and unquestionable bond as that which he shared with Oliver made Owen feel ugly, as if he were a stranger to his own self. The shadow eyes were gone, but the seeds that they had planted in Owen's head had taken root. Such was their power over an innocent mind.

Owen spoke very quietly, "Oliver?"

Oliver did not respond. He was still too upset. *His poor Mommy...*

Owen moved so that he could see Oliver's face.

"Oliver?"

Oliver's eyes were shut. The moaning was farther away now, but both of the boys still twitched at each of the loud thuds that continued.

"Oliver? Please...open your eyes?"

Oliver opened his eyes and looked at Owen. When the brothers' eyes met, Owen gathered his brother in his arms and pulled his feet out of the snow. It was Oliver. It was his brother. Owen held him tight and wept with relief. He untangled the blanket and wrapped it around them both, covering Oliver's head and feet. Oliver snuggled against Owen for more than just warmth. He was safe now. Owen had saved him again.

The boys were utterly exhausted but they did not immediately fall asleep. Owen looked up at the bright white moon, which had come out from behind a cloud. There was a faint corona around the moon, whose light diffused in a fading circle through the clouds around it. The distant moaning and thudding continued. The sound was coming from the mist.

From beneath the blanket Oliver asked in a frightened voice, "S'at Mommy?"

"What? *Mommy?*" Owen was confused by his brother's question. "No, Oliver! That's not Mommy!"

Owen listened for a few moments. He grew calmer and realized that the moans were nothing more than the lowing of the cow-pies and that they must be ramming into each other, making the dull thuds.

"It's the moo-moos," he said.

"*Moo-moos?*" There was both relief and concern in Oliver's voice.

"I think the eyes got 'em," Owen answered.

Oliver poked his head out and looked back in the direction of the sounds. "*Moo-mooooos!*"

Owen said, "It's okay. They'll be okay in the morning."

Oliver made a sad sound, "Mmmm*mmm*."

Owen picked up some snow and held it to Oliver's mouth.

Oliver gobbled it and said, "Sanks, Owen."

Owen tucked Oliver's head back under the blanket and then gathered some snow for himself. He heard Oliver's sleepy voice, muffled by the blanket.

"Owen? I 'ove you."

"I love you, Oliver."

Owen ate his snow for a while and thought. The shadow eyes left him feeling sad and afraid, but he knew now that none of the terrible thoughts and images that they fed him were real. Still, though he didn't know it, gentle tears ran down his face.

He said, "Tomorrow we can go back up the hill and look for somethin' ta eat. We'll just make sure we come back here before nighttime."

Oliver didn't hear him. He was already asleep.

CHAPTER EIGHTEEN

It was still dark when Owen awoke. He could no longer hear the lowing of the cow-pies. He was sitting up with a sleeping Oliver wrapped up in his lap. Owen couldn't remember the dream he'd been having, but its impression remained, leaving him feeling very small, very alone, and very frightened. He looked around at the starlit winter landscape and saw that there was nothing to be afraid of, yet he couldn't shake the vague and overwhelming fear that he felt. Some things were just too big for him to cope with.

He was lightheaded and weak. He was hungrier than he'd ever felt before and he knew that Oliver would be just as hungry when he woke up.

Owen felt very cold. He was also painfully stiff, but when he tried to shift his position, Oliver moaned in his sleep. Owen flexed his legs as gently as he could so as not to disturb his brother. The ache in his legs and his empty belly filled his mind and kept any thoughts from forming but to stand the pain for Oliver's comfort. Owen did not go back to sleep. He sat and endured his suffering for his little brother, keeping his lonely vigil until the sun spread its light into the sky.

At first light, Owen gently roused Oliver so that they could share what would be the first and last sunrise they would ever see over the snow-covered forest of Winterland. Endless clouds of red and gold reached across the sky, warming the boys' spirits if not their bodies. The brothers forgot their hunger as they gave themselves over to the magnificence of the winter dawn, whose colors reflected in the icy landscape, leaving not a single patch of white. Everywhere the snow glowed with pale color. Glistening crystals flashed like sparks in the snow-encased trees and across the frozen steppe beyond. The air itself seemed saturated with warm hues.

The boys did not speak for some time. When the sky finally revealed the light blue cast that it would keep that day, the boys remembered their plight.

"Owen, huuuungwyyyyy..." Oliver whimpered softly.

"Me, too," said Owen. He tried to think of a way to reach those strange apples.

Oliver continued to whimper softly. Unlike Owen, he did not quite see that the images of the night before were not real. He broke his brother's thoughts when he voiced the true source of his misery.

"Mommy gets me?"

Owen looked at his brother in surprise. "What d'you mean, Oliver?"

Oliver did not know how to explain the image of Mommy trying to find him with her terrible moans. He repeated, "Mommy *get* me!"

His whimpers turned to sobs. The shadow eyes had tortured poor Oliver with his mother in many ways. In finally making him afraid of her, it was as if they stolen her from him.

Owen saw that Oliver was frightened but he didn't understand why or how his baby brother could be frightened of Mommy. He said, "But that would be a *good* thing! Wouldn't it, Oliver?"

Oliver continued to sob as his memories of Mommy grew tainted with fear.

Owen was only four, but he knew, perhaps all the more for his tender age, that Oliver needed Mommy to comfort him.

"Mommy *loves* you, Oliver! There's no reason to be scared."

Oliver sobbed harder. The fact that Owen didn't understand made it worse.

Owen went on. "It's not real, Oliver! It's like a bad dream. It's the shadow eyes! That's all!"

Oliver sniffled. He was beginning to clam down. "No' whee-uhl?"

"No! Our real Mommy loves us. She would never scare us! She's at home with Daddy, missing us. When she finds us, she's gonna hug us and kiss us and make it all better."

Oliver smiled gently through his tears, but Owen began to cry now. He wanted more than anything for what he had just said to come true.

He had been trying so hard to take care of his little brother, but he needed someone to take care of him, too.

Oliver was confused by his big brother's tears. He asked, "Why you cuh-why, Owen?"

Owen looked at his little brother. The love and concern that he saw in his eyes helped him very much.

"I'm sorry, Oliver. I miss Mommy and Daddy."

"Me, too!" said Oliver, and he gave his big brother the hug and kiss that Mommy couldn't.

The boys held each other, Oliver with his head buried in Owen's chest, and Owen with his eyes cast up at the snow-covered branches on the trees.

A gust of wind blew a clump of snow from a large branch. Owen watched it fall to the ground. He paused, tilted his head, and opened his eyes wide. He'd had an inspiration.

"Oliver! I know how to get those crazy pumpkin apples! C'mon!"

At the promise of food, Oliver caught his brother's sudden zeal and got to his feet, only to be reminded that he had no shoes. He hopped from one frozen foot to the other with his arms held out to Owen, trilling in his happy impatience to eat. The terrors of the night before had retreated behind his love for Owen, and for Mommy and Daddy, and left him eager to return to Autumnland.

Owen got down on his hands and knees so that Oliver could climb onto his back. Oliver jumped on him with a little too much enthusiasm and both of the boys toppled over, face first into the snow. They laughed in spite of themselves as they brushed themselves off and tried it again. On their second try, Owen succeeded in getting to his feet with his burden intact but they forgot the blanket which was still lying in the snow. Owen bent down to pick it up, careful not to dislodge Oliver, who giddily chimed, "Whoa-uh-wwwwwhoa!" as he held on. Owen wrapped the blanket around his middle to cover Oliver's bare feet and then set off, back toward the wooded hill on the other side of the mist.

The boys' initial excitement for the prospect of food soon wore off and left each of them struggling to endure the long walk back to the autumn trees.

Owen felt dizzy. Every tired step he took felt like it was the last one that he could manage, but each time one of his feet fell, the other lifted and carried him on. Owen learned something that morning. He learned that he could keep going, even when he thought he couldn't. He felt Oliver shivering on his back and so he pushed himself past his limits, his love for his brother giving him the strength that his body no longer had. Oliver was counting on him.

Oliver shivered uncontrollably. His teeth chattered in Owen's ear. It was the boys' third day without food and Oliver's little body had no fuel to produce the energy needed to keep him warm. He was in the beginning stages of hypothermia. He snuggled against Owen's body heat, but he was weak and had a difficult time holding on.

Oliver thought about little but the cold. Unlike his big brother, he had nothing to learn that morning. He had already found that he could count on his brother to take care of him and he blindly trusted that he would.

The boys entered the mist that separated winter from autumn and the warmer air encouraged them to hold on a little longer, though the deep fog seemed to go on much further than it had the night before.

Owen walked, hunched over, watching his feet through the mist as if they belonged to somebody else. Just when he was sure that he had become lost in the whiteness, the mist began to clear. He lifted his head to watch the autumn colors slowly reveal themselves.

Oliver was huddled against his brother's back, staring at the seam on Owen's shirt where his sleeve met his shoulder. The sun appeared, shining in a clear blue sky. Oliver felt its warmth on his back. His teeth stopped chattering and his chills grew slightly less convulsive.

When the boys finally reached the bottom of the wooded hillside, Owen dropped to his knees and fell forward with Oliver landing on top of him.

They disturbed the layer of leaves on the ground and Oliver had a moment of panic. He was terrified that the shadow eyes would still be there like black beetles burrowing in the soil. Owen did not share his fear. He felt himself blacking out and was fighting to remain conscious.

There was of course nothing under the leaves but dirt. Oliver rolled off of his brother but still held tightly onto his warmth. Owen's head began to clear. He felt Oliver shaking and he, too, rolled over and gathered him in his arms to warm him. The boys lay arm in arm on their backs and rested, staring up at the light of the sun that shone through the autumn leaves.

Funny little red and gold animals chased each other up and down the trunks of the trees and jumped from limb to limb. The sight lightened the boys' hearts. They both began to giggle.

Owen mused aloud, "They look like chipmunks."

"Pipchunks!" Oliver yelled. He thought that Owen was making fun of them because they were fat. He was quite amused.

Owen tried out the name. "Pipchunks..." He started to laugh.

The boys said it together several times until they broke out into a song of which *pipchunks* was the only lyric. They drew up their knees and swung them together in time with their singing, rolling their heads and shoulders from side to side. The song went on for an obnoxiously long time. The boys ended it on a high note and Oliver let out a long and amused sigh, "Haaaahhhhhh."

"Ready to eat, Oliver?"

Oliver jumped up and nodded his head up and down, repeating, "Yups yups yups yups yups yups yups yups!"

Owen stood up and looked around on the ground. He found what he was looking for and picked it up. It was a long stick. He yelled, "Look out below!" and swung it up into the branches of the tree above the boys' heads. The stick smacked off of a branch and came crashing back down as the boys laughingly jumped out of the way.

Owen did it again, calling, "Look out belooooow!"

Oliver screamed and squealed with delight at the game, and in anticipation of the coming meal. It took Owen several tries but eventually he managed to hit a cluster of the strange purple and gold fruit and down it came, landing with a rustle in a pile of autumn leaves. The boys jumped on the fruit, which were still attached by their stems. Each brother grabbed one with both hands and pulled until they came apart and the boys fell over backwards. They laughed as they landed in the soft leaves, each with a piece of fruit in his hands.

Oliver did not wait for Owen to give the "okay." He immediately bit into the fruit and was delighted by the taste. It was crisp like an apple, but the taste was something between a pear and a peach, with an aftertaste of honey. Underneath the purple and gold splashed skin, the flesh of the fruit was a soft pink that deepened to a magenta core.

The boys ate noisily, making many a crunch and a slurp and a "yummy" sound. The pumpkin apples were so big that the boys needed to use two hands to hold them. Neither boy was able to finish.

Once Owen was full, he began to play with his food. He broke it open and found tiny seeds in the center. They were a bright lime green and almost seemed to glow in contrast to the magenta core. He tasted one but it was terribly bitter. He immediately spat it out and took another bite of the fruit to get the taste out of his mouth.

"Don't eat the seeds, Oliver. They're terrible!"

So of course Oliver broke open the core of his pumpkin apple and put a seed in his mouth. He, too, spat it out.

"Ucky!"

"I *told* you they were terrible!"

Oliver was holding out his tongue to keep the bitterness out of his mouth. "Ehhhhhh! Uhhhhhh!"

When Owen stopped laughing he said, "Take another bite, stupid-head!"

"*Uuu ahhhh ooooo*," which translates to "but I'm full" with one's tongue stuck out.

"Well then just lick it!" Owen was growing ever more amused.

Oliver licked the pink fruit until the bitterness was gone. "Whew! Sanks, Owen!"

Owen laughed at his brother, who was breathing hard as if he'd just escaped some catastrophe. Oliver looked at him and started to laugh with him. He didn't understand what was funny, but Owen's laughter was contagious.

After eating, the boys lay next to each other in the soft leaves for a while and looked up at the colorful trees, enjoying their full bellies. Owen showed Oliver how to make a leaf angel by swinging his arms and legs. This released the smell of the dried leaves. It was a comforting scent: the scent of autumn.

A soft wind began to blow. It roused the boys to get up and explore. Oliver's feet were cold, but not so much that he couldn't easily ignore them to have an adventure.

They didn't go very far before Owen spotted Odie leaning against a tree. He hurried to pick him up before Oliver could see and then he stuffed the dog in his shirt. He planned to surprise Oliver with Odie by magically producing him when they reached the top of the hill.

Oliver hadn't noticed. He was concentrating on climbing. He wasn't yet very coordinated and he almost fell back down the slope several times. His little legs ached but he ignored them as he did his chilly feet. Children can ignore all sorts of discomforts that threaten to get in the way of their fun.

The autumn air awoke something special in Oliver. Strange as it may be for an eighteen-month-old boy to feel nostalgia, that was indeed what he felt. He didn't understand, but then he was so young that he didn't *know* that he didn't understand. He felt a sense of things past and a fresh newness, all at the same time, as if he were exploring a familiar place. It made him feel alive and yet safe, a feeling of home. Owen had felt something similar in Springland, which would grow to be his favorite place, but Oliver would always love the autumn best.

Owen reached the top of the hill first. He made sure to stay in sight of Oliver so that his little brother would not get scared that he had left him. Owen watched Oliver climb. He wanted to help him but he could see that Oliver wanted to do it himself. As Owen watched his brother's clumsy determination, he was filled with admiration for him. He loved him more than anything else in the world. When Oliver reached the top of the hill, he held out his hand and Owen took it and pulled him up into the long yellow grass.

The boys stood on top of a grassy ridge that sloped gently down into a copse of evergreen trees. They were anxious to climb down into those trees, but Oliver was exhausted and needed to rest. He sat down and Owen sat next to him. A wind was blowing the tops of the evergreens and sweeping up the hill toward the boys. They watched a flock of black birds fly overhead ("Owen! *Buhds!*"), then turn all together and fly into the distance until they looked like tiny dots in the sky. The boys listened to the sound of the birds' fading caws as it was replaced by the swishing sound of the grass blowing in the wind.

Oliver picked a long blade of golden grass and put the end in his mouth as he had seen in pictures of farmers. He wiggled his lips from side to side, making the grass dance and making him giggle to himself. Owen noticed this.

"Oliver! Are you eating *grass?*"

This made Oliver giggle even harder, until it was a struggle for him to keep his lips closed on the blade of grass. He sat and giggled and made the grass dance until his body was shaking with mirth. Each time Owen would say, "No! Bad Oliver! Don't eat the grass!" Oliver would rock back and forth, squealing with closed-lipped laughter. It took several minutes for the boys to tire of this game.

When Oliver seemed rested, Owen asked, "Ready?"

Oliver spit out the grass and nodded. "Yah! Yah! Yah! Yah! Yah!"

When the boys got to their feet, Oliver noticed an orange glow through the evergreens. He remembered his dream.

"DADDYYYYYYY!"

He ran down the hill crying out for Daddy. He was so excited that he almost fell at every awkward downhill step.

Owen made a sidestepping jog down the hill after him, feeling somewhat confused. He couldn't see Daddy anywhere. Still, there was *something*, and it made him feel happy. Oliver disappeared from his view amongst the trees but Owen could still hear him calling their Daddy's name. Owen finally saw the orange glow and his loping jog turned into an eager charge down the hill, though he had no idea what the glow might be.

Oliver ran through the trees and came out on the other side of the copse to find an enormous pumpkin sitting all by itself in the middle of a clearing. He ran up to it and stopped. He tilted his head sideways and scrunched his face in confusion for a moment, then he hugged the pumpkin, closed his eyes and whispered, *"Daddy..."*

Owen emerged from the trees to find Oliver leaning against the pumpkin with his arms outstretched. It was a fat, round pumpkin, so big that the top of Oliver's head only reached about two thirds of the way up its heavily ribbed shell. Swirls of autumn colors danced about in the air all around it. Owen knew right away that it was a magic pumpkin. He ran toward it and stopped right behind Oliver.

Owen reached over Oliver's shoulder and put a hand on the pumpkin. It was nice and warm. Little wisps of color danced around the spot where his hand touched its shell. It was only for a moment and then the colors dissolved into nothing.

Owen felt very happy. A spontaneous giggle escaped him and it felt so good that he giggled some more. He lifted his hand from the pumpkin and put it back down in a different spot to watch the colors swirl again. His giggles mounted into high-pitched peals of delight. Still reaching over his brother's shoulders, Owen repeatedly slapped both of his hands on the pumpkin.

Oliver's ear was pressed to the glowing orange shell. The hollow sound of Owen thumping the pumpkin sounded almost like a heartbeat. The thought made him giggle, but only once before he resumed his blissful state of joy. He murmured again, *"Daddy..."*

Owen heard him and looked at his brother with amusement. "What? Oliver, that's not Daddy! It's a pumpkin!" Owen did feel something familiar about the pumpkin, but he dismissed it as being impossible, and even a bit silly.

Oliver turned his head and looked at Owen with a mischievous and knowing smile that Owen couldn't quite decipher, but that amused him and made him feel happy nonetheless. Oliver then leaned back and smacked the pumpkin as Owen had done, laughing at the colors that rose from its shell. The boys were both enrapt by their discovery, though only Oliver had sensed just *what* they had discovered.

As the sun traveled to its highest point, the boys laughed and played around the pumpkin. Their hearts had found a new lightness. They didn't bicker or fight, not even a little bit. They played tag, using the pumpkin for home base. They chased each other around it, hidden from each other's views but able to hear each other's laughter. They pretended that they were little pumpkins that released colors of their own. They pretended that the pumpkin was a fort, and then their house, and then a castle; and finally, Owen pretended that it was a horsey.

With some difficulty he managed to climb atop the pumpkin and swing his legs around either side of its giant stem. He grabbed the loop of its vine, kicked his heels and yelled, "Hyah! Hyah!"

The pumpkin rose into the air.

Owen screeched with surprise and delight.

Oliver had been leaning on the pumpkin when suddenly it wasn't there anymore and he fell forward on his face. He lifted his face from the ground and screeched as well, but it was hardly with delight. Owen was taking the pumpkin and leaving him. Oliver's tears flowed large and hot, and instantly. He cried the way that any child would when an older sibling has taken their new toy away from them. Oliver started screaming angrily and fearfully at Owen to come back.

As Owen soared away into the sky, he heard Oliver's cries die away and he felt free. He had never experienced anything to compare with this. He couldn't tell if he was controlling the pumpkin or if the pumpkin was taking him wherever it wanted. He didn't care. He almost felt like he could let go of the pumpkin and still soar through the air without it.

For a brief moment, Owen had a vision. He could ride the pumpkin anywhere. He need never worry about Oliver's dirty pants or his whining again. There need be no more finding food for him or waiting up for him. Owen could be on his own, just him and his pumpkin, with no one to worry about but himself. He could be truly free...

The vision startled him. He didn't want that at all. He wanted his brother. Owen could no longer hear Oliver's cries and their absence scared him. No sooner did he desire to go back to him than the pumpkin looped around and flew back the way it had come.

Oliver was curled up on the ground, weeping loudly, when he heard Owen calling his name. He looked up and saw him coming back fast, trailing wisps of color behind him. Oliver stood up.

"*Owen!*"

Oliver started jumping up and down in excitement. As the pumpkin softly floated back to the ground, Oliver marched around it in a circle clapping his hands in time with his steps. He was too happy for words. Owen climbed down from the pumpkin and picked up his little brother in a hug. Oliver hugged him back, cooing softly.

When Owen put him down, Oliver scrunched his face and pointed at Owen's chest.

"Shuht?" Oliver had felt the lump under Owen's shirt.

"Oh! I forgot!" Owen retrieved Odie and handed him to Oliver.

"Odieeeeee!" Oliver hugged his stuffed dog and squeezed him as tightly as he could.

"I found him when we were climbing the hill," Owen explained.

Owen looked at Oliver and smiled. He waited for a couple of moments, very amused that Oliver was so excited to have Odie back that he had apparently forgotten that he had just watched his brother fly through the sky on a giant pumpkin.

"Oliver?"

Oliver raised his eyebrows. "Whut?"

"Dontcha wanna fly on the pumpkin?"

Oliver tilted his head and looked at the pumpkin. It was a very mischievous light indeed that danced in his eyes. He knew that *this* was not allowed. He was scared, excited, and suddenly very impatient to fly through the air like Owen had done.

His eyes opened wide and he started making a strange warbling noise. He was practically hyperventilating. He started to dance in place in front of the pumpkin, holding Odie behind him at arm's length. He shook the stuffed dog at Owen, waiting for him to take it so that Oliver could climb up onto the pumpkin.

Owen laughed and took the dog. He stuffed him back in his shirt and watched as Oliver tried to mount the pumpkin. Owen didn't help him, at first. The sight of his baby brother jumping and trying to climb up the pumpkin was much too comical to be interfered with. He may as well have been trying to jump over a ten foot wall.

Finally Oliver yelled, "Owen! Help!"

This was a process that the boys would refine over time, but that first attempt to get an overexcited Oliver up and seated on the pumpkin was hardly a graceful affair. Owen picked him up under his arms and lifted. Oliver swatted at the pumpkin and kicked his legs in a fruitless effort to climb until Owen put him back down, feeling silly. Owen then got down on all fours so that Oliver could stand on his back. Oliver tried jumping from there but he still came up short and eventually Owen yelled at him to stop breaking his back.

Owen tried to think while Oliver danced from foot to foot looking like he had to pee, and making very impatient noises. The pumpkin released its swirls of color as if it were goodnaturedly teasing the boys.

Finally, Owen told Oliver to stand in front of the pumpkin, then he knelt down behind him. Owen put his hands on the back of Oliver's thighs and pushed him up the side of the pumpkin. Oliver wasn't ready (indeed, he hadn't known what Owen was going to do), and he leaned too far back, toppling over and landing on his head.

Once Oliver had stopped crying and angrily smacking his brother, they tried it again. The second time, Oliver managed to get a hand on one of the pumpkin's vines, but he couldn't pull himself up. Owen stood, planted his hands on Oliver's bottom and pushed him the rest of the way to the top.

Oliver was a ball of nervous energy. He felt very unbalanced on top of the pumpkin so he spread out and held on tightly to the stem. He was terrified that he was going to slide off but at the same time he was giddy with anticipation.

"Oliver! Sit up and put your legs around the stem!"

Owen had no room to climb up himself with Oliver lying spread eagle like that.

Oliver very carefully inched his way into position. Owen threw the blanket at him, climbed up and sat behind him. When Oliver got a little bigger he would sit behind Owen, but until then Owen always placed him in front so that he wouldn't fall off.

"Ready, Oliver?"

Oliver gave a squealing giggle in answer to this and yelled, "No!"

"Too bad!"

The pumpkin rose into the air.

The movement made Oliver feel weightless and tickled him in his belly. He was terrified and filled with rapturous joy. He screeched with laughter as Owen had done the first time. Owen was laughing, too. Now that the brothers were riding the pumpkin together, they left all else behind but the euphoric rhapsody of their magical flight.

Chapter Nineteen

The pumpkin soared across the sky, safely transporting its precious passengers to a new and wonderful place. The boys saw the sun sparkling on the Gold River long before they reached it. The river ran in a straight line across fields of long, golden grasses and weeds. Slender trees with light, milky brown trunks and branches dotted its banks. Their red, star-shaped leaves fluttered in the same gentle breeze that carried autumn seeds through the air, attached to their bits of fluff that caught the sun like floating points of light.

Oliver pointed toward the river in amazement. Even after Owen had excitedly cried, *"I see it! I see it!"* Oliver kept pointing and glancing over his shoulder to make sure that Owen was still looking. As the river drew nearer, Oliver realized that it was their destination. He pointed even more vehemently, his arm fluttering with fervent anticipation. He did not yet understand that it was water, a discovery that would shock his senses with sheer delight.

The pumpkin gently landed in a tuft of swaying yellow grass with what would become a very familiar, hollow *fwump*. The boys' first flight together had been fairly short, but to Owen and Oliver it had seemed endless.

The boys had been transformed by the joy atop which they sat. The pumpkin could not return to them the innocence that the shadow eyes had stolen, but its joy permeated them, renewing their childlike faith in the power of goodness and love. The nightmare of the shadow eyes had not tainted the purity of the boys' youthful spirits, but only forced it to hide. The joy of the pumpkin brought it back into the light where it could shine unafraid; the essence of childhood: an openness of heart and mind that thrilled in love and generosity, discovery and imagination.

Owen slid off of the pumpkin first, then talked Oliver through the process of swinging one leg around its stem and sliding into his arms. He put Oliver down and the boys raced the few steps to the Gold River. They perched on the grassy bank and stared at their reflections in what appeared to be a gold mirror. Oliver was shocked by what he saw.

"Go'ss *hay-uh?*"

Though the boys had only been in the land for a week, the magic in the rivers and in the fruit they had eaten had been at work in Oliver's little body. He was looking at the reflection of a little boy with a full head of hair that was almost an inch long, long enough to lay down on his head. His hair was bright red, having not yet had time to lighten in the sun.

"Owen! Go'ss hay-uh!" Oliver tilted his head and peered harder. "I'ss *wed?*" The last time Oliver had seen himself with hair, it had been blonde. Still staring at his reflection, Oliver ran his fingers over his head and started to laugh.

Owen laughed with him. "Yeah, it started growing when we were in the snow. I just forgot to tell you."

Oliver continued to run his fingers through his soft, new hair. "I'ss wah-ummmm!" The shining sun had warmed his hair, but Oliver thought that it was warm because it was red. This made him very happy. Owen reached over and ran his fingers through his brother's hair.

"It *is* warm! You'll never need a hat, Oliver!"

Both of the boys laughed, to each other and to themselves. They were in quite the jovial mood.

Oliver reached down to touch his reflection and was amazed to find that his fingers went right through it. "Whut zuh heck!" He could see his fingers dancing just beneath the surface, making tiny ripples in the river's slow current. "What its *doing*? I'ss move!"

Owen put his hand in the water and made a splash. "What the heck? Oliver, it's water!"

Both boys cupped a handful of the gold water and took a sip. Their eyes widened and Owen took a deep breath of pleasure. The very thirsty brothers drank handful after handful of the delicious water.

This was why the pumpkin brought them to the Gold River. The boys were thirsty and so it brought them to the nearest water. Of course, the pumpkin couldn't *think*, exactly, but it was almost certainly aware. It seemed to sense the boys' needs as well as their desires and to do its best to respond to them. This was what actually steered the pumpkin. Owen always held the vine as he would the reins on a horse, but it was his thoughts to which the pumpkin responded.

The pumpkin was even able to guide the boys to places they didn't know, for though it had come to be with them, it had grown from the land. When the magic in the soil had passed into it and given it life, the pumpkin had absorbed most of its memories, although some things the pumpkin couldn't know. Everything in the land was connected, but only its beauty went into the pumpkin. None of its darkness had had a hand in the pumpkin's growth, for being made of joy, shadows could not touch it.

The boys drank their fill of the gold water. It gave them a relaxed feeling of contentment. They continued to lay on their bellies on the river's grassy bank and to watch their fingers drifting to and fro in the current. Owen noticed that Oliver was shivering in the crisp autumn air so he got up and retrieved Odie and the blanket. He gave the stuffed dog to Oliver and then covered his little brother with the blanket before he lay back down next to him. That was when the boys noticed a soft, beautiful singing. There were no words, just harmonious voices unlike any they had ever heard.

Oliver started and spoke in hushed tones so as not to disturb the singing. "Owen! Fiss!"

Owen peered through his fingers and saw that Oliver was right. There was a school of fish swaying in the water a few feet below them. The fish had iridescent red scales and long, gently billowing fins that resembled the ruffled, lavender petals of hibiscus flowers.

After watching the fish for a few moments, Owen splashed his hand in the water, hoping to watch them dart away. As one, the school twitched a few feet to its right and resumed its stillness. When the fish moved, the singing built up to a crescendo and then steadied back to its peaceful, sonorous notes.

Oliver and Owen both wore a querulous tilt to their heads. Oliver splashed the water with more gusto, using both hands. With a flash of sunlight on their scales, the fish swam a ways upstream. The music ascended with their movement and faded slightly, now that the fish were farther away.

The boys turned to each other with a comically slow movement, their brows raised high over wide eyes that were having trouble believing what they had just seen. The fish were *singing*. The boys were so thrilled by this that their bodies shook with merriment. They tried to stifle their laughter so as not to scare the fish away, but that only made it build up inside them. Finally Oliver's mirth burst from between his tightened lips with a sound that was very like the razzberries. Owen continued his soundless, laughing breaths and the boys turned back to stare in awe at these mesmerizing fish.

The boys slowly calmed down, enthralled by the alluring notes of the school's voices. They weren't like human voices, nor like any instrument that the boys had heard. The notes were less airy than a flute's, but didn't cut as deep as a violin's, nor did they blare out like a brass horn's. The notes were soft yet clean; clearer than a whisper but with a delicate vibration, as if the water through which they traveled to reach the boys' ears added its own movement and life to the music. Oliver unconsciously reached out his hand. Owen took it and held it as the brothers were slowly lulled to a peaceful, dreamless sleep.

The sun inched its way across the cloudless sky. A cool breeze rustled the dry grass and the leaves in the few trees that dotted the riverbank, caressing the boys' slumber with peaceful sounds. Pipchunks played and chased each other up and down the trees.

After a time, the boys awoke together. They each opened their eyes to find the other looking at them and smiling. They felt truly rested, like they hadn't since they had first awoken in that magical land.

The boys didn't speak at first. For a few moments they were all that existed in the world, and this made them happy. They simply enjoyed each other and the pure love that they shared. They started to giggle softly as this enjoyment welled up and overflowed. Little by little the world around them came into focus. They heard the sounds of the wind. They felt the grass beneath their heads. Together they watched a strange and tiny insect crawl across a blade of beige grass between them. The insect looked very friendly as it trudged along, its wings hidden beneath an orange and green shell. The insect's wings buzzed once, twice, and away it flew. The boys lifted their heads to watch it fly away and then they finally sat up and looked through new eyes at the autumn grandeur all around them.

It is amazing how much easier life's goodness and beauty penetrate the heart of a well rested child. Neither of the brothers could remember ever feeling this good. Long before they came to this land, the brothers had suffered restless nights and tired days. Owen's nights had long been haunted by loneliness and fear for his little brother. Oliver's rest had always been tainted by sickness and pain. When he fell into a deep sleep at the hospital, it was always interrupted by the beeping machines or the procedures and medicines for which he needed to be woken every few hours, even throughout the night. Now Owen had awoken to his brother's hand in his, and Oliver's sickness was gone.

"Owen, hungwy."

Owen took a deep breath and looked around. An ear-to-ear grin spread across his face when his eyes rested on the pumpkin. He stood up and helped Oliver to his feet. "Let's ride the pumpkin to some food!" he said.

An identical grin spread across Oliver's face. He ran to the pumpkin and got into position to be lifted atop it. A few squeals of anticipation escaped him and his hands balled into excited fists. Owen knelt down behind him and boosted him up. Oliver kicked his legs and grabbed wildly at the pumpkin's vine, his bottom resting on Owen's shoulder. Owen couldn't help but notice that Oliver needed to be changed but he was in too good a mood to care about that right then.

Shortly Oliver was up and Owen was seated behind him. The pumpkin lifted into the air and the boys giddily enjoyed the sensation of their tummies being left behind, breaking out into laughter when they finally settled.

Having no clear idea of what he wanted to eat, Owen simply pretended to steer the pumpkin while it took them to the nearest food. The pumpkin crossed the Gold River and flew a short distance over the rolling hills. It followed the rising land up and over a ridge to unveil for the boys a majestic sight. Climbing the slopes of a series of golden-brown hillocks was an entire forest of fire trees (though of course, the boys had not yet given them that name).

"*YEH-WOHHHH!*" Oliver cried out excitedly.

"Whoa, pumpkin! Whoa!" Owen thought that the pumpkin was going to fly them straight into what he mistook for flames.

The pumpkin brought the boys to rest several yards from the nearest trees. The boys hopped down and ran to them, but were confused when they could feel no heat. A slight wind blew through the yellow leaves causing them to flit about, adding to the illusion that they were flames. Oliver walked right up to one of the slender white trunks and jumped at a low hanging branch. Owen yelled at him to stop, but Oliver pulled the branch down and grabbed a handful of the feathery leaves with a giggle. Owen had followed behind him and now grabbed some of the strange leaves himself.

"What the heck? I thought they were on fire!"

Oliver looked over his shoulder at his older brother as if he were being silly and gave him a flippant chuckle, although truth be told, Oliver had also thought that the leaves were flames but had wanted to grab them anyway. He was only a year and a half old, after all.

Owen pulled on the branch until with a loud crack it broke off of the tree. He landed hard on his bottom to the sound of more of Oliver's amused chuckles. Owen tore a leafy sprig from the branch and handed it to Oliver to play with and then he inspected the rest. He was fascinated by the smooth, white bark and the softness of the leaves. He ran his fingers over the wood while Oliver ran about waving his sprig and pretending that it was a torch.

The breeze was warmer here than it had been by the Gold River, for the boys were near the border of Summerland. The sunshine bounced off of the white trunks, filling the copse with an airy light. Above the boys, a blanket of sunlight dappled through the delicate yellow leaves, lending an intangible weightlessness to the boys' spirits. There was a sweet and rich scent in the air that vaguely reminded the boys that they were hungry.

The boys switched places. Owen stood up with the yellow leaves between his fingers and began to run around pretending that he was on fire. Oliver, while swishing his "torch" at the ground, had noticed some beautiful, deep red leaves growing out of the wheat-colored grass and sat down to inspect them.

Oliver suddenly missed his Mommy very much. He thought that she would like the pretty leaves so he decided to pick some for her.

He pulled on the leaves and was surprised to find that their potato-shaped root came easily out of the ground. Oliver's rumbling tummy overrode all else and he broke the root open, exposing its orange flesh and releasing the scent of cinnamon and sugar.

A scene followed of covetous feelings and angry words between the two brothers, but eventually more roots were found, tears were dried, and happy bellies were filled. Even Odie had gotten to eat his fill. The boys sat facing each other, each with his back against the trunk of a tree and a half-eaten root in his hands.

Owen said, "What *are* these crazy things?"

Oliver concurred, "Deh's *cuh-waaazzzzzy!*"

"I know! They're like potatoes on the outside and carrots on the inside, but they taste like french toast!"

"Fwence toas-tuh!" (followed by giggles).

"They're *ca-french-toes!*" laughed Owen.

"*Whut!* 'At's cuh-wazy, Owen!"

"Okay then, potarrots!"

"Pawwots!"

Owen smiled at his brother and agreed, "Fine, they're parrots."

He laughed at the joke that Oliver would never get, and Oliver laughed with him, feeling very pleased with himself.

Owen sniffed and caught a waft of his brother's dirty pants. "I wonder if the pumpkin can take us to the Green River," he said.

Oliver perked up at this idea. "I'ss *wah-ummm!*" He was tired of feeling chilly.

The boys got up and went back to the pumpkin. Owen was about to boost Oliver up when Oliver remembered the pretty red leaves. He told Owen to stop and then ran back to collect some for Mommy, carefully and lovingly folding them up in the blanket to keep them safe. He walked back with a beaming smile on his face and explained to Owen, "Mommy!"

The boys again clumsily mounted the pumpkin. Owen held the vine and the pumpkin lifted the boys over the fire trees toward open fields. The boys' laughter grew more excited as the yellow grasses of Autumnland grew green with life and the air grew ever warmer. They passed an orchard of flutter trees whose branches were bare in the still-bright sunlight. The boys saw the Green River sparkling through the thick limbs and the pumpkin sped up, fed by the boys' anticipation.

Fwump!

The boys ran through the soft green grass, enjoying the feel of the hot sun. Oliver stopped by the bank of the river and shivered the last of his chills away. Owen ran along the bank looking for a shallow spot in which he could bathe his brother. He soon found a suitable place and started to undress.

Oliver was still catching his breath, but when he saw Owen taking off his clothes he yelled, "Baff? Woo hoo!" He ran to where Owen was standing and without slowing down Oliver jumped in the water, making as big a splash as he could.

Owen finished undressing and walked to the edge of the water where he proceeded to pee in Oliver's direction. Oliver did not find this amusing.

"Soppit, Owen! Sop! Sop! SOP!" Oliver angrily beat at the water, trying to splash Owen.

Owen didn't answer. He laughed and jumped in the water, splashing Oliver and making him even more angry. Owen waded over to Oliver and tried to undress him but Oliver batted him away, grunting his wrath with each swing of his little fists.

Owen stood back. He said with mock indignation, "Fine! Just be dirty, then!" and submerging himself, he swam away under the water.

Oliver stood in water up to his chest and pouted. By the time Owen surfaced, Oliver was crying. He had forgotten to throw Odie aside before he jumped in the water and now he held the soaking-wet dog in his hand, his little heart broken.

"Aww, it'll be okay, Oliver. He'll dry!"

Owen swam in a graceless doggy paddle over to his brother and took the stuffed dog. Oliver nervously wrung his hands and watched with sad but hopeful eyes as Owen squeezed the excess water from Odie and waded to the bank, carefully placing him in the sun to dry.

Owen said, "Besides, I bet he was thirsty anyway."

Oliver tried not to smile at his brother's joke but he couldn't help it. It was hard to stay upset in the Green River. He struggled to take his pajama top off but got stuck halfway with the shirt over his face and with his hands in the air.

"Owen! Help!"

Owen couldn't stop laughing at the way Oliver's arms were waving in a panic, but he rushed to his side to help.

"No waff, Owen!"

Oliver was annoyed again. The sound of his muffled voice made Owen laugh even more, as well as the effort to remove the pajamas from a fiercely struggling Oliver. However, once Oliver was naked, he immediately cheered up again and happily played in the water while Owen did his best to rinse his soiled clothes. Once the clothes were "clean," Owen joined his brother in splashy play.

An hour later, the brothers sat in the emerald water in silence, watching the sun go down.

Oliver felt so very warm. He did not want to go back to the frozen sweeps of winter, but the shadow eyes were coming for him. He wasn't quite crying yet, but his tears were close and the anxiety in his chest made it feel weightless.

Owen did not know what to do. He couldn't bear the thought of either course of action, but he also was thinking that he must choose one or the other. The sun was almost to the horizon.

The boys watched the sinking sun and felt their spirits sink with it. Oliver could no longer hold back his tears. The first ones fell silently, but soon his face contorted and he began to sob in that high-pitched, wordless wail of very young children. Owen began to cry with him. The boys didn't look at each other. They kept their eyes to the horizon, unable to look away from their coming nightmare. They felt utterly helpless.

The brothers saw shadows appear on the opposite bank of the river. This made them both squeal with fear, but they needn't have been afraid. The shadows were surrounded by an orange light.

Owen realized that the shadows were their own, cast by the growing light of the pumpkin behind them. He turned around and then grabbed his brother's arm.

"Oliver! *Look!*"

Oliver turned and saw that the pumpkin was pulsating with warm light. He felt as if it were calling to him.

The boys stopped crying and climbed out of the water. They both ran to the pumpkin and hugged it, feeling safe. The pumpkin's radiance dimmed back to its normal glow, but it released its bright swirls of color everywhere around the boys, enveloping their naked bodies in its joy.

Owen didn't want to move, but he forced himself to let go and as quickly as he could, he gathered up their clothes, the blanket and Odie. He rushed to get dressed and then pried Oliver away from the pumpkin long enough to dress him, too.

Oliver whimpered in his urgency to finish so he could press himself against the pumpkin once more. He'd seen that the sun had touched the horizon.

Moving very quickly, Owen shoved his brother up and onto the pumpkin and then climbed up himself. No sooner had he grabbed the vine than the pumpkin was in the air and flying fast across Summerland, taking the boys to a destination which Owen could not guess.

Oliver thought that it was taking them to Winterland and he began to moan, "No, Owen...*i'ss col'...i'ss col'...*"

Owen said nothing as they passed a grove of melon trees and reached the bottom of a hill. He felt time running out but he also felt a fierce determination to escape the shadow eyes and to protect his little brother. He was filled with a blind trust that the pumpkin would somehow help them. He saw the pinkberry vines rush past on his left and suddenly knew that they'd been there before.

Up the hill the pumpkin flew in a flash. The light of the pumpkin was now the brightest light left in the land. The tip of the sun was about to disappear.

Oliver sobbed hopelessly. The pumpkin was not taking them to Winterland. He knew then that he would rather be cold for the rest of his life than to face even another minute of the shadow eyes' darkness, but then he saw the pale light in the hillside.

Owen saw it, too. The pumpkin was speeding the boys right toward it. Owen became filled with desperate hope. If only they could reach that light...and before he could even finish that thought...*FWUMP*!

The brothers were bounced off of the pumpkin and onto the soft grass just as the last of the sun's rays faded. Oliver had dropped Odie. He screamed his name as he frantically looked all around for him. Owen grabbed his little brother. With Oliver in his arms still screaming for Odie, Owen dove into the light.

CHAPTER TWENTY

Owen's eyes were closed. Oliver was still in his arms, crying out for Odie, whom he had abandoned to the shadow eyes. It didn't matter that Odie was only a stuffed dog; he was Oliver's friend, and he was outside, all alone in the dark, so Oliver cried for him.

Owen had closed his eyes when he had leapt. There was a moment when he thought he'd made a terrible mistake. A sensation of sliding had caused his stomach to turn and his body to be flooded with adrenaline, which was already starting to wear off. The slide had ended after only a few short feet.

Owen opened his eyes and looked around. He could see the pumpkin in the entrance to the cave, warm and glowing as it ever was. He could also see that a dim light lit the inside of the cave, though he couldn't find its source.

Oliver's sobs grew louder. He was still terrified. Owen saw that his eyes were squeezed shut.

"Oliver! We're okay! Open your eyes and look!"

Oliver did not open his eyes. "Odieeeee!"

"He'll be okay, Oliver! The shadow eyes can't hurt him! Besides, the pumpkin will protect him. Look!"

Oliver opened his eyes. He saw Owen smiling at him but he was still frightened for his stuffed dog. He asked in a worried voice, "Odie scayud?"

"No, Oliver! Odie *can't* get scared. That's why Granny got him for you in the first place!"

Oliver thought about the many days and nights that he'd held his stuffed dog. He saw that maybe Owen was right. He stopped crying and did his best to smile through his drying tears.

Owen looked into his baby brother's wet and sparkling blue eyes and saw trust and belief. Owen's smile grew, and Oliver's grew with it. The boys sat up and looked around at what they did not yet know would be their new home.

"Owen, whut?"

"I don't know, but it's *awesome!*"

"Oss-tummm!" Oliver repeated.

The boys stood up. They looked down into the bowl of the cave. Owen still couldn't see where all the light was coming from. It was Oliver who figured it out.

"I'ss gwoh-wing!"

"What? It's not growing, stupidhead!"

"No, Owen! No' gwoh-ing! Guh-*wohhh*-wing!"

Oliver had an exceptional vocabulary for a child his age. Sick as he was for so long, and in the company of adults, his mind had developed in place of his sick body, which could not. Since he hadn't been able to *do*, he had learned.

Owen looked again, all around. His eyes opened wide. "It *is* glowing! Whoa!"

The boys ran onto the lip of the bowl and pressed their hands to the side of the cave. It felt like normal rock. The boys started to giggle. Soon they were laughing. There were no shadows anywhere. They would always be safe here!

Owen ran along the lip of the bowl to the back of the cave. Oliver followed, moving more cautiously on his clumsy legs. The boys explored the narrow crevice on the far left and peered down the bottomless shaft. They had nothing to throw so they both spit into the nothingness and laughed. Next they found what would become their bedroom. They turned and saw the pumpkin across from them, glowing in the opening to the cave. The sight made them feel giddy.

From the back of the chamber, Owen yelled, "Echo!" The sound bounced around the walls quickly and then disappeared.

Oliver joined in. "Et-toh!" He started to giggle, and now noticed that this sound, too, echoed.

The boys yelled and shouted for a while and then Owen stepped out to the lip of the bowl and yelled again, "ECHO!"

This time, in the larger open space of the cave's main chamber, the echoes came slower and lasted much longer. Oliver mimicked his older brother, following with his high-pitched "Et-tohs" until the boys had filled the cave with sound.

Owen was standing on the rim of the bowl that formed the main chamber of the cave. He stepped over the edge, ran down into the large cavity and up the other side, yelling, "Whoooooo!"

Oliver was amazed by this feat. He immediately ran over the edge but only made it three steps before he tripped on the steep incline. He fell head first, skinning his hands and knees, and giving his forehead a good, sound knock. Oliver started screaming in pain and surprise before he finished sliding to the bottom. His hot tears had already wet his red face when he looked up at Owen, expecting him to make it all better.

Owen ran to his brother's side. He was actually more frightened than Oliver and he didn't know what to do. This was Mommy and Daddy's job.

"Are you okay, Oliver?" It was a stupid question. Obviously Oliver was not okay, but what else could a four-year-old boy say?

Oliver lay on his belly, wailing loudly and straining to lift his head. He looked like he was trying to get up so Owen put his hands under Oliver's arms to help him. Oliver reacted to this with a loud shriek that may or may not have included the word "NO!" Owen couldn't tell. He took his hands away and acted like he thought Mommy would.

"It's okay, Oliver. You're awright. C'mon, Oliver. You're *awright!*"

"I...want...my...MOMMY!"

"Shhhh, Oliver. Shhhhh, lemme see."

"*I want my MOMMY!*"

"C'mon, Oliver. Please? Lemme see!"

"I...WANT...MY...MOMMMMYYYYYYYY!"

Owen started to cry. He tried so hard not to, but he couldn't help it. He wanted Mommy, too.

Now that the boys were safe from the night and from the shadow eyes, from the cold and from hunger; now that they had the pumpkin to take them wherever they wanted to go; now that they had nothing else to be afraid of, they missed their home and their Mommy with every fiber of their being. In their innocence, they did not understand this natural process. They didn't understand why suddenly they needed their mother so badly. This wasn't the work of any outside force. This was a pain born of love that came from inside their own hearts, hearts that were breaking.

Owen curled up next to Oliver and put his little arm around him. Oliver rolled over and wrapped his arms around Owen, and the brothers cried together for a long time. It didn't occur to the boys to go and sit by the pumpkin. The pumpkin's joy could have helped them to feel safe and loved, but from where they lay, the pumpkin couldn't be seen.

The scrapes on Oliver's hands and knees soon stopped bleeding but they still stung painfully. The lump on his head was red and very tender. Oliver hardly noticed these things. He dreamed of Mommy's warmth, of her arms around him and of her soothing voice, and he wept because she wasn't there.

Owen held Oliver and pretended that Mommy was holding *him* in the same way. Owen gently squeezed his brother and could almost feel Mommy's arms giving him the same affectionate squeeze. He was sure that she would do just that, if she could. He knew that somewhere she was missing him as much as he missed her. The knowledge started to make Owen feel a little better, though he still felt sad and scared, too.

He got up and retrieved the parrot leaves. He laid them out before Oliver and then wrapped him in his arms again. Oliver lightly stroked the velvety leaves with one finger. Owen started to speak to Oliver in a soft voice that gently shook through the tears that continued to leak from his eyes.

"Remember how Mommy tickles us? That's funny. And when she reads to us? She always makes the crazy noises. *Buzzzzzz! Buzzzzzz!* They always make you laugh. Remember when we were feeding the gooses and they scared Mommy?"

Oliver smiled at the memory of Mommy being chased by an angry goose and said, "Wan away!" He made a noise that was almost a giggle.

Owen continued, "I like when she pushes us onna swings. And she slides down the slide with us on 'er lap. And she dances *crazy*."

The boys gently laughed together at their memories of Mommy kicking her legs out, dancing to no music.

Oliver sighed, "Mommy cuh-wazy," and made himself smile.

Owen talked on. "I bet when she finds us she'll flip us on our beds. That's fun when she does that."

Oliver had been sick for so long that he'd almost forgotten how Mommy used to flip him. He said, "Swing uh-wownd?"

"Yeah! Swing us!" Owen answered. "I bet Mommy misses us."

"Mommy sad?"

"Uh huh, but Daddy will take care of her and help her not be sad."

"Mmmmm."

Owen stopped talking. The boys thought about their Mommy and Daddy. They missed them so much. The brothers went to special places in their own minds where memories of Mommy and Daddy blended with fantastic dreams that they created for themselves. The boys still felt sad, but their fantasies gave them enough comfort to fall asleep and to dream good dreams.

The boys awoke to find the cave glowing more brightly than ever. They soon realized that it was the light of the sun shining into the cave and bouncing all around. Morning had come. The night had passed without fear or cold or hunger. For a while the boys lay quietly, each thinking their own thoughts. There was a brand new reality to explore.

Owen didn't understand this new feeling. He couldn't realize that he had found the very thing that he did not know he had been searching for. He had found a safe place that he and Oliver could call home. He looked around at the glowing walls of the cave and felt his brother in his arms. They would be okay here.

The possibility was slowly sinking into his mind that he and Oliver could live their days without anyone to take care of them. *He* would take care of them. This was a very grown up thought, and it confused him. After all they had been through, to feel safe didn't make sense to him. The possibility of spending his whole life without adults had been inconceivable to him right up until about ten minutes before, when he had awoken to this new feeling. The idea was altering his very consciousness.

Up to that point, his thoughts had been that Mommy and Daddy would find them and take them home. It was only a matter of time, and of what he and Oliver would have to do in the meantime. He now began to think in much longer terms, which was a foreign concept to his child's mind. It frightened him. In the end, his mind compromised with itself. He kept the thought that Mommy and Daddy would someday find them. This actively kept Mommy and Daddy a part of his daily life, and helped him to reconcile with his ability to live without them.

Oliver was having both an easier time with this, and finding it more difficult than his brother. Oliver was much younger so that he adapted to change easier, not having such a set idea (as Owen already had), of what life was supposed to be. However, being so young and having had his Mommy and Daddy so close to him for so long, they were still the defining truth of his existence.

How he identified himself had been ripped away from him, leaving an empty place inside him. That emptiness would be refilled with love and joy and beauty. This would happen rapidly, so that although he would be left with scars, they would fade until Mommy was a thought and an image that would bring laughter more often than longing. Of course, nothing could ever quite replace Mommy, and there would always be times when Oliver would miss her terribly, when he would cry for her and call her name, but he was young enough to forget most of what had been left behind, replacing it with what he now had. He had Owen and a magic pumpkin, and a world that was his playland.

Though all of this would come in time, that morning he still associated happiness with the face and touch of Mommy and he was confused by this contented feeling of peace and stillness without her. Oliver did what he always did when he was too confused or overwhelmed by his thoughts and emotions. He retreated into puppy mode and took a break from reality.

The boys both lay quietly, each adapting in their own way to this new life into which they had landed. Owen would be pained by his longing for home long after Oliver had let his go, but even as young as Owen was, he could see that having Oliver alive and well was worth it all, and through this he would find his own happiness, and his own empty place would be mostly filled. Although Oliver would all but forget that he was ever sick, Owen could never forget that his brother had been going to die, and that now he wasn't. Owen would keep it a secret from his little brother. He remembered what Mommy had told him: *He doesn't need to know.* It was just one more burden that Owen would bravely carry, and carry alone.

Oliver stirred. "Yip! Yip! Yip!"

This made Owen smile. "Good morning, puppy!" Owen sniffed. "Did puppy poop?"

Puppy answered with a guilty whimper. "Hmm hmmm hmm hmmm!"

"Okay, puppy. Let's go clean you up!"

"Yip! Yip! Yip!"

"And then we'll have pinkberries for breakfast!"

Puppy answered this last with excited panting and a vigorous wagging of his backside.

It wasn't easy to get Oliver on the pumpkin while he was in puppy mode and refusing to stand up, but Owen eventually managed it and tossed up the blanket. Before he climbed up himself, he spotted Odie, none the worse for wear after his night outside, and handed him to a very relieved Oliver. The pumpkin took the boys to the Green River where they swam and played under a pale golden sky until their rumbling bellies drove them back onto the lush grass of Summerland.

"Oliver, let's race back to the pinkberries!"

Oliver hesitated. "Punkin?" He was reluctant to leave the pumpkin behind.

Owen looked at the pumpkin. He tilted his head and rubbed the blanket's silky tag against his nose while he thought. "Hmmmm..."

He walked over to the pumpkin and put his free hand on its side. It lifted just a bit and hovered, gently bobbing up and down a few inches off the ground. Owen ran a few steps and the pumpkin moved with him.

Oliver's eyes opened wide in surprise and delight. He ran to catch up and put one hand on the pumpkin's other side. In his other hand he held Odie by one of his back paws. Together the boys ran across the grassy fields with the bobbing pumpkin between them and the stuffed dog flopping about in Oliver's hand. They laughed at the swirls of color that the pumpkin trailed, not because they were funny, but because it was such a happy thing to exist.

What had seemed like such a great distance just eight days before, now passed beneath the boys' happy feet in a matter of minutes. When they had come the opposite way in search of water on that first day, they had been scared and dirty and Oliver had had little strength. They had miserably hobbled along, constantly stopping to rest. Now they were filled with energy and the joy of the bright summer day. They stopped only once to quickly catch their breath and then they continued to run until they reached the pinkberry patch.

And so the days passed. The boys explored the many wonders of that magical land. They bathed and swam in the rivers of spring and summer. They jumped in the leaf piles of autumn and chased the black birds from the trees. They ate their fill every day, bickering over which strange fruit was their new favorite food. They played amongst herds of cow-pies, laughing at the animals' long ears and funny mooing. They even sang with the fish that lived in the Gold River. They discovered the paint plants, the leaf-catching spot, and most importantly the make-place.

The boys found the clothestone first and abandoned what was left of Oliver's torn and ragged pajamas for jeans and t-shirts and sweaters. Oliver had been most excited to find new shoes for himself. He'd been having an especially hard time walking through any kind of wood in his bare feet, and when Owen had splashed along in the White River, Oliver had had to walk in the grass beside him because the pebbles hurt his tender soles.

The boys' reaction to finding the clothestone was complicated. They were overjoyed by the discovery, but it also made them long for home. The simple clothes that they found seemed peculiarly out of place in that magical land. The first thing that the boys did upon discovering them was to look around to see who had left them. They vaguely expected to see Granny waiting nearby to see if they liked their new clothes, and were somewhat deflated when she wasn't there. Their disappointment was short-lived, however, swallowed up by their anticipation of a trip to Autumnland now that they could finally dress warmly enough.

There was only one article of clothing that Owen wished for but that never appeared, and that was diapers for Oliver. He still had to take his baby brother to the Green River almost every morning to clean him, although he now had clean clothes to wear afterward instead of always having to put on the same damp pajamas. Oliver was trying to learn to use the bathroom shaft, but it would be another month or so before he would get the hang of it. Even then, the occasional accident would greet the boys upon waking to the otherwise fairly clean cave.

Two weeks had gone by since the boys had found the glow cave. They had found the far right room in the back of the cave and had divvied up Owen's treasures from home into two small booty piles, though Owen had yet to climb up and explore the shelf that lined the right side of that room. The boys had made the chamber opposite the entrance to the cave into their bedroom, and had brought back blanketful after blanketful of fire leaves to sleep on and to cushion the bottom of the slide.

The boys often cried themselves to sleep at night, but it seemed almost as often that they peacefully drifted off, or fell asleep huddled together under the blanket and talking about what they would do the next day. The boys shared the blanket at night, but during the day it belonged to Owen, just as Odie belonged to Oliver. Sometimes Owen left the blanket behind in the cave (generally because he forgot it), but he usually carried it with him. Oliver never left the cave without Odie in his arms.

The boys had already shared many adventures, but had not yet returned to Winterland. One night, as they lay on their bed of leaves deciding what to do the next day, Owen had an idea.

"Oliver, let's make a snowman!"

"Whut? So-man?"

"Yeah! Don't you remember?"

Oliver did *not* remember, but the idea of a man made out of snow intrigued him. "Tocks?" he asked.

"No! Of course he can't talk! He's made of snow! *I'll* show you."

"T'ss col'!"

"It's okay, we'll go to the clothestone first and get coats and hats."

Oliver patted his red hair. "No hats!"

The next morning, after a trip to the Green River and a breakfast of pinkberries, the boys climbed on the pumpkin and laughed through the air to the make-place. Owen went straight to the clothestone where, as he'd expected, he found winter coats, hats and gloves, as well as boots lined with warm fur. He turned to help Oliver dress but Oliver had run to tell the gray stone wall about playing with the moo-moos the day before. Oliver liked to watch himself laughing in the images that appeared.

"C'mon, Oliver! We'll come back after, I promise!"

Oliver tilted his head and smiled at the wall before waving goodbye and then he obediently went to his big brother to be dressed for their winter adventure. He refused the hat, still believing that he didn't need it. Owen shoved the knitted hat in his coat pocket just in case, and the boys mounted the pumpkin.

The boys enjoyed their ride, as they always did, but soon the temperature began to drop and Oliver wished he'd worn the hat. His regret didn't last very long. His chilly ears were forgotten as soon as the snow-covered fields of Winterland came into view.

The sky was a light purple that day, with big, puffy white clouds floating along at their leisure. The combination of white and purple gave a very friendly feel to the landscape, as if it were inviting the boys to come and play.

A few evergreen trees, laden with heavy snow, grew in scattered copses. Oliver stared down as they flew over the trees and pretended that he was a bird.

The pumpkin landed and the familiar *fwump* was enriched by the sound of the snow crunching beneath it. The boys hopped off and Oliver immediately asked for his hat.

Owen felt his brother's red hair. "Your head's still warm, Oliver."

"Ee-yuhs huht!"

Owen looked at his brother's ears and saw that they were very red. He pulled the warm hat out of his pocket and put it on Oliver's head. Oliver pulled it down over his ears and Owen smiled at the sight of him. The rim of the knitted cap was pulled so low that Oliver had to tilt his head back to see.

"C'mon, Oliver."

The two little boys trekked through the snow to a spot that didn't look any different from any other spot, and then Owen stopped, announced that this was the place, and fell backward into the deep snow. Oliver laughed out loud and then mimicked his brother, falling straight on his back and landing with a quick, dull crunch. Owen showed him how to make a snow-angel and then the boys got up and inspected their work. Oliver was delighted.

"Ready to make a snowman, Oliver?"

"Yups! Yups! Yups!"

Owen gathered up some snow and pressed it into a large snowball while Oliver watched with keen interest. When Owen set the snowball down and began to roll it, Oliver's eyes grew wide with surprise at what happened. The snowball was growing! Oliver laughed with delight as he watched his big brother work.

Soon the snowball was so big that Owen could no longer roll it by himself and he told Oliver to help. This being his first try, Oliver's excitement got the best of him and he clumsily pushed his hands right through the snowball, causing half of it to collapse.

"Oliver*rrrr*! Aaaaagghhhhh!"

Oliver was so overcome with remorse that he started to cry. Owen was rather perturbed but his little brother's tears helped him to find patience.

"It's awright, Oliver. We'll make another one. Just do it more softer next time." Owen looked around. As far as the boys could see there was nothing but flat, snowy tundra. "It's not like we're gonna run out of snow!"

Owen kicked the lopsided snowball and laughed at the pieces that exploded from it to show Oliver that it really was okay that he'd ruined it. Oliver then kicked it, too, and started to laugh. After the boys had completely demolished the failed attempt, Owen started over and working together, the boys soon had three colossal snowballs of slightly varying sizes.

Owen explained what came next. "Okay. That one's the bottom. That's the middle, and that's his head."

However, the snowballs were far too heavy for the boys to lift. After many a grunt and a failed try, Oliver started to cry again. Owen felt very discouraged himself, but then he was struck with an idea.

"Oliver! Help me make one more, but a little smaller."

The boys soon had a fourth snowball made. They were all lined up, biggest to smallest. Owen now explained his idea.

"We'll just make *all* of these bottoms! That one will be Daddy, that one Mommy, this one will be me, and the last one is *you*! Yeah! That's a *great* idea!"

Oliver happily clapped his gloved hands and stomped his feet in approval of the great idea, then he squatted and immediately started to make more snowballs. It took the boys a long time to finish their work. They stopped to rest and to eat some snow a few times, and Oliver had a cranky and frustrated moment when he collapsed another snowball, but he soon cheered up and the brothers got back to work. When the boys were finished, they stood back and admired this magnum opus of snowmen. They were panting and exhausted but they felt good. It always feels good to create.

Owen walked a few feet away and had a jolly pee in the snow. While his back was turned, Oliver made one more small clump of snow next to his snowman. Owen finished peeing and turned back to see what Oliver was doing.

Oliver pointed at the new clump and proudly announced, "Odie!"

"Ya know what, Oliver? I bet these will be here forever! I bet the snow never melts here!"

"Fuh-evuh?" Oliver looked at the snow family again with a new respect and sense of accomplishment. He then proceeded to march around them, clapping his hands in time with his steps as he tended to do when he was too thrilled for words.

Now that their creation had been properly appreciated, Oliver was ready for lunch. He wanted to ride the pumpkin back to Autumnland to find some parrots, but Owen wanted to fly around and explore a bit more of Winterland. After a brief argument, Owen bribed Oliver with the promise of letting him play with the bouncy balls when they returned to the cave. The boys mounted the pumpkin, thoroughly enjoying its warmth, and rose into the sky.

It wasn't long before the boys saw a line of intense blue cutting across the frozen landscape. Owen steered the pumpkin closer and the boys realized that they had found another river. In the distance, the Blue River flowed into the Winter Forest, but the boys had landed at a point where there were no trees at all. Oliver was so excited to see the water and look for fish that as soon as the pumpkin landed he slid off into the snow in a heap, and then he was up and running through the deep snow with his comically awkward goosesteps.

The river appeared to still be about ten feet away when suddenly the snow collapsed beneath Oliver's feet and into the icy water he went with a piercing scream that would haunt Owen's memories for a long time.

Not knowing what else to do, Owen ran straight to him. The current was taking Oliver away, but Owen caught up and jumped into the water face first with hands outstretched, grasping one of Oliver's legs. Owen was immediately paralyzed by the shock of the frigid water to his system. He dimly registered that Oliver had already stopped screaming. Owen was so cold that he could barely move his arms and legs. He couldn't think. He could hardly see. He was holding Oliver's head above the water, terrified by his face which had turned blue, and his lips which had turned a deep purple. Owen began to lose feeling, too. The boys helplessly floated downriver. Just when Owen was too cold to hang on to Oliver for even a moment longer, he bumped into something warm.

Both brothers would have died that day if it hadn't been for the magic pumpkin. The boys didn't see it come. The pumpkin was suddenly just *there,* next to them in the water, blocking them from being washed away.

Owen felt his head clear just enough to realize that a vine was loosely held in his hand. He tightened his grip and immediately he and Oliver were on the snowy bank, shivering and wet. They huddled against the pumpkin for warmth, wrapped in each other's arms and sobbing.

Oliver was crying for Mommy, though his voice shook so badly that Owen couldn't tell that he was actually speaking. Owen couldn't make a sound. It was all he could do to breathe. The boys had thought that they knew what it was to feel cold, but this was much worse than even that first night in Winterland alone under the stars. The boys shook so violently that it appeared to their eyes as if the world were breaking apart. They were jolted where they sat, frightened by the intensity of their tremors and the hammering din of their uncontrollably chattering teeth.

Slowly, the pumpkin's warmth crept into the boys. As their bodies slowed and calmed, their emotions took over and left both boys crying for Mommy, for surely if ever there was a time for Mommy to gather up her little treasures and reassure them that they were okay, it was that moment. But Mommy wasn't there.

The pumpkin, however, was. It smothered the boys in its warmly colored swirls until they stopped crying. Strange, that the boys didn't know where the comfort came from. They simply felt themselves cheer up, at least until Oliver noticed that Odie was gone. He had been holding him when the snow had given way beneath his feet, and the stuffed dog had floated away. Oliver had lost him.

He cried out for his friend every bit as mournfully as he had cried for Mommy. Owen tried to comfort him, but Oliver was inconsolable. With Odie lost, the boys grew suddenly afraid. Even the pumpkin couldn't take away the boys' fear. Oliver's tears froze on his cheeks as he scanned the river for any sign of his friend. There was none. The fear ebbed and was replaced with heartache. Oliver would miss him dearly.

The boys sat in the snow for a long time, neither of them willing to let go of the other, even for the moment it would take to mount the pumpkin for the ride back to summer's warmth. A comrade had fallen there and the boys were reluctant to leave to scene of their parting.

As time went by, the boys grew calm, for this was not a place that lent itself to sadness, but to stillness. They watched with reflective eyes as the beautiful blue waters flowed past. In spite of their experience and the terrible loss of Odie, the boys fell in love with the Blue River that day, though they would always be afraid of it. It would be some time, but both of the boys knew that they would want to come back here, and oh-so-carefully climb to the edge to drink its cold beauty.

Instilled with this new calm, the boys eventually climbed upon the pumpkin without a word. It took them back to Summerland to recover from their icy adventure under the hot sun. Owen held his brother tight as they rode across the sky, reflecting on how close he had just come to losing him. He was totally unaware that the most earth-shattering discovery of that cataclysmic day still lay before him.

Night had fallen outside the glow cave, and the boys lay curled up under the blanket in their bedroom. Oliver had cried himself to sleep, missing his friend. Owen lay awake listening to him dreaming of his stuffed dog.

Oliver was talking in his sleep, calling Odie's name as if he were looking for him. He took a deep breath and said his name one last time, with great relief. In his dream, he had found him. Oliver spoke no more, but a calm look smoothed his worried brow and his breathing became deep and slow.

Owen lay wide awake in the silence of the cave. He felt restless. He stared at the pumpkin in the entrance of the cave and the sight slowly calmed him, but just as he was drifting off, he thought he heard a strange noise. He raised himself up on one elbow and tilted his head to listen. It was a gentle sound, like a woman softly crying. Owen could just barely hear it over Oliver's breathing. The sound was so faint that it did not even make an echo in the cave.

*In the cave...*it was coming from the booty room.

Owen got up, careful not to wake Oliver, and slowly crept into the chamber where the boys kept their treasures. He saw nothing, but the sound was slightly clearer now. He was sure that it was someone crying.

He looked up at the shelf which he had not yet explored. With a struggle, he pulled himself up. He found himself on a ledge about six feet wide which ran the length of the room. In the corner farthest from the entrance was a dim spot from which there was no glow. Owen was frightened, but he felt himself pulled to the spot. He very slowly inched his way toward it. He finally reached it and looked down. What he saw took his breath away.

Owen was looking into his own dark bedroom, in his home with Mommy and Daddy. He was directly over his own bed, on which Mommy lay crying. She held his and Oliver's pillows to her face, breathing in their scent between her sobs. Her eyes were closed tight. He called to her softly but she didn't seem to hear.

Owen was so excited that he didn't know what to do. He called a little louder. Mommy still didn't hear him. Owen's mind was overloaded. There was home! All he had to do was jump down and he would be bouncing on his own bed, to be swooped up in Mommy's arms and covered with the kisses that he needed so badly! She wouldn't be sad anymore! After all the boys had been through, home had been right here all along!

Owen stood up and got ready to jump. He had to be careful so that he wouldn't land on Mommy. He took a deep breath, bent his knees... but then he stopped. He looked back toward where Oliver lay sleeping. He couldn't leave him. Owen turned to go and wake him up, but again he stopped. Oliver couldn't go back this way. What if he got sick again? Oliver *would* get sick again. He would die. Owen felt absolutely sure of this. He looked back at his weeping mother and started to cry. It wasn't fair. Mommy was so sad. She missed him. He needed her. Owen sat down, and from his own side of the portal he wept with his Mommy, even though she didn't know that he was there, so close.

If only he could somehow let her know that they were all right; that they thought about her and loved her. Owen climbed down from the shelf and picked up a small, slender stick that he'd found in Autumnland. It was pure white, from one of the fire trees. He climbed back up and held the stick above the portal. He poked its tip through and felt it taken from his hand. He watched it fall softly onto his bed next to Mommy's elbow, but she didn't notice. Owen hoped that she'd find it eventually. He wanted to follow the stick so badly that he could feel the tangible ache of his longing.

It wasn't fair that he had to choose between going home and staying behind in the magical land with Oliver. But, there really was no choice at all. He loved his baby brother more than anything.

Owen whispered, "I promise to take care of him, Mommy. I promise not to ever tell him that he was gonna die. I love you, Mommy."

This would be Owen's greatest desire, and his heaviest burden. He would keep it a secret from his brother. Oliver must never know. He wouldn't understand. Once the decision was made, Owen felt more than ever like a grownup, and he hated it.

He would send nothing else through the portal, afraid that if Mommy and Daddy knew he was there, they would make him bring Oliver back. They wouldn't understand, and he had no way to tell them.

In the entrance to the cave, the magic pumpkin glowed brighter, as if it sensed that the joy of which it was made was needed now more than ever, but Owen didn't see it. He sat and cried with his Mommy until she left the room, and then he crept back to his brother and lay awake until morning with Oliver in his arms.

END PART TWO

Interlude

The man's joy left him on the day that his sons disappeared. He felt it going, as if it were a physical sensation. It seemed to drain out of him until ultimately there was none left. His boys were the source of his joy, and they were gone. What the man couldn't know was that his joy had gone to be with them. It would play with them and watch over them, show them safe places and wrap them in its colorful swirls, its comforting orange glow a constant reminder that they were loved.

Had the man known this, he could have found great solace, but since he didn't know, he searched for his joy where none could be found.

The man let himself hope in his heart that his sons were alive somewhere, that he may even see them again, but even this gave him no joy. In a vague way, in places in his mind that he dared not look, the thought of the boys alive filled him with a nameless anxiety, and fear. The little voice would just whisper, *what's happening to them...?* and the man would run from those fears, replacing them with grief, for surely his boys must be dead. In some ways, it was easier to think so.

In this way his turbulent mind never settled, never rested. It had been this way for more than a year now. The only reason he clung to what bits of his crumbling mind were left was that if the boys ever did come back, they would need him. If he could only know that they'd never return, he could let go, finally give in to that consuming grief that he so longed for.

The man always thought *they* instead of *he* because to accept the obvious truth was too difficult for him. The man's mind could not cope. His baby boy had been so sick. He could not possibly have survived, probably not even another day. And so whatever had happened to his first born son, wherever he might be, he had faced it, or *was still facing it*, alone. But these were the thoughts that the man's mind ran from the fastest.

When the woman had found herself left without her sons, she had found herself left without love. She thought of her boys all day, every day, trying to feel what she had felt when she had them near to her. She cried throughout each day, and every night she went to the boys' room and cried in their beds. She had lost the most precious part of herself and could not find it again. She looked at the man through cold eyes, trying to find even a bit of the love that she'd lost, but she felt nothing.

From the moment that each of her sons was born, her love had no longer been something inside of her. It lived outside of her. It went where her sons went. She felt its absence when they were out of sight, and she soaked it up like warm light when they were in her presence.

The boys had been gone now for so long. She no longer dwelt on what may have happened to them. She simply accepted that they were gone, and that all of her love had gone with them. She didn't know that deep down, well hidden even from herself, she held on to a tiny seed of impossible hope. It was all that kept her alive.

A few weeks after the boys disappeared, the man had found what he took to be a sign in his older son's unmade bed. He had knelt before the bed and grabbed at the covers, wrapping himself in his son's essence, when something had poked his arm. It was a little stick, perfectly smooth and pure white - just the kind of stick that his son would have picked up and brought home. The man had shown it to the woman, and together they had held it and cried. They searched everywhere but could never find another like it, nor could they ever discover where it had come from or how it had come to be in their son's bed. The man and the woman broke the stick in half, and each of them wore a piece of it as a necklace, keeping it close to their hearts. Against all reason, they knew that it had been a gift from their oldest son, and when the man's fear and the woman's emptiness became too much, they could rub the smooth, white wood and find just a bit of hope in the pale shadow of the joy and the love they had lost. But that had been so long ago, and they had found no signs since.

PART THREE

CHAPTER TWENTY-ONE

The sun had already gone behind the crest of the steep hillside, leaving the boys in the shadows of an early twilight that shrouded the ravine long before actual nightfall. The rain had stopped while the boys were sleeping. Owen was awakened by pattering drops of rainwater falling from the soaked black hole trees. The drops made a tapping sound on the blanket of dead leaves that covered the floor of the ravine and that clung to the banks of the Black River as if afraid to be washed away in its darkness. Owen saw the deep shadows all around him and fear immediately coursed through him. He looked up at the narrow strip of gray sky above him and saw that night had not yet come, but he knew that it soon would.

Oliver was moaning in his half-sleep.

Owen studied his brother's face. It was so pale beneath the smears of dark mud. His long blonde hair was dirty and knotted. Owen's eyes moved over his brother's mangled body. He was already scared, but the blood that still seeped from Oliver's wounds made him feel something very close to panic.

Owen looked all around for the dark creatures. He kept thinking that he heard them creeping up on him, but it was only the sound of the dripping trees. The boys were sitting so close to the twisted black hole trees. Owen eyed them nervously. Could the tentacles reach him where he sat?

Owen's mind filled itself with these if's because it was afraid to face a dread certainty. Finally he couldn't block the thought from his mind anymore: the shadow eyes were going to get them.

Owen started to cry. He felt so helpless. He *was* so helpless. The sadness in the river drained his will. The air was close and filled with the dank smell of rotting leaves. Owen stirred and the small movement made him cry out in pain. He hurt all over. He began to cry harder. He did not know what to do.

Owen's crying disturbed Oliver's sleep. Oliver's moans grew louder and he started to shiver. He opened his eyes, saw where he was and remembered. Immediately his bottom lip began to quiver and in another moment he was like a siren, belting out a continuous, high-pitched wail.

Owen tried to calm him. "Shhhh, Oliver! Shhhhh! It's okay…" but as soon as he said this he began to wail himself because he knew that nothing was okay.

The sky continued to grow darker high above the sobbing boys. Soon Oliver had exhausted himself. His cries weakened to whimpers. Owen knew that he had to do something. He pulled himself away from Oliver. It wasn't easy because Oliver was clinging to him with what strength he had left.

Oliver began to plead with him. "No, Owen. No…don't leave…I'm sorry, Owen…no no noooo."

Owen rose to his knees in front of Oliver. "I'm not leaving, Oliver. I promise I won't ever leave, no matter what."

Oliver whimpered a sigh of relief and closed his eyes. Owen started to remove his brother's raincoat. At the smallest movement Oliver screamed at him to stop and hit his hands away. He was in so much pain that all he wanted to do was stay perfectly still.

"Oliver, just watch. I'll take my clothes off first so I can wrap them on your cuts. Remember like you did when I hit my head that time?"

"No, Owen!"

"Oliver, we *have* to. You're *bleeding*!"

That made Oliver start to cry again. It wasn't the high-pitched wail but a guttural screeching. Owen proceeded to take off his own raincoat and the mostly dry shirt he wore underneath. Oliver watched him do this and screamed even louder.

Now it was Owen's turn to plead, "Please, Oliver! Please stop crying! Please!"

Oliver didn't stop.

Owen pointed at the stuffed dog that Oliver had forgotten he was holding.

"Look, Oliver! It's Odie! Remember? I found him for you!"

Oliver squeezed his dog and began to calm down a little. "Odie..."

Owen took a deep breath and as gently as he could, started to slip Oliver out of his torn raincoat, his nimble fingers working with a slow delicacy. This hurt Oliver too much for him to cooperate, but he did his best not to struggle. It took a long time, but Owen eventually succeeded in removing the coat. Oliver had cried and squealed in pain the whole time, never easing his grip on Odie.

Now that Owen could see the wounds better he grew even more frightened. He was very glad that Oliver's eyes were closed. He tried to cry silently as he wrapped his shirt around the wounds on his brother's shoulder and chest. By then, his normally agile fingers were shaking badly. Again, Oliver cried and screamed until it was finished.

Owen was cold so he put his raincoat back on, not that it offered much warmth. He peered through the failing light at the punctures on Oliver's stomach from the creature's claws and at the blood on Oliver's jeans from the wounds on his leg. He couldn't do anymore. He couldn't take hurting his baby brother and making him scream like that anymore. He hoped it would be okay.

Owen saw that Oliver was shivering again so he sat back down next to him. Oliver cried out once more as Owen pulled him onto his lap, and then the brothers rested. Oliver's bare skin felt cold on Owen's belly.

There was still a bit of light in the sky when the boys felt a familiar though almost forgotten fear begin to seep into their minds, and into their hearts. The shadow eyes had at long last found them again. In fact, the boys had come right to them. The Black River was where the shadow eyes hid from the light. They dwelt in the bottom of that ravine because it was the first place that the sun abandoned, and the last place that its light returned to. They didn't need to wait for nightfall to prey upon the brothers.

Oliver's whimpers grew and changed in pitch. The hopelessness in his cries broke Owen's heart. Whereas Oliver was being probed with fear, Owen felt the sadness in the river seeping into him, as if he were a bit of white cloth dropped in a pool of ink until no white was left.

The shadow eyes enjoyed this appetizer. Everything in the boys rebelled against what they knew was coming, and the shadow eyes feasted on their dread.

When the first eye opened on the surface of the river itself, the boys went into hysterics. They couldn't run. They couldn't move. Oliver's wounds were far too severe and Owen would not leave him, no matter what he had to endure to stay by his side.

More eyes opened on the water and they continued to probe the boys' minds. The dull black eyes fed the brothers no images, not yet. The brothers were so afraid of the shadow eyes themselves that they needed nothing to bring the boys to the desired state but simply appear.

Appear they did, like never before. Soon the Black River was filled with eyes. The boys stared in horror, unable to look away, and unable to cease their screams. It looked to them as if the water itself was nothing but eyes, a river of lifeless black eyes, more than the boys could count in a lifetime.

It was very dark now. Through their screams, the boys heard the black hole trees come alive with movement and a terrible groaning, for all living creatures were prey to the shadow eyes, even the tentacled beasts that lived within the trees. The river of eyes appeared to overflow its banks and like a rising tide it crept toward Owen and Oliver. The boys' fear approached a state of madness as the eyes opened ever closer, swallowing up everything before them. This was so much worse than it had ever been before. It was the difference between a single sting from a wasp and being engulfed by an endless swarm.

Oliver's screams began to form words that would return to haunt Owen for the rest of his life.

"Owen...no more eye shadows...you promised...you PROMISED!"

And then Oliver fell silent and stopped moving.

The boys were surrounded. Owen could feel the eyes opening all over his body. Just as the last bit of light faded from the patch of sky above, Owen turned to look at his brother. An eye had opened over Oliver's mouth, silencing him. Oliver looked back at Owen with utter terror in his eyes. It was for but a flash before his eyes went dead and Owen found himself looking into two lifeless, pitch black orbs. Then the blackness took Owen and he saw nothing more.

Throughout that endless night, the boys were trapped inside their own minds, shut off from the outside world and from each other. When the boys had first endured the torments of the shadow eyes so long ago, they had been fed twisted visions which they took to be true. This night was different. The boys had been overwhelmed. They did not just witness the unspeakable scenes that the shadows brought up from the depths of their darkest fears, the boys were taken *inside* their fears, so that they experienced them as if they were actually happening.

Oliver watched as the pumpkin's glow faded and went out. The pumpkin began to rot. Oliver tried to climb it, to *save* it, but its shell caved in under his hands, releasing the stench of death. Oliver fell into the dark slime of its rotten innards. He couldn't find the way out...

Owen stood outside of Oliver's hospital room. He could hear Oliver screaming. He was dying. If only Owen could get into his bed he could save him, but the door was locked...

Oliver was mauled and eaten over and over. He watched the dark creatures devour Owen, and Daddy, and Mommy. They ripped Odie to shreds. Oliver could hear the stuffed dog squealing in pain and fear...

Owen watched as his brother succumbed to his wounds. Oliver was gone. Owen left the land, going through the portal alone, but was not welcomed back by Mommy and Daddy. They screamed at him and told him that it was all his fault. They blamed him for Oliver's death and told Owen that they hated him. They struck him with awful violence and forced him from his home. No one would ever take care of him or love him again...

Over and over the boys lived these and worse nightmares. In the land there was silence. The boys sat motionless in their catatonic states. There were no screams or tears...just eyes, watching and feeding.

The boys did not witness the dawn. It was long before the rays of the sun reached into the deep vale to drive the shadow eyes back into the Black River. The eyes had lingered as long as possible to devour every succulent morsel of the boys' pain and then all at once, they were gone.

Released from their nightmares, the boys found no solace at first. They didn't understand what had happened.

Owen returned to his senses first. He felt Oliver breathing in his arms. His brother was alive. Owen released a torrent of tears. He sobbed uncontrollably, with such force that he found it hard to breath. His relief was such as he'd never before known, and never would again.

It took Oliver longer to come back. It had all seemed so real. He thought that *this* was the dream. Owen's sobs scared him, but he had watched Owen being eaten. Oliver wept at the false memory and lost himself in his tears. His heart and mind were breaking together and he was far too young to comprehend what he was experiencing.

Owen was the first to stop crying. He rocked Oliver back and forth and whispered soothing things to him, but he couldn't relieve his brother's fear. Oliver was terrified by his own confusion. Owen didn't understand this. He didn't realize that Oliver didn't know what was real and what was not. Owen saw that Oliver was bleeding again. He had to do something.

"Oliver, they're gone! No more shadow eyes! They're gone! It's okay."

Owen's words shocked Oliver into silence. *Shadow eyes?* What was Owen talking about? It was light out. *It was light out.* Slowly Oliver began to see what had happened. He was racked by the same sobs that had made Owen fight for breath.

"*Th-th-the...muh-monsters...ate mee-eeee...ate...muh-muh-muh...muh-muh-muh...Mommy!*"

"No, Oliver! It's not real! Mommy's okay! Mommy's okay, I *promise!*" Owen felt a sharp jab at hearing his own words as he remembered Oliver's rebuke from the night before. He paused before he went on. "Look! Here's Odie!"

Oliver grabbed at the stuffed dog but did not stop sobbing. He held Odie to him with his good arm and retreated back into himself.

Owen was already feeling an intense urge to get away from that place. He pleaded with his brother, "We have to get up, Oliver! We have to leave!"

The panic in Owen's voice only scared Oliver more and he retreated deeper within himself. *Oh, he hurt so much.* He wished Owen would stop yelling at him.

Owen was crying, too, now. He stopped talking for a while and the boys each cried, feeling very far apart. When Owen spoke again, it was gently.

"I miss Mommy. I wish she was here."

At the mention of Mommy, Oliver tuned into his brother's voice, though he did not yet open his eyes.

"Do you miss Mommy, Oliver? She loves us. If she was here, she could make everything better. She would make us sandwiches and give us juice. She would give us a bath and let us splash her."

Oliver stopped crying. Images of Mommy floated through his mind, pulling its pieces back together. He loved her so much.

Owen had learned long ago that he could use his brother's love for their Mommy to comfort him. He had only needed time to calm down and remember. He went on, comforting himself as well.

"Mommy used to take us to the park. She picked flowers and put them in our hair. When you cried too much, Mommy would take us for a ride in her car and sing to you and call you snuffer." Owen had finally made himself smile.

Oliver opened his eyes. His voice was quiet but he spoke. "Snuffuh?"

"Yeah, and lots of other stuff but I forget. Wait...she called you snuffer-butt!"

"*Snuffer*-butt?" Owen heard Oliver giggle weakly and knew that he'd be okay now.

Owen continued to talk about Mommy and to share his memories of her until Oliver felt himself thinking almost clearly again.

Owen's head had somewhat cleared, too. He stopped to think. He looked all around. They couldn't go back up the hill. Even if there were no monsters in the trees, it was too steep for Oliver to climb. Owen shuddered when he thought about those tentacles. He would never look at the trees again without remembering what lived inside them.

He looked at Oliver, who had closed his eyes. His wounds weren't bleeding but they looked very painful. He was moaning softly. Owen was still afraid that he might not get better.

Owen was at a loss. Now that he had quieted Oliver he didn't know what to do next. He felt fear creeping back in and fought back tears. Where could he go? He was just about to give up and give in to despair when his eyes rested on Odie. He paused and waited for a missing piece to fall into place. What was it about Odie that could help him? Owen's eyes opened wide and he suddenly knew what to do.

"Oliver! Wake up! Odie!"

Oliver opened his eyes. Owen's excitement had startled him. "Odie whut?"

"We lost Odie in the Blue River, remember?"

Oliver did not remember. He stared at Owen, waiting for him to explain what he was talking about.

"The Blue River is in Winterland!" Owen waited for his brother's happy reaction, but Oliver just continued to stare at him through half-closed eyes. "You know! *Winterland*! Uhhhhh! Oliver*rrr*! The shadow eyes can't get us in Winterland! Remember?"

"Can't finds us?"

"Nope!" Owen was thrilled with his new plan, which he had neglected to actually explain to Oliver.

Oliver looked at Owen with big, open eyes, waiting for him to finish.

"Uhhhhh! Oliver*rrr*! If Odie got *here*, then we can just follow the river back to Winterland!"

Oliver eyed the Black River warily. He didn't understand why Owen was so excited about following it. "No, Owen! Not the rivvuh!"

"Oliver, trust me! We'll follow it until it turns blue and then we'll be safe!"

"*Safe*?" The word *safe* had Oliver warming to the plan. "But whut about the punkin?"

"We'll come back and find it tomorrow."

Oliver sighed. He still wasn't sure about Owen's plan, but he did trust his big brother. "Okay, Owen."

Over the next hour, Oliver lay back and endured the pain from his wounds as Owen tried to cheer him up with all of the things that they would do when he got better. Owen got more and more animated as he talked. He truly believed that the very next day they would be riding the pumpkin again. He even managed to convince Oliver. The boys stayed there by the Black River, wrapped in their bubble of imagined safety, and hid from the reality of their situation.

Oliver could not be moved, let alone get up and walk. His wounds were too severe. He had lost so much blood that he barely had the strength to keep his eyes open. The boys had no clean water and they were afraid to drink from the Black River.

Oliver had soiled himself in the night, but Owen hid even from this. He couldn't remove Oliver's jeans without him screaming in pain, so he left him dirty and pretended that he didn't notice the smell. Owen even ignored the bright green sky overhead. If he didn't watch it, it couldn't grow dark.

Children dream of all sorts of fantastical adventures that they have the ability to truly believe in. They see a simple, straightforward path and neglect to consider any obstacles that might stand in their way. Owen was trapped in one of these fantasies. The day was passing but he still saw himself arriving safely in Winterland before the sun went down. He needed to believe this, and so he did.

Oliver passed the day in a haze of pain and thirst. He heard Owen's voice, but could make no sense of the words. Oliver was fading, but he was able to focus on his brother's presence. Owen was with him, talking to him and keeping him company. At one point Oliver became vaguely aware that Owen was trying to get him to eat something.

Owen had found the parrygus stalks in his pocket, but Oliver couldn't eat. Owen held the stalk to his mouth and Oliver nibbled a bit from the end of it. He wanted to please his big brother, but the bite sat in his mouth, unchewed and unswallowed. It only made Oliver feel his thirst all the more. Owen had said that they were going to Winterland to be safe. Oliver focused on eating the snow and maybe even drinking from the Blue River.

The day wore on. As the shadows in the ravine deepened, cracks began to form in Owen's mind. Still he fought against what was about to happen. When he felt the shadow eyes' presence and his tears started to fall, he went on telling Oliver that they would be safe.

He spoke softly with trembling, weeping words, "We're going to Winterland, Oliver, where the shadow eyes can't get us. They'll never get us again. We'll be safe there."

The shadow eyes took the boys and Owen spoke no more.

CHAPTER TWENTY-TWO

The brothers spent three nights, there on the banks of the Black River.

By the second morning, Oliver had gotten much worse. He groaned and cried for a long time after the shadow eyes had gone. He was feverish, and barely knew what was happening around him. He drifted in and out of the lingering nightmares that the shadow eyes had tortured him with, alternating between moans and whimpers as his pain competed with his fear. The strength to scream and cry drained out of Oliver, so that Owen didn't know just how badly he was suffering. Oliver spoke only twice that day. The first time was in answer to something Owen said to him.

It'll be okay, Oliver. We'll go to Winterland today. It'll be all right...
Okay, Owen...

The second time Oliver spoke was in the afternoon, to beg Owen for something to drink. After what seemed an eternity to Oliver, he had felt Owen's wet hand pressed to his mouth. The water had been awful and it had made Oliver very sad. Though he was still very thirsty, he did not ask for another drink. Oliver couldn't quite sleep. He was in too much pain. He tried not to move as he suffered through that long day.

Owen's suffering that second day was hardly less than his brother's. He never really recovered from the long night. He was very shaken, and he mistook Oliver's daze for apathy. If Owen could have known what was taking place in his brother's mind, he would have at least felt less lonely. As it was, he thought that he alone was left with the night's terrible thoughts and images.

Owen was a nervous wreck, jumping at shadows and at the slightest sounds. He insensibly clung to the idea that he and Oliver would go to Winterland that day and be safe. He told Oliver this, and Oliver had simply said "okay" before drifting back into his moaning.

Owen looked at his brother. His skin was pale white, except for patches of red that were creeping out from beneath the shirt that Owen had wrapped around him, and from the exposed punctures on his bare belly.

Owen was very afraid, but he did not know what to do. He had promised Mommy that he would take care of Oliver, but he had failed. Owen couldn't help but start to believe that what the shadow eyes had made him experience were not illusions but visions of a very real future. Would Mommy and Daddy still love him if he went back without Oliver? He didn't think so, which meant that he would have to stay in the land all alone for the rest of his life.

He tried to comfort Oliver and himself in the same way that he had the day before. He talked to Oliver about Mommy and nice things, but his words felt hollow, even to himself. He couldn't tell whether Oliver could even hear him.

In the afternoon Oliver started to beg for water. Owen told him that there was none but it seemed that Oliver couldn't hear him. He kept pleading for something to drink until, in desperation, Owen scooped a handful of water from the Black River and gave it to him. Oliver fell silent after that.

Owen stared at the lightless water. He, too, was very thirsty. He cupped his hands and dipped them in the water. He felt all happiness draining from him before he even brought his hands to his mouth. He drank greedily, then lay back overwhelmed with sadness. He, like Oliver, would not want to drink the black water again.

Throughout the day, Owen thought about the spot in the cave that could take him home. The land had changed. It frightened him now. He couldn't bear the thought of being there alone, but he didn't know how to save his little brother. Maybe it was time to take Oliver home. There were doctors who could help Oliver. Maybe when Oliver got sick again, Owen could make another birthday wish and bring them both back again...but Owen knew this wasn't true. He didn't know how he knew, but he did. Once they left the land, they would never be able to come back. Oliver would get sick and die.

Owen couldn't stand it anymore. He had to go home. He couldn't take care of Oliver anymore, but he couldn't live without him. He didn't know how to get Oliver to the cave, even if he did decide to go back. The water of the Black River was working in Owen. He sat by his brother, held his hand and cried while he waited for the shadow eyes to return.

On the third morning, Oliver didn't wake up. He wasn't moaning. His breathing was shallow. He was deathly still. Owen shook him, shouted at him, pleaded with him to wake up, but Oliver never stirred. His skin was so cold. Not knowing what else to do, Owen removed Oliver's jeans and cleaned him as best he could. He dressed him again and placed Odie on his chest and then he sat and cried.

The sky was gray and overcast. Owen cried out with his thoughts. He needed help.

Daddy, what do I do? What do I do? Daddy! Please, Daddy, help me! Mommy? Mommy!

He was answered by silence.

Owen stood up. He looked at Oliver and broke down one last time. He doubted himself very much. He thought about his brother running through the White River and laughing. He took a deep breath. He wasn't sure if he could do it, but he would try. Owen tucked Odie in his pants and then picked his brother up so that Oliver's head was resting on his chest and his bent legs dangled from Owen's hips. Owen clasped his hands under Oliver's bottom and began to walk, following the Black River to its source.

It was a difficult journey. Owen hurt all over. He was exhausted and Oliver's weight was hard for him to bear. He made slow progress. Every misstep made him feel like crying. Time passed too quickly. He stopped often to rest, and to shift Oliver's weight, but always he marched on again. More than once, he stumbled and fell. Each time, he managed to twist his body around so that he wouldn't land on his brother, yet each time Oliver's wounds bled anew.

When Owen reached the edge of the Deadwood Forest, the black hole trees were replaced with strange new trees that did not look any friendlier. These trees grew right to the edge of the Black River, hindering Owen's path. They were short with long branches that twisted like horns, and roots that grew up out of the ground to trip him. They had stiff, pointed leaves that poked Owen like needles. At times he had to put Oliver down, climb through a narrow space in the branches and then pull Oliver through after him. Owen felt relief that Oliver was not awake to scream in pain at his rough handling, then he punished himself for thinking those thoughts.

If only the hillside would grow a bit less steep he could abandon the river and climb out of the ravine, but the hills only became steeper as he went. Owen tried to fight the sadness emanating from the Black River. It did little good. Owen could barely remember that it was possible to feel any other way but sad and frightened.

The day was half gone when the narrow ravine opened up into a wide basin. The hillside had been gradually growing lower so that Owen thought he might soon be able to climb out. When he looked around now, he finally started to sob. He had walked into a swamp that was contained on both sides by sheer rock walls that rose ten feet straight up. The walls were pale gray and spotted with emerald green moss. They were topped with more of the strange, twisted trees whose roots hung down over the rock, but not low enough for Owen to grab. As if to add to his woes, the gray skies finally opened up and released a cold and heavy rain that drenched the brothers.

Owen was so discouraged that he didn't notice a change in the air, as if the melancholy was less stifling. He did notice, however, that the trees were less dense, leaving spaces of open grass that grew green and soft. He laid Oliver on the grass and sat by him. He shielded his brother's face from the rain with his raincoat. Owen let the swollen drops beat on his own face and head, and on his bare back. He didn't care about himself. He closed his eyes. His idea seemed so stupid now. They would never reach Winterland. Owen could take no more. His mind shut down, emptying of thoughts. He stopped crying. He felt numb.

As Owen sat, the magic in the land worked in him. He didn't feel it at first, but the rain was washing away much of his weariness and despair. He also hadn't noticed that in spite of the rain, he was no longer quite as cold as he'd been. He was no longer in Autumnland and yet he hadn't reached Summerland. He had found somewhere new, and soon he would open his eyes and see this new place with the wonder befitting the little boy that he was.

Oliver felt a nudge.

Mmmmm...

He felt another. He realized that it was raining and that he was wet.

Hmm-mmmm...

"Oliver? Are you waking up?"

Nooooo...

"Oliver, look!"

Oliver opened his eyes to see his brother's smiling face. He immediately started to moan. The pain in his shoulder was unbearable.

When Oliver opened his eyes, Owen bowed, rested his head against Oliver's thigh and wept with joy. He had not thought that Oliver would wake up, but the rain had worked a bit of magic in Oliver as well.

"Owen, get offuh me."

Owen lifted his head and started to laugh. He had been holding his arms up, careful not to spill what was in his hands. His heart felt so light that Oliver's crankiness could only amuse him. "Look at the water, Oliver!"

Oliver looked to see that Owen's cupped hands were filled with perfectly clear water.

Owen had sat patiently waiting for the rain to collect in his hands and then he had nudged Oliver awake. He had not yet taken a drink for himself.

Oliver wanted the water so badly that instead of speaking he simply opened his mouth wide and stuck out his tongue. He drank the water and said, "More!"

"You have to wait 'til I get more." Owen held out his cupped hands to gather more raindrops.

Oliver laid his head back and thrilled at every drop that landed in his open mouth. He was distracted when Owen said a word that he'd never heard.

"Oliver, look at the darkles!"

Oliver was still hazy, but he thought he heard Owen say *darkles*. He didn't know what that was. He looked up and saw that Owen was motioning with his head (he was still collecting rain with his hands), but Oliver was lying on his back and couldn't see anything. He was in too much pain to sit up.

"Whut, Owen! Whut's darkles? I can't see."

Owen brought his cupped hands to Oliver's mouth and let him drink what little rain he had collected, then he very gently put his hands under Oliver's back and lifted him. Oliver grunted and cried out. Owen quickly scooted in behind him. He sat up and brought Oliver to rest against his chest. Oliver could now lean back on his brother in a sitting position. Owen cupped his hands to catch more rain and motioned out over the wide swamp that had formed in the Black River.

This was the first still pond that the boys had seen since they had come to the land. A scattering of the strange horn trees (as Owen had already begun to think of them), were growing out of the stagnant water, water that didn't seem to be moving at all. It spread across the basin in a round body. Roughly a hundred yards past the boys, the rock walls narrowed like the neck of a bottle and rounded a bend, taking the opening of the swamp out of sight. On the near side where the boys sat, there was a grassy strip of land just wide enough for the boys to walk around the pond. On the far side there was no ground. There, the sheer rock wall dropped straight into the water.

Oliver had winced sharply when Owen had moved him. He kept his eyes shut and took several deep breaths while he waited for the intense pain in his neck and shoulder to subside. When the worst was over he opened his eyes and looked out over the water. Oliver saw the darkles and actually smiled through his pain at this simple, new wonder.

Oliver was looking at what he thought to be an intensely bright, lime green pond. Over the entire surface of the water, endless tiny black specks were rapidly flashing. Oliver thought that they were winking at him. He cupped the hand at the end of his uninjured arm and stared at the funny sight while he collected raindrops.

"Can't we drink the green water, Owen?"

"Nuh uh, that's still the Black River. It's only green on top."

Owen had already inspected the strange green layer close up. He didn't know the word algae, but he saw that the black water was covered with tiny leaves that were smaller than his pinky fingernail. What he called darkles were actually the individual raindrops hitting the surface, each one exposing the black water underneath for an instant before the tiny plants closed up again.

He tried to explain to Oliver, "The green is little leaves on the water. The darkles are raindrops."

"Whut? Wain drops?" Oliver tried to tilt his head to think but it hurt too much to do so. He sighed. He'd just have to figure it out later. He slurped the rainwater from his hand and lowered it. He was very tired.

Owen watched the darkles on the water while he continued to gather the rain. He was pleased by his own cleverness. He called them darkles because they were the exact opposite of sparkles. What Owen didn't know was that the layer of algae did more than just entertain him. The tiny leaves acted as a filter, absorbing much of the sadness that emanated from the dark water. It was this, as well as the cleansing rain, that had allowed the boys to finally smile.

When the rain eased and then stopped, Owen stood up. The reprieve from fear was over. The boys had to keep going. They had to get away from the Black River, or as Owen thought to himself as he looked at Oliver, he had to try.

He asked Oliver if he thought he could walk. He was feeling better so he naively assumed that Oliver felt better, too. He was quite wrong. Oliver could barely move. The water had refreshed him, but not healed him. Oliver had actually started to think of the shadow eyes again and was feeling panic build inside him.

"Owen, carry me!"

The urgency in Oliver's voice, weak though it was, was contagious. Owen felt a surge of adrenaline and went to scoop up his brother. However, Oliver screamed and swung his good arm when Owen tried to pick him up.

"Oliver, we have to get away from here! I have to pick you up!"

Oliver was sobbing now and Owen's own tears were very close.

"Wait, Owen!"

But Owen didn't wait. He tried to be gentle, but he also had to be quick. He felt a cold fear in his belly and it was about to take him over. Oliver screamed again as he was lifted. He managed not to swing at his brother this time, but it hurt so much. Owen told Oliver that he was sorry over and over as he hefted him into the same position as before. Owen's arms ached. His legs were sore. But he would go on. He had learned that he could.

Once Oliver was in Owen's arms, he tried to be still. Owen started to walk. Every step caused pain to shoot through Oliver's shoulder and through his wounded leg that rubbed against Owen's hip. He had meant to tell Owen that he was sorry for hitting him, but instead he cried because he hurt so much.

"It hurts! It hurts!" These were the only words that Oliver managed before he gave in to loud sobs that accompanied Owen's every step.

The clouds were breaking up to reveal a rare and bizarre sienna sky. When the sun appeared, Owen saw that time was running out. He wanted to walk faster but he was afraid that he would fall if he did. It had been a long time since he had had to flee with Oliver in his arms. Never had he felt this tired. He hadn't eaten since the scanty meal of smashed parrygus the day before. Owen tried to ignore his own body's hurts. He hadn't been bitten or clawed by the creatures, but his tumble down the side of the hill from the leaf-catching spot had left him bruised and battered all over.

As the boys neared the neck of the basin, the rock walls gradually grew darker and took on a brown hue. The horn trees disappeared from their summit. Owen began to think he heard a strange noise between Oliver's sobs. It was almost like a dull roar.

Owen stopped to look around. He was very frightened now. He saw nothing so he continued his march, but he kept expecting the dark creatures to leap out at him. The roar was growing louder. Just before the boys reached the curve in the wall Oliver finally heard the roar, too, and began to squeal and whimper as if he were having a fit.

Those final steps toward an unknown terror were the second bravest that Owen would ever take. His legs had turned to jelly. His whole body was trembling. Whatever was making that noise, it was right around the bend. Owen started to cry, but he kept going. He had to save his baby brother from the shadow eyes, no matter what lie ahead.

Oliver was scared senseless. His wounded arm hung lifeless at his side and his other was wrapped tightly around Owen's neck. He existed in a haze of pain and fear. The nightmare replayed in his head over and over. He was going to be eaten while the shadow eyes watched. He, too, was trembling all over. He buried his face in Owen's chest. Owen was holding him. Whatever happened, they loved each other and they were together.

Owen rounded the bend. He stopped and stared. Oliver's head was still buried in his chest, facing toward the setting sun, back the way they had come. The terrifying noise was deafening. It bounced off of the rock walls, seeming to come from everywhere.

Then Oliver heard Owen make a noise that made no sense to him. He couldn't tell if Owen were laughing or crying. *Laughing*; Owen was laughing. Oliver felt himself spun around as Owen turned to let him see.

It was a waterfall, a brilliant orange waterfall. The two sides of the rock wall came together and where they met, the Orange River flowed over them and crashed into the algae-covered rocks ten feet below. The sun was setting through the clouds behind the boys. Its bright red rays reflected off of the orange waterfall in an ever-changing dance of crimson shines. A glowing pink mist rose from the murky blackness of the mire that the waterfall fed.

Oliver stared at this sight. He didn't laugh with his brother. He cried. His sobs abated until silent tears ran down his face. Then he closed his eyes and saw nothing more. His strength was gone. He felt nothing as Owen turned around and approached the waterfall. The strain had been too much for Oliver. He had given in to the sweet oblivion of a little child's deep and dreamless sleep.

Owen continued on and soon reached the crashing waters. The grass beneath his feet had given way to solid rock the color of stained wood. Owen found that this rock at the base of the wall formed a ledge that ran beneath the waterfall. He carried Oliver through the dampening pink mist and stopped behind the falling water, where the sun's rays shone through the beautiful orange cascade, bestowing it with luminance as if it were made of light.

For a moment Owen was transfixed. He wondered if he and Oliver would be safe there. He was so very tired. All he wanted to do was sit and rest. He felt hidden, so well hidden that even the shadow eyes would not be able to find him. He held out his hand to touch the curtain of orange and red light. Where his fingers broke the veneer, rills of light appeared around them in the shape of upside down V's that moved smoothly and unbroken when he moved his hand. The water was very warm.

Owen pulled his hand back and licked the moisture from his fingers. The taste was vibrant and sweet. It was like drinking the nectar of some marvelous fruit that he'd never before tasted, only it wasn't sticky, and there was a strange aftertaste of exotic spices. The little sip of the Orange River began to clear Owen's head.

As the Green River healed the boys' bodies and the White River lightened their spirits, so the Orange River now opened and sharpened Owen's mind. He immediately saw that when the sun went down, the light would disappear and leave him in darkness. He was standing right at the mouth of the Black River. He drank a handful of the enlightening waters and then hurried on. The shining waterfall was already beginning to dim.

Owen fought a losing battle to hold back his tears. Now that Oliver was unconscious, Owen felt incredibly alone. He hefted his brother higher up on his hips and walked along the rock and into the mist on the other side. He stepped carefully. The ground was hidden under the spray and was wet and slippery.

Owen safely emerged from under the waterfall and saw that on the other side a large diagonal crack had split the rock wall, forming a steep and narrow path to the top. At first he tried to ascend this incline with Oliver still in his arms, but the extra weight threw off his balance. It was too steep.

Panic was struggling to overcome the effects of the orange water and to cloud his thoughts. Owen began to emit a whimpering cry as his tears fell. He tried laying Oliver down and scuttling up the slope backwards, dragging Oliver by his armpits, but he could find no traction and his feet kept slipping. Owen desperately kicked out with his legs but he went nowhere.

Owen was again at a loss. He stopped and sat, feeling hopeless. He tried to think but by now he was frightened almost completely out of his wits. He looked around wildly. He shifted himself to climb up alone on his hands and knees and finally the answer came to him. He turned back to Oliver and gently lifted him to a sitting position. Owen sat in front of him and pulled his brother's arms around his neck. He then leaned forward onto all fours, shifting his weight to lift Oliver onto his back. Keeping his legs straight and his arms bent, Owen was able to keep his back level so that Oliver stayed put, allowing Owen to use his hands and feet to scurry up the slope. He slipped only once, and felt a surge of fear like the world was ending when he felt Odie slip from his waistband, but he quickly recovered and made it to the top.

The ground on top of the wall was wet; a layer of soft and silky mud. Before Owen even looked around, he rolled his brother off of his back and slid down the crack in the wall to retrieve the stuffed dog. By the time he reached the top again he was incoherently blubbering, certain that he could feel the shadow eyes, or worse, reaching for him from below. But when he turned there was nothing there.

Owen laid Odie on Oliver's chest and wrapped his brother's uninjured arm around him. Then he stooped and gently placed his hands under Oliver's arms and dragged him through the mud, away from the edge of the rock wall and from the bank of the Orange River. He wasn't looking where he was going. He just needed to get away from the Black River.

Owen was facing the setting sun as he backed up through the silt. He saw that only a sliver was still visible on the horizon. After only a few steps the ground became dry and Owen found himself dragging his brother through very soft sand. It was unlike any sand that Owen had seen, even in picture books. It was dark brown, and so fine that it moved almost like a light and airy liquid.

When Owen had gone a short distance he stopped. He ran to the Orange River and retrieved two handfuls of water for Oliver. He tried to wake him up but Oliver would not open his eyes. Owen used his forehead to open his brother's mouth, spilling most of the orange water from his hands. He poured what was left into Oliver's mouth. Oliver sputtered and choked but did not wake up. Owen felt discouraged and scared. Oliver had woken up before to drink. Owen didn't understand why he wasn't waking up now.

Owen looked around for the first time. He was in another new place, more bizarre than the last. As far as he could see, the brown sand spread before him. He and Oliver were on a large, perfectly smooth expanse of lifeless desert. It rose in the near distance to the ruddy brown sky in dunes and ridges, and the Orange River cut a straight line through it all. A gibbous orange moon was rising over the river opposite to where the last piece of the sun had just dipped below the horizon. Stars began to pierce the darkening brown sky, creating the illusion of bringing its vast, endless movement to a sudden stop.

Owen felt something brand new awaken in him. The sublime beauty of this desolate landscape actually offered him comfort. Not for the first time, Owen felt very small. But this was different; it felt okay to be small. The vastness would protect him. His insignificance would hide him from danger. Owen didn't understand that this was what he felt. He simply knew that a calm was washing over him and making him feel brave.

As with the unbroken snow of Winterland, there was nothing here to cast a shadow. The eyes would not feast on the boys that night. Again, Owen had saved his brother. They were safe.

Owen looked at Oliver. There was fresh blood seeping from his wounds, blossoming into the thick mud that covered him. Loneliness overtook Owen. His chin dropped to his chest and as the last of the day's light drained from the sky, his shoulders shook with quiet sobs.

CHAPTER TWENTY-THREE

The boys slept through the sunrise. Owen had eventually lain next to his brother for warmth and had fallen asleep looking up at the stars. He had tried to wake Oliver so that he could see them, too, but he hadn't been able to rouse him.

Owen had had a night of intense dreams, perhaps an effect of the moon moving across the night sky, or perhaps it had been the magic in the Orange River. Some dreams take such hold that they are an exhausting ordeal, whether scary or not. Owen's dreams had been of this kind the entire night, and he'd had both scary and not.

He woke up feeling tired and dizzy under a bright purple sky. His body felt tingly. It wasn't until he stretched that he noticed he and Oliver were three-quarters buried in the warm, dark brown sand. It didn't scare him; in fact, he felt safe and snug, like the land was giving him a warm hug.

Childish as the notion may seem, it actually wasn't far from the truth. The air over the lifeless desert was dry and did not hold the heat of the sun once it was gone. The sand, however, stayed warm all through the night. When the boys had started shivering in their sleep, the vibration on this impossibly fine sand had caused the boys to sink until they were nice and warm. Owen did not want to get up. This was like lying in air. He stayed where he was and did something that felt almost alien for its recent absence: he smiled.

Owen finally had to emerge from the sand to pee. He walked to the edge of the rock wall and peed over the side, making his own little waterfall next to the crashing orange waterfall to his right. He then walked back to where Oliver lay and tried to wake him, but Oliver wouldn't stir. This stole Owen's smile away. Oliver did not look good at all. He looked like he was wasting away.

A sharp hunger pang cut through Owen's belly, doubling him over. He must find food today. Maybe *that* would help Oliver to get better. Owen went to the Orange River and drank his fill of its water. This helped to take the edge off of his hunger and it awakened his mind. He had an idea.

Keeping Oliver in his sight, Owen edged along the bank of the river until he found a spot where he could reach in and touch the bottom. The current was swift, but not swift enough to carry away a little boy and his brother. Owen drew a large arrow in the sand to mark the spot and then went to retrieve Oliver.

Owen had taken off his shoes and socks and was enjoying the feel of this soft sand on his bare feet. He sank to his ankles with each step, but his feet sifted through it effortlessly. He thought to himself that it was like walking in powdered sugar, except that it didn't taste good.

Owen gently dragged his brother through the powdery sand until he reached the arrow. He then started to undress Oliver, but his clothes were stuck to his wounds. Owen immediately wanted to give up on his stupid idea. He had found great strength and bravery, but the traumas of the last few days had left him very fragile. He hit at the sand and let his hot tears flow for a few moments, and then he calmed down and tried to think. What had Mommy done when his band-aid had stuck to his cuts? It was hopeless! He couldn't remember! He beat at the sand and shouted in frustration. Owen looked at his poor little brother. He would do anything if Oliver would only wake up and talk to him. When Owen stopped trying to remember, the memory came to him. Mommy had left the band-aid on until bath time, and then it had fallen off all by itself! Owen stepped into the Orange River with all of his clothes on and pulled Oliver, fully dressed, in after him.

Oliver was dreaming. The dark creatures were surrounding him. There were lifeless black eyes hidden all over them, under their fur. The creatures kept circling ever closer without reaching him. Every time he saw an open space he tried to run but he just fell forward because only his top half worked. Every time Oliver fell, he heard the creatures roar and pounce, but then he would roll over and stand back up to find them circling, circling. This seemed to go on forever. Then all at once, they fell upon him. He shrieked and screamed as their teeth and claws ripped through him.

Oliver awoke to intense pain crackling like fire through his many wounds. He screamed and struggled and drew in breath to scream again, but there was no air. He drew in lungfuls of water. He felt himself lifted roughly and then he was choking. He vomited violently and then he was gasping for air. The pain had already subsided. He heard Owen yelling his name.

When Owen had pulled his brother into the Orange River, he had suddenly come to. Owen was taken by surprise by Oliver's fit and he dropped him. Just as Oliver's head submerged, Owen heard him gurgle as the water entered his mouth. Owen instantly pulled him up and beat on his back. He was terrified that he had drowned him.

Oliver finally opened his eyes. He was completely disoriented. He felt something holding him and he continued to struggle. He heard Owen's voice. Where was he? He was in the Black River! Oliver closed his eyes and panicked.

"Oliver! Oliver! It's okay! You're okay! It's me, Owen! It's Owen! Oliver!"

Oliver stopped struggling and cried. It was the loud, angry wail of a very small child who has just been very scared. Owen held him and explained.

"We're at the top of the waterfall, Oliver. It's safe up here! It's just like Winterland! See? It's a new river. It's *orange!*"

Owen held him from behind. Oliver settled down and leaned his head back to feel his brother.

Owen said, "You okay, Oliver?"

When he felt Oliver nod, Owen let him go and maneuvered around so that they sat in the water face to face. He smiled at his brother.

Oliver sat and breathed heavily. He looked down at the pretty orange water and all around at the dunes and ridges of dark brown sand. A few breaths of surprised laughter forced their way out through his nose. He looked at Owen and said, "*WHUT?*"

His simple, confused question made Owen laugh, which, of course, made Oliver laugh.

"Aren't you going to take a drink, Oliver? It's okay."

Oliver was still trying to clear his head after his long sleep. He looked down at the water for a moment, as if seeing it for the first time, and then he scooped handful after handful into his mouth. Owen sat and watched him. He felt very happy. Oliver was back. Owen waited in amusement to see how Oliver would react to the magic in the water.

Oliver finished drinking and tilted his head. His neck didn't hurt so much now. He did that thing that Owen so loved to watch him do. Keeping his head perfectly still, Oliver's eyes grew wide and looked all around, trying to make sense of his surroundings.

"Where's Odie?" Oliver asked.

Owen was now very glad that he had gone back to retrieve the stuffed dog. He pointed to where Odie lay in the sand, safe and sound. "He's okay. I dropped him climbing the cliff but I went back and got 'im."

Oliver breathed a sigh of relief, but then his brow crinkled in confusion. "Cliff?"

So Owen told him the story of what he had slept through. Oliver's favorite part was when they went *under* the waterfall. He was amazed by what his big brother could do.

"You cay-weed me? Thanks, Owen!"

For no reason at all, both boys laughed at Oliver's thank you. They enjoyed a little break, sitting in the Orange River. The bed of the river was soft clay. It felt to the boys like they were sitting on firm cushions. Owen rolled balls of the clay and threw them as hard as he could, trying to get them to go over the falls. Oliver yelled, "Close!" after each throw landed short. The boys giggled to each other and made silly faces, wasting time and not thinking about what to do next.

When they had soaked long enough, Owen undressed his brother. Oliver winced in pain, but it wasn't nearly as bad as it had been. After soaking in the water, his skin was not as tight around his wounds. Owen inspected the wounds, being very careful not to touch them. They were still inflamed, but now that all of the gunk and dried blood had been washed away they looked much better, cleaner. Oliver did not look at them. He was afraid to see. Owen was relieved by this. As scared as the gashes made him, he thought that they would scare Oliver even more.

"Do you think you can walk, Oliver?"

"No! Cay-wee me!"

Owen sighed and then laughed. It was the answer he expected, although he suspected that Oliver was being tricksy.

Oliver smiled, too. He liked being carried. It reminded him of Mommy.

Getting dressed was difficult for both boys, sore as they were, but especially for Oliver. Luckily the sand that caked on the boys under their clothes was so fine that it didn't irritate them. It did just the opposite, as if the boys had rolled around in baby powder. Still, Owen had to be very careful with Oliver's wounds. They were very tender to the touch, and the damp clothes were much harder to put on then they had been to take off. Oliver squealed and insisted on remaining naked, but Owen said no, mostly because he didn't want to have to carry both Oliver *and* his clothes, at least that's what he told Oliver. What he didn't tell him was that he didn't want to have to see those scary slashes in Oliver's skin.

Owen pulled Oliver out of the water and gently set him on his feet in the sand. When Oliver sank to his ankles he started to laugh. This changed everything. He now wanted to walk through the funny sand by himself, but when he tried to take a step, pain flared in his injured thigh and he collapsed. He started to cry, as much out of frustration as from the pain in his leg. He wanted to play.

Owen saw that he wasn't being tricksy, after all. He said soothing things to comfort his little brother, telling him that they would come back when he was better, and then he gently picked him up as he had before, face to face with his hands clasped under Oliver's bottom. Oliver wrapped his good arm around Owen's neck and the boys set out.

Oliver stared at Owen's feet moving through the sand as he fought between hunger, pain and exhaustion. He slipped in and out of a light doze throughout the afternoon.

Owen scanned the horizon for any sign of something that they could eat. He saw nothing but sand. He, too, was very hungry.

A growing fear was gnawing at each of the boys. They were lost. It had been a very long time since the boys had felt lost in the land. It was hard for them to cope with this forgotten feeling. They both wished fervently that the pumpkin were there, not only to take them home but so they could feel its joy.

They stuck close to the river where the sand was flat and shadowless, stopping often to drink and to rest. They talked about finding the pumpkin and eating parrots and rainbowberries. They looked forward to going back to their cave and playing with their cars and bouncy balls. Owen said that it was time to take a bunch of his rocks down to the Green River and throw them in. He said that they would pick them out together and that Oliver could throw half of them. They talked about Mommy and Daddy and Owen shared some of his favorite memories of them. The boys did not talk about their fears. Both of them were trying very hard to be brave for each other.

When the sun started to set, the boys' fear rose to the surface. They were afraid that the shadow eyes would find them. They were afraid that they would starve to death. They were afraid that they would be lost forever.

Oliver started to whimper.

Owen had barely been holding back his tears, but when he heard Oliver's quiet whimpers, he couldn't hold them any longer. He marched on anyway, trying to sniffle the tears back in. Oliver was still watching his brother's feet. Owen had long since stopped looking around and was also staring at his own feet. Both of the brothers were willing the night not to come, but it was coming anyway.

Owen stopped and looked up. What he saw drained what little strength he had left. He dropped to his knees and held his brother tightly enough to make him cry out, then a torrent of tears flowed from his eyes.

"It's okay, Owen. It's okay!" Oliver tried his best to comfort his big brother, but he was facing the other way and hadn't seen what Owen saw.

Owen yelled out in anger, frustration and hopelessness. "It's *not* okay! *Look!*"

Oliver couldn't twist around to see, so he patted Owen and continued to try and make him feel better. "Shhhh, Owen. It's okay. Shhhhh."

This made Owen cry out even louder. He turned so that Oliver could see.

The Orange River disappeared into a line of hills not twenty feet from where the boys had stopped. It had formed a tunnel under the hills out of which it flowed. There was no way around and the boys would not brave the darkness of the low tunnel.

Oliver couldn't make sense of this. "Where's the river?"

"I don't know!" Owen squealed.

"What do we do, Owen?"

"I don't *know!*"

Oliver began to cry with his brother. Owen didn't have the answer. This shook the core of Oliver's courage. His confidence in Owen had been unwavering up to that moment. He had grown to see him as he used to see his Daddy, able to do anything. Now he saw Owen just as he was: a scared little boy. Oliver's mind recoiled from this glimpse of frightening reality. It didn't seem possible that Owen didn't know what to do. Oliver couldn't comprehend it. He refused to believe it. He grew angry with Owen for scaring him.

"Owen! Stop it!" He screamed.

This shocked Owen into silence. He lifted his head and looked at the terror in Oliver's eyes. Oliver was counting on him. Owen took a deep breath. "I'm sorry, Oliver. It'll be okay. I promise."

The boys cried themselves to sleep that night under the bright starlight. As the night air cooled, the sand pulled them in and kept them warm. In the morning, Owen would indeed find the answer. The boys would find many answers. Eventually, they would find the way home, but it would not be what they remembered.

CHAPTER TWENTY-FOUR

It was Oliver's turn to wake up first. He lay in Owen's arms enjoying the warmth of the sand as Owen had done the day before. He didn't lay there long, however, before he began to remember the events of the last several days. He relived just a glimpse of each terrifying and painful moment before moving on to the next. In this way he tried to outrun the terrible traumas in his mind, only to end up at the unwanted conclusion that was the boys' current predicament. Oliver quickly hid from this, too. He retreated back into the moment, feeling safe in his big brother's arms.

The sky above him was chartreuse. It was a cheerful color. Oliver decided that he would not get up from the sand that day. He would lay there in his warm cocoon and let Owen sleep all day. He played with Odie, telling him about the nice things they had found, like the darkles and the orange waterfall, and sparing the stuffed dog (as well as himself), from the bad things that scared him.

Although Oliver's mind was happy to hide, his body had other plans. It wasn't long before he needed to go to the bathroom. He managed to hold it, but he was also getting very thirsty. Soon his tummy was rumbling angrily, and then painfully. When he shifted to relieve the ache from his full bladder, pain flared in his wounds, threatening his serenity with the memory of how he had gotten them. He didn't want to be alone anymore.

"Owen? Wake up." He nudged his brother. "Owen."

Owen stirred and opened his eyes. He enjoyed the realization that he was in the warm sand again.

"Owen, I'm hungry...I'm thirsty...my arm hurts...my neck hurts..." Oliver was close to tears.

Owen tried to clear his head. It wasn't easy with Oliver hitting him with so much at once. He sat up, and then had to lean forward until a spell of dizziness passed. Oliver was looking up at him expectantly.

"Do you have to go to the bathroom, Oliver?"

"Uh-huh! Uh-huh!"

Owen stood up and then pulled Oliver to his feet, supporting him under his good arm. This had happened too fast. Oliver blacked out. When he went limp, Owen wasn't ready and he nearly dropped him. The movement was painful enough to snap Oliver out of his stupor. He leaned forward and retched into the sand.

Owen didn't know what to do. He held on to his brother, feeling scared. Old, old memories came back to him. He hadn't seen Oliver so sick and weak since...but he banished the thought before it could finish forming.

"Are you okay, Oliver?"

Oliver didn't answer. He felt awful. He concentrated on breathing. He had felt okay when he was lying still, but all of that movement had made him feel nauseous and very weak. He wished that Owen would put him down, though he said nothing; it was taking all of his focus just to breathe. Owen held him and waited. Oliver tried lifting his head just a little bit...so far, so good. He didn't notice that he had wet himself. He managed to raise his head almost level. He stared out at where the bright green sky met the dark brown hills.

Oliver whispered, "Thuhsty."

Owen carried him to the riverbank as gently as he could. He set Oliver down and then cupped some of the orange water in his hand. Oliver sipped the water from his brother's hand and felt a little better. His head cleared, though he still felt very weak.

Once Oliver could sit up on his own, Owen drank his own thirst away. He then took Oliver's shoes and socks off so that he could dangle his feet in the water. Owen did the same for himself and the brothers sat for a while by the sandy riverbank.

Owen was thinking. He looked around at the hills out of which the river flowed. They weren't very high, after all. He thought that maybe he could climb over them, but he couldn't leave Oliver behind. He wished he had his blanket.

"Whattuh we gonna do, Owen?"

Owen said nothing at first. He knew that Oliver wouldn't like the answer.

"Owen?"

"We gotta climb over the hill."

Oliver did not react as Owen expected. He looked at the hills that were hiding the river's source and simply said, "Okay, Owen."

Oliver *wanted* to climb the hill. He liked to climb. The fact that he was far too weak to do so never figured into his thinking.

It was, however, all that Owen was thinking about. Owen knew that he'd have to carry him. He wasn't sure that he could. Maybe the hill was soft and he could drag him. Oliver wouldn't like that.

"Ready, Oliver?"

Oliver took a deep breath. It was a comically adult mannerism and it made Owen smile in spite of the circumstances, as did the resignation with which Oliver answered, "I'm ready."

Owen put their shoes and socks back on and helped Oliver to his feet. Oliver winced and hissed in air through his teeth, but he managed to not cry out. Owen kept his supporting arms around his brother so that he wouldn't fall, doing his best to avoid his wounds.

"Can you walk now?"

With a nod, Oliver said, "Uh huh."

Of course, Oliver could *not* walk, but Owen pretended to believe that he could. He wanted to keep his little brother in good spirits as long as possible. The boys made their way to the bottom of the lowest hill, Oliver shuffling the foot at the end of his uninjured leg through the sand as Owen half-dragged and half-carried him.

Too soon came the part that Owen had been dreading. He set Oliver down with his back against the slope and waited to see what he would do. Oliver awkwardly looked down at his feet. He hurt all over. He knew that he couldn't do it. All of a sudden, he didn't seem to know what to do with his hands. He sat there, waiting for Owen to do something, and making embarrassed movements with his fingers.

Owen asked, "Do you need me to carry you?"

Oliver nodded without looking up.

"*Okay*, but it might hurt."

"No, Owen! *Don't* make it hurt!"

"I have to carry you on my back. Okay?"

Oliver didn't see what Owen meant. "With your *back?*"

"Not *with* my back, *on* my back. I'll show you."

Owen knelt in front of Oliver with his back to him and leaned back until the boys were almost touching. "Now put your arms around me."

Oliver raised his good arm to Owen's shoulder. "Like dis?"

Owen grabbed Oliver's forearm and leaned forward, lifting Oliver onto his back. Oliver cried out and started yelling at Owen to stop. His tender wounds were flaring with pain. Owen quickly turned around and started up the hill on all fours as he had done when he climbed the rock wall. Oliver wanted to struggle but it hurt too much to move and also he was afraid that he would fall off.

Oliver screamed at his brother. "Stop! Stoppit! Owen! *Please stop!* Put me down! Owen *please! Pleeeease!* Please stop HURTING MEEEEEEEE!"

Owen said nothing. He let his own tears fall and continued up the hill. Oliver continued to scream and cry. His agony was his brother's agony. Owen slipped and his face hit the dirt, jarring a piercing shriek from Oliver. Owen had bloodied his own nose. His vision blurred with even more tears, but he kept going, swallowing the blood that was filling his mouth. All the while Oliver's shrill cries deafened him.

And then, they were at the top. Owen set his brother down and then held his own bleeding nose. All that blood scared him and he wailed right along with Oliver. When Oliver saw the blood running down his brother's face and through his fingers, he cried even harder, his own pain forgotten in his concern for Owen, who sat hunched over with his hands over his face and sobbed.

"I'm sorry!" Owen squealed. "I'm sorry, Oliver!" His voice broke with remorse. He had hurt his little brother so badly. He had made him *scream.* Owen rocked back and forth, chanting, *"I'm sorry...I'm sorry..."* over and over. He was afraid to look at Oliver.

Oliver tried to pat Owen on the shoulder but he couldn't reach him. He told Owen that it was okay, that *he* was okay, but Owen wouldn't calm down. The brothers sat for a long time, each sobbing out their anguish for the pain that they had caused the other.

When many minutes had passed, Owen snuck a timid peek at his brother. Oliver was all right. He was crying softly, but he was all right.

In a calm and gentle voice, Owen said, "I'm sorry I hurt you, Oliver."

Oliver was startled by his brother's voice. He looked up at him and started to cry harder. Oliver felt that he had been bad. He didn't quite understand how, but he knew that it was his fault that Owen had cried. Oliver didn't say anything. He was waiting, not for Owen's apology, but for his forgiveness.

Owen wiped the blood from his face and spat until he couldn't taste it anymore. Oliver looked back down at his awkwardly positioned hands and moved them over Odie's back. He picked up the stuffed dog and offered it to Owen, who finally smiled and took the dog. He gave it a squeeze and asked it if it was all right. Oliver answered for the stuffed animal with an affirmative *yip*. Owen handed Odie back to Oliver and looked out from the top of the hill for the first time. What he saw left him stunned as he stared in disbelief.

"*Whoa...*Oliver...*look,*" he whispered.

Oliver turned to see what was waiting for them on the other side of the hill. He sat and stared for a few moments. He smiled, then he chuckled once, and then he was laughing, even though it hurt to do so. Owen laughed with him.

When Owen had recovered from the initial shock he said, "Okay. Going down will be easier. You can sit on your butt and scoot. We'll go real slow, I promise."

It would have been difficult to keep that promise, for Owen was barely able to contain himself, but he needn't have worried. Without waiting another second, Oliver started shuffling down the hill with his good leg as fast as he could.

Though the boys had seen many beautiful and wondrous places throughout the land, they all paled in comparison to the sheer grandeur of the valley that now spread below them. The boys had found the very heart of that magical land, where all things came together. It was the core, the center, hidden in this remarkable place. As they had looked out from the crest of the hill, their eyes had been met by all four seasons at once. The four rivers: Gold, Green, White and Blue, were all flowing toward the boys, cutting the valley floor for miles into long narrow wedges.

From the far left came the Gold River through all the magnificence of Autumn. From the far right came the Blue River, bringing the peace and stillness of unbroken snow. Forming a perfect "V" between the two came the Green River sparkling through lush grass and fruit-laden trees, and the White River, floating over its bed of stones through an endless shower of blossoms and fresh, bright flowers. The four rivers met at the base of the hill and disappeared under the earth, where their waters mingled unseen, transforming through unknown mysteries to emerge on the other side as the brilliant Orange River, whose waters had granted to the boys the land's final gift of unlocking their intellects to help them better understand.

All of the different trees that the boys had seen throughout the seasons were scattered across the valley floor. The bright colors of Autumn leaves swirled around the pumpkin apples. Fire trees let fall their yellow flames over endless red parrot leaves. The woods of Summer beckoned the boys with pinkberry patches, melon trees, flutter trees and paint plants, sprinkled throughout with rainbowberries that stretched across grassy fields. Purple parrygus stalks bloomed in the Spring, as well as fields of rain peas, orchards of blossom trees and more of the magenta rainbowberries.

Birds filled the sky. Black birds swooped and cawed, the little blue birds sang and played with their large, red-plumed cousins. Cow-pies grazed peacefully in Spring and Summer and pipchunks chased each other through the fallen leaves of Autumn, and up and down its trees' bare branches. Accompanying the music of the breeze in the swaying trees, the flowing waters and the birdsong, were the harmonies of the singing fish in the Gold River.

After the desolate sands, this vibrant vision of life and contrasts affected the boys as if they were awakening, refreshed and eager, from a long sleep.

Where the four rivers met, a tiny isle poked out of the water. The island was made of stark white rock and was topped with a patch of vibrant green grass. Aside from this lush grass, there grew only a single, pure white orchid in the center of the bit of land. The boys' hunger forgotten, it was to this giant flower that they now hurried. They were irresistibly drawn to it, as it was the most beautiful thing they had ever seen.

Oliver had started down the hill first. Owen followed close behind, impatiently urging him on. Oliver was too excited to take notice. Every tooth was showing as he panted through a smile that felt like it would never leave his face. Pain flared in his leg and was easily ignored.

Owen saw that the hill ended in a short drop to the mixing waters below. The boys were directly above a strip of the Green River. Owen yelled at his brother to stop, but Oliver never even slowed down. When he reached the drop, he pushed himself right over the edge and fell face-first into the water below. Owen jumped in after him to find that the water was just deep enough to cushion his fall.

Oliver had cried out when he'd landed but his face had instantly reemerged and was already smiling again. The green water had immediately gone to work in him, soothing his pain and healing his wounds, for there the magic in the rivers was at its strongest. Owen, too, felt his aches and bruises disappear as he helped his brother to wade through the sparkling emerald water.

The boys reached the tiny island. It was just wide enough for both of them to comfortably spread out on its soft grass. Owen helped Oliver climb onto it and the boys lay next to each other on their tummies with their elbows and knees bent, resting their chins in their hands and their feet in the air. They lay in front of the beautiful orchid as if in a trance, soaking up the love of which the flower was made. It was the love that the boys had missed and needed most. It had been right there all along, at the heart of everything, gently seeping into the land to find the boys wherever they went, though they had never known it. The flower was larger than Owen's two hands together. Its long lower lip swooped down in a graceful arc, releasing its sweet fragrance: the scent of Mommy.

The boys stayed by the orchid for more than an hour. They didn't speak; they didn't need to. They could feel each other's happiness. When they were filled up with the flower's love, they turned to each other and smiled. Oliver climbed onto his brother and gave him a kiss, then they both rolled into the water and made their way to the green shore of Summerland.

The boys feasted on pinkberries and melons and had rainbowberries for dessert. The rivers were shallow and the boys splashed in them all, even the frigid Blue River. They ran across the flowered fields of Springland and jumped in the leaves of Autumnland. They rolled in the grass of Summerland and built a snowman in Winterland. For a time, all of their hardships and fears were forgotten. They ran about and played tag, hide-and-seek, and a strange game that they called "spit-threes."

When the sun began to set, the boys were not afraid. Oliver stopped and picked some of the pretty red parrot leaves for Mommy, as he always did. The boys calmly waded back to the little isle to say goodnight to the white flower. Owen then turned toward the hill but Oliver stayed a moment. He pulled the parrot leaves from his pocket, carefully smoothed them out, and lovingly laid them before the orchid. Owen had stopped to watch this, and he smiled at his brother's innocence.

Oliver was much younger than Owen. Truly, it *was* his innocence that allowed him to know some few things that Owen did not. Just as Oliver had recognized the joy of which the pumpkin was made, so now he knew the love that was the orchid. He rearranged the pretty red leaves so that they were perfect and then he beamed up at the orchid, as if for approval. The flower seemed to shine a little brighter, just for a moment, making Oliver very happy. Before he turned away, he leaned toward the flower and whispered something that Owen didn't hear, then he joined his brother at the foot of the hill.

The boys helped each other to climb out of the water. Oliver's wounds were barely sore by then. The brothers held hands and leisurely scaled the hill. They paused at the top for one more look at the hidden valley and then climbed back down the other side to spend the night safely under the bright stars, snug in the warm, shadowless brown sand.

The boys sat up for a while and talked before lying down to sleep. They wanted to enjoy the stars, and to watch the Orange River as it flowed across the desert plain.

"Aw we gonna find the punkin tomorrow, Owen?"

"Yup! All we have to do is follow the river."

"The Green River? That one take us home!"

"But the pumpkin's not *at* home. Remember? It's still waiting for us by the leaf-catching spot."

"I don't wanna go back *there*, Owen!"

"We have to! That's our *pumpkin*! What if it misses us? And how're we gonna get anywhere without it?"

"I dunno." Oliver paused. "So how'uh we gonna find it?"

"Easy! We'll follow the *Gold* River."

Oliver tilted his head and squished his mouth to one side. "Okay, Owen! I like the Gold River!"

"But first we'll sit with the flower some more before we say goodbye."

"Yeah! Can we come back here, Owen? Aff-tuh we find the punkin?"

"*Yeah*-uh! We'll come back here every day!"

"Whoo-hoo!" Oliver clapped his hands excitedly. "But first we'll see the flower?"

"Yup."

"Okay, Owen."

The boys talked on, making plans for when they found the pumpkin and could go back to their cave. They spoke no more of the white orchid that night. Neither one knew how to express what the flower made them feel. It was almost as if it were too special to say out loud, and must be kept inside them where it would be safe. No matter what the boys said, the white flower's love was there, just behind their words. It had always been there, and always would be, even when the boys didn't think they could feel it.

The boys stopped talking and stared up at the stars. They felt safe, and at peace.

Oliver fell asleep, happily repeating in his mind what he had whispered to the flower. It was a secret; one that he knew Owen wouldn't understand. It had been only two words: *Goodnight, Mommy.*

The next morning Oliver woke to find that he was alone in the sand. He sat up and saw Owen sitting by the Orange River, splashing his feet in the water.

Owen was deep in thought. He'd woken up and come to the river to clear his head. He didn't want to leave the valley. He was thinking that he and Oliver could just stay there forever, but he also missed the glow cave and his treasures. He thought about the make-place and the blossom-filled meadows of Springland. A piece of Springland was there in the valley, too, but it wasn't quite the same as when it stretched as far as he could see. Most of all he thought about the magic pumpkin. He missed it very much. He missed falling asleep to its warm glow and he missed the way it would do whatever he wanted. He missed the way he felt when the pumpkin was near and more than anything he missed flying through the air.

Oliver came and sat next to him. "Good morning, Owen!"

"Mornin', Oliver."

Oliver took his brother's hand and held it. He sensed that Owen needed this.

Owen gave his hand a squeeze and said, "Let's spend one more day here and then tomorrow we'll go and find the pumpkin and go for a ride."

"Okay!"

Oliver was excited to climb the hill by himself that morning. His wounds were all but healed. He now wore Owen's shirt that had been wrapped around him as a bandage. It was much too big for him. The neck kept slipping down on one shoulder and then the other. Oliver wanted to give the shirt back to his brother, but Owen made him keep it. They had left Oliver's shredded raincoat and sweater at the bottom of the ravine by the Black River, and as Owen pointed out, he couldn't walk back to the pumpkin with no shirt on.

The boys stopped to rest at the top of the hill. They looked out over the wide valley in awe. The sky was the color of warm gold. Towering cumulus clouds slowly floated across its vastness. The clouds were white, but they seemed to radiate pale reflections of other colors. The early morning sun sent its rays through the clouds, so that patches of beautiful light roamed the landscape, exploring the four seasons and their rivers. The birds in the air followed the sunbeams, playing and swooping about in the slanted planes of light.

After a few moments, the boys turned to each other with giddy smiles and hurried down the side of the hill to splash into the water as they had done the day before. They went straight to the white orchid and spent an hour soaking up its love. By coincidence or magic, a sunbeam constantly shown on the flower so that its giant yet delicate white petals glowed steadily, surrounded by dazzling particles in the air that danced a slow waltz all around it.

The boys were enthralled by the sight as if it were a dream. Time seemed to slow down. The movement of the orchid as it caught the light breeze was an instantiation of grace. The boys experienced the flower with all five of their senses, each of which was heightened in their rapt absorption. They heard the faint sound of the orchid's bending stem, and the caress of its petals against each other. The flower's delicate fragrance filled the boys' noses and tickled their tongues. They could feel the flower's love as if it were holding them in a gentle embrace.

The boys hardly stopped laughing that day. They lost themselves with utter abandon to the noble merriment of childhood play. There in that hidden valley, fear did not exist. Everything became a game, even sitting in the grass. The boys ate and drank their fill. They took off their clothes and frolicked in the White and Green Rivers. They rolled naked in the snow and then ran back to the warmth of summer, laughing and squealing at the cold. They played hide-and-seek among the cow-pies. They climbed on the animals' broad backs and leapt from one to another, laughing at the gentle beasts' annoyed snorts and grunts and swishing tails. They buried themselves under piles of autumn leaves and burrowed through them pretending to be pipchunks. They held each other's hands and danced in a circle until they fell to the ground in a dizzy pile.

When the sun finally began to set, Oliver picked the day's parrot leaves and placed them before the white orchid. This made him very happy. Owen watched this with a smile as he had the day before. He loved his brother so very much.

CHAPTER TWENTY-FIVE

Owen and Oliver sat by the orchid, whose pure white light was untouched by the rosy hues of the dawn. The boys were saying goodbye. They planned to visit the flower every day, but it was still difficult for them to leave it. Every time that Owen thought he was ready, something stopped him. The words would be in his mouth, *okay, Oliver, let's go find the pumpkin*, but they wouldn't come out. He was afraid to leave.

It was Oliver who finally slid off of the little isle and splashed his way to the banks of Autumnland. Owen stayed by the flower and watched him. Oliver gathered up a bunch of the pretty red parrot leaves and waded back to the orchid. He climbed out of the water and carefully set the leaves in a circle all around the white flower, like the rays around a child's drawing of the sun. As Owen watched him, he felt his heart grow heavy. Oliver sat back and inspected his work with a beaming smile on his face. Owen watched this, too, and couldn't hold back his tears any longer.

Owen was experiencing emotions that he didn't understand. He didn't understand why he couldn't be happy like his brother. Owen felt the orchid's love flowing into him, and it made him weep. He was too young to understand that this, too, was love.

Oliver saw his big brother's silent tears. He smiled at him and held his hand. Sometimes Oliver understood things that Owen did not. He was young enough so that he didn't fill his head with the questions and doubts that Owen had. Oliver just felt and accepted, and this allowed him to see these things more clearly.

"It's okay, Owen. It'll be okay here without us. It's everywhere!"

Owen looked at his little brother. He didn't quite understand what Oliver meant, nor why his words made him feel a little better. They just did. When Owen smiled back at him, Oliver let go of his hand and hopped into the water. Owen paused another moment. He reached out to touch the orchid's beautiful petals. His hand stopped when his outstretched fingers were still an inch away. He let them hover there for several seconds, and then withdrew his hand without touching the flower. He felt unworthy. His eyes filled with tears once more as he whispered a secret to the flower and said goodbye. Then he slid into the water where Oliver was patiently waiting for him.

When the boys climbed onto the banks of Autumnland, they each picked a parrot from the ground and stuffed it into their pockets. Then they skipped over to Summerland, grabbed as many pinkberries as they could carry to eat while they walked, and crossed back to the side of the Gold River. The brothers both turned and waved goodbye to the orchid, and their journey home began.

The boys thoroughly enjoyed their walk through Autumnland, especially Oliver. The boys had had the pumpkin since before Oliver could really remember. They had never taken very long walks because it had been so fun to fly. Now, as they hiked out of the valley, their little bodies, refreshed from two days of eating and drinking and playing, thrilled at the exercise of walking.

The crisp autumn air was perfumed with the scent of dry leaves and sweet golden grass. Black birds flew through the bright pink sky overhead. The colorful foliage filtered the sun's rays, deepening the warmth and richness of the landscape. The boys had each found long sticks to help them climb, and to swing about like swords.

When the boys reached the crest of a slope they turned back for one more sight of the hidden valley. It was gone. The Gold River flowed into the distance but the other three rivers could not be seen. The hill into which the rivers flowed was no longer there, nor was the little isle upon which the white orchid grew. The boys stood in confusion for a few moments with their heads tilted to one side.

"Owen? Where'd it go?"

"I dunno."

Together, the boys' heads straightened and lifted, as if pulled gently back by their own rising brows. They looked at each other with wide eyes for a moment, then gave a sly, sideways glance in the direction from which they had come. With strangely knowing smiles they looked back at each other, reached out and took each other's hands, and turned away to continue their journey back to the magic pumpkin. The brothers would never see the hidden valley again.

The walk was very peaceful, aside from what adventures and games the boys' imaginations concocted. Owen had convinced both himself and his little brother that there was no danger; that they would find the pumpkin and be safely back in their cave before nightfall. This was based on nothing more than the fact that being caught by the shadow eyes seemed too unfair after the spell of safety that the hidden valley had cast upon the boys. It couldn't possibly happen again. Owen believed this because he had to, just as he had believed for those two long days on the banks of the Black River that he and Oliver would escape the ravine, even when it was clear that they would not. This time, however, luck or magic was on the boys' side.

It was late afternoon when the boys turned a familiar bend in the Gold River and left its course to make their way through a stand of evergreen trees. Their steps quickened in anticipation until they were running with excited smiles on their faces. They had no thoughts of the dark creatures. They broke through the trees together and there was the pumpkin, its orange glow pulsating as if it were as happy to be found as the boys were to find it. They ran to the pumpkin, pressed themselves to its side and were wrapped in its warm swirls of autumn colors. The pumpkin's joy filled the boys. It welled up inside them and poured out of them in the form of laughter.

All day, the boys had been dreaming of climbing on the pumpkin and flying through the air, but that was not what they did; at least, not at first. All at once, both boys started to talk to the pumpkin, telling it of their adventure. They interrupted each other and talked over each other. They repeated each other's favorite parts, each so eager to be the one tell of them. In the embrace of the pumpkin's joy, the boys even told it about the scary parts. The bad things had no power over them now that they had found their magic pumpkin and would be safe. The boys were so excited that they told everything out of order. They forgot parts and went back to add details, jumping around in an incoherent jumble of events and discoveries. To anyone listening to the boys' chaotic storytelling, it would have made little sense, but the pumpkin seemed to glow brighter and to release its swirls at each of the appropriate moments. It was clear that the pumpkin had missed the boys very much and was happy to hear their animated little voices and to feel their touch, whether it understood what they were saying or not.

When the pink sky became streaked with the red and gold of sunset, the boys climbed atop the pumpkin. The familiar giddiness overtook them as they felt the tickles in the bottoms of their bellies and then they were in the air, flying back to their home in Summerland. The pumpkin's joy bubbled out of the boys in the form of laughter that didn't stop until they had landed at the entrance to their cave.

It was not quite the homecoming that the boys had expected. They slid down the slide into the pile of fire leaves and looked around their cave. The same glow was all around the boys, but it felt different.

The boys did not run down the slope of the bowl as they usually did. They were very quiet. Owen looked at Oliver and put his finger to his lips. Oliver understood that he was to be silent. Owen carefully got up and tiptoed around the rim of the bowl to the back of the cave with Oliver close behind him. Both boys crouched as they stepped. They were tensed and ready to run back to the pumpkin.

They checked the bathroom shaft first. Owen was almost afraid to look into the shaft, though he did. There was nothing there. He didn't know what he could have possibly expected to find, but he was afraid nonetheless. The boys checked their bedroom next, but found nothing out of place. Finally, they crept to their booty room.

Owen stopped before the entrance and held an arm out to Oliver, in a silent gesture of *wait here*. Owen poked his head into the chamber. It was empty except for Oliver's untouched booty pile. Continuing on his tiptoes, Owen walked into the room, crouched low so that he couldn't see above the shelf where his own booty pile sat. Oliver watched from the entrance, holding his breath. Owen leaned against the shelf, working up his courage, and then lifted his head just enough to peek over its edge.

Everything was just as he had left it. So then why did he still feel afraid? He turned back to Oliver with his finger to his lips once more and then climbed up onto the shelf as quietly as he could. Owen went straight to his leaf zoo and slowly pulled the elephant ears aside. That was when Owen finally realized what he had been so afraid of. He had thought that the portal would be closed, but there it was, the same as ever. His bed on the other side was empty, but it was there.

Owen replaced the elephant ears and turned to his brother. "It's okay, Oliver. There's nothing there."

Both boys jumped at the sound of Owen's voice echoing off of the walls of the cave. They laughed nervously at themselves. Owen hopped down from the shelf. The boys had talked excitedly about their booty piles and the slide and running around the bowl of the cave, but now they simply stopped.

Neither one of them knew what to say or do. They didn't understand what was wrong. The boys couldn't see that it wasn't the cave that was different, but themselves. They had been through too much. Their innocent illusion of safety had been shattered by the dark creatures.

The creatures had introduced the boys to the concept of vigilance, but being so young, the boys couldn't grasp it. Indeed, against such monsters, what good would vigilance do anyway? The fact that such things existed at all would ever be a source of fear to the boys. Would the monsters find them again?

Oliver felt a need and gave in to it. "Owen, let's go where we can see punkin."

Oliver turned and walked back out to the edge of the bowl. He looked at the pumpkin as Owen followed and then stood beside him. The pumpkin's warm glow comforted the boys, as it always had. Oliver smiled and ran down the slope of the bowl and then looked back up at Owen expectantly.

"I have to go to the bathroom, Oliver."

"No, Owen! Don't go bathroom." Oliver was afraid to be alone.

"I'll just be a minute!"

Owen went to the bathroom shaft. As soon as he'd started to go, he heard Oliver's loud, wailing cry erupt out of nowhere. The cry was so sudden that Owen thought that Oliver must have fallen and hit his head. He hurried and ran back to his brother. He saw Oliver sitting in the bottom of the bowl, bawling. Owen ran down to him.

"What's wrong, Oliver? Did you hurt yourself?"

Oliver screamed at him. "You *leff* me, Owen!"

"I was just going to the bathroom! I was still here!"

Oliver continued to bawl, holding his arms out to his brother. Owen picked him up and sat down with him on his lap. He gently rocked him back and forth as he cried. Oliver had simply gotten scared when Owen had left his sight.

Oliver would often feel scared now, as would Owen. The boys had felt safe in the hidden valley, even after all they had been through, and the journey back had been filled with happy thoughts of finding the pumpkin again and of being comfortably back in their own cave. Now that they were back, now that they had stopped moving toward something, they felt the absence of that safety which they had felt in the valley. They felt unprotected and alone. The pumpkin could cheer them up, even make them forget for a while, but it could not erase the fear which had tainted them.

Oliver continued to sob. He didn't know why; he just knew that he felt sad and frightened. Owen began to wish that they had never left the hidden valley. He sat and rocked his brother and tried to cheer him up.

"How about we get up early and ride the pumpkin back to the flower tomorrow?"

Oliver answered between hitching breaths. He was beginning to calm down. "How wi' we find its, Owen?"

"The pumpkin can find it...I think."

"Aw you shu-uh, Owen?"

"I dunno. But it finds everything else. Then we can have the pumpkin *and* the flower!"

"Punkin *aaaand* flowuh?"

"Uh-huh! That's a *great* idea! Isn't it, Oliver?"

Oliver smiled, and even chuckled. "Yeah, Owen! 'At's a *great* idea!"

"Let's go up where we can see the pumpkin. Okay, Oliver?"

The boys climbed out of the bowl and went to their bedroom. They sat in their soft bed of leaves and watched the pumpkin's glow as they finally ate the parrots that they'd been carrying in their pockets.

The next day, the boys searched for the hidden valley. They followed the Gold River but it never seemed to end. Owen retraced their course and even flew the pumpkin over the leaf-catching spot, a place that made Oliver whimper with fear. He did not explore the ravine. The boys couldn't see the bottom and they were too afraid to fly the pumpkin down to where they knew the Black River flowed. The boys knew that the valley must be there, but no matter which direction they approached from, they couldn't find it. They did not find the Orange River, either.

Every day, the boys searched. They followed each of the rivers but they all seemed to flow endlessly on, leading the boys nowhere. As the days turned into weeks and the weeks turned into months, the boys stopped searching every day.

The water of the Orange River was still working in the boys, especially in Owen. He began to understand that they would never find the white flower, that some magic hid the valley, though he didn't understand why. It wasn't fair. It made him frustrated, angry and sad all at the same time.

Oliver didn't so much realize these things as accept that the flower had gone somewhere beyond the boys' reach. This made him, too, very sad, and vaguely afraid.

Owen became aware that no one was ever going to come for them, nor make everything better and take them back home. The knowledge was yet another affliction of the Orange River's gift. At times it filled Owen with a loneliness that he'd never felt before.

The boys still played and enjoyed the land for a time, although they never went back to the leaf-catching spot. The White River still lifted their spirits. The make-place still showed them their stories. The boys still had their weekly birthday parties, though each one was a little less exciting than the last. The cow-pies still made them laugh for a while and the paint plants still stirred their creativity, but it was never the same as it had been. Their laughter left them ever more quickly.

The boys' joie de vivre, that had been so well-protected for so long, was slowly seeping from them. As time went on, the boys' enthusiasm for these things that had always brought them such joy began to dull. Their nightmares, which had been terrible after they had first returned to their cave, had come less often for a while, but after a few weeks had passed, the boys' sleep once more became increasingly troubled. The boys stayed closer to the pumpkin, hesitant to stray from its glow, for the pumpkin eased their anxieties and still gave them a feeling of joy. The boys grew even more dependent on each other's presence, each afraid to leave the other's sight for even a moment. A poison festered in the brothers that they did not know was there.

When the boys had each drunk the waters of the Black River, seeds of sorrow and fear had been sown in them. There was nothing that the boys could do to stop the seeds' growth. Over time, they grew weary of the land. They dreamed of home more and more, Oliver just as much as Owen.

Owen became aware that if he were to go through the doorway that led to home, this growing depression would not follow. This unnatural sadness would be left behind in the land and he would be free to laugh as he once did. This was the final bit of understanding that the Orange River granted him, and its most cruel; for if they went home, Oliver would die, leaving Owen with a heartache far worse than what he now knew, but how much longer could he watch his little brother continue to grow more and more sad? Wouldn't he at least be happy at home, even if it were just for a while?

As with most of his grown up thoughts, these left Owen feeling scared and very unhappy. He envisioned the joy that Oliver would know if he were reunited with Mommy and Daddy, as well as how happy Mommy and Daddy would be themselves. He, himself, yearned to be covered in the kisses that he had dreamed of for so long. These fantasies tormented him. Owen watched his brother drifting away and did his best to keep him happy, but his best was not enough and this made him feel that it was all his fault. He thought that he was failing the love that was most sacred to him.

Oliver's accepting nature had been refined long ago by the terrible illness that he had all but forgotten. He had learned to take what comes. Perhaps more tragic than Owen's struggle and natural rebellion against what he was feeling was Oliver's almost apathetic regard of his own despondency. He didn't question why he felt less happy as time went on. He realized that things like the make-place and paint patch weren't as fun anymore, and for him that's just the way it was. He didn't look for new things to take their place. The pumpkin still made him happy, and he loved his brother more than ever, almost desperately, but everything else had lost its glimmer. Oliver was fading away, and he felt it, but it never occurred to him that there was anything to be done about it. Hope was a thing that he no longer knew.

Oliver had also drank from the Orange River, but in his fewer years the understanding of things came to him differently. In some deep place inside him, he knew that his sadness was connected to the land, but he didn't know about the portal that could take him home. He simply stopped thinking of going home altogether, though he wanted to, more than anything. He missed Mommy terribly, and cried for her often.

Since Oliver had found the white flower, Mommy's face came to him more and more. He somehow knew that Mommy would never come for him, but this understanding translated into his conscious thoughts only as a deep longing for her. He had little grasp of the future or of a lifetime without her. Oliver lived in the present. His thoughts only went as far as *Mommy's not here and I wish she was*. His mind was far too young to digest such an illimitable concept as *I'll never see Mommy again*.

As the months passed, Oliver began to do no more than go through the motions of childhood. He followed his brother and did the things that he knew were supposed to be fun, but without feeling any real pleasure. What he felt was eventually no more than a faded memory of that all-consuming joy that is the hallmark of childhood. When enough time had passed, he could no longer tell the difference between this pale shadow of happiness and the true happiness that he used to feel. He gave in to the growing darkness inside him because he forgot that there had been a time when it wasn't there.

CHAPTER TWENTY-SIX

It was Oliver's fourth birthday, though he didn't know it. It had been nearly a year since the boys were attacked by the dark creatures. Although the waters of the Green River had soon healed the boys' wounds, they had never recovered emotionally. They still kept a watchful eye whenever they left the cave, ever wary of a danger that no longer existed. They could perhaps have felt a measure of safety return to them when enough time had passed, but the poison in the Black River had continued to slowly spread throughout the boys' little bodies until their inner joy was overrun with sadness and an obscure fear that became their constant companion.

The light of childhood innocence that had once shone so brightly in the boys had dimmed to dying embers. Soon, it would go out altogether, snuffed out by the poison in the waters of the Black River, and when it did, nothing would be able to rekindle it. It would be gone forever.

But, that had not happened *yet*. The boys' spirits were strong, and held on. They found strength in each other, as they always had. What small bit of happiness that still lived inside them came from each other; a touch, a smile, a word - these small gestures of love gave them a reason to go on trying, each for the other's sake more than for their own.

Owen would suggest a bath in the White River in an attempt to lift Oliver's spirits, and Oliver would agree because he wanted to please his brother. Although neither boy truly felt like going, in this way they still found the will to make the effort, and after all, the magic in the White River did still have the power to lift the boys' spirits for a while, as did other wonders of the land. However, this cheer did not permeate the boys as it once had, and when they moved on, they left it behind.

The magic pumpkin was the greatest source of joy that remained to the boys. They took it with them wherever they went, and yet, though the boys were the source of the pumpkin's joy, this joy existed outside of them and could not penetrate the darkness that was poisoning them. The boys stayed close to the pumpkin, as to a fire on a frozen night, but it could only warm the surface of their spirits.

Owen continued to be tormented by the portal that could take the boys home. Now six years of age, his soul was already weary, worn down by his many lonely burdens. His tears fell often. Though he tried his best to hide them from his brother, Oliver saw, and said nothing. Oliver felt that he was failing his big brother, just as Owen felt that he was failing Oliver.

This made the boys try harder for a while. When either of them forced a smile that they did not feel, they would sometimes be rewarded by a genuine smile from the other, which would in turn leave them both feeling better, just a little bit. Although not the intense joy of the pumpkin, this small bit of comfort was stronger for that it came from deep down inside them. The boys would try to make it last, but always their melancholy would again overtake them.

Oliver woke up and opened his crying eyes. He had been dreaming of the dark creatures, only it had been Owen that had been held in the massive jaws and not himself. That dream was always worse. Oliver closed his eyes against the world around him and snuggled more closely against his brother.

It was early morning. The sun was rising in a bright yellow sky. Oliver wanted to do nothing that day but ride on the pumpkin. He felt a little safer in the air, and the pumpkin always made him smile. The idea brought him no real cheer as he lay there; it was simply what he was going to ask Owen if they could do that day.

Oliver opened his eyes again. "Owen, wake up. I have to go the bathroom." Owen was deep in his sleep and didn't stir. "Owen! I have to go to the bathroom!"

The boys had long since only gone into the narrow shaft together. The tight space that had once so amused them now frightened them.

Owen groaned and lifted his head without opening his eyes. "So go! I'll watch you and make sure nothing happens."

"Owen, open your eyes, then!"

Owen opened his eyes and forced a smile for his brother to help him to not be scared. It didn't work.

Oliver whispered now. "What if somethin's in there?"

Owen's smile faded. He got up and dazedly followed Oliver to the bathroom shaft. Of course, nothing was there. When Oliver finished, the boys went back to their bedroom and Owen laid back down to sleep. He was so tired. He already knew that this was going to be one of those days when he would have no energy.

Oliver did not lay back down. He sat by his brother and watched him sleep, trying not to think sad thoughts. He looked at the pumpkin and that helped. Here were the two things that made him feel as good as he was able: Owen and the magic pumpkin.

After a while Oliver got up and went to the edge of the bowl. He looked at the yellow sky that framed the pumpkin in the entrance to the cave. There was a time when he would have eyed that particular hue of sky warily, even while he enjoyed seeing his favorite color, but now he felt nothing.

Oliver was hungry but he wanted to let Owen sleep, and he wouldn't leave the cave by himself. He saw Odie half-buried under some fire leaves but he might as well have seen a plain rock for the reaction he felt. Months ago he had tossed the stuffed dog aside and never picked him back up. The comfort that Oliver had found in his friend had seeped away until Odie had become only a lifeless bit of stuffed fabric to him.

Oliver looked toward the booty room. He wanted to go in there to look at his Daddy's matchbox bus but he was afraid. He really didn't want to ask Owen to get up again. Oliver stood there for a few minutes, trying to work up the courage to go into the room by himself. The fact that he wanted something and couldn't bring himself to get it made him depressed. He didn't cry, he just stood there, feeling very sad and small.

Finally Oliver crept toward the room on his tiptoes. He sensed that there was something about that day, something different. He didn't know what it was but it helped him to overcome his fear. His heart pounding, Oliver poked his head into the room. He let out the breath that he had been holding and very carefully edged his way into the room.

Oliver saw the little bus, but it offered no comfort. He didn't even bother to pick it up. Feeling dejected, Oliver knelt by the parrot leaves that he still kept for Mommy. He didn't gather them every day anymore, and these leaves were wilted. He caressed one of the red leaves and started to cry. The leaves used to fill Oliver with warm memories of Mommy and dreams of her pleased and smiling face when she would someday enjoy his pretty gift to her. They had always made him happy, but now they always made him cry. He wanted his Mommy so much but he would never see her again.

When he was finished crying, Oliver got up to leave the booty room. When he reached the opening, something made him stop and turn back. He looked at Owen's shelf. He was tall enough now to just see over its edge, but he had never climbed up there. It was Owen's, not his.

Oliver went to the opening of the bedroom and saw that Owen was still sleeping. Surely Owen wouldn't mind if Oliver just peeked at his treasures? Oliver tiptoed back to the treasure room and approached the shelf. He felt a childlike curiosity that he hadn't known for a long time. He peered over the edge. He saw the bouncy balls and the matchbox Lamborghini, the pile of rocks and the old, dried out sticks. On top of the sticks was the necklace of pinkberry vines that Owen had made for Mommy. It was old now, and falling apart. Oliver looked at the withered remains of Owen's leaf zoo. Owen had added no new leaves in a long time.

Oliver started to look away when his eye was caught by the bright green of the fresh elephant ears. They were strangely out of place. *They* were new. Oliver remembered now that Owen had brought them back fairly recently. He wondered why Owen would keep bringing only *those* leaves back to the cave when he had stopped caring about the rest. He tilted his head and listened for any sign that Owen might have gotten up. When he heard nothing, Oliver lifted himself up onto Owen's shelf.

Oliver felt a nostalgic memory of his former mischievousness. He sat on the shelf and looked down at his own booty pile. He was vaguely aware that he should feel something, sitting in Owen's special place and looking down from where only Owen had looked before. He knew that he was missing something and he didn't care. The capacity to appreciate the profound had left him.

Oliver crawled on all fours to the elephant ears. Did he hear something? No...but there *was* something. He just couldn't tell which of his senses had let him know. Oliver touched one of the giant leaves. Nothing special happened. He was afraid to pick it up. What if Owen knew that he had been there? He struggled with this for a few moments and then finally picked up the leaves and saw what they were hiding.

At first, Oliver just looked. He could make no sense of what he was seeing. Was it a picture? It sure did look real. He wanted to touch it. Was that a bedroom? A real one? Something was awakening in him, something light and fluttery. What *was* this? He stared down at Owen's unmade bed with his hand outstretched but hesitating. Dreamlike images floated through Oliver's mind: the ocean, his doggy, Mommy's smile. Oliver's hand dipped a bit lower. He would touch it and see...

"Oliver, STOP!"

Oliver froze. Owen had caught him and was already climbing onto the shelf. Owen wrapped his arms around his brother in a panic and fell back with Oliver on top of him. Oliver was already crying with shame and guilt and fear. He felt hot.

Owen held his brother tightly and started to cry himself. He had almost lost him. He had almost lost Oliver! Owen knew that if Oliver's fingers had broken the plane of the portal, he would have been pulled through forever.

"Oliver! Don't ever ever ever ever touch that!"

Owen was just scared but Oliver thought he was angry.

"I'm sorry, Owen! I'm sorry!"

Owen released his brother and helped him to sit up. "It's okay, Oliver. I promise I'm not mad."

Oliver was very upset. He heard Owen say that he wasn't mad, but he had been so startled by the ferocity of Owen's initial reaction that he had to take the time to cry it out. Owen held him and kept repeating that it was okay, that he wasn't mad.

"You just scared me, that's all."

"I'm sorry, Owen. I didn't mean ta scare you."

Owen sat behind Oliver with his arms around him as if he were afraid that if he didn't hold him back, Oliver might still fall through the portal. The boys grew silent, both staring through the doorway into their bedroom. Finally, Oliver spoke.

"What *is* that?"

Owen didn't know what to say. How could he explain?

"Owen?"

Owen's mind raced. He felt like he was drowning, grasping at anything that might keep him afloat, but he found nothing. "That's home," he said.

"*What?*"

"That's home, Oliver. Our *real* home, where Mommy and Daddy are."

Oliver stared at the bed and at the drawings on the wall. "Is 'at my bed?"

"No, it's mine. Yours is over there." Owen pointed to his left, to where Oliver's booty pile lay. "But that's your pillow."

Oliver didn't comprehend what all of this meant, not at first. He continued to stare as the realization slowly sunk in.

"Are all those stuffed animals *yours?*"

"I think some are yours. I can't remember. Sometimes there's new ones."

Oliver felt the embers of his happiness growing brighter, even as Owen felt his slipping away. After a very long silence, Oliver asked, "We can go *home?*"

"No, Oliver. We can't."

"What? Why not?" Oliver could feel his brother's sadness but didn't understand it.

Owen took a deep breath. He had feared this moment for so long. "Oliver, do you remember how we got here?"

"I remember! Ummm...I dunno."

"Do you remember being sick?"

"I was sick?"

"Yeah. You were very, very sick. You were in the hospital. Don't you remember the hospital?"

Oliver tried to think. "Was there a fountain?"

"Yeah. We used to throw coins in it and make wishes."

"Like when we throw rocks in the Green River?"

"Uh huh."

Owen leaned over to his booty pile and scooped up the quarters that he'd had in his pocket on the day that they had come to the land. He showed them to Oliver. "I brought these to the hospital to throw in the fountain and wish for you to be all better, but it was my birthday so Granny let me keep 'em and gave me some of *her* coins to throw in."

Oliver thought about this. "You wished we'd come here?"

"I wished that you wouldn't be sick anymore so you could play with me. Then when me and Granny went to see you, Mommy and Daddy let me snuggle with you and when we woke up, we were here and you weren't sick anymore. That's why we can't go home, Oliver. You'll get sick again."

"But I'll get better again, too."

Owen closed his eyes. He was very close to tears. He had promised Mommy that he would never tell Oliver...

"Won't I get better, Owen? At the hospital?"

"I don't know. But if you got sick again we wouldn't be able to play anymore. You'd have to stay at the hospital."

"But we'd be with Mommy and Daddy?"

"Uh huh."

The boys fell silent, each lost in their own thoughts, each gazing at home, just a few inches away. They were both thinking that they could be happy again if they went through the portal, at least for a while.

The boys had been through so much, so many changes, but one thing that had never changed was that they still lived for each other. What made each of them happiest was seeing the other happy. For a long time now, neither brother had found much reason to feel happy, try as they might.

Oliver was thinking about how happy Owen would be to go home. He didn't mind being sick if Owen wasn't sad anymore. Owen cried every day. He cried in his sleep and called out for Mommy and Daddy. Oliver remembered the many times that Owen had curled up and wept, softly chanting that he wanted to go home.

Oliver finally realized that all this time, he *could* have. Owen had stayed here for him, so that he wouldn't have to be sick. Oliver's poor little heart was breaking for his brother, breaking with love and gratitude, and with remorse.

Owen was thinking about how sad Oliver had become. Even worse was when Oliver didn't seem to care about anything. Sometimes he seemed like he didn't even care that he was so sad. Owen's heart had been breaking every day, wishing that his little brother would just laugh, but a low-spirited smile was all he ever saw. Owen knew that if they went home, this sad feeling would be left behind. Oliver would laugh again. Could he let his brother go so that he could laugh again, even for a little while? But how could he live without Oliver? Owen started to cry.

Oliver felt a teardrop land on his head. He said, "Let's go home, Owen."

This made Owen cry harder. His arms tightened around his little brother, his treasure.

"It's okay, Owen. I don't mind if I'm sick. You can come and play with me at the hospital!" Oliver wanted so to see his big brother happy again. He wanted him to be with Mommy and Daddy.

Owen was just a little boy. This was all so unfair. "Oliver, you'd get so sick that you wouldn't be able to get out of bed."

"But you could lay in my bed and snuggle with me, right, Owen?"

"But we'd never be able to come back here."

Oliver thought about this. "I don't like it here anymore, Owen. I wanna be with Mommy and Daddy. I wanna go home."

Owen breathed in the scent of his brother's hair as he stared at the doorway home. He was so tired.

"Okay, Oliver. Let's go home."

Oliver tilted his head back and smiled up at Owen, who wiped away his tears and smiled back.

The boys stood up and hopped down from the shelf. They went to the pumpkin. Its glow shone out with a radiance that the boys had never seen. This filled the boys with an inner peace. They were doing the right thing.

The boys wrapped their arms around the pumpkin and whispered their goodbyes. They did not feel sad about leaving the pumpkin. It couldn't come with them, but deep down, where the boys couldn't see, was the knowledge that the joy from which it was made would follow them home.

Oliver looked out across the land and said a silent goodbye to the white orchid as well, although he knew that its love would come home with them, too. Owen may not have understood, but Oliver knew that he'd get to take the best parts of this magical place with him. He turned and took his brother's hand. Together, the boys walked along the edge of the bowl. They stopped when they were directly across from the pumpkin and took one last look.

Oliver said, "Thank you, punkin!"

Owen said, "I love you, pumpkin!"

Owen reached down and picked up Odie from where he lay at the entrance to the boys' bedroom. Oliver would soon need his friend again.

Owen boosted Oliver up onto the shelf and then climbed up himself. The boys stood before the portal home and held each other's hands. They looked at each other once more, communicating what there are no words to say, and together they stepped through the portal. Their love for each other took them home.

Epilogue

On the day that the boys stepped through the portal, the white orchid and the magic pumpkin left the land. The orchid did not explode in a shower of light, nor did the pumpkin vanish with a poof and a swirl of colors. They were simply there...and then they weren't.

Seven months, twelve days, and five hours after the boys had gone, a new flower appeared in the hidden valley. It was smaller than the one that had been, but it shone with a brilliant white light that never dimmed. It would shine forever, though no one would see it.

At that same moment, in a clearing in Autumnland, a pumpkin sprouted. It did not grow slowly throughout the day. Like the orchid, it appeared all at once, and was smaller than the pumpkin that had been, but it, too, glowed with an even warmer light. It would never be seen, for no one was coming to find it. The pumpkin would never leave the clearing, for no one was coming to play with it. It would never fly, and it would never disappear again.